Praise for
What Lies Within

"Karen Ball writes from the heart. The journey of *What Lies Within* will capture readers from the first page. Another winner from this master storyteller."
—KAREN KINGSBURY, best-selling author of *Sunrise* and
Between Sundays

"Karen Ball is a skilled novelist whose stories are not only entertaining, but credible and authentic. In fact, those of us who are Karen's friends know that's exactly what she is: authentic and entertaining, a delight to be with, and a delight to read."
—RANDY ALCORN, best-selling author of *Deception*

"Karen Ball brought me to tears with *A Test of Faith*, gave me renewed hope with *The Breaking Point*, and left me breathless with *Shattered Justice*. She is an author who never fails to please. Don't miss *What Lies Within*."
—ROBIN LEE HATCHER, best-selling author of *Return to Me*
and *A Carol for Christmas*

"Karen Ball writes from the heart *to* the heart and never fails to reach her target. With skill, emotion, and wit she creates stories that reflect our world and the loving heart of God. Whenever I see 'Karen Ball' on the cover, I know I'm in for an engrossing read."
—ANGELA HUNT, author of *Doesn't She Look Natural*

"Anytime you pick up a novel by Karen Ball, you can count on an adventure: an adventure that explores the emotions, the struggles, and the triumphs of her always engaging and unforgettable characters. She never fails to deliver an intense, compelling story that remains with the reader long after the last page has been turned. This is an author who makes a promise to her readers at the very beginning of each novel…and always keeps that promise with her unique blend of warmth and humor and sensitivity."
—BJ HOFF, author of the Mountain Song Legacy and
An Emerald Ballad series

WHAT LIES WITHIN

WHAT LIES WITHIN
PUBLISHED BY MULTNOMAH BOOKS
12265 Oracle Boulevard, Suite 200
Colorado Springs, Colorado 80921
A division of Random House Inc.

The characters and events in this book are fictional, and any resemblance to actual persons
or events is coincidental.

ISBN 978-1-59052-415-2

Library of Congress Cataloging-in-Publication Data
Ball, Karen, 1957–
    What lies within : a novel / Karen Ball.
      p. cm.—(Family honor series ; bk. 3)
    ISBN 978-1-59052-415-2 (trade pbk.)
  1. City and town life—Oregon—Fiction. 2. Oregon—Fiction. I. Title.
    PS3552.A4553W47 2007
    813'.54—dc22

                                    2007031613

Printed in the United States of America
2007—First Edition

10 9 8 7 6 5 4 3 2 1

FAMILY HONOR SERIES BOOK 3

WHAT LIES WITHIN

A NOVEL

KAREN BALL

MULTNOMAH
BOOKS

~~~

Other Novels by Karen Ball

Family Honor Series
Shattered Justice
Kaleidoscope Eyes

The Breaking Point
A Test of Faith
Reunion
"Bride on the Run" in the *3 Weddings and a Giggle* anthology

For Daddy.
My encourager, my anchor,
the one who taught me from the very beginning
what a man wholly devoted to God is like.

Simply wonderful.

Thank you for a solid foundation of faith
and a lifetime of laughter and love.
I am who I am because of you and Mom.

I love you.

AUTHOR'S NOTE

This story came in answer to prayer.

Years ago, I realized I lacked something I desperately wanted. Regular time in God's Word. It wasn't that I couldn't do it. I just wasn't disciplined enough. So I asked God to give me a love for His Word. To make me hunger for it the way I hungered for novels and beautiful writing.

Well, as always when we come to God with sincere hearts, He answers. I started reading the Bible, and every word hit me as never before. Funny thing was, He drew me to the book of Nehemiah. A book I'd never read. But as I went through the story of rebuilding the wall, I was struck by one verse: "Shallum son of Hallohesh and his daughters repaired the next section."

And his daughters.

All the men who worked on the wall were named, along with their fathers and father's fathers. But these women? They were just "and his daughters."

That got me wondering. What must it be like to be a woman in a male-dominated field? Suddenly, a story emerged. Exploded, is more like it. I pulled out my journal and wrote as I read the book, and there, in the story of Nehemiah, was another story.

The story of Kyla Justice.

That was twenty-two years ago. So you can imagine my delight at finally bringing this story to life. And that's why you'll find so many verses from Nehemiah as chapter headings in this book. Because that's where the story came from.

Of course, it took a lot of additional research. The book of Nehemiah didn't offer much insight into gangs or construction companies. But research is fun. It's fascinating and educational. I've been immersed in search and res-cue, synesthesia, allergy to bee stings, languages, stained glass, meth labs—and those are just a few of the topics I've explored as I wrote the Family Honor series.

The research for *What Lies Within*, though, has taken me beyond anything I've done before. It sent me into a world I knew existed but didn't begin to understand. The world of gangs—where they're located, how they form, what draws people to them, how they talk and dress, what their goals and motivations are, and more.

As a result, I've discovered new words for research.

Sobering. Disturbing. Chilling.

Terrifying.

The gang I've portrayed in this book, the Blood Brotherhood, is fictitious. But their actions are true to life. And, as unsettling as it may be, their actions are mild compared to what some gangs do. If I learned anything from researching this book it's that those involved in combating gangs—and in resisting them—need our prayers. The world of gangs is a dark, pervasive, spiritually oppressed place where humanity gives way to violence, mercy to degradation. There's only one source of light in such darkness: Jesus Christ. May we call upon Him with passion and determination to speak to the hearts of those lost in a life many of us can't even imagine.

And now, the flip side.

May I just say to anyone involved in the military…

Thank you.

The research I've done for Rafael and his Force Recon team has been fascinating. Uplifting. Inspiring. And, at times, terrifying. I can't believe what those in the military, especially the Special Forces and Force Recon, are called to do to secure our country and our freedom. I've seen photos, listened to audio recordings of radio transmissions, read firsthand accounts of battles—both victories and losses—and it has moved me to tears. The men and women in the U.S. military deserve our respect, our support, and our eternal gratitude for all they are and do. As President Ronald Reagan once said, "Some people spend a lifetime wondering if they made a difference. The Marines don't have that problem." I'd add that anyone in the military shouldn't have that problem.

They make a difference. A big one. May God place His hand of protection upon each of them.

Two notes, just for the record: Rafe's Force Recon team, the Pride, is fictitious. (Their motto is an adaptation of the motto for the "WolfPack," the

3rd Light Armored Reconnaissance Battalion.) While I've done my best to ensure accuracy in the military and battle details, I also took some creative license for the sake of the story.

Also, my sources on gangs informed me that many, if not most, gangs similar to the one in my book name themselves after the streets they live on. I wanted to be sure I didn't use a real gang name, so I didn't follow that standard.

Finally, because I know some folks like them, there is a glosssary at the end of the book for the Yiddish, Spanish, and gang terminology used in *What Lies Within*.

And now, I give you the final episode of the Justice clan. May God use this story to bless and encourage you richly.

In His service,
Karen Ball

*"The LORD looks down from heaven
and sees the whole human race.
From his throne he observes
all who live on the earth.
He made their hearts,
so he understands everything they do.
The best-equipped army cannot save a king,
nor is great strength enough to save a warrior.
Don't count on your warhorse to give you victory—
for all its strength, it cannot save you.
But the LORD watches over those who fear him,
those who rely on his unfailing love.
He rescues them from death
and keeps them alive in times of famine.
We depend on the LORD alone to save us.
Only he can help us, protecting us like a shield.
In him our hearts rejoice,
for we are trusting in his holy name.
Let your unfailing love surround us, LORD,
for our hope is in you alone."*

PSALM 33:13–22

*"What lies behind us and what lies before us are tiny matters
compared to what lies within us."*

RALPH WALDO EMERSON

PROLOGUE

*"We crucify ourselves between two thieves:
regret for yesterday and fear of tomorrow."*
FULTON OURSLER

*"O LORD, how long will you forget me? Forever?
How long will you look the other way?
How long must I struggle with anguish in my soul,
with sorrow in my heart every day?
How long will my enemy have the upper hand?
Turn and answer me, O LORD my God!
Restore the light to my eyes, or I will die."*
PSALM 13:1–3

The night was a chameleon. Sometimes soft and welcoming, like a warm hug when you return home. Other times...

Oppressive.

Threatening.

For a moment Kyla's mind hovered on the thought, probing. What felt so wrong? Then she understood. It was too dark for a city street.

Her hand gripped the railing on the church steps; her feet felt their way down to the street. She was a few feet away from the building when it hit her.

The streetlights were out.

With a glance front and back—was someone out there, watching her?—she walked toward one tall light pole. Something crunched beneath her foot. She crouched, fingers exploring the ground—and her lips compressed.

Glass. Someone had broken—or, more likely, shot out—the streetlight. Her senses went into overdrive and she straightened. It wasn't hard to figure out who'd done it. Or why.

They hadn't been able to stop her with threats. So they were taking the next step.

Kyla spun and ran back toward the building, pounding feet sending an ominous echo through the oppressive night. As she drew near the church, she heard a door open. Could just discern someone stepping outside.

"Kylie?"

For a moment stark fear lodged in Kyla's throat. It took two hard swallows, but at last the words were freed. "Annot, get back inside!"

"Miss Annie, do what your sister says."

Tarik. Thank heaven. If Tarik was with Annot, then surely she'd listen. Wouldn't risk endangering the boy.

Kyla should have known better. She watched the dim outline of her sister as she came down the stairs toward her.

"Kylie, what's wrong? What are you—?"

Two sounds split the night: Tarik's alarmed cry, and something else.

Something sharp and terrifying.

It took Kyla's frantic mind a heartbeat to identify the sound.

A gunshot. Followed by a second.

Kyla bolted the last few feet and grabbed her sister's arm. "*Get inside!*"

No response. Kyla could just make out her sister's features...the wide eyes, the mouth opening and closing without making a sound.

"This is no time to fool arou—" The scold died when Annot slumped against Tarik—and Kodi's howl echoed, a chilling sound in the night.

"They were after me." The boy's low, choked words made no sense—but his eyes spoke volumes. Anguish. Sorrow. "She threw herself in front of me. If it wasn't for her, I'd be... They were shooting at me."

No. It wasn't possible. "Annot?"

Her sister just looked down, her usually smooth forehead creased. Annot's hands pressed against her ribs, but they couldn't halt what bloomed behind them, on the white of her shirt. Dark petals reaching out, spreading, covering the white.

Blood.

"Annot!" Kyla's cry tore through the night as Annot's knees buckled. She sank to the cold concrete steps, pulling both Kyla and Tarik down with her.

God! God, please!

Pure desperation lifted the prayer skyward. "*Someone,* help us!" She pressed down on Annot's hands despite her sister's pained groan, trying to staunch the flow. To no avail.

"Miss Kyla—"

"Somebody call 911!"

"Miss Kyla!"

The urgent words jerked Kyla from her panic. She focused on Tarik.

"Help me." He struggled to stand, his hands under Annot's arms. "We have to get her inside."

Nodding, Kyla gripped Annot's legs, and they carried her through the entry, into the vestibule, dodging a frantic Kodi.

Tarik pressed Kyla's hands against the sticky flow escaping her sister's body. She welcomed the solid feel of Kodi leaning into her.

God...God, please...

"Keep the pressure on. I'll call an ambulance."

Biting back tears, Kyla nodded again. She watched as the young man bolted toward the phone. Then she let herself look down at Annot's white face.

What if they couldn't get here in time? What if it was already too late? What if Annot was—

No! Kyla squeezed her eyes shut. There was only one thing her stunned mind could take in, a single fact it could grasp.

One person. One person had caused it all. The anger. The danger. Annot getting shot.

Annot dying...

Don't even think that!

"I'm sorry." Kyla's remorse weighted her like a sodden cloak, bending her, breaking her. "Oh, Annot, I'm so sorry."

Her sister's eyes opened. Her fingers closed over Kyla's. Forgiveness drifted on pained gasps. "Not...your fault."

But Kyla knew different. Her sister was dying. Before her eyes. In her arms. And there was no doubt in Kyla's mind.

It was all her fault.

ONE

*"Don't seek God in temples. He is close to you.
He is within you... Surrender to Him and you will rise
above happiness and unhappiness."*
LEO NIKOLAEVICH TOLSTOY

*"Here I sit in sackcloth. I have surrendered,
and I sit in the dust."*
JOB 16:15

Death was waiting.

Staff sergeant Rafael Murphy didn't have to see Death to know he was there. He could feel him. Feel the icy fingers inching up his spine. The disquiet shivering beneath his Kevlar. The heaviness in his chest, like a claymore aching to go off.

Back off. You're not getting my guys...

He glanced over his shoulder. He could have sworn the DZ was still in sight, but all that met his searching gaze was the fog cloaking them. The Huey had no sooner dropped them than the blasted fog moved in. Like it was waiting for them.

It took a little longer for the sand to start up.

When Rafe was a kid, he used to go to the Oregon Dunes with his buddies. When the wind picked up, the tiny grains whipped and stung like needles. So when he heard the stories about Iraq sandstorms, he wasn't worried. He'd been through sandstorms before.

Wrong.

The storms at home could be fierce, but these storms... They were flat evil. Roiling, roaring clouds that rose out of nowhere; monsters that traveled as fast as sixty mph, billowing down on everything in their paths. Like ravenous demons, they engulfed the world, turning the brightest day into hazy black night. As if that weren't freaky enough, there were times when the storm reached out and snatched the sun's light, absorbing and diffusing it until everything was tinged orange or red.

Blood red.

Iraq sandstorms weren't just nature flexing its muscles. They were living entities, bent on destruction.

At least the storm that met them today was a baby. Just enough to blend with the fog and limit their vision. That wasn't good, but it was better than it could have been. At least he could see a little—thirty meters or so. About a third of a football field away.

It wasn't great, but Rafe would take it.

He turned his eyes to the front, snugging his M4A1 assault rifle just a fraction closer. The Pride's mission was clear. Secure the area around a small town north of An Nasiriyah. Battalions were already on their way and would be moving on the town at 0 Dark 30.

It was 1600 hours now, which gave his team about two hours before dark. So far they'd had limited contact. One group of civilians passing by. A large group. Moving en masse.

That's when Death first spoke to Rafe. Whispered a low, rattling chuckle in his ear.

Sure, civilians often left town in twos or threes, but all together? That said one thing: "See ya later. Enjoy the ambush."

He and his team eyed the group of men, women, and children as they went by, watching…waiting…but nothing happened. The fleeing civilians made their way past, bowing their covered heads against the increasingly wind-whipped sand.

That they passed without incident should have eased Rafe's tension. Instead, it amped it up a notch.

"So what?" Death's mockery was deep and jagged. *"So those civilians weren't the ambush. Doesn't mean there isn't one waiting for you up there, just behind the curtain of fog and sand—"*

"This don't feel right."

The voice in his headset drew Rafe's attention to the left. So his ATL felt it too. No surprise there. Rashidi's instincts were as honed as his fighting skills, making him the perfect assistant team leader for the Pride. Rafe opened his mouth to reply, but a low southern drawl beat him to the draw.

"What is with this sand?"

"S'matter, Thales? You don't have sand in Gaw-gia?"

"Stuff it, Monroe."

Rafe's fingers tightened on his weapon. "Okay, Pride, can the chatter."

"C'mon, Asadi. How we supposed to secure the area when we cain't see spit? I cain't see a dang thi—"

"City at twelve o'clock, Asadi."

Leave it to Jesse Green to be focused on the task at hand. The guy was as grounded as any Marine Rafe ever met. Sure enough, about fifty meters ahead, buildings took shape.

The team tightened up as they moved into the city. They walked down the debris-scattered dirt road, scanning the buildings lining the road. The city might as well be a ghost town for all the activity they found there.

"Ghost town. How appropriate."

Rafe shook off the dark voice taunting him—until he noticed the street suddenly narrowed. Buildings seemed to spring up out of nowhere, looming over them left and right. Debris and abandoned cars—perfect booby traps— lay scattered all around. And Rafe knew.

This was it. What he'd been dreading.

He opened his mouth to warn the Pride when dust kicked up around his feet.

"Contact!"

Rafe turned at Jesse's yell, looking up, and flinched as something sang through the air from above. Bullets. It was raining bullets. "They're on top of the buildings!"

Through the fog Rafe saw the hazy forms. How many he didn't know. Nor could he tell who was shooting and who wasn't.

"Ah, the rules of engagement. Hard to comply now, wouldn't you say?"

Rafe's teeth clenched. *Shut up. Shut up before I shut you up!*

But again, Death was right. Soldiers in the U.S. military could only fire on those they knew were firing on them. That meant waiting for a muzzle flash in the fog.

And that would be too late.

Images flooded his mind. His men, bloodied, broken, dead eyes wide as their limp bodies were dragged through the streets by hooting Iraqis—

No! The Pride was *not* going down here. "Suppression fire! Thales, call for support!"

Moving into a tight three-sixty of defense, the team peppered the top edges of the buildings on either side, sending their attackers diving for cover as they made their way back out of the city.

Rafe heard Thales radioing in, yelling out their location. But he knew, as the others had to, as their grim features attested, that there wasn't time for support to reach them.

They were in a kill zone.

The street, the walls, everything channeled the enemy fire. The abandoned cars around them offered no cover; they were probably booby trapped. All their attackers had to do was keep shooting. Eventually, if Rafe and his team stayed there, they'd go down.

They had to get out of this on their own.

"Move out! Back the way we came!"

Still firing, Rafe looked behind them, measuring the distance. Ninety meters to safety. The hardest target to hit was a moving target, so—

"Move!"

His men responded without hesitation. Eighty meters to go. Sixty. Forty. Yelling and gunfire all around. Deafening. Bullets hitting walls, bricks, sending chips flying like tiny daggers.

Twenty meters. Ten! They were going to make it. Just a few more feet—

The searing pain came out of nowhere, exploding in Rafe's knee and hip.

Everything shifted to slow motion. Rafe looked down. Saw, as though it were some perverse scene on TV, the bullets pierce flesh, driving deep, shattering bone. As he fell, he watched the red gush forth. Soak his cammies. Seep into the ground, flowing across the desert, ballooning until everything was angry red—the color of his heartbeat.

"Man down! *Man down!*"

Rashidi's cry echoed around him. Rafe clawed at the ground and screamed, as much in anger as pain. Screamed and screamed again—

"*God!*" The cry ripped from Rafe's gut, echoing in the darkness of his room as he sat bolt upright.

Images shimmered behind his lids. Swirling sand and fog faded into muted darkness. The debris-littered street morphed, then settled into more benign shapes. A dresser. Bedside table. Lamp.

Muzzle flashes glittered and died. Became the first rays of daylight streaming in through his bedroom window.

Home.

He was home.

It was a dream. Again. The same dream that had tormented him for nearly four years.

Breathe. Memories can't hurt you. He threw back the covers, moved to slide out of bed, and winced. Yeah. Memories may not hurt, but torn tissue and muscle, damaged bone...

That hurt. All the time.

Rafe leaned forward, listening. No sounds from the other room. Good. He didn't wake Tarik this time. He hated disturbing the boy's sleep with his nightmares.

The ache in his leg worsened, and with a deep sigh, he turned to the ruby eyes watching him. "Mornin', fella. Ready for another day?" He lifted the cane beside his bed, letting his fingers trail across the silver lion's head handle. A farewell gift from his unit. A lion for the lion, they'd said.

Since their team was known as the Pride, it only seemed fitting they called him Asadi. Swahili for "lion." Which was cool. Shoot, it beat what they'd *started* to call him.

The image of that night sprang to life, and he closed his eyes. Now *this* memory he'd take.

As clear as if it were happening again, the night sky darkened overhead. Rafe and his team, bivouacked after an especially grueling day of training, sat around the fire, absorbing its warmth. Jesse Green, Rafe's assistant communicator, and David Thales, the primary communicator, sat there, MREs in hand, studying their sergeant.

"You're something else, sir."

Rafe wasn't sure who Jesse Green was talking to, but one look at the misplaced surfer told Rafe the comment was directed at him. Even if Green's sunbleached hair hadn't given away his L.A. roots, his lanky swimmer's build would have.

"He's right, Sarge. You somethin' else." David Thales looked like he'd been born in cammies. The southerner stood six foot four, was solid muscle, and lacked only one thing: a neck. First time Rafe saw the one-time star of his high school and college football teams, he hadn't been too sure Thales could move with the stealth they'd need on their missions. But years of bow hunting had made the kid as silent as a heart attack. And equally deadly. Good thing his small-town southern upbringing made him bona fide nice.

Rafe trailed his gaze from Thales to Green. "I'm nothing special."

"Gotta say I agree with them, Sarge." Pride shone in Rashidi Martin's dark eyes. "Like the motto says"—he jerked his chin toward the Force Recon tattoo on his coffee-colored upper arm—"'Swift. Silent. Deadly.' That's you, Staff Sergeant." He glanced at Thales and Green. "Oo-rah?"

Agreement sounded swift, certain. "Oo-rah!"

Thales stretched his tree-trunk legs in front of him. "Never seen no one move like you, Staff Sergeant. You remind me of somethin'—" He pursed his lips, then a big grin broke across his broad face. "I got it. I was out huntin' one weekend with my pappy and gran'pappy. We was sittin' around the campfire one evenin', jus' like this. 'Cept it weren't quite dark. And it weren't in Iraq. Anyways, the dogs was secured, an' we was just sittin' and drinkin' coffee." He leaned back. "Man…I loved being out there like tha—"

"*What* are you talking about, boy?"

Rafe eyed Kevin Monroe. His dark hair blended into the night, but that pasty midwesterner skin glowed like a beacon. At just this side of twenty-three, Monroe claimed the spot of youngest unit member. Pure farm boy from the heartland of America. "You saying the staff sergeant looks like coffee?"

Jesse Green pushed his boonie hat back off his forehead and hooted. "Naw, man. He's sayin' he looks like one of the dogs."

"No sir!" Thales's spine stiffened. "I ain't sayin' that at all, Staff Sergeant, sir."

Rafe didn't even try to respond. Didn't need to. His team was doing just fine without him.

"Well, what *are* you saying?" Kevin Monroe might not be as tall as Thales, but he boasted an equally powerful build. "I swear, Thales. Does everyone from the South take this long to spit something out?"

Thales's jaw tightened. One thing you did not do was impugn the South. Not in this man's presence. "Look, farm boy, just 'cuz you puke out words without givin' 'em a thought—"

"*What?*" Thunder settled on Monroe's bushy brow and he started to rise. Rafe's muscles tensed, but he needn't have worried.

"*Siéntate,* Monroe." Tom Sabada's quiet command stopped Kevin cold. No threat in the words, but there didn't need to be. Everyone in the Pride knew there was one team member none of them could take. Not even Rafe.

Thomas Sabada.

The man hailed from a blip on the map called Glorieta, New Mexico. Grew up in the mountains, where, as Sabada liked to say, the air was thin and tested your will. He learned to hunt and track with the best of them, which made him an effective point man. Nobody Rafe would rather have responsible for early detection of the enemy.

Rafe watched as Monroe eyed Sabada. The farm boy had the Hispanic by a good four inches—six foot two to Sabada's five foot ten—and probably fifty pounds. To a bystander, there was little about Sabada to make Monroe stand down. Until you met the man's eyes. Then you knew: here was a force to be reckoned with.

Sabada was a 7th Dan in Taekwondo, which earned him the title Master. Only thing that kept him from being an 8th Dan, a Grandmaster, was his age. You had to be at least forty-four to advance to the 8th Dan; Sabada was only thirty-eight.

Monroe did as Sabada commanded, and Sabada nodded at Thales. "Go on."

"Anyhow, there we were, sittin' and drinkin' coffee—"

"Have *mercy.*"

"—when the dogs started making a ruckus. Whinin' and pacin'. We hollered at 'em, but they wouldn't let up, so my granddaddy told me to go check on 'em. An' there it was."

Jesse Green was hooked. He leaned forward, that fresh face alive with curiosity. "There what was?"

"A cougar. Florida panther. Just walked outta the woods and right by us, slick as you please. The way that thing moved"—Thales rested those massive forearms on the weapon hanging across his chest—"whooee! All smooth and relaxed, but with those muscles and teeth, well, you knew it could be on you in a second and you'd be in a world of hurt."

"A puma." Sabada eyed Rafe. "*Si,* I can see that."

"Mountain lion, huh?" Green's teeth shone white in the dimming light. "We should call you *Simba,* Staff Sergeant."

Great. Nothing said *dangerous* like a Disney-character nickname.

"No." They all turned to Rashidi. "Not Simba. *Asadi.*"

Thales frowned. "*Asadi?* Whatssat mean?"

"It's my mother's native tongue. Swahili. It means *lion.*"

Thales leaned back and gave the name a test drive. *"Asadi."* His crooked grin broke out. "I like it."

"Who cares what you like, redneck." At least Monroe's jibe was friendly this time. "Question is, does the staff sarge like it?"

Five pairs of eyes peered at Rafe through the growing darkness.

"What do you say, *jefe?*" Sabada chewed the toothpick. "Work for you?"

Rafe studied the faces of his men, men he'd come to trust without hesitation during the year and a half they'd been together. "Yeah." He allowed a slow nod. "Works for me."

Works for me...

Words so full of confidence. Of the certainty that the day, and the next and the next, would be his. Rafe sighed and lifted his cane, caressing the exquisite silver lion's head with his thumb. Light from the lamp beside his bed caught the ruby eyes, making them glitter.

Works for me...

"Some lion I am now, eh, *compa?*" He set the cane down, leaned on it, and stood. "You know what happens to crippled lions in the wild, don't you? They die."

He'd almost done that.

But you didn't.

Rafe pressed his lips together. No, he didn't. He wasn't sure why, what he was still here for. Of course, others had their ideas…his sister, his team, and the one childhood friend who'd stuck with him.

That friend in particular was sure why Rafe was still there. At the thought of her, his gaze drifted to the computer desk next to his bed. Working the stiffness out of his gait, he made his way to the chair and plopped down.

Two quick clicks of the mouse, and his e-mail was open. Sure enough, a message from AngelEyes was there, waiting for him. He opened it up, his grin spreading as he read.

To: Asadi
Fr: AngelEyes
Subject: Something special's coming
Rafe, I woke up this morning thinking of you. God just plunked you down in my heart, so I've been praying. And as I did so, I had the coolest feeling. Can't explain it other than to say this:
Something's coming.
Something great.
Don't know what God has in store for you, but I'm betting it has to do with YKW.

Rafe's grin spread. YKW: You Know Who. This girl was so funny.

Talked with YKW yesterday. Busy, as always. But something was…off. Can't explain that either. Just know things aren't quite right.

Rafe frowned at that, unease stirring in his gut. Not quite right… What did that mean? Maybe he should try to find out. Maybe.

I know you said she hasn't been around lately and you're worried. But Rafa, she's in God's hands. As are you. And I know, my friend, that He's in control. So don't let things get to you, okay? Just relax and let Him lead. His timing is perfect. Don't ever doubt it.
Hey, look at me! If He can bring such beauty out of my life, you

KNOW he can do a number with yours. 'Cuz you're a great guy. And you may not like to admit it, but your heart is for Him.
Peace today.
A

His mouth tipped. Okay. Message received. Stay out of it. Angel was so sure of herself. Of her God. So sure of him. Even after all these years, he hadn't figured out why. He hit Reply.

To: AngelEyes
Fr: Asadi
Subject: You always seem to know…
…when I need to hear from you. Had another nightmare. Ugly stuff. Wonder if I'll ever get those images out of my mind. But it helped to find your e-mail waiting for me. Always has. You know I printed out all the e-mails you sent me overseas? Store them and your letters in a folder. I pull 'em out to read sometimes. Helps me keep the good memories alive, not just the bad ones.
It's okay, though. I was there for a reason. I don't regret it. Things didn't turn out like I wanted, but hey. That's life, eh? Yeah, yeah, I know. That's God. Unpredictable, but good. Someday I may believe that for myself. Until then, you keep on believing. For both of us.
Give your honeys—two- and four-legged—my best. And have a great day.
Asadi

As the animated e-mail envelope vanished into cyberspace, Rafe's fingers curled around the lion head atop his cane, and he pushed himself to his feet. "Come on, compa. Time for our morning workout." He tapped the cane against his right leg. "Gotta get loosened up and ready for the day." Rafe allowed a small smile. "I may not be King of the Pride anymore, but I'm still a force to reckon with, eh?"

He made his way to his workout room, determination building with each step. Because he knew it was a gift. Being around to get ready for anything. And more than that, he knew there was a reason. Some reason he'd survived.

Had to be.

So he'd keep doing what he knew to do until that reason chose to reveal itself.

He'd barely walked out of his bedroom when the fragrance hit him. Coffee. So. He'd roused Tarik after all. Rafe made his way to the kitchen, and sure enough, the boy was there, just pouring the black brew into two heavy mugs.

Tarik glanced up at him, and one dark brow lifted. "Oh yeah. You look rested." He held out a still-steaming mug.

"Funny boy." He heard the edge in his tone and softened it as he came into the room. "As rested as you feel, most likely." Rafe accepted the mug with a nod. "Sorry I woke you."

The boy's shrug offered grace, understanding. "No worse than I've done to you, man."

True enough, but at least Tarik's nightmares were growing fewer and farther between. Rafe wished he could say the same. He pulled a chair out from the kitchen table and eased himself down. "You didn't have to get up, you know."

There was the edge again. Tarik's bland look told Rafe he'd heard it and dismissed it. Rafe took a sip of the hot liquid, letting it burn his throat. Served him right for being a grouch.

Again.

Silence stretched and deepened, and Rafe drank it in even as he savored the strong coffee. He hadn't been sure about opening his home to Tarik, but it had been a good decision. He'd given Tarik a safe home. And the boy had given him a solid friend.

One who knew the value of quiet camaraderie.

Rafe leaned his elbows on the table. "So, big plans today?"

Tarik's chuckle balanced between manly and boyish. At fourteen he was perched on that precipice, his heart telling him he was a man even as his age tied him to childhood.

"Oh yeah, the biggest. School. Homework. You know, fun, fun."

The boy's wry tone didn't fool Rafe. He knew how grateful Tarik was to have such things, how determined the boy was to succeed. Overcome. Leave the past in the dust.

It was one of the many similarities that bound them. Blood. Race. Backgrounds. All those might differ, but at heart, Rafe and Tarik were the same.

"You gonna have time for a workout this morning?"

The boy's question drew Rafe's gaze to the clock, and he gritted his teeth. How did time keep getting away from him? No workout meant he'd hurt more, but taking the time now would put him at the shop late. A curse almost escaped him, but Tarik's warning look halted it. Though Rafe's stint in the military had turned his language somewhat salty, having the kid live here had been as effective in setting Rafe's mouth straight as if his mother were still alive. "Doesn't look like it. I'd better get a move on if I want to get to the shop on time."

Tarik leaned back in his chair. "You'd *better* get there on time. You may be the owner, but your sister…"

Rafe grinned. "Yeah, I know. She's the boss." He pushed to his feet, nodding at Tarik. "Thanks for the brew."

"No problem. And Rafe?"

He turned back to face the young man seated at his kitchen table. "Yeah?"

"I'm prayin' your lady shows up today."

His lady. If only that were so. "You are, huh? Since when are you so concerned with my"—his mind halted, searching for the right word—"friendships?"

The boy's lips twitched as he reached out to grab Rafe's now-empty mug. "Since not seein' her made you so crabby."

Rafe rested against the kitchen doorway. "Crabby, huh?"

"Yeah, like a bear—"

"Ah, well—"

Tarik set the mugs in the sink. "With blisters."

"Okay, I get the—"

"On his behind."

It was Rafe's turn to fight a grin at the boy's half-scolding tone. Which of them was the adult again? "Sorry, bud. I'll do better."

Tarik's smile was entirely too smug. "I knew you would." He glanced at the clock. "Now you'd better hit the showers before your sister starts callin' to see where you're at."

Rafe couldn't help himself. He saluted. And chuckled, all the way to his room.

Having Tarik come to live with him had brought some adjustments, but it had also brought something else. Something Rafe had been missing for too long.

Joy.

TWO

*"Restlessness and discontent are the
first necessities of progress."*
THOMAS ALVA EDISON

*"So I turned in despair from hard work. It was not the
answer to my search for satisfaction in this life."*
ECCLESIASTES 2:20

If joy came in the morning, then it had to be a hair past nighttime, because
the one thing Kyla Justice did *not* feel was joyful.

She pushed the driver's door open and stepped out into the mall parking
lot. She'd parked at the outer edges, intent on getting in for the dedication
and getting out. She hit the lock button on her remote—and froze.

What was that sound? A soft, distressed squeak.

Great! Just what she needed. A malfunctioning remote. That couldn't
have been a good soun—

But no. The mewling cry came again. From behind her car.

It was hard to spot at first, but then Kyla caught a shiver of movement
beneath a bush. She moved closer—and caught her breath. A kitten. Multicolored fur matted and damp from the misting rain that morning. Trembling.
A pathetic, barely discernable mew tore at her heart, and Kyla reached for the
bedraggled creature. Then stopped. Tiny or not, if this was a feral cat, she'd
get shredded for her efforts. She cast a glance this way and that.

Where was the mother?

No lurking feline met her searching gaze. "Come on, Mama. Where are
you hiding?" Another soft cry drew her gaze once more to the little bundle

huddling under the bush. Wide eyes beseeched her. The weary fright in them tugged at her heart.

Take it home with you. The thought was as immediate as it was startling. Feelings Kyla didn't recognize flooded her. They were positively…maternal. But take it home? How could she do that when she was on her way to a grand opening?

You can just tuck it inside your suit coat.

The animal was certainly small enough. Poor thing couldn't be more than a few weeks old. Her body warmth would probably put the little puff-ball right to sleep.

Are you crazy? Now *this* voice she knew. *You paid a mint for this suit!*

But if she didn't help the kitten, it would probably die.

Not your problem. You can't risk standing up there at the podium, trying to look professional, only to have this little beast snag the expensive threads beyond repair.

Kyla straightened but couldn't leave.

Fine. Don't blame me if it decides to turn Tasmanian devil on you. Can you see a shot of that on the front page of the paper? Be smart, Kyla.

Smart. She was always smart. Always did what made sense. Kyla looked at the kitten. It just lay there, its little head on its paws. It was probably too late to do anything anyway.

Then just put it in your car. On the floorboards in the backseat. Enough to shelter it.

And risk letting it claw the leather interior? You have *lost your mind!*

Stop!

Kyla strode across the parking lot, trying to ignore the heaviness in her chest that grew with each step away from the tiny creature in need.

"Kyla?"

She spun. "Oh! Mason. You startled me."

The man came to her side, took her arm, and planted a circumspect peck on her cheek. "Sorry, dear. Have I told you today how proud I am of you?"

Kyla forced a smile to her lips. Would he feel that way if he knew what she just did?

Yes, she realized as she fell into step beside him, he would. Mason was all about common sense. Not letting warm and fuzzies hinder good judgment.

Well, it didn't get much warmer or fuzzier than what she'd faced. *And resisted*.

"Kyla, darling?"

She started, forcing her attention back to the man at her side. "Yes, Mason. You've said you were proud of me. A number of times."

His arm slid around her waist and tugged her close. "Well, forgive a man for delighting in his beloved's accomplishments."

Her smile was a bit more sincere this time. *Beloved*. What a nice term. She brushed his designer jacketed arm with her fingers. "Forgiv—"

The word turned to a little yelp when Mason's arm ushered her forward. "You're on, darling. Be brilliant."

"Wait! I…here, take this." She pushed her cell phone at him. She didn't have time to turn it off, and last thing she needed was to have it pipe up while she was standing in front of everyone.

Then, gathering her composure, Kyla advanced to the podium, ignoring the flashes as reporters shot their photographs. She shook hands with Mr. Belkins, her client—whose cat-that-ate-the-canary grin demonstrated his pleasure with the finished project—then turned to offer a welcome for the grand opening of the Mountain's Edge outlet mall.

Applause followed her and Mr. Belkins as they moved toward a large green ribbon stretched across the mall entrance. A perfectly shaped and coiffed woman stepped forward to cut the ribbon. Applause sounded again, and Belkins turned to the crowd.

"Please, come inside and see for yourselves why Mountain's Edge is more than just a mall. It's a step into the future of retail."

Kyla nodded and smiled as people filed past, heading for the refreshment tables. What she wouldn't give to have Mason whisk her away from this. Take her someplace for a quiet celebration. But that was like wishing for the sky to turn chartreuse. Mason was, first and foremost, a businessman. And in business, one simply did not walk away from positive—and free—publicity.

"Great job, Miss Justice."

She turned to Mr. Belkins, noting the satisfied smile stretching his too-smooth features. "Thank you, sir. It's always good to know my clients are happy."

"You really are unique, you know that?"

Kyla glanced over her shoulder to where Mason stood in the background, content to let her shine this time. "So I've been told."

"I mean, look at what you've done."

She followed the effusive sweep of his hand, taking in the line of buildings before them. Mountain's Edge was, without a doubt, stunning. She'd constructed the mall with an eye to every detail. From the buildings' log-house facades to shaded coves holding benches that beckoned weary shoppers to sit and recoup, the design was that of a woodland hideaway. But the crowning touch was a hewn-log trellis overarching the walkways. Branches, complete with pine needles that looked so real you could almost smell them, stretched between the buildings, giving the sense of walking through the woods.

It was a masterpiece. Or as close as she'd come yet in her work.

"People are going to love coming here." Belkins's manicured hand clapped her on the shoulder. "I'm going to make a mint off this place, and I owe it to you."

The effect the gleeful words had on Kyla was probably the exact opposite of what the man intended. Her stomach clenched, and the ache inside her kicked into overdrive. Still, she dredged up a gracious smile. *"Always be professional,"* her father had told her. *"Don't ever let your emotions get the better of you."*

"I'm glad you're pleased."

"Pleased?" Belkins chuckled. "I'm delighted. And I'm going to see to it that you have more contracts than you know what to do with."

Kyla forced out the appropriate words of gratitude, then glanced toward the crowd around the refreshment table. One woman's features caught her eye. Soft white hair framed a round, smiling face that glowed with some inner radiance. There was a face of kindness. Love.

There was someone who wouldn't leave a kitten to die.

Kyla almost choked on the thought.

"Are you all right, my dear?"

She fended off Belkins's conciliatory hand on her arm. "I'm fine. Now, you probably need to go talk with the reporters you invited."

"Won't you join us? I'm sure they'd love to talk with you as well."

A revolting idea, if ever she'd heard one. "Regrettably, I have another appointment." She glanced at Mason.

It wasn't a lie. Not really. She and Mason *were* having dinner together. Okay, not for a few hours, but still…any port in a storm.

"Ah." Belkins patted her hand. "I see. Well, give my best to Mr. Rawlins." He leaned in a bit closer. "I hope there are no hard feelings that I awarded the mall contract to your company, and not his. I just knew you'd understand my vision—"

Kyla assured him Mason was as professional as they came. Her client thus mollified, she finally made her escape. Her height had been a bane when she was younger, but she was glad for it now. For the long legs that brought her to Mason's side in a few quick strides. "Please, for the love of heaven, get me out of here."

He frowned at the vehemence in her tone. "You're not going to talk with the reporters?"

She looped her arm in his. "No. I have…things to do." Again, not really a lie. She *did* have things to do. Nothing that couldn't wait, but she wasn't telling Mason that. "Besides, I need to get ready for a very important dinner this evening."

"Ever the voice of wisdom, my dear." Mason took her arm as they headed for the parking lot. "You did a phenomenal job on this project."

Yes, she could admit that was true. So why wasn't she more excited? Pleased? *Some*thing other than…

Empty.

How she hated the word. The feeling. That gut-deep sensation she'd done everything she could to avoid. She'd been empty—truly, tragically empty—once in her life. She'd sworn then she would never feel that again.

And yet here she was, fighting it again. All because of some silly, soggy kitten?

"The fact that you were so involved in the design on this one, and that it turned out so beautifully, will open more doors than you can imagine."

Kyla's stomach roiled. She narrowed her gaze, trying to see if the animal was still there. It had been nearly two hours. Would the little creature be lying there, stiff? Mute testimony to just how hardened she'd become?

"Perhaps I should sell my company and come to work for you?"

Of course, Mason was teasing. Well, as much as he ever teased. "Don't be ridiculous." Was that a movement beneath the bush? Her heart raced, and she grabbed Mason's arm, directing him toward her car. She wouldn't let him see. Neither would she look. "Rawlins Building is just as successful as JuCo."

"A bit more so, probably."

He was right, as usual. She hit the remote unlock, and Mason opened the door for her, then handed her into the car. Kyla loved his old-world manners.

Mason leaned his forearm on the top of her car, smiling down at her. "Still, it might be interesting to sit about, answering the calls for your talented services all day—oh! Speaking of which. Your phone."

He reached down and pulled it from his suit coat pocket—just as a cheery tone sounded. Those fine brows of his arched. "Well. How's that for timing? What say I give it a go now?" He leaned close to Kyla as he answered the phone. "Justice Construction, may I help you?"

"Oh! Is this you, Mase?"

Oh dear. Annot. With the phone held between them, Kyla heard her sister's every word. Better catch her younger sister before she said anything she shouldn't.

Mason forestalled Kyla's hand. "Yes, Annie, it's *Mason*. How are you?"

"Me? I'm fine. Yup, just fine. And you. You're…well, you're still around, huh?"

Kyla grimaced. Ouch. When would Annot learn not to express every one of the multitudes of thoughts that flitted through her mind?

The tiniest bit of umbrage sneaked into Mason's usually calm tone. "Obviously so, Annie. How nice of you to ask. I assume you called to speak with your sister? She's right here."

Kyla pressed her lips together and took the phone from his extended hand. She pressed the phone to her chest and sent Mason a tacit apology, then raised her head for his peck on the cheek.

"Well"—he straightened, and Kyla tried not to let the sardonic twist to his lips bother her—"I'll leave you to your conversation. See you at your place? Around six?"

"You have the key I gave you?"

"Indeed."

"Thanks again for the offer to fix me a celebratory dinner. I appreciate it, Mason."

"Yes, well, I like to think I treat you as you deserve to be treated." His gaze drifted to the phone. "Though I'm sure there are some who don't agree."

She should say something, but her mind was as void as her heart. So she just sat there, watching the man she was supposed to love walk away.

Doing nothing to stop him.

THREE

> *"I have always been delighted at the prospect of a new day, a fresh try, one more start, with perhaps a bit of magic waiting somewhere behind the morning."*
> JOSEPH PRIESTLEY

> *"If I had the gift of prophecy, and if I understood all of God's secret plans and possessed all knowledge, and if I had such faith that I could move mountains, but didn't love others, I would be nothing."*
> 1 CORINTHIANS 13:2

Where was she?

Rafe lifted a cup of steaming black coffee to his lips. A week. Seven days since Kyla had been here—eight if you counted today. Every day he watched for her, waited to see her smile as she came in, to catch that tantalizing perfume as she drew close. Something simple and elegant. A kind of vanilla, like the cookies his mom made him after school when he was young. Warm and subtle, but with enough impact to reach him through the scent of good, strong coffee.

After three days with no sign of her, he began to worry. Had he done something wrong? Somehow made her uncomfortable? No, impossible. He'd done everything he could to accomplish just the opposite. To make this place a haven for her, a place she longed to be.

Two more days went by. Then two more.

Maybe she was ill. He plunked his coffee mug down on the counter.

Why hadn't he found out where she lived? Yes, he'd wanted to move with care. To make each advance in their budding acquaintance as cautious and strategic as possible. He wasn't going to risk scaring her off.

But what if something had happened to her? With her sister and brother so far away, who was around to help her if she needed it?

You think a woman like that hasn't got friends? Hasn't got a man?

A man. The thought pierced him, but only for a moment.

No, not the way she'd smiled at him. The way her eyes warmed whenever she looked at him. Even if there was a man in her life, it wasn't someone who owned her heart. Rafael was as certain of that as he was his own name.

Worry stuck in his gut. He'd waited long enough. Time to do something. He could go to her company's office, but that seemed too…intrusive. Then he remembered. She'd mentioned the mall her company was building. Perfect. He'd just drive past the construction site. Surely he'd see her there, and then his worries would be put to rest.

He turned and went to find Olivia. His sister listened as he asked her to carry the shift on her own.

"You crazy, Rafa? You know I stay in the background. You're the front man, si? I don't deal with those people. Six bucks for a cup of coffee? Those people are nuts."

"My coffee is worth it, sis."

She tossed her hair. "*No*body's coffee is worth that much money. Not unless there's gold dust in the grounds."

He waggled his brows at her. "Heeey, there's an idea."

She waved him off and started to walk away, but he caught her. Curled his arms around her shoulders and put on his best puppy-dog face. "For me, Livita. Please."

Her heavy sigh signaled surrender—the childhood nickname had done the trick, as he'd known it would. But she didn't give in without a price.

"So, what you going to say to this *chica* if you find her?"

"Say to her?"

"Si, Rafa. You'll have to speak to her one of these days. Maybe even tell her how you feel." She pinched his arm. "That should be interesting. My little *chato,* too tough to express his emotions, telling a woman he loves her."

When he didn't take the bait, she nudged him with her hip. "Come on, Rafa. Practice with me. *Te amo, mi cielo.*"

"Liv…"

"*Mi amor.*" She batted her eyelashes. "*Mi corazon.*"

"*¡Córtala!*"

Her laughter rang out as she complied. "All right, Rafa. No more teasing."

He handed her his barista apron and was out the door and behind the steering wheel in two heartbeats. He gunned the engine, racing through traffic and brushing aside the thought that he was acting just a bit crazy. If he saw Kyla at the construction site, fine. He'd know she was okay.

If not…he'd be placing a call to his Force Recon buddy David Thales. Thales would find Kyla. In record time. Thales could find anyone. Anywhere. Anytime.

He braked for a red light—and frowned. Thales would want to know who Kyla was. What she was to Rafe.

And what, pray tell, is she? A customer at your coffee shop.

He hit the gas, focusing just enough to maneuver around a snarl of traffic. Kyla was more than that. She'd been coming to Rafe's coffee shop every day for the past four months. Every day. And she didn't just buy coffee and walk out. She stayed to talk. Sometimes he even took a break and sat with her at one of the small round tables.

That was more than just a customer, right?

Yeah. He could just hear what Thales and the others from his Force Recon team would say.

"Sure, Asadi. Whatever you say."

"You taking up stalking, Staff Sergeant, sir?"

"You wiggin' out, Asadi?"

But Rafe would tell them what he kept telling himself: Kyla Justice was just a friend. Nothing more. He spotted the construction site ahead, and his heart rate picked up speed. He'd just drive past, nice and slow—but not too slow. Didn't want to draw attention.

His plans faded, though, as he pulled into the parking lot. There were cars everywhere. And from the looks of things, this job wasn't in process. It was done. In fact, unless he missed his guess—which didn't happen often—there was a grand opening in progress.

Rafe peered into the milling crowd but saw no sign of Kyla. His concern flared to life, and he reined it in, turning the wheel to circle the parking lot—

There! Her car. Sitting at the back of the lot. And perched on the driver's seat, legs stretched out the open driver's door, was Kyla. Talking on her cell phone.

Relief so powerful it made him lightheaded swept through him. She was okay. And then, on the heels of relief, came the gnawing unease. He managed to ignore it as he steered his car out of the parking lot, back onto the road. Even held it off until he shifted the car into park back at his coffee shop. But it crawled through him as he pushed out of the vehicle and headed inside.

Because if she wasn't sick, something else was keeping her away.

~~~

"Stop it this minute! Kylie? Are you daydreaming again? He-*llo!*"

Issuing a heavy sigh, Kyla put the phone to her ear. "Annot, for heaven's sake, must you be so belligerent to Mason?"

"I'm not belligerent."

"All right then, rude."

"Not that either."

Kyla leaned forward, resting her forehead against the steering wheel, then straightened with a jerk. There it was. A mewing sound. She was sure of it!

She slid from the car, the cell phone to her ear. "Fine. Then what would you call that idiotic remark you made to him about his still being around?"

The silence drew out. "You heard that, huh?"

"Yes, Annot, I heard it." Kyla reached the back of her car and peered down at the bush.

Nothing.

The kitten was gone.

Pain—sudden and blinding—shot through Kyla. Piercing her heart.

"Kyla? Are you okay?"

The alarm in her sister's voice told her she'd somehow given herself away. "I'm fine. Just"—she pressed trembling fingers to weary eyes—"frustrated."

More silence. "Look, I'm sorry, Kylie. I guess I'm just ambivalent when it comes to Mason."

Why hadn't she come back sooner? Why hadn't she at least called the Humane Society? "He's a fine man."

"But is he the *right* man? That's what bothers me."

"What matters, my dear sister, is whether or not it bothers *me.*" Kyla let the overwhelming emotions fill her tone, welcomed the outlet even as she knew Annot didn't deserve her response.

"I've seen you two together, and I've listened to your voice when you talk about him, and there's just…"

Kyla closed her eyes. "What? There's just what?"

"Nothing."

The word fell like a stone. How horribly appropriate. "Annot—"

"No, that's what there is. Nothing. No longing. No sense that you can't wait to be with him. No *passion.* You need a man with passion."

"Our passion is doing just fine, thank you."

"Oh?" Long pause. "Anything I should know about?"

"Don't be absurd, Annot. You know me better than that."

"Exactly. Which is why I know Mason is fine as a friend, but he's just not the one. Not for you, Kylie."

Kyla didn't cry. Hadn't done so in years. And yet as she stood there, listening to her sister's voice, her eyes burned and filled.

Think of something else. Tell Annot your name isn't Kylie…

She didn't have the energy to try to stop her sister's use of the childhood nickname. What was the point? Annot gave everyone nicknames. *Annie* rather than *Annot, Dan* in place of *Avidan.* Even her dog was everything from Kodi, the animal's actual name, to Beast, Monster, and—Kyla's personal favorite—Kodi-o-dio. And that was fine. For Annot.

Kyla chose to hold to the true names they'd been given. Out of respect.

Not, no matter *what* Annot said, out of rigidity.

"So how's life down south?" Annot lived in Medford, which was three hundred miles south. A nice area, though a bit too arid for Kyla. She much preferred the lush green of the Portland area.

Unfortunately, her sister didn't take the distraction bait. "Don't you ever get tired of it, Kylie?"

"Of what?"

"Being so sedate."

At least that made Kyla laugh. A little. "Are you calling me dull?"

"Well. Yeah. I mean, think about it. You and Mason are both so unaffected by life. So controlled."

You should see me now. She pressed two fingers to the bridge of her nose. This conversation was going nowhere. Just like her life. And that had to change. "Was there a reason you called?"

Another pause. Then a sigh. Her sister could communicate *volumes* with one sigh. "Two reasons. First, I wanted to know how the opening went."

"Fine."

"You don't sound very excited."

Kyla stared at the clouds studding the sky. "It's a mall, Annot. It's not like I built something that will change anyone's life." Her own words struck her, and she straightened her back, brows furrowing, realization nudging at her.

"Anyway, the second reason I called is to let you know that Jed and I are getting married." Delight lilted across the phone waves.

"Yes, I know. You've been engaged for almost seven months now."

By all rights, the two should already be husband and wife. They'd planned to marry back in December.

It surprised everyone when they, hand in hand, had gathered the family in Annot's living room and Jediah explained. "Annie and I love each other, but God has made it clear we should take our time." He looked at Annot, and the love in his features was undeniable. "This is going to last all our lives. We need to do it right."

Kyla's mouth had fallen open. Something she seldom allowed but couldn't stop this time. "You're taking time to *think* about something?"

Annot laughed. "Yes, Kylie, as out of character as that may seem. But hey, isn't it about time I was sensible about something in my life?"

"Yes, it is." Kyla had smiled at their brother, Avidan, and he winked his agreement.

Kyla drew her focus back to the phone call. "So, you're getting married is supposed to be news because…?"

"Because we've set a date."

"Oh, Annot! Really? When?"

Her sister's laughter trilled. "Now *that's* more like it. You need to get excited more often, sister mine."

"Just tell me the date, brat."

"December 21."

Kyla grabbed her purse and tugged her day planner free. "That's barely three months away!"

"It's a good deal more than we'd have had with our original plan."

True enough. That would have given them a week. "Okay, then, December 21 it is." She set her day planner on the seat beside her. Her sister's wedding. Now this was something that mattered. "You'll tell me what you want me to do and when?"

"You mean other than be my maid of honor?"

Kyla bit her lip against the sting at the backs of her eyes. How did Annot do that? Know exactly what to say to tug Kyla's heart to life? "I'd love to. Thank you."

"Yeah, like I'd ask anyone else, goofball."

"You'd better not. Anyway, let me know when you want to get together to talk about things or try on dresses, or whatever."

"Will do. And Kyla?"

"Yes?"

"Get some rest. You don't sound right."

"Annot—"

"I won't say another word. I promise."

Kyla couldn't hold back the wry smile as she bid her sister good-bye. Annot not say another word?

Now *that* would be a miracle.

FOUR

"Associate with men of good quality if you esteem your own reputation; for it is better to be alone than in bad company."
GEORGE WASHINGTON

"Yes, I will punish those who...fill their masters' houses with violence and deceit."
ZEPHANIAH 1:9

It was a miracle nothing had happened so far.

He stood back, concealed by the concrete building, and watched what was happening across the street. Frustration warred with apprehension in his gut.

That ladder rung should have given way by now. He'd been here the last two days, waiting. It shouldn't have taken this long. He'd chosen the old extension ladder because it was tall enough to do the trick, but not so tall the accident could kill. He chose a middle rung, about five feet up, and made a perfect cut. Just enough to weaken the rung but not so obvious anyone would notice. Lucky for him the construction crew was using the ladders owned by the church as well as their own aluminum equipment.

Wood ladders were far easier to sabotage.

Another construction worker climbed the ladder in question, and he held his breath. But the worker made it to the top of the ladder without event.

Foul thoughts flew through his mind, curses against whatever guardian angels hovered nearby. Sure, it was a church. But that shouldn't matter. Accidents happened everywhere, even on so-called holy groun—

A loud snap and a man's alarmed cry jerked him from his dark reverie. Anticipation wrapped around his heart, making it pound as he leaned for a better view. Ah, success!

The worker lay on the ground, writhing in what clearly was agony. Chaos erupted as his fellow workers ran to his side.

"Call 911! Now!"

Music to his ears.

He slipped behind the building, leaning against the cold concrete, and smiled.

～〜

"I'm done."

Fredrik Tischler looked up from the ledger he was studying to peer at the tall man standing in the doorway of the church office. He hadn't known James Lawton long, but he liked what he knew of him. He'd worked hard these last few months, keeping his construction crew past sunset more often than not.

Speaking of which…Fredrik glanced past the contractor at the still-sunny day outside. He frowned and almost questioned James, but reason seeped in. The crew deserved to get off a little early once in a while. He waved a hand. "Fine. We'll see you first thing tomorrow."

"No." The contractor's tone hardened. "Not done for today. *Done.*"

Sudden understanding brought Fredrik to his feet. How such a man, a professional, could be saying this was more than he could take in. "You're quitting?"

Lawton buried his large hands in his pants pockets. "I'm sorry—"

"But we only have two more months to finish the project!"

"Mr. Tischler, I'm sorry. But we can't keep working with these conditions."

"Please—"

Words spilled forth, frustration evident in the clipped tone. "No. I just sent another man to the hospital."

"Oh no." Fredrik pressed his hands against the desktop, steadying himself. "I heard the sirens but didn't know they were coming here."

"This man has worked for me for five years. Never been injured on the job, not once. And now he's the fourth man injured on this job." He shook his head. "If that weren't enough, every order for supplies has come back wrong, no matter *how* careful we are with the measurements. It's not my guys. I *know* it's not."

"I know, but—"

"Tools have gone missing. Permits have been delayed or lost. Vehicles have been broken into. And these accidents…" Lawton clamped his jaws on the tirade.

"Mr. Lawton, please—"

"No, I'm sorry. I know you're trying to do a good thing here. I respect that. I wanted to be a part of it. Really. But I won't put my guys at risk any longer." He held out a folder Fredrik hadn't noticed before. "Here's everything you need to give the new contractor."

Fredrik took the folder, then did the only thing he could. He held out his hand.

Lawton hesitated for a second, then accepted Fredrik's hand. "I'm sorry, sir. I really am."

Fredrik believed him. "You do what you must, sir. With such there is no arguing."

Lawton turned and walked toward the doorway, where he hesitated and turned back, concern heavy on his features. "You've got somebody working awfully hard to keep this project from happening. Are you sure it's worth the cost?" He didn't wait for a reply. He just walked out of the office.

Fredrik stood there, folder in his hands, mind spinning. Finally, with a weighted sigh, he laid the folder on the desk and picked up the phone.

~⁓~

Father, we need a miracle.

"I see you're praying again."

Fredrik turned as Willard walked toward him. "I'm Jewish. I'm in a temple. I should do something else?"

With the ease born of long friendship, the white-haired man came to stand close beside Fredrik.

Fredrik stated the obvious. "You got my message."

"About the contractor?" The older man's words were as heavy as Fredrik's heart. "Yes, I got your message." They stood in silence for a few moments. What could either of them say? They both knew how hopeless the situation was.

"By the way, you're in a church, Fredrik, not a temple."

Fredrik glanced at his friend. "Yes?"

"You said you were in a temple." Willard shrugged. "Just thought I'd point out that it's a church."

"Church, temple." Fredrik lifted a hand to touch the wood of the sanctuary wall. "Youth center…it's all the same to me. A house of God. Old habits die hard. Besides, they all point us to God, though my Orthodox brethren wouldn't agree."

"On that, and a number of other things."

So true. But Fredrik knew the time would come for the truth to touch God's chosen. He stared up at the wooden cross that had hung in the sanctuary for over a hundred years. How he'd hated that symbol as a child. Almost as much as he now loved it. "It has seen much of life, hasn't it, old friend?"

The eyes that angled his way held a depth of affection and humor. "It's a cross. Inanimate wood. It hasn't 'seen' anything."

Fredrik shook his head, *tsking*. "Ah, Willard. It must be a sad place, your mind. So lacking in imagination."

The older man's lips twitched. "I'll leave that to you, Fredrik. You have enough imagination for a dozen men."

"It's a gift."

"It's a nuisance."

Fredrik lifted one wrinkled hand to pat his friend's shoulder. "Aren't you glad I know you're not serious?"

Willard's deep laughter rang out, echoing off the warm wooden walls as it had so many times over the years.

How can we bear it, Father? We love this place. The ache in Fredrik's heart was almost more than he could bear.

As though he could read Fredrik's mind, Willard released a sigh. "It's too hard." He looked around the empty sanctuary. "Closing the doors was bad enough. At least we had the hope of seeing this building turned into something good, something to help the community."

Fredrik nodded. Yes, a youth center would definitely help this community.

"But to lose it now, after all we've done—" Willard's voice choked.

Fredrik tightened his hand on his friend's shoulder. "We're not going to lose it."

"Fredrik…"

"No." He gave a hard shake of his head. "I will not listen to such talk. God brought us to this place and time for a reason. He's had His hand on this old church for more years than even you or I have been alive. He made it clear to us that we were to have it renovated into a youth center. That has not changed. *God* has not changed." Fredrik's voice—and heart—filled with renewed confidence. "His purposes will be fulfilled."

"Without contractors?"

Good question.

"Why can't the police stop him?"

Fredrik didn't ask who Willard meant. No need. He knew who was behind their woes. Some in the church thought it was the Blood Brotherhood, but Fredrik didn't think so. The gang had left the small church alone so far.

No, he was convinced their opposition came from a far more professional source. "No proof. Without solid proof, they can't do a thing."

Willard swallowed, his gaze drifting back to the cross. "I just can't believe one of our own would do this to us."

One of their own.

Sam Ballat had definitely been that. His parents were married in this church. He grew up in it. It was Sam's grandparents who donated the land for the church to be built nearly a hundred years ago. Land that had been in their family for years. Land they wanted to dedicate to God's service. Which was why they'd put that clause in the deed. The clause causing all the trouble now. A clause that made it clear: should the land ever cease being used to benefit the community, ownership would revert back to the Ballat family.

"We knew this day was coming."

"Yes, we did." Attendance at the small church, located as it was in the midst of warehouses and a rapidly decaying neighborhood, had been dwindling for years. "I was so sure we'd lose this place, that it would revert back to

Ballat when we had to close the doors." He patted Willard on the back. "But your wonderful idea saved us."

It had been Willard's idea to take the money saved up from donations—a substantial amount for such a small congregation—and convert the building into a youth center.

The response was immediate: everyone loved the idea.

"Saved us for a while. Until Sam heard about it."

Indeed. "Hindsight, it's twenty-twenty, yes? I guess it was a mistake to invite him to our discussions."

They'd done so out of consideration for his family, but he did everything he could to discourage them. Pointed out how the church leadership was too old to manage a project this big. How such things always cost more than anticipated. How they'd be wasting valuable property. On and on he went, making point after point.

None of which changed their minds. They wanted to give back to the community, to help the families still living there. They all knew gangs were a growing concern among the parents, especially since the Blood Brotherhood had been gaining membership.

"And this gang. We had no idea it would grow so much in just five years."

"Has it only been here that long?" Willard nodded, and Fredrik sighed. "Time. So fast she goes when you're old, eh, my friend?"

The gang came into the neighborhood not much more than a graffiti crew. But it had grown from just a few members to, as best they could figure, over fifty now. Suspicion abounded that the gang was no longer penny ante, that they'd gotten into theft and street drugs, but no one could ever prove anything. All the neighbors and church members knew was that the gang was doing everything it could to recruit kids from the neighborhood. Providing an alternative to hanging with the Brotherhood would be a definite help.

"I really thought Sam Ballat would be proud of what we wanted to do."

"So he should have been."

But he wasn't. When Sam realized they were moving ahead with the youth center plan, he was furious.

Willard lowered himself to a pew. He was less and less able to stand these days. One more worry for Fredrik.

"I don't suppose we can fault him for that, Fredrik. After all, there were companies champing at the bit to level this place and put up any number of warehouses."

"True, true. Should Sam sell this land, it would fetch more than a tidy profit. I should blame a businessman for doing good business? No. But I *do* fault the good Mr. Ballat for the underhanded way he made sure he got what he wanted."

Willard didn't reply. There was no use. They couldn't prove Sam was doing anything wrong. He was too clever for that. But they all knew who was behind the problems. The threatening phone calls that motivated the first contractor to quit. It took awhile, but Fredrik and the elders finally found another contractor. That one lasted six months, but he didn't get anything done. When Fredrik and the elders finally challenged him, he gave a host of excuses. None made any sense. They were left with one conclusion: someone had paid the man to waste time. It had seemed a miracle when they found James Lawton. Finally, they could see progress being made. They were all so excited. And now, just two months shy of their deadline for completing the project, to have the *third* contractor walk away...

It was a deathblow.

Or it would have been, if not for God.

"If not for God..." Fredrik repeated the thought out loud.

Willard turned to him. "What?"

"Mr. Lawton, the contractor, asked me an interesting question before he left. He said someone's working to stop us. Asked if I thought the cost was worth finishing the project. I admit to you, old friend, I wasn't sure it was." He let his gaze wander to the cross. "Not until this very moment."

"And so?"

"If not for God." He patted Willard's stooped shoulder. "We'd be defeated, if not for God. But *with* Him"—Fredrik's heart lifted, and he grinned—"we have more than we need to accomplish the task *He's* called us to."

Now Willard was smiling. "If God be for us, who can be against us?"

"Exactly. So come." Fredrik started down the aisle toward the front door. "We have much to do."

"And time is running out."

Indeed, it was. But time wasn't the determining factor in their success.

God was.

That fact should be enough to calm all their fears. At least, that's what Fredrik told himself as he held the door open for his friend to pass through. But as he closed and locked the door behind them, he couldn't help wondering.

How much time did they really have left before they had to close this door for good?

FIVE

*"Change is the essence of life. Be willing to surrender
what you are for what you could become."*

ANONYMOUS

*"Leave your foolish ways behind,
and begin to live; learn how to be wise."*

PROVERBS 9:6

God is in control... God is in control... God is...

Kyla leaned back against the car seat, eyes closed. It wasn't helping. No matter how much she repeated it to herself, she still felt as though everything was spinning out of control. Especially her.

"Get some rest. You don't sound right."

Annot's words kept ringing in her mind. She'd assured her sister she'd do that, then rung off. But as she dropped the cell phone into her purse, she knew it was more than fatigue. More than not sounding right.

She didn't *feel* right. She hadn't for a very long time.

Kyla glanced out the windshield, staring but not seeing anything. Finally she turned to her day planner and started to flip the cover shut, then noticed the photo she kept tucked at the front. She tugged it free...and smiled.

It was a picture taken a few years ago of Kyla and her two siblings—Kyla in the middle, Avidan and Annot on either side. Her brother and sister wore teasing smiles as they mugged for the camera, pretending to throttle Kyla. Kyla studied her own expression.

Tolerant. Enduring. Long-suffering.

She turned the photo over and read what Annot had written there: "To our beloved Sister-Mommy. From the brats, Annie and Dan."

Emotions swarmed through her, and Kyla bit her lip again. This was getting ridiculous! She was *not* an emotional woman. She tucked the photo back in place and noticed her hand was trembling.

Stop it. You have no reason to be so upset. It's been a good day. You're doing your job, and doing it well. Dad's business is everything he wanted it to be. You should be proud.

But she wasn't.

She pounded the palm of her hand against the steering wheel. What on earth was *wrong* with her? She should be ecstatic with the way things were going. She'd fought long and hard to make a place for herself in the world of construction, a business that was still very much a man's business. And she'd succeeded. The workers who'd been so hesitant to accept her when she took over her father's company now respected her, counting her one of their own. In fact, the men on the crew who'd worked with her dad had all but adopted her. It was like having a team of dads watching over her, counseling her. She loved it.

And she loved the work. Loved creating welcome and a sense of home no matter the environment. Loved bringing what looked to the untrained eye like a confusion of lines on the blueprints to full, glorious life.

Yes, she was her father's daughter. Building was her passion.

A fact her clients confirmed over and over. Gregory Belkins wasn't the only customer who'd been delighted with her work. As far as she knew, all of her clients in the last ten years had only praise for Justice Construction.

Yes, she still had to overcome what sometimes felt like an abundance of prejudices against a woman working in a male-dominated field. But Kyla had never let other people's prejudices hold her back.

So why, then, when things were going so great, was she sitting here feeling so miserable?

It didn't take long for the answer to come.

She'd lost perspective.

It was at the beginning of her second year with the company that her father took her up on the steel girders, high above ground. Amazingly, she felt no fear as she looked down at the ground far below. In fact, she felt safe there, with him. With God.

Her dad waved a hand out at the city beyond. "Look out there, hon. All the people, all the hearts, longing to be touched. That's what it's about." His large hand would come to rest against the upright. "These buildings, they're just steel and concrete. Wood and wallboard. It's not the buildings that matter: it's the people you touch with what you create. What God helps you create."

She could still see his tender smile as he turned and laid his hand on her shoulder. "It's about serving people, Kyla. Letting God use you to touch them."

She'd known, in those moments with the two of them together, that he was passing on more than just the tools to run his business. He was passing on his heart.

When her father fell ill, though Kyla was only in her midtwenties, the mantle of leadership fell squarely on her shoulders. Her father remained involved, her constant advisor. But heart complications forced him out of the day-to-day operations. It hadn't been easy. Not at all. But her dad had been a constant support, right up to his death nearly six years ago. During those last few months, she'd sit by his bedside and brief him on the events of the day, and nothing made her happier than to see that twinkle in his eye in response to something she'd handled well.

"God has gifted you for this work, Kyla. And you're using your gift well. I'm proud of you."

Her father's words undergirded her when after his death, the employees questioned her ability to run Justice Construction…when during those first few months, clients pulled their projects, saying that without her dad, Justice Construction was on its way out.

"I've run this company for years!" she'd stormed to Avidan and Annot. "And now not just the employees, but the clients doubt me?"

"Give them time." The quintessential sheriff's deputy, Avidan was a man's man, ready and able to handle whatever came his way. "You've been in charge, but to their minds, Dad was there in the background running things."

Before she could protest, Annot put her hand on Kyla's arm. "We know that wasn't true. Dad told us often enough you've been the heart and mind behind JuCo for years. Dad believed in you, Kylie. So do we."

"And so will others. In time."

She wished she were more like Annot, so she could do something to vent her frustration...like kick a table. Instead, she clamped down the irritation trying to push free and nodded. Annot was right. Her father believed in her.

That was enough.

Day by day, she showed up, did what her dad had taught her to do, and refused to give up. Thankfully, a number of Justice Construction's major clients stuck with them. And when JuCo brought the jobs in not only on time, but under budget, the clients made sure everyone knew it. By the end of the first year without her father, the company had regained any lost ground. And last year, just five years after her father's death, the company he'd founded was more successful than she—or Dad—ever dreamed.

But the company wasn't just about profit. As she'd learned during those times on the girders, it never had been. From the very beginning, her father decided that his company would do more than construct buildings. Justice Construction would work on projects that bettered the world. And Kyla had honored that decision. Yes, she'd do the commercial projects, the malls and subdivisions. But she'd always work on projects that mattered too. And anyone who came to work for her company would have to be willing to do both as well.

In the last few years, though, as her reputation had grown, Kyla found herself working on more and more projects like the one she'd just finished.

Projects that didn't matter. Projects that skewed her perspective.

She shifted in the seat, trying to evade the sense of weight on her shoulders. On her spirit. But unease had chosen her as its resting place, and she couldn't dislodge it.

Why this unrelenting restlessness, Lord? I'm doing good work. Work Dad would be proud of. And these projects may not matter that much to me, but they matter to the clients.

As though some tiny devil's advocate had flown in on the wings of her unrest, a response sounded within her almost before she'd finished the thought.

Right. They matter because they bring in a great deal of money, both for you and for the clients. But is that enough?

Kyla's grip on the steering wheel tightened. No. It wasn't. Not even close. *It's not that I don't want to do the other projects. The money's there. I've set it aside after every project, just like Daddy did.*

She should have known she wouldn't get off that easy.

Yes, but your father didn't let the money just sit there. He used it. He helped people.

Frustration—or was it guilt?—pierced her heart. *I just haven't had any opportunities come up lately.*

Right. Like the chance to help something? Like the kitten? You wouldn't have noticed them if they did. You're too focused on the next accomplishment.

It was hard to argue with truth. Which explained why, with the completion of each of the commercial projects she'd done the last few years, one feeling was growing and threatening to overwhelm her. A feeling she'd spent her life doing everything she could to avoid.

Failure.

Enough!

Enough thinking. Enough feeling sorry for herself. She had to get out of here.

Now.

She jabbed the key into the ignition, then froze.

Was that…?

Her senses sharpened, Kyla jumped out of the car and ran toward the bush near the trunk. Sure of what she'd seen. But the spot where the kitten had been was still empty. Stabbing disappointment stole her breath—until another sound jump-started her breathing, drawing her around the bush, along the landscaped section to another smaller bush nearby.

There, cowering beneath the leafy branches, was the kitten.

This time, Kyla didn't hesitate. She reached down, cupped the tiny animal in her hands, and drew it close. She tucked it inside her suit jacket, nestling it next to her racing heart, and made her way back to the car.

Easing into the driver's seat, Kyla rubbed the kitten's fur, doing her best to dry it and warm it at the same time. Its coat was a mixture of black, orange, and white—though the white was more of a dingy gray at the moment. The animal's shivering body and heart-wrenching squeals tightened Kyla's throat.

"I know, little guy. I'm sorry. I'm so sorry I left you there…"

The kitten rested its forehead against her, and the simple trust in that motion nearly undid Kyla. She met her own gaze in the rearview mirror, noted the red-rimmed eyes, the tears streaming down her face. "You look terrible."

Funny thing was, she was smiling as she said it.

Holding the kitten with one hand, she leaned down to pull out the phone book she kept beneath her driver's seat. It only took a moment to find a nearby animal hospital. A few minutes more to call for directions and let the person on the phone know she was coming in.

"Is this your pet?"

The woman's question stopped Kyla, and she looked down at the bundle now sleeping against her. She couldn't keep it. Of course she couldn't. For one thing, she was gone all the time. For another, there was Mason to consider. She didn't even know if he liked animals. Shouldn't she ask him first?

"Ma'am? Is this your pet?"

Be smart, Kyla.

She opened her mouth to answer, and one word jumped out. "Yes."

Kyla had to bite her lip to keep from laughing out loud. She tightened her hold on the kitten, and this time her answer came out solid and sure. "Yes, it's my pet."

So it wasn't smart. So what? This little creature nestled against her seemed to think it belonged to Kyla. And for the life of her, she couldn't disagree.

All those years of telling Annot you weren't an animal person, and now you do this? You're knocking on crazy's door, you know.

The kitten shifted, rubbing its soft face against her hand and releasing a soul-deep sigh. Kyla's heart melted.

Crazy or not, this kitten was exactly where it belonged.

And if Mason doesn't agree?

He would. Of course he would. Because it was important to her. And when someone loved you, they cared about what mattered to you. Right?

She didn't give herself time to ponder the answer. She'd faced enough crises for the day.

It was time to give her heart—and her doubts—a rest. At least for tonight.

SIX

"*The dream was always running ahead of me. To catch up,
to live for a moment in unison with it, that was the miracle.*"

ANAIS NIN

"*Your heavenly Father already knows all your needs, and he
will give you all you need from day to day if you live for him
and make the Kingdom of God your primary concern.*"

MATTHEW 6:32–33

"Rafa, if you stare at that doorway any harder, it will melt."

Rafe took another sip of his coffee and angled wide-eyed innocence at
his sister. "I don't know what you're talking about."

Her eyes scolded. "Do me favor, *porfa?*"

"Whatever you ask, *'manita.*"

"Keep in mind that just because I'm your sister, that doesn't make me
una cretina."

"I would never call you an idiot."

"*Vale,* but you try to treat me like one, hmm?" She waved at the door
he'd been staring at. "You tell me you've come to work early so you can have
everything ready before the first *clienta* comes in. And then you sit there,
drinking your coffee, waiting for her to show up. The morning passes, and
still you sit there for every break. Watching the door. Hoping. And *tu creo que*
I don't know that's what you're doing?" She swatted at his shoulder. "Besides,
you know as well as I do it's still too early for her. She doesn't usually show
until at least early evening." She winked at him. "A little touch of heaven on
her way home, si?"

"My coffee heaven?" Rafe let a broad grin spread across his lips. "Si, *hermana.* I'll agree with that."

Olivia flounced past him. "Not your coffee, you! Ooo, you make me crazy when you do that."

He held up his hands, still laughing. "I'm not trying to annoy you, *mija*—"

She planted her hands on her slim hips. "Oh, don't give me that. You love annoying me. And all I'm trying to do is help you."

Rafe fought hard against the laughter. He really did. But there was no holding it back.

Olivia tossed back her long black hair, pressed her lips together, and glared at him. *"¿Qué?"*

He stood, going to slip his arms around her. "Sorry, mija. I don't mean to laugh at you. You just look so much like *Mamá* when you scold."

Olivia's frown melted into a warm smile. "Look like her, si. But not sound like her. Mamá scolded in *Español.*"

"You do too. Sort of."

Olivia went back to the glass display case she'd been stocking. "Spanglish, Rafa. You know Mamá hated Spanglish."

"She didn't hate it. She just chose not to participate in it." Rafe set his coffee cup on the counter. "I miss her." Hard to believe their parents had been gone for five years. Killed in a car crash when he was twenty-eight and Olivia had just turned thirty-four.

A soft hand came to rest on his shoulder. "They would be so proud of you, Rafa. Of all you've done here. That you didn't let your injury destroy you." She waved her hand at the shop. "That you used all you've learned, all you are, to make this."

Rafe couldn't say he was sure about a lot of things. But this place? He'd known the day he opened Cuppa Joe's that his coffeehouse would be a success.

Oddly enough, he owed that to the military—prime territory for coffee addiction. Especially in his Force Recon team. Now, Rafe had always liked coffee. Good, strong coffee, the way his *abuela* made it. He smiled. Nobody made coffee like his grandmother, but these guys…just the smell of the stuff put a gleam in their eyes and a blissful grin on their faces. But it was watching them consume the liquid that opened his eyes.

True coffee lovers didn't just drink the stuff. They lived for the whole crazy experience.

It was the one thing that Thales, Monroe, and Green shared. Those three were hooked, big time. A fact proven the day Thales came back from a street market with a package stuffed with bags of coffee. It wasn't long before the three men disappeared. When they showed up again, it was with one of those fancy coffee makers—the kind that makes coffee and espresso.

Thales and Monroe handled the machine with a reverence usually reserved for their weapons. Sabada watched over their shoulders. "How much did that thing cost you guys?"

Monroe's eyes went wide. "Who cares, man. It's coffee!"

Rafe frowned. The kid might have problems keeping his temper, but he was a pro at not letting his money get away from him. "You can get coffee free at the mess."

Green opened the bag of beans like it was some sacred, long-awaited treasure. He held the bag beneath his nose and inhaled, drawing the fragrance in like it was purest oxygen. Monroe held out the grinder as Green poured beans in, then pressed down the button. "That's not coffee, Asadi." Monroe held up the grinder. "*This* is coffee."

"Not just coffee, Farm Boy." Green took the grinder and dumped the grounds into the holder and tamped it down. "We're talkin' *great* coffee."

As black liquid flowed into a mug, Thales poured milk into a small pitcher, stuck it over a protruding tube, and turned a knob. The machine responded with spitting and hissing.

Rafe sat back, torn between laughter and amazement. There were these three big Marines, men he'd seen take fire with total calm, acting like little kids waiting for the go-ahead to tear into the gifts beneath a Christmas tree. When the rich, dark liquid was perfectly doctored with cream and bottled syrups, they drank.

No, not drank.

Savored.

Rafe's eyes were opened that day. Suddenly he saw coffee hounds everywhere. From every branch of the service. And the amount of money they forked over for what they considered good coffee? Unbelievable.

"Tell Mamá and Papá you should all invest in coffee companies," he wrote Olivia a few weeks later.

After his honorable discharge, when he was wondering what to do with his life, Olivia reminded him of that letter, and something clicked. He started looking around, and sure enough—you couldn't swing a dead cat in Portland without hitting a new coffee kiosk. But there were only a few true coffeehouses. And his sister was an amazing cook...

Opportunity wasn't just knocking. It was driving a Humvee through the door. Within the year he'd found the perfect location, and Cuppa Joe's opened to its first customer. But Rafe's place wasn't your usual coffeehouse. Sure, he offered the usual—mochas, lattes, blended drinks, and just plain coffee—but he also let himself create, making personalized concoctions to match people's personalities. And Olivia provided his customers with amazing pastries and sandwiches. Then there were her desserts. Several men had proposed to Olivia when they tasted her creations. A number of his women customers told him they should be outlawed.

All of which confirmed what Rafe had known for years. His sister was an artist in the kitchen.

But while those things gave Cuppa Joe's a foot up on other coffee places, what really set it apart from the rest was the décor. Rafe decided providing coffee and sweets wasn't enough. Not for him. He wanted his place to show people the military. The *real* military. The people—men and women in uniform—from the inside out.

Olivia thought he was nuts. "Rafa, the war polarizes people. They hate it or they love it. No middle ground."

"This isn't about the war." He stepped back from the picture he'd just hung—a desert sunset–framed Rashidi, in full combat gear, head bent, deep in thought as he read a small Bible. Rafe had snapped the shot because, despite a rifle strapped to one shoulder and a knife on the other, the man's features had shone with peace.

Rafe turned to face his sister. "That's the point. It's about people. Good people. And what they do for all of us, whether we support them or not."

It took awhile, but his sister finally caught his vision. Which was good, because she was far better at creating the look he'd hoped for. Soon the walls

held perfectly grouped displays of paintings and pictures, textiles, and arti-
facts from all the places Rafe and his team had been. And she didn't stop
there.

Olivia was a genius outside the kitchen too. Especially when it came to
finding what she wanted for next to nothing. Rafe never knew what would
show up next. One day he was lugging in bistro tables and chairs; the next,
overstuffed chairs; the next, fabric for what she called "window treatments."

The final effect was more than he'd hoped. The day before his grand
opening, Rafe and Olivia stood together, surveying what she'd created: a
warm environment that welcomed his customers, inviting them inside to
ample seating for groups as well as private corners for conversation. Rafe's pictures and mementos complimented the ambience. And then there was
Olivia's pièce de résistance—a communications corner, complete with com-
puters and a Web site for customers to send e-mails to the troops. "You really
are brilliant."

Olivia's smile was more than smug. "Si. I am."

Rafe walked around the shop, finally stopping in front of a photo of him
and his team, just before they'd headed out on their last mission together. He
pressed his palm to the cool glass covering the picture. "Thanks, guys. I owe
this to you."

It felt good, being surrounded by his buddies like this. It felt right. All he
needed now was for customers to agree.

Happily, they'd done so.

"Earth to Rafa. Time to stop daydreaming and get to work, *manito*."

Pulled from his thoughts, Rafe touched a finger to his sister's smooth
cheek. "Thanks, Livita."

She pursed her lips. "For what?"

"Everything. I couldn't have made it these last few years without you.
Your encouragement and support…" Emotion clogged his throat and he
looked down.

"And my pastries, eh? Don't forget my *deliciosa* pastries."

Her teasing words eased the tightness in his throat, but before he could
thank her, the bell above the door jangled.

Rafe turned, ready to serve the customer, and found instead a friend.

"Fredrik." He moved forward, hand extended. "Have you finally decided to take up the fine art of coffee drinking?"

"I should be so crazy? And if I were"—his hand swept toward the menu board behind the counter—"I should spend so much on hot water?"

The old man's insults were belied by the twinkle in those blue eyes. Rafe took the proffered hand in his own. "Ah, but what wondrous flavor lies in that water."

The old man's white brows waggled. *"Narishkeit."*

"No, Fredrik. What's foolishness is that you come to a place with such delectable treats and don't partake." Now it was Rafe's turn to waggle his brows. "I thought Jews didn't do self-denial."

"There's more here to enjoy than your flavored water, my boy." He lowered himself into one of the overstuffed chairs. "The company of friends..." A cloud passed over his features, and all merriment melted away. "And sound counsel from a man of God."

Rafe could count on one hand the number of times the old man had been troubled in all the years he'd known him. It didn't sit well to see disquiet on a face so accustomed to joviality. He turned to signal Olivia, letting her know he was taking a break, and then took the chair next to Fredrik. "What troubles you so today?"

Sorrow was an ache in his friend's aged eyes. "Our contractor quit."

Rafe leaned back. "But...I thought this one just got started."

"So he did. But the obstacles, they were too many. A number of his men were injured. Accidents that no one can explain." The stooped shoulders lifted in an eloquent shrug. "We've tried and tried, but everything seems against us doing what God has called us to."

Rafe debated voicing his question but decided it was better to ask now than wish he'd done so. "You're still sure it's His call? Renovating the church into a youth center?"

Fredrik stared down at his hands, lips pursed. Then his head moved in a slow, weary nod. "You know the people who live in this neighborhood, Rafael." His gaze met Rafe's. "And you know the opposition."

Rafe's lips compressed. Yes, he knew them. When he left the military he'd thought his days as a warrior were over. Then God brought him to Fredrik's little church. Rafe thought it was to join the congregation. But he soon discovered that wasn't his only purpose.

"The 22s?"

Fredrik's forehead creased. "The who?"

"I'm sorry. The Blood Brotherhood."

"Oh yes, of course. They do call themselves the 22s, don't they? I've never quite understood why."

Rafe shrugged. "Simple. B is the second letter in the alphabet. BB for Blood Brotherhood becomes 22. So…"

"The 22s. See? That makes perfect sense." Fredrik steepled his fingers. "So, are the 22s involved? That I don't know for certain. I didn't think so, but others? Well, they're convinced the gang is working with Ballat to stop us."

"How so?" Rafe braced himself for the answer, disappointment gnawing deep in his gut. When God called him to involvement with the gang, he'd argued long and hard. He just wanted to run his coffee place and be at peace. But God didn't turn loose. He kept putting members from the 22s in his path. First a young kid he caught stealing from the construction site. Then two thugs who tried to intimidate him as he left the church one morning. Rafe smiled at the memory. They'd found themselves on their backs, staring up at the sky.

And, of course, Tarik.

That's when Rafe finally gave in. Accepted that he was being called to build some bridges, to help the 22s understand the church wasn't a threat. He'd worked so hard with these kids, been so sure they were going to leave the church alone. "What makes the elders think the 22s are involved?"

"The elders at the church believe the gang is being used. Hired thugs. But have I actually seen them do anything? No."

"Well, if not the Brotherhood…"

Fredrik tapped his two index fingers together. "Ballat."

Of course. No one else had more motivation for stopping the renovation. "What can I do to help?"

"Pray." Fredrik let his hands fall into his lap. "And suggest a good contractor. One who won't be frightened away by opposition." He heaved himself out of the chair, laying a hand on Rafe's shoulder as he passed by. "But mostly, pray. That's what will see us through this."

"You got it."

"Thank you." Fredrik blessed him with a fond smile, then made his way to the door. "Now, it's home for me. I need to spend time with the Father. I may not know what the next step is, but He does. I just have to listen so He can share that knowledge with me."

As Fredrik reached the door, it opened toward him. He stepped aside so the man coming in could pass by. "Come, enjoy!" Fredrik waved a hand at the menu board. "Such nectar even heaven hasn't got." He tossed a wink at Rafe and was gone.

Rafe stood, laughing to himself, and went to greet his customer. It was a man Rafe hadn't seen before—blue-collar type. Interesting. With all the construction going on, road and buildings, he was seeing more and more strangers lately. Even so, his usuals normally came in before anyone else. "Mornin'."

The man glanced around as he came to the counter. "Morning." His gaze came to rest on Rafe, who fought a smile. Clearly, this guy wasn't overly comfortable in a coffeehouse. "I hear you got good coffee."

"Nope." Rafe crossed his arms. "We have great coffee."

The man's lips twitched. "So prove it."

"Let me guess…you want black. Straight up. No frills."

The man's smile widened. "You got it."

As Rafe went to pour the coffee, he watched the man glance around. His eyes widened a fraction when he saw what was on the walls, and then, as so many had before him, he walked to study one of the photos displayed there.

The same photo that seemed to catch everyone's eye.

It was a typical shot of a Marine. Military-issue green tank over desert camo pants. Muscled arms, one with a tattoo from shoulder to wrist, projecting strength despite their relaxed state. Gloved hands rested with familiar comfort, much the way many men's hands rested on their briefcases, on the assault rifle hanging in front of him. Everything about the picture said gung-ho, hard-as-they-come, Semper Fi Marine.

Until you noticed a splash of color.

There, out of the side pocket of the Marine's camos, peeked a brightly colored bouquet of wildflowers.

That unexpected sight never failed to impact. Especially when the viewers spotted the two items next to the photo: one was a picture of a beautiful little girl of about six, dark eyes wide and happy; the other held a bouquet of dried wildflowers.

Rafe's customer studied the photo, glanced back at Rafe, then went back to the picture. His hand came up to touch the glass over the dried wildflowers.

"Coffee's ready."

The man eyed the picture a moment longer, then returned to Rafe. He took the cup Rafe held out, eyes traveling to the tattoo on Rafe's left arm. He gave a slight nod. "It's you."

"It's me."

"Marine, huh?"

"Yup."

He sipped the coffee. "Where'd you find flowers in the desert?"

Rafe picked up a rag and wiped down the counter. "The little girl whose photo is with the flowers? She gave 'em to me. Just came up and held them out. She'd been trailing after me for days. I guess she decided she liked me. When I hesitated to take them, she opened the pocket on the side of my camos and slid them in."

"You wouldn't take flowers?"

Rafe shrugged. "Didn't trust anyone. Couldn't. I'd seen too many guys who did, and it cost them their lives."

"So she gave 'em to you anyway, huh?"

"Yeah. My buddies got a kick out of it, this little bit of a kid comin' up to a guy with a gun and giving him flowers. One of 'em took a picture with his new digital camera. Said he was going to print it out and give it to the little girl."

"Did he?"

Every time he told the story it got to him, but he schooled his features not to let it show. "Didn't get the chance. She and her family were killed when a suicide bomber attacked a nearby marketplace."

The customer halted mid-drink, his gaze riveted to Rafe's.

As hard as Rafe tried, he couldn't escape the blow of that memory. If only he'd taken the flowers, opened his hand to a little girl...

The man lowered the cup from his lips, then looked down. After a beat, he let out a pent-up breath. "You're right. It's great coffee." He looked up at Rafe and held out a hand. "Doug Franklin."

Rafe shook the proffered hand. "Rafael Murphy."

"Well, Mr. Murphy—"

"Rafe."

The man inclined his head. "Rafe, I don't generally come to places like this. Too froufrou for me. But the guys on the job said your place is different. I can see they were right." He lifted the cup in a salute. "I'll see you tomorrow."

Rafe tipped his chin. "Look forward to it."

The jingle of the bell over the door signaled another customer had entered, and Rafe saw three of his regulars coming in.

No doubt about it. His business was a success, and then some. It brought him great satisfaction and a reason to get up every day. But he never imagined it would bring him the dream he'd given up so many years ago.

The dream that was Kyla Justice.

SEVEN

> *"Twenty years from now you will be more disappointed*
> *by the things that you didn't do than by the ones you did do.*
> *So throw off the bowlines. Sail away from the safe harbor.*
> *Catch the trade winds in your sails.*
> *Explore. Dream. Discover."*
>
> MARK TWAIN

> *"But when you ask him, be sure that you really expect*
> *him to answer, for a doubtful mind is as unsettled as*
> *a wave of the sea that is driven and tossed by the wind."*
>
> JAMES 1:6

Rafe saw it the moment she pulled up outside his shop. Kyla's car, easing into the parking space.

She was back. He held his breath. *Come on, Kyla…come inside…*

Seemed like he'd been wooing this woman most of his life. Even back when she was just a friend…

Friend? Who you tryin' to kid? You've been in love with her from the time you met her.

In love? Hardly. He'd been twelve. It was a crush, nothing more. Still…

He allowed himself a smile as he remembered. It might not have been love, but he'd had as serious a crush on Kyla as a kid that age could have. He glanced at her again. She'd been beautiful back then.

She was stunning now.

Come inside…

As though she'd heard his silent call, she nodded, then turned to push open the car door and, her steps firm, walked around her car and headed for the door.

His heart raced as he watched her, waiting for her to look at him. One step, two, and then she stopped, eyes drifting shut, and inhaled.

Ahhh.

Rich, dark, earthy…the fragrance of fresh-roasted coffee filled her senses. Though her fingers remained disciplined, her taste buds took up the tap dance.

Oh yes, she needed this.

Coffee. Was there anything more enticing, more uplifting than coffee? Not just any coffee, of course, but *good* coffee. The darkest, richest brews that served as a base for tantalizing concoctions. Blends of flavors she'd never think to combine. These creations were as much a masterpiece as anything she built, and Kyla indulged in trying new ones when they were posted on the colorful blackboard. Here, she could take risks. This was the one place she didn't have to keep herself in strict control. The one place that eased the empty sense, deep inside. That felt like a haven. Like home…

And not just because of the coffee.

She opened her eyes, and there he was. Standing at the counter, dark eyes watching her, that enigmatic smile tipping his lips. Odd how at home he seemed behind the counter. If she'd seen him walking past her on the street, she never would have pegged him for a coffee barista. No, with that no-nonsense stride of his—a stride hindered only slightly by his use of a cane—that athletic build, and the flame tattoo traveling from shoulder to wrist on his left arm, she'd have figured him for someone who ordered his coffee black and strong.

No frills.

Maybe with the grounds still in it.

And yet, here he was. Not just a good barista, but a great one. She'd been hesitant at first to stray from her standard grande-caramel-macchiato-skinny-no-whip. But he'd coaxed her, bit by bit, until she finally gave in and let him make one of his creations for her. From the first sip of the frothy concoction, she'd been hooked. When he saw her reaction, his smile deepened, and those dark eyes danced as though he reveled in her delight.

No doubt about it, the man was every bit as enticing as the aromas filling her senses. Which was exactly why she'd decided she mustn't come here anymore.

"Hey, Miss J. Haven't seen you for a few days."

So old-school respectful—*Miss,* not *Ms.*—and yet beneath the propriety there lingered a touch of warmth that never failed to up her pulse a notch. That calm voice, with a feather-touch of an accent, soothed her weary heart. So much so that his voice started to join the dance, but Kyla sent it to sit in the corner. Facing the wall.

She was here for coffee, nothing more.

You can say that again! You're not even supposed to be here at all. You're supposed to be back at your apartment. With Mason.

The shock of reality jolted her. Oh dear. Mason.

Yes. Mason. Mason Rawlins. You remember him? The man you've been dating for almost six months? The man who has asked you to marry him?

A glance at her watch told her how late she was. For a second, she considered just turning to leave, but the sweet scent of coffee wooed her. It would only take a minute, then she'd be on her way. Besides, she'd given Mason the extra key to her town house, just in case. That way he could start on dinner if she was delayed.

"Uh, Miss Justice?"

Kyla frowned at the alarm in Rafael's voice. Forehead creased, he was nodding at her jacket.

"I think your coat's alive."

She looked down, and sure enough, her jacket was wriggling to beat the band. So, her little friend had finally awakened. Before she could soothe the kitten, its head popped up, and a yowl split the air.

Mortified, Kyla reached into the generous inner pocket where she'd settled the little tyke and lifted the kitten free. "I'm so sorry." Her face had to be as red as the cherry syrup sitting on the counter. "I know I shouldn't have brought an animal in here, but—"

Rafael waved off her concern. "There's no one else here, so it's fine."

"But the health code—"

His brows waggled. "You don't tell anyone, neither will I. Deal?"

Her agreement slipped out on a nod and a smile, and she looked down at the little troublemaker in her arms. "Rafael, I'd like you to meet a friend of mine."

Warmth lit his features as he held out his hands. Kyla set the kitten in those large palms, noting how gentle his fingers were as he cupped and stroked the little animal. Rafael lifted the little head so the two of them were eye to eye. "You"—his gaze lifted to Kyla—"are adorable."

Quick heat filled her face, and she dropped her gaze to the kitten, reaching a finger out to pet the tufted head. Anything to distract herself from the look in his eyes.

"What's her name?"

Kyla's finger paused, and she stared at Rafael.

"Now, how did you know she's a she?"

He inclined his head toward the kitten. "Calico. Most calicos—"

"Are female. Yes, I know." The vet had explained that while giving the kitten fluids and food. When she showed her surprise, he lifted a brow and asked what she knew about kittens. Her blank stare was all he needed. He'd given her a list of supplies and instructions.

Who knew something so little could be so much work? But one look in those sweet eyes and any hesitation faded. This kitten was hers.

She lifted the animal back into her arms. "As for her name, I don't know yet. I'm waiting for her to tell me."

Rafael didn't blink at that. "Sounds reasonable."

Really? She hadn't thought so. In fact, the idea was far more an Annot kind of thing than it was Kyla. But she hit a dry well when she tried to unearth a name. Patches. Lucky. Chance. Noah (you know…saved from the rain).

They all seemed too cliché. Normal. Run-of-the-mill.

Either that or stupid.

The way this little one came into her life was definitely none of those things. And almost in spite of herself, Kyla felt the little kitten deserved a name as unique as her circumstances.

"So she's a new part of your family, huh?"

Kyla liked that. A part of her family. "Yes, as of today, in fact." She explained what had happened that morning, and Rafael listened. He was so attentive. As if he really cared about what she had to say.

There was something so…comfortable about this man. So familiar. She'd felt that way from that first visit to his coffee shop. As though she'd known him forever, not just a few months. Which only made it that much more appealing to stop in and indulge. In the coffee.

And his presence.

When she finished, he leaned against the counter. "I think that's great. That the kitten chose you, and that you accepted. Too many people would have left it where it lay."

I almost did.

She wanted to tell him that. To be honest about herself. Her struggle. But she just couldn't. She couldn't stand seeing the disappointment in those dark eyes.

"You just have to love those little serendipities in life." He chucked the kitten's little chin. "Don't you, little one?"

"Serendipities." Kyla let the word roll off her tongue. "That's exactly what it was. A serendipity." She looked from the kitten to Rafael, a smile easing across her mouth. "Serendipity. What do you think, girl? Is that you? Serendipity?"

The kitten yawned, bringing one paw up to rest on Kyla's fingers. Rafael's deep chuckle sounded. "I think she likes it."

Kyla was sure he was right.

"And when she's mischievous, you can call her Dippity."

"Mischievous?" Kyla's smile turned lopsided. "Ha. My cat will be perfectly well behaved."

Clearly, Rafael was doing all he could not to guffaw. "I was going to ask if you wanted your usual"—he motioned toward the kitten—"but it's clear you're feeling adventurous today."

Her? Adventurous? Only this man would ever think her so. She hugged the newly dubbed Serendipity close, feeling lighter than she had in days. Maybe even weeks. "Adventurous, eh? What have you got in mind?"

He studied her a moment—those eyes so dark brown they almost seemed black—and she forced herself not to react. Should a traitorous tint of warmth fill her face she would simply pretend it wasn't there. Because it wasn't. Or shouldn't b—

"I know just what you need."

She didn't doubt him for a second.

Kyla leaned against the counter, one finger entertaining the kitten as she watched him work. Despite his limp and the ever-present cane, the man's movements were a study in precision. Even if the décor in the coffee shop hadn't told the story, one look would tell her he once was in the military.

"Here, try this."

She looked down at the creation he held out to her. "Oh my."

The edges of his mouth lifted as he took the kitten so she could curve her hands around the cup. "It's a new drink I created. A caramel-chocolate coffee shake topped with whipped cream and caramel drizzles. I call it *Sabor a Cielo.*" Her eyes lifted to his as he translated. "A taste of heaven."

Oh…my… Her gaze drifted back to the drink.

"Go ahead, give it a try."

She shouldn't. The thing had to have a million calories. Still, just a taste couldn't hurt, could it? She put her lips to the straw.

Her eyes drifted shut. Taste of heaven was right.

"You like it."

She smiled at him, taking another long draw on the straw, letting the rich flavor wash away the remnants of the day.

"You okay, Miss J?"

The caring concern in the question startled her. "I…" Words struggled to fall into place, to form some kind of cohesive response, but the look in Rafael's eyes tipped her composure on its ear.

Why did this man affect her this way? More to the point, why did he look at her the way he did? Like she was something precious. Treasured…

"Miss J?"

Thank heaven. A distraction. She tilted her head, painting a scold on her features. "Rafael, how many times have I asked you to call me *Kyla?*"

His generous mouth barely betrayed a smile as he transferred his gaze to the kitten. "About as many as I've asked you to call me *Rafe.*"

This was much better. Safer. Teasing repartee between friends. She arched a brow. "There's nothing wrong with your full name."

"Nobody calls me *Rafael*, Miss Justice." His wry smile peeked out again. "Nobody but my mother."

She almost laughed at that. "Please, won't you do as I ask? Then I'll know we're really friends." She reached out to lay her hand on his arm, intending only to add emphasis to what she was saying. But the moment she touched him, she knew.

It was a mistake. A terrible mistake.

Because deep within her chest, her heart exploded.

It was just a touch.

A simple gesture of friendship.

So why did his arm suddenly feel like a landing pad for lightning?

She must have felt something too, because her eyes went wide and her face… Well, to say she was startled was an understatement.

He'd seen that look before. On young Marines during their first battle. Half terror, half exhilaration, one hundred percent adrenaline.

Sure enough, she jerked her hand away and backed up. "I'm sorry!"

"It's okay." He kept his tone low, calming. He didn't want her to leave like this. "You're fine."

"No…I…" She looked around, seemed relieved they were alone. Then she plucked the kitten from his hands and blurted out, "I'm late. I have to go."

Spinning on a heel, she was gone, the echo of the tinkling bell above the door the only sign she'd been there.

That, and the lingering scent of her perfume, which, he thought as he drew the fragrance in, was the perfect sign an angel had been there.

A sweet breath of heaven.

EIGHT

"Nothing is easier than self-deceit."
DEMOSTHENES

*"Therefore, since we are surrounded by such a huge
crowd of witnesses to the life of faith, let us strip
off every weight that slows us down, especially the
sin that so easily hinders our progress. And let us run
with endurance the race that God has set before us."*
HEBREWS 12:1

Good heavens, I really have gone crazy.

Kyla couldn't believe she'd just scampered out of the coffee shop like a mouse with a tomcat on its tail. Her breathing didn't return to normal until she pulled into the garage of her town house and hit the remote button to lower the door. She sat for a moment, letting the silence infuse her and still the shaking deep within.

What's wrong with me, God? Why did I act that way?

"Kyla?"

She jumped, then felt herself relax when she saw the man standing in the light of the doorway to her home. She tucked the sleeping kitten into her inner jacket pocket, opened the car door, and stepped out.

"Mason, I'm so sorry I'm late."

He stood aside as she passed through the doorway, then followed her into the kitchen. "Is everything okay? I tried your cell and it went right to voice mail."

She bit her lip. Oh yes, her cell. It was still in the backseat of her car.

"Then I called your office, and they said you were still at the opening of the mall." He laid a hand on her shoulder. "Did something go wrong?"

Kyla put her hand over his—See there? She *could* touch a man without her knees nearly buckling—and patted it. "No, Mason. Everything's fine. I just…" She stopped, letting her breath out on a huff. "Do you like cats?"

Mason angled a look at her. "Do I…? Are you all right?"

"Yes, I'm *fine*. Do you?"

"Do I what?"

"Like cats? Or more to the point, kittens. Do you like kittens?"

The deepening crease on his brow showed his confusion was downshifting to frustration. "What are you talking about?"

"Mason, it's a simple question."

He looked like he wanted to shake her. Instead, he crossed his arms over his chest. "Fine. No."

Her heart dropped to her stomach. "No?"

"No. I don't like cats. Or kittens, considering that they become cats. In fact, I detest the creatures."

"Detest them?" Past the stomach, straight to the floor.

"Precisely. Now, your turn. Where on earth have you been?"

"I…uh, I had an errand to run." She finished the explanation in a rush, then hurried to her bedroom. "I'll be right out."

Once there, she slipped free of her coat, letting it fold onto the bed, becoming a makeshift cushion for the kitten. She went into her master bath, gathered several large, fluffy towels, and came back to use the towels and her bed pillows to create a warm nest for the animal.

The vet had fed the kitten a bottle of formula and supplied Kyla with enough cans of the stuff to get her through the next few days. She lifted the now-drowsy kitten from her jacket, settled it in the middle of the nest, and stroked its soft fur.

"Now, you just sleep and be quiet, okay? Not a peep."

The last thing she needed was for Mason to see she'd brought an animal home. And a cat at that.

Mason detested cats.

How could she not have known that?

Because you never asked.

She frowned, thinking hard. It was true. She'd never asked what he thought about cats or dogs or even children, for that matter. In fact, she hadn't asked him a lot of things.

Why do you suppose that is?

She brushed the nagging question aside. She didn't have time to think about it now. He was waiting for her. Exiting the bedroom, she smoothed her clothes to remove any remnants of cat hair and returned to the dining room, where she exclaimed over the exquisitely laid table. Fortunately, Mason didn't ask for further details on why she'd shown up late. And why should he? He trusted her.

The thought sent a pang of guilt zinging through her, but she brushed it aside. So she stopped for a coffee. So what? She just wanted to show Rafael her kitten.

Rafael. You wanted to show Rafael…and not Mason.

That made her pause, but only for a heartbeat. Never mind. Mason would be fine once he had a chance to warm up to the idea of her having a cat. After all, he loved her. And if she wanted a cat, he'd be fine with it.

Eventually.

Anyway, she was home now, where she belonged. With Mason Rawlins, the man who was even this moment in her kitchen, fixing her a wonderful celebration meal.

She studied him as he prepared two tall glasses of iced tea. His trim, sandy hair showed touches of white at the temples. He had everything laid out just so in the kitchen, perfectly placed for when he needed it. Annot would call him rigid—had done so, in fact.

But his propensity for order was what drew Kyla to him. He was the only person she'd ever met who did more preparation and planning than she. That and the fact that his construction company was as successful as hers.

Well…nearly.

Though they'd known each other on a professional level for years, it wasn't until last Christmas that something else grew between them. She'd been at the stunning Hotel Vintage Plaza—rated as one of the "Top 500 Hotels in the World" by *Travel + Leisure*—attending a Christmas gathering thrown by a client. Kyla had done her duty, talking and schmoozing with the appropriate people, and had just made her way to the coatroom. She was so relieved to be free of the crowded room that she didn't realize she'd cut in front of someone until the coat check woman gave her a stern look.

Cheeks burning, she turned to the man she now saw standing beside her. Good grief. Bad enough to shove in front of someone. Even worse to have it be one of her top competitors. "Oh, Mr. Rawlins! I'm so sorry."

His forgiveness was as immediate as his smile. He held his hand toward the woman. "Please, Miss Justice. Be my guest."

Miss, not *Ms*. She liked that. "No, really, you were here first. I just didn't see you."

He plucked the ticket from her fingers and held it out, along with his own, to the coat check woman. As she went to retrieve their coats, he gave Kyla another smile. "Believe me, Miss Justice. I understand wanting to get out of here."

The heat in her cheeks went up a notch. "Nothing of the sort."

Fortunately, the woman returned with their coats. Mason took Kyla's and held it out for her.

"Please don't misunderstand me"—his voice spoke close to her ear—"I'm not making a judgment. You see, I'm in the same boat."

She stepped away and turned. His smile really was quite nice. "How so?"

He picked up his coat and shrugged it on. "I realize these kinds of gatherings are a necessity for good business, but given my druthers, I'd be at home."

Her lips twitched. "Sitting on the couch."

"With a good book and an even better cup of coffee."

Her brows arched. "Decaf, of course."

Now his lips lifted. "This time of night? Of course."

They fell into step as they headed for the spacious lobby.

"I have an idea."

She glanced up at him. "Oh?"

He motioned her to exit the front doors before him. "Did you taste the coffee in there?"

She almost giggled at that. "It was…passable."

"Exactly. We've clearly been deprived, and I'd suggest, since we were so good about performing our professional duty this evening, that we treat ourselves."

She nodded to the uniformed doorman, who raised an arm to signal a taxi. Then she turned to study Mason Rawlins. "What do you suggest?"

"I know a wonderful little coffee place not far from here." His smile widened. "Might I buy you a cup of coffee?"

The taxi pulled up to the curb, but Kyla hesitated.

"Good coffee."

The doorman opened the taxi door, and Kyla handed him a dollar. But she paused, hand on the open door.

"Even extraordinary coff—"

"Yes."

One word. That's all it took, and she was on her way. Not just to coffee, but to a relationship. Funny how life could take a one-eighty when you least expected it.

"My dear?"

She shook herself from her thoughts of the past six months to take the tall glass of iced tea Mason offered. He lowered himself to the overstuffed chair beside her, took a long drink, then leaned back. "Dinner will be ready in about fifteen minutes."

He was so sweet to fix her a celebratory meal. This was what she wanted in a man. Someone who understood the intricacies of her work. Who wasn't in the least bothered when she was late or distracted or even had to cancel their dates. Nothing ruffled the man.

And nothing about him ruffled her.

He held out a hand, and she placed hers in it. Who needed sparks? This was better. Calm and serene and—

Boring.

Before she could tell that irritating inner voice to take a leap, Mason tugged at her hand.

"So tell me about your day."

She did so, giving him all the pertinent details. Oh, none of the emotional stuff, of course. They never burdened each other with such things. Still, that dull ache within her grew. She did her best not to let it show, but the crease in Mason's normally smooth forehead told her she was failing. Miserably.

For a moment she thought he would ask what was going on behind the story she gave him. He even opened his mouth, but then his reserve slipped back into place and he looked down.

The forehead crease deepened.

Never mind. Don't get into it. Just focus on being together.

"What's wrong, Mason?" Oh well. So much for not getting into it.

He contemplated the ice in his tea for a moment, then set the glass on the table and contemplated her. "That's what I was just wondering." He tipped his head. "Why do I have the sense you're not telling me everything? Maybe even the most important thing?"

His acuity should have pleased her, but it was just so…uncharacteristic.

"Kyla, please, what aren't you telling me?"

She looked at their joined hands, the relaxed way they rested together. It was the perfect symbol for what she and Mason were together. Tranquil. Controlled.

Dispassionate.

She shifted in her chair. *We are not. There's plenty of passion between us.* She looked at Mason, searched the smooth blue depths of his eyes for a ripple of emotion.

Nothing.

Well, so what? We're just more reserved than most couples.

Her inner voice actually snorted at that. *Yeah. Right. Reserved. Whatever. Fine. You want passion? I'll show you passion.*

In one smooth move, she was out of her chair and plunked down next to Mason in the easy chair. He turned to her, eyes wide, but before he could say anything, she planted her hands at the side of his face and kissed him.

Hard.

His hands came up to grip her arms—and Kyla tensed. Was he going to push her away? But he didn't. His fingers relaxed, then spread against the backs of her arms, pulling her even closer as the kiss deepened. Triumph danced through her. For a whole second. Then Mason stiffened and pushed himself away from her. In one fluid motion he was up and out of the chair.

They stood there, staring at each other. Unadulterated shock painted Mason's features, and he spun away from her. In three long strides he reached the glass doors leading out to the deck, jerked them open, and went outside.

"Ohhh, what an idiot!" Kyla slumped back against the chair, covering her burning face with her hands. What must Mason think of her? She'd never been like this before. Emotional upheaval was her younger sister's forte, not hers. Annot had never met an emotion she didn't embrace and, at some point, express.

If only Annot were here now to tell Kyla what to do. How to deal with the lunacy that was human emotions. Because Kyla didn't have a clue. As evidenced by this moment of insanity. And the fact that she'd just sent Mason skittering.

It's not like this is your first such moment, though, is it? Of course, you like to forget those other moments ever happened...

Kyla brushed the thoughts away. This wasn't about the past. That was over and done with. This was about here and now. Which would also be over and done with if she didn't get a grip.

With a deep sigh, she stood and went outside.

Mason leaned against the deck rail, looking out over the Columbia River. Kyla moved to stand beside him, careful not to touch him. When the silence grew so heavy she thought she would scream, he lowered his head and spoke.

"Don't...ever do that again."

She'd thought she couldn't be more humiliated. She was wrong. Heat surged into her cheeks. "Mason, I'm so sorry."

He lifted his head and turned to her, and any words she'd been about to utter dissolved in the face of the smoldering emotion in his eyes. She'd never seen him look that way.

Never.

He gripped the railing with one hand, as though the solid contact helped center him. Restrain him. "I've always treated you with the utmost respect. With care and consideration."

She swallowed at the vehement words. "Yes, you have."

"I've never presumed to take our relationship a direction we weren't ready for." His gaze burned into her. "That *you* weren't ready for."

"Mason, please—" She reached out to touch his arm, but he pulled away.

"I'm only human, Kyla."

The hoarse quality of those words stunned her. How had she ever been so foolish as to think this man dispassionate?

Because you mistook control for not caring.

On the heels of that truth, came another.

And because you mistook your emotion—or lack thereof—for his.

She cringed. Wanted to deny it. And couldn't. Her gaze lowered to the deck rail. Had she ever felt this miserable?

Oh, yes. She had. But not in a very, very long time.

Berto.

Kyla's fingers dug into the railing. No! She would not go there. Would not think of him. Would *not* allow those memories to taunt her now.

You loved him.

It took all her will to hold back a bitter laugh. She'd been young. An utter fool controlled by her emotions. Controlled—and destroyed.

Memories started to flow. Images of faces she hadn't allowed herself to recall for years.

No. Stop! She gritted her teeth, forcing the scenes away, back into the recesses of her mind. Berto was in the past. She was done with him. With the mistakes. With being a fool.

Tears slipped free, despite her best efforts to restrain them. Fine, let them fall. But she wasn't giving way to the memories. Not for a second. They were over and done with. That the merest hint of them made her cry only firmed Kyla's resolve.

Nothing would ever hurt her like that again.

NINE

> *"All truths are easy to understand once*
> *they are discovered; the point is to discover them."*
>
> GALILEO

> *"Lord, when doubts fill my mind,*
> *when my heart is in turmoil, quiet me."*
>
> PSALM 94:19 (TLB)

Kyla, I didn't mean to hurt you. Please, don't cry."

Mason's voice, so remorseful, so *astonished*, gripped her, making it hard to choke out words. "I'm sorry. Oh, Mason. I'm so sorry."

At her wretched whisper, gentle hands closed on her arms. She let him pull her close against his chest, cradle her there, stroke the back of her head. "It's all right, Kyla. It's all right."

His voice was familiar again, even and calm. She burrowed her face into his chest. "Mason, what's *wrong* with me?"

He slid an arm around her shoulders and led her back inside. They sat on the couch, his arm still around her. She leaned into him. If only she could close her eyes and erase the evening. The day. The month.

The year.

"Are you really so unhappy?"

She snuffled against him. "I don't know. I'm just so…weary."

"I've seen that, for weeks. Maybe even months." His arm tightened, as though to shelter her. "I've been worried about you."

She pulled back at that and looked up at him. "You have? But you never said anything."

The smile that tugged at his lips was as ironic as it was brief. "Would it have done any good?"

They both knew the answer to that.

"Kyla." Lines appeared in his forehead, and she could tell he chose his words with care. "Have you ever considered—" He looked away. "No, never mind."

Kyla tugged at his shirt front. "What?"

"It's not fair of me to even suggest it."

She watched the play of emotions on his face, disquiet wrestling with deference. Kyla's heart warmed. She really didn't deserve this man. "Mason, please. Tell me. What's on your mind?"

"Why don't you just give it up?"

Her lips twitched. "What? Stress? Sure, but how does one go about doing that?"

The warmth in his gaze dimmed, and he eased his hands free of hers. "Like I said, never mind."

Quick alarm shot through her. She started to lay a hand on his arm but stopped. Instead, she pinched at his sleeve. "No, wait. I'm sorry. I was just trying to lighten the mood."

He stood and paced to the open doorway out to the deck, looking at the wide river beyond them. "Kyla, it's not my place to tell you how to live your life."

She held her silence. He had more to say, and she'd give him time to sort through it.

"It's just…" He turned back, and there was no denying the concern weighing his face and his words. "I worry about you. You seem more and more on edge lately. You don't laugh or smile nearly as often as you used to."

Kyla frowned. Was that true? She hadn't realized—

"And I hardly ever hear you say anything positive about your work."

She leaned back in her chair, thinking over the last few months. "I think that's because it's become just that, Mason. Work."

"Then why don't you walk away from it?"

Kyla came out of her chair. "Walk away? From Justice Construction?"

Mason covered the ground between them in two long strides, taking her hands in his, pressing them to his chest. "Kyla, you know how I feel about you. I've made it clear I want this relationship to be a permanent one."

"I know, but—"

"If we were married, you wouldn't need to work any longer. You're meant for better things than letting the stress of running a construction company weigh you down."

"I'm not weighed down." She stood and went to look out the french doors leading to the balcony. "I've worked hard to get JuCo to the place it is now."

"Darling, I know that. And you're amazing at what you do." His gentle tone firmed. "But what point is there in doing it if it doesn't bring you a sense of joy or accomplishment?"

She bit her lip. What point, indeed?

The touch of his hand on her shoulder told her he'd come to stand behind her. "Sweetheart, you know the last few years have been good for Rawlins Building. More than good."

Kyla nodded. Mason's company had won a number of lucrative contracts from Ballat Enterprises, one of the top investment developers in the Northwest. She'd been so proud of Mason when those contracts came through.

"Why don't you let me buy you out?"

She turned, eyes wide. "Buy me out?"

He took her by the shoulders, his grip gentle. "Think about it. We could merge the two companies. Even combine the names, so your father's business continues to exist. And you could rest easy, knowing all you've done, the business you've built with such devotion, would be taken care of, that the employees would be treated fairly, and that the fine reputation you and your father built would go on. If you wanted, you could still be involved a little. But really. Wouldn't it be nice to be able to travel at will? To spend your days relaxing and even having a little fun? Isn't it time you enjoyed some of the nicer things in life?"

He lifted her fingers to his lips and, much to her surprise, kissed the tips. "Please, darling, let me set you free."

His lips on her fingers, his gaze caressing her face, Kyla waited for the surge of relief, for the overwhelming sense that this was the right thing to do.

And waited.

Nothing.

Well, that wasn't quite true. She did feel something—a shiver skittering across the top of her skin, like a smooth stone skipping over water, touching down just often and long enough to send ripples through her. But they weren't ripples of delight. Far from it.

They were ripples of unease.

The silence between them stretched—along with Kyla's nerves. Finally Mason let out a low sigh and released her hands. "All right, Kyla. I won't press you." His gaze caught hers, held it. And she saw something deep in those eyes.

Something that sent the stone skimming again.

"But someday soon, darling, you're going to need to make up your mind. About your business." He eased back into his chair, his gaze still locked with hers. "About me."

Remorse swept her then. "Oh, Mason…" She moved toward him, and he held his hand out without hesitation. That simple act—acceptance in the face of her doubts…and in the face of what she'd put him through that night—moved her deeply. She took his hand and perched on the arm of his chair.

"I've already made up my mind about you." She traced the long fingers laced with hers, and he chuckled.

"Have you, now?"

"I trust you, Mason. And I know you only want what's best for me."

"And?"

She bit her lip.

His smile tightened a fraction. "And you love me?"

Kyla straightened. "Oh, of course. Yes, of course I do."

"Then say it."

Kyla pulled back, but his arm encircled her, keeping her perched on the arm of his chair.

"Kyla, just say it. You love me."

She tried to do as he asked. It was such a small thing, after all, to say those words to him. But when she opened her mouth, all that came out was, "I do."

"You do what?"

"I…" What was wrong with her? Why couldn't she just say those words to him?

"Good grief! What is *that*?"

Kyla spun at Mason's exclamation, just in time to spot a flash of tricolored fur skittering across the kitchen floor, then scooting inside the open lower cabinet.

Oh no! She glanced down the hallway to her bedroom. Surely she'd shut the door, hadn't she?

"A rat!" Mason's eyes were wide. "You've got a *rat!*"

For a moment she considered letting him think that, until he strode into the kitchen and pulled a broom from the closet.

"Mason!" She put herself between him and the kitten, which must surely be cowering in the corner of the cupboard. "No!" She took hold of the broom and wrested it from him. "It's not a rat."

"It's not?"

It took a few moments to return the broom to its proper hiding place, and she used that time to think through what she was going to say.

Why? What's the big deal? So you got a cat? So what? This is your house, after all. The man doesn't live here.

Kyla shook the troublesome thoughts from her head and knelt on the floor.

"Be careful! It might bite you."

She angled a look over her shoulder, then went back to the task at hand. Sure enough, the kitten was pressed as far back in the corner as it could get. Kyla reached toward it, crooning. "Come on, Serendipity. It's okay..."

"Seren—! Kyla, *what* are you doing?"

She spun around at his impatient bark and stood to face him, hands on her hips. "I'm trying to calm down a defenseless kitten that *you* terrorized. Now *hush*, Mason."

To say he was astonished was far more than an understatement. The poor man's face was mottled with color, and his mouth hung open.

He looked like something was trying to throttle him.

Probably his indignation, but Kyla couldn't worry about mollifying him right now. She knelt again and, after a number of minutes, finally coaxed the kitten from the cupboard. She lifted it into her arms, noting how natural it felt to cuddle the little creature, and stood again to face the still-steaming Mason.

Kyla cleared her throat. "Mason, I'd like you to meet a fr—"

"It's a kitten." He looked like he'd just downed an unripe persimmon.

She couldn't restrain her wry tone. "Yes, *she's* a kitten."

"But…what is it doing here?"

She turned sideways, as though to shelter the animal from his acerbic tone. "More to the point, she's my kitten. Her name is Serendipity."

"Your—"

She waited, but nothing else was forthcoming. He just stood there, staring at her as though convinced she'd taken leave of her senses.

So much for hoping he'd warm up to the idea.

She went into the living room, Mason following close behind. They sat, and Kyla told the tale again, just as she'd told it to Rafael. Mason listened, but the tightness around his mouth never lessened. When she finished, he sat there, hands on his knees, eyes fixed on the kitten in her lap.

"You're keeping it." Half statement, half disbelieving question.

Her reply was one hundred percent absolute. "I'm keeping *her*."

His gaze lifted to hers, and she saw a hard edge there. "I see. So the fact that I don't care for cats…?"

Kyla bit her lip. Why couldn't he understand what this meant to her? "Mason, I'm sorry. But I really think if you'd just let yourself relax and spend some time with her, you'd find she's really quite delightful."

"And you know this after, what, a few hours?"

No. She'd known it within seconds. But she wasn't about to say that out loud. She stood. "Let me get her settled in the bedroom, and make sure the door is closed this time, and we can discuss it more, if you like."

By the time she'd dealt with the kitten and returned to the living room, Mason had his coat on. Alarm coursed through her.

"Mason, please—"

He took her outstretched hand. "Never mind, Kyla." He tugged her close and slipped his arms around her. "It's just a kitten. We'll work it out. Somehow. I mean"—he almost smiled—"everyone can use a little Serendipity in their lives."

Hope sparked as he hugged her, trailed a finger down her cheek, and pressed a soft kiss to her lips. "I'll call you tomorrow."

She followed him to the front door, then watched him walk to his car and drive away. As she closed the door and walked back into the living room, one question taunted her.

What is wrong *with me?*

Mason was a good man. A man of faith and integrity.

Faith?

She pursed her lips at the hint of doubt. Yes, *faith.* All right, so Mason wasn't as vocal about his relationship with God as others—say Avidan or Jediah Curry, her sister's fiancé. And yes, there were times Kyla wondered whether Mason's profession of belief wasn't more because he knew it was so important to her…

She shook off the troublesome thoughts. Mason's faith was real. And it was private. There was nothing wrong with that.

Or with the man. Who, by the way, loved her. Wanted to marry her. Any woman would be thrilled to have a man like Mason offer to take care of her.

Any woman, it seemed, but her. Because no matter how much sense it made, no matter how hard she tried to sell herself on the idea that it was time to accept Mason's proposal…

Her heart just wasn't buying it.

TEN

> *"The heart has eyes which the brain knows nothing of."*
> Charles H. Perkhurst

> *"God knows all hearts, and he sees you.*
> *He keeps watch over your soul."*
> Proverbs 24:12

I don't buy it."

Kyla plopped back against the pillows on her bed. "Don't buy what, Annot?"

"You say you're okay, but you don't *sound* okay. Are you *sure* you're—"

"I'm *fine.*" Oh dear. Best tone it down or her sister would be on the next plane to Portland. "Really. I'm just tired, that's all."

"I didn't wake you, did I? I mean, you're usually up and running by now."

A glance at the clock confirmed Annot's words. Nine o'clock! Kyla couldn't remember the last time she'd slept in this late. What was more amazing was that it actually felt good. "I was just about to get up."

"*Me-oww!*"

The sound was followed by a ball of fur landing on Kyla's head. Kyla yelped and caught the kitten.

Wonderful. The beast was a morning person.

"*Kyla!* Are you all right?"

"I'm. Fine." Kyla forced the words through gritted teeth, then forced herself to relax. "My cat just jumped on my head."

"Your...what?"

Ha. Take that, Miss You're-Not-Spontaneous. "My cat. Or kitten, to be precise. I just got her yesterday."

Annot's squeal rivaled any sound Serendipity had made. "You got a pet! That's so great."

"Hmm. I wish Mason thought so." She cuddled Serendipity close, loving the way the kitten's purrs rumbled against her chest. "Anyway, I was just relaxing this morning. I did just finish a big job yesterday."

"Oh, no, no, no. You don't get off that easy. What's the kitten's name? Where'd you get her? What's she look like? I want details. *And* pictures."

"Okay, okay. Soon. But right now I have to get up and get busy."

"New project already?"

"I'm working on it." And so she was. But this time she was going to do something different. Something she should have done long ago.

The ensuing silence told Kyla her little sister had something on her mind. "What is it, Annot?"

"What is what?"

"Whatever you're deciding whether or not to say."

Her sister's heavy sigh was ample confirmation. "I'm not going to ask it."

"Ask what?"

"If you're okay."

Kyla would have screamed if she'd been given to such displays.

"I'm sorry, Kylie. I'm just worried about you, that's all."

Annot's gentle words eased the tension in her shoulders. Her sister knew her so well. And loved her anyway. She rolled on her side, reaching with one hand to pull the comforter around her as she moved. "I'm just so"—she shrugged into the blanket—"I don't know. Restless, I guess."

"Kylie, really. What's going on?"

I've realized I lost my way and didn't even know it. "Nothing." No need to worry her sister. This was her problem to sort through, and so she would. Now that she'd realized what was gnawing at her, why she felt so empty, she knew what to do to make it right.

That's what she was best at. Making things right. "I think I'm coming down with a cold or something. You know how I hate summer colds."

Annot's chuckle warmed her even more than the comforter. "Summer is over, goof."

"Not yet. Autumn doesn't officially begin for another two and a half weeks. I refuse to surrender summer one day sooner than I have to. Annot, about the wedding? What would you think about making it a double wedding?"

"*What?*"

She couldn't blame her sister for her shocked reaction. The question had shocked Kyla as well. *What* was she thinking? "I don't know. I mean, Mason asked me to marry him again—"

"*Again?*"

Kyla kneaded her temples. "Annot, would you please stop shrieking? You're killing my head."

"Kyla Marie Justice, are you telling me a man proposed to you and you didn't tell me when it happened?"

"Actually, a man proposed to me three times now—"

"*Kylie!!*"

Her temples pounded. "Shrieking. Again."

"Sorry. Again." Annot softened her tone. "Okay, I'm speaking in calm tones now. Kyla, beloved sister, this man who proposed to you three times. Is it Mason?"

Kyla vented her exasperation to the ceiling. "Well, who else do you think it would be? The hunky barista down at the coffee shop?"

She could have bitten off her tongue. She was getting as careless as Annot about letting words just blurp out of her mouth. With any luck, her sister would pay no attention—

"What hunky barista?"

Of course. Why should she think she'd have any more luck today than usual? "Never mind."

"Kylie—"

"Would you please forget about the barista?"

"*Hunky* barista, you said."

"Hunky schmunky! I'm talking about Mason."

"Schmunky?"

"He asked me to marry him again last night—"

"Did you really just say *schmunky?*"

"What I just said was that Mason has asked me to marry him."

A pause. Apparently Annot needed to absorb this news. Then, "So…what did you say?"

Kyla rolled onto her side. *Why* had she opened her mouth about this? She should have known her dear sister would ask question after question. None of which she was prepared to answer. "Nothing."

"Nothing."

Kyla sighed. "Right. Nothing."

"See! I told you he wasn't the one for you—"

"I didn't say that."

"You don't have to! I mean, if you loved him, the answer would have been immediate."

Oh, now that was going too far. Kyla sat up, sending poor Serendipity tumbling across the bed, and clutched the receiver. "Now listen. Just because I want time to think about the most important decision I'll ever make doesn't mean I don't love Mason. Of course I love him. Why shouldn't I? He's intelligent, cultured, an excellent businessman—"

"Kylie, will you *listen* to yourself? You sound like you're discussing a potential employee, not your soul mate."

Kyla's brows rose. "I never said Mason was my soul mate."

"Exactly! But don't you want that? Someone who's part of your heart in a way no one else ever could be?"

"Please, forget I said anything."

"Right! Forget my sister said someone proposed to her."

"Annot, please. I shouldn't have said what I did. I'm not even sure Mason will like the whole double wedding idea. He's rather—"

"Persnickety."

"—particular." She flopped onto her back, making her tone as scolding as she could without hurting her sister's feelings. "He's already mentioned a couple of times that he wants us to be married someplace exotic."

"Is that what you want?"

"I don't know."

Another sigh. "Okay, I'll let it go for now. And I promise I won't bug you about marrying or not marrying Mr. Thrillsville."

Kyla threw an arm over her aching eyes. "You're not bugging me, Annot. Not really. It's just that I'm not ready to make a decision on all this yet."

"Listen, Kylie, try to get some rest, okay? You don't sound good."

"Gee, thanks."

"You know what I mean."

Yes, she did. And as she hung up the phone, she knew she couldn't ignore it any longer. All these years, she'd managed to keep the past at bay. So why, all of a sudden, was it there, haunting her?

Condemning her.

Something was going on. What, she didn't know. But something *was* there on the fringes.

And it was headed for her.

Well, fine. Whatever was coming, there was only one way to prepare for it. Kyla leaned forward to lift her Bible from the side table.

~~⌒

Arroow-rooww!

Annie Justice swatted at her German shepherd, who was walking in circles, that heavy tail pummeling her for added emphasis. "Look out, you crazy moose-dog! You're gonna knock me over."

Kodi's cold nose came to nudge at her, and she stood. "Okay, okay. I surrender. Let's go for a run."

The dog's joyful bark resounded in the room, and Annie laughed as she made her way to the front door to grab Kodi's leash. She glanced back at the clock on the wall as she pulled open the door. She had a half hour until Jed came over. Plenty of time.

Besides, she needed to run. She always thought better when she ran.

Five minutes of warmup later, they were off, Kodi trotting along beside her, tongue flopping in happy rhythm to their steady footsteps.

Annie let herself go on automatic pilot, her body falling into the easy rhythm of running. She took in the flowers blooming along the path, the sun that was already starting to grow warm, the fragrances all around her.

What a great day.

Only one thing cast a pall on her full enjoyment. That conversation with Kyla. She'd sounded so…what? Upset? Not really. Frustrated? Yes, but something more. There'd been something in Kyla's tone she'd never heard before.

Her sister was hiding something.

What, Annie wasn't exactly sure. Was there a problem with her work?

Possibly, though that made no sense. With her relationship? Now, that was a definite possibility. Kyla and Mason seemed more like work associates than two people in love. People in love touched and shared private jokes and couldn't bear to be apart.

Like you and Jed, you mean?

Annie allowed herself a little smile. Exactly. Of course, Kyla and Mason might just share something different than she and Jed. A more sedate relationship. But Annie wasn't convinced that was what her sister really wanted.

Or, for that matter, needed.

Kodi nudged her around a corner, and Annie realized they were in the homestretch. Remembering Jed should be at the house by now, she lengthened her strides, eating up the distance.

Sure enough, the gate to the driveway was open, and Jed's car was parked by the front door. Annie knew she should slow to a walk for her cooldown, but at the sight of Jed's tall form standing by his car and the smile on that handsome face, her feet developed a mind of their own. She sprinted the last few yards toward him.

His smile shifted to a full-blown grin as he watched her, and he opened his arms. She didn't hesitate; she jumped into his embrace. He caught her, laughing as he spun her around, Kodi circling them and barking up a storm.

After a breathless kiss, Jed set Annie on her feet. "Now that's what I call a welcome."

Annie paced back and forth, letting her muscles cool down from the run. "Hey, can I help it if I missed you?"

"You mean those whole nine hours we were apart? After all, I didn't head home last night until a little after midnight." He stretched. "I swear, woman, you're gonna be the death of me with all this late-night carousing."

She sat on the grass, stretching. "It was *your* idea to watch four John Wayne westerns in a row, genius."

His grin reappeared, and he leaned back against his car. "Start off with *The Shepherd of the Hills*, then on to *The Sons of Katie Elder* and *The Undefeated*, and finish up with *Rooster Cogburn*. You have to admit, it was a great way to spend an evening." Kodi stuck her snout in Annie's face, that long tongue slurping up the side of her face, and Annie shoved the dog away. "Thanks a lot, Moose." She wiped her sleeve across her face. "And yes, it was a great evening." She reached out to pet Kodi, who'd taken her rebuff by circling a couple of times, then plopping down on the grass beside Annie with a doggy huff.

"Okay, what's up?"

Annie looked up at her intended. "What do you mean?"

He tilted his head at her. "I mean, what's wrong. And don't say nothing, 'cuz I can see it in your eyes."

Letting out a heavy sigh, Annie told him about the call with Kyla. "She's my only sister, Jed. And I can tell when something's off. I can't pinpoint it, but something's just not right with her."

"You're worried?"

She pondered that, then gave a slow shake of her head. "I'm...bothered, but not worried yet."

Jed pushed away from the car. "Well then, I say we take some time and pray for her." He held his hand out to Annie, and she let him pull her to her feet and into his arms. "And if you shift into being worried, we'll know it's time to do something else."

She snuggled against him. "Such as?"

"Such as send you and your beast to Portland so you can check up on your *only sister.*" He nudged her. "Like I didn't know that's what you were hinting at, brat."

Annie framed his face with her hands. "I don't deserve you."

"No"—he pressed a kiss to the side of her mouth—"you don't. But you've got me."

Ample proof, Annie thought as she melted against him, of how very, very much God loved her.

ELEVEN

"An evil life is a kind of death."
OVID

*"God...reveals deep and hidden things;
he knows what lies in darkness."*
DANIEL 2:20, 22 (NIV)

He loved these windows. Too bad he had to trash 'em.

You couldn't tell now, not with the streetlights shot out to make sure there wasn't even a sliver of illumination, but when daylight shone through those windows, it was beautiful. Just let the sun come out, and the windows rained color down on the room. He used to sit there, holding out his hand so those colors washed over his skin. Skin the color of ebony, his mama always said. He'd study the pieces of glass, how they fit. Like those puzzles he and Mama used to put together.

One side of his mouth drew up. They never had all the pieces. And his mother's patience only lasted through a couple drinks. Then she started grabbing pieces and pounding them into place. He'd learned early on not to complain, to point out that the picture wouldn't be right if she did that.

Better a messed up picture than a broken jaw.

He touched a finger to the cool, stained-glass window before him. No pounding here. Just color and perfect fit; rippled colored glass from ceiling to floor, forming pictures. Beautiful, terrible pictures.

Yeah, these windows were older than he was. Probably twice as old. He didn't know anything else in the neighborhood as old as this church. Made him sad, what they had to do.

But the old men hadn't left them any choice.

"King K, we got it all in place. Time to light it up, man."

He didn't respond. Just splayed his fingers across the glass, let his gaze rise to where Jesus hung on the cross. *You shoulda made them listen.*

"King—"

One look was all it took to shut his boy up. If it ever took more, he was in trouble. "We light it when *I* say, Chato."

He almost smiled at the fear that sprang to the kid's eyes. But this wasn't the time to smile. Kid needed to fear him. He'd stay alive a lot longer that way.

"Naw, man, I know. I wasn't sayin' nothin'. Just, you know, letting you know we ready. Nothin' more, man."

This boy talked too much. They'd have to break him of that. "Go wait for me with the others. Tell 'em I be there"—he sharpened his gaze and words—"when I'm ready."

The boy's hands came up. "Sure, sure. I'll tell 'em. Just what you say, man. We wait 'til you're rea—"

"Chato."

If the kid been a dog, he'd have wet himself. "Yeah?"

"Go."

Chato went.

King Killa watched the boy scramble. Kid wasn't afraid of anyone—except him. King respected that. Kid was jumped in a few weeks ago. Took the beat down better than King expected. Even managed to get back on his feet when it was over. He'd stood there, face split and swollen, clothes soaked in blood, chin up.

This kid…he was gonna be a player.

The door closed behind Chato, and King turned back to the scene before him. He studied the face as he'd done so often as a child. Saw how pain twisted those features. God's features, if what his mama told him was true.

Why'd You do it?

Son of God, right? God made man. More power in His little finger than all those religious leaders had between them.

Man, You coulda taken 'em all out. Just like that.

He pressed his palm to the cold glass. Fit his hand to God's. Let his fingers cover the rigid fingers that spread out, as though trying to escape the nail holding Jesus's hand to the cross. The tats traveling King K's hand blended in, became part of the scene. The dagger cutting across the back of his hand followed the rough line of the cross; the blood dripping down the blade, the drops circling his wrist, flowed from the red stream escaping the center of Jesus's hand.

What did his mama always say? "God sees all and knows all. He's in all things, and more powerful than anyone can begin to imagine. All power. That's what God is. All-powerful."

So why'd You lay down and die?

King K dropped his hand and turned away. *God made man? So what? You let Your crew down. Let the Man dis them. Hunt them down. Torture them. Kill them.*

He looked down at his hand, at the red drops of blood circling his wrist. The blood of his brothers. His fingers clenched into a fist, and he walked toward the door.

Mama was wrong. God wadn't no hero. No all-powerful being. He was a coward. Let God die. Let Him give up His blood.

King Killa didn't work like that.

He didn't die. And neither did his crew.

He pulled open the door, walked out into the cool night. The Blood Brotherhood were there. As he'd known they'd be. King K lifted his chin to the largest of the crew. "You got the lighter? It's Sunday, man. Time to have church?"

Dancer's scarred lips curled into a dark grin as he pulled his hand out of his pocket and tossed the lighter to King K. King caught it, then flipped it open. A flame jumped to life. He eyed his crew standing there, watching him. Waiting.

They knew he wouldn't let them down. Just as he knew they'd stand for him to the last breath. They were family. A brotherhood tested in blood. They didn't lie down. They didn't give ground. Not one inch. Nobody—not a bunch of old men, not God Himself—could change that.

And anyone who thought they could—He flipped the lighter through a broken-out window in the parsonage—was about to see just how wrong they were.

TWELVE

*"I haven't failed; I've found ten
thousand ways that don't work."*
BENJAMIN FRANKLIN

*"I said to them, 'You know very well what trouble we are in.
Jerusalem lies in ruins, and its gates have been destroyed
by fire. Let us rebuild the wall of Jerusalem and end
this disgrace!' Then I told them about how the gracious
hand of God had been on me.... They replied at once,
'Yes, let's rebuild the wall!' So they began the good work."*
NEHEMIAH 2:17–18

Ashes. That's all that was left. Of the parsonage. Of their dream. Smoldering, ruined ashes.

The contractor quitting wasn't enough? We have to suffer this baleydikung as well?

Anger grappled with sorrow deep within as Fredrik stepped over the charred remains of what once was the three-story church parsonage. At least the fire didn't spread beyond that portion of the building. The church sanctuary still stood. As did the classroom section.

But was it enough? Was there enough left for them to fulfill the calling God had given them?

Yeshua, it's in Your hands. You know what they will say. How this will pain them. Discourage them. How they already feel time is running ou—

Oh! Time. His fingers felt for the gold chain hanging from his vest pocket, then tugged his pocket watch free. He thumbed the spring release so the cover flipped open to reveal the face of the timepiece. So. Ten minutes. In just ten minutes he'd sit at a table and face them. The church elders.

Followers of God. Friends. Treasured advisors.

Willard and his two sons, Von and Don. Steve, Alden, Sheamus, Wayne, and Hilda. Dear Hilda. Faithful believers whose years on this earth had granted them wisdom. Fredrik could almost guess what they'd say.

No, don't guess. Wait. Listen. They may surprise you.

Perhaps. He eased the watch cover shut, then slipped the timepiece back into his pocket. He turned and made his way through the rubble. To the sanctuary, where they were most likely waiting.

I wouldn't mind it, Yeshua. Being surprised. He stepped over a charred board. *But would it be such trouble, just this once, to let the surprise be a good one?*

He hoped not. He'd had all the bad surprises he could take.

~~~

"It's over."

So. Fredrik had waited, and he'd heard. Sheamus's two words, spoken with such conviction, were pretty much as he expected. A clear reflection of years of running his own business.

Sheamus's pronouncement told the tale.

It was okay to keep up the fight so long as there was a solid payoff in sight. But now? The only thing before them was ruin.

But is Sheamus right? Help me know what's right.

Fredrik stilled his troubled thoughts—which had sprung to life with Sheamus's heavy words—and folded his hands on the tabletop. Then he frowned. *Yeshua, how can these be my hands? My hands are strong. Carpenter's hands, like Yours.* Or they were last time he looked at them. When had they become so pale and wrinkled?

"How can you say that, Sheamus?" Steve, who'd never turned away from a challenge, entered the discussion. "We still have time."

Optimism speaks up. Thank you, Steve. I needed to know not everyone is ready to give up.

"Two months!" Wayne was usually the quiet one, speaking only when he had something he absolutely needed to say. For him to blurt out such an exclamation swept Fredrik's relief aside. "Steve, be realistic. What can we do in two months? Especially after the fire. The parsonage is in ruins…" Wayne turned to the man sitting beside Fredrik. "Don, you tell him. Tell him he's talking crazy."

Don's strong hands—hands that had run a dry kiln at the mill with both precision and skill—rested on the table. Fredrik waited as the man pondered his response. Like his brother, Don loved to tease and laugh. But both men were as solid as the concrete foundation of the church and, when the situation called for it, thoughtful and solemn.

And if ever a situation called for it, this one did.

Finally, drawing in a heavy breath, Don met Wayne's eyes. "I don't know, Wayne. Seems to me if God has called us to this, He has to be the One to tell us to give it up."

If. Yes, Yeshua, there is the question. If. Did You call us, as we thought You did? Then why so many obstacles? Fredrik rubbed his fingers across the back of his hand. *And when did my skin turned to rice paper draped over eighty-year-old blue veins?*

Old, Fredrik? Yes, I suppose. But life flows through them. Your life. My life.

Yes? He drew in breath, felt his lungs fill. *Yes, Abba. Life, still. And I thank You for every new day. But the dream. What of the dream You gave us? Is that alive?*

"Surely God doesn't expect us to run what's left of this church into the ground." Sheamus shook his head. "How is that good stewardship?"

Fredrik wove his fingers together. *Sheamus is right, Yeshua. How can we continue to throw good money after bad?*

Hilda looked down in her lap, where her ancient Sheltie lay curled. There was more Sheltie than there was lap, but Hilda didn't care. Doggy Dog was her family, and the animal went wherever she did. Even church.

She stroked the dog's fur, and when she spoke her gentle tone ushered calm into the room. "None of us wants to run the church into the ground. That's what we're trying to avoid."

Don fingered the edges of the paper he was doodling on, then directed a question to his brother, Von. "Where are we with our finances?"

Von opened the folder on the table in front of him. "As of this week, we're down to about a fourth of what we started with."

"That's not enough."

"Maybe not if we were in this on our own." Steve met the troubled gazes around the table. "I know you understand business, Sheamus. The success of the company you founded shows that. But this isn't about just business."

Alden nodded. Years working in the forests as a ranger had given him a quiet astuteness. "That's true enough. If it was, we'd have pulled out long ago." He gave another slow nod. "No, obedience. That's what this is about."

Such a team You put together here, Yeshua. Such a blending of personalities and temperaments. Only God could have done this—knit their hearts and spirits into a tapestry of faith. Made them more than members of the church Fredrik had pastored for over forty years. God made them friends.

No, more than that. *You made us family.*

"Fredrik, what do you say?"

He lifted his eyes to those sitting around the table, studying the faces almost more familiar to him than his own. These people he respected and loved.

Which was why it tore him apart to hear them do little lately but debate.

This time the breath he drew in made him weary. Old friends at odds. It shouldn't be. "What do I say about what, Wayne?"

The man's back straightened a fraction more—something Fredrik hadn't thought possible. "Weren't you listening?"

"Listening?" He let his gaze travel to the seven faces watching him. The church elders. The heart and soul of what, until six months ago, was the Blessed Hope Fellowship Church. Seven elders and one deaconess, all as timeworn and tested as he. Well, almost. He did have most of them beat in the age category, but not by much.

"Listening to what, Wayne? More arguing? More debates?" He slid his hands beneath the table, resting them in his lap. "I should listen to this, instead of what God told us?" He shook his head. "No. I wasn't listening. But I was asking."

"Asking?" Wayne leaned his elbows on the table. "Asking what?"

"If we believe this call we've been given, to make our church over into a community youth center, is from God."

Slow nods answered Fredrik. Hilda's blue eyes encouraged him to go on.

"And do we trust the Scripture we've held to since this church opened its doors? The psalm we chose for our mission statement?" He indicated the framed psalm on the wall.

"Absolutely." There was no doubt in Wayne's tone, nor in the echoes of agreement from the others.

Fredrik folded his hands on the table. "Then I ask you this: does this fire mean God has released us from that call?"

Not one of them hesitated. They shook their heads, and Steve voiced their reply. "No, it doesn't."

Fredrik planted his hands on the table and pushed himself to his feet. "Then, old friends, we have our orders. We must move forward."

Grumbles sounded on every side, and Sheamus frowned. "I just don't see how we can possibly do that."

The sharp sound of metal scraping wood jerked their attention to the right. Willard had pushed back his chair and, hands resting on the table for support, pushed himself to his feet. At eighty-seven, he was the eldest elder, both in age and in wisdom. His large hands reflected his heart, equal parts strength and tenderness. He'd endured a season of suffering—thanks, as he often said, to his own choices as a young man—and come out, by God's grace, cleansed. Grounded. Joyful. This was a true man of God. Though the newest elder to the church—he'd been attending since he moved to Portland after retiring ten years ago—it seemed he'd been a part of them forever.

That was most likely because Willard's sons, Don and Von, had been. Just two years apart, they'd started coming to the church as young men. Fredrik had married them to their sweethearts, baptized, and married their children, grandchildren, and even a few great-grandchildren. And through it all, Willard was there. Visiting at first, and then as much a part of their church family as anyone who'd ever attended.

And Fredrik's most trusted friend.

He watched now as Willard made his way to the whiteboard on the wall. Lifting a marker, he pulled the cap free, the snap sounding like a thunderclap in the suddenly silent room. His movements slow but steady, Willard wrote on the whiteboard. The silence stretched. One minute. Three. Five. When he was finished, he put the cap back on the marker, walked back to his chair, and sat down.

Such a simple answer, Yeshua. Fredrik raised a hand, letting his finger touch the board beneath Willard's paraphrase of verses they all knew so well. *Why didn't we see it sooner?*

For a moment, no one spoke. Then Wayne let out a low sigh. "Point taken. Let's take the night to pray. To seek God's guidance as to our next step. Then talk again tomorrow and form a plan."

Murmurs of agreement sounded, and the group rose and left the room. Fredrik waited until he was the only one left, then went to stand before a frame hanging on the wall. Like similar frames in every room of the church, it held selections from Psalm 89—words that had undergirded their lives as a congregation:

> *I will sing of the LORD's unfailing love forever!*
> > *Young and old will hear of your faithfulness.*
> *Your unfailing love will last forever.*
> > *Your faithfulness is as enduring as the heavens....*
>
> *Who in all of heaven can compare with the LORD?*
> > *What mightiest angel is anything like the LORD?*
> *The highest angelic powers stand in awe of God.*
> > *He is far more awesome than all who surround his throne.*
> *O LORD God of Heaven's Armies!*
> > *Where is there anyone as mighty as you, O LORD?*
> > *You are entirely faithful....*
>
> *Powerful is your arm!*
> > *Strong is your hand!*
> > *Your right hand is lifted high in glorious strength.*
> *Righteousness and justice are the foundation of your throne.*
> > *Unfailing love and truth walk before you as attendants.*
> *Happy are those who hear the joyful call to worship,*
> > *for they will walk in the light of your presence, LORD.*

They rejoice all day long in your wonderful reputation.
*   They exult in your righteousness.*
You are their glorious strength.
*   It pleases you to make us strong.*
Yes, our protection comes from the LORD.

Fredrik let the words seep through his soul, strengthening him anew. He patted the framed Scripture, then walked toward the door, a wry smile teasing his mouth. He opened the door, turning back for just a moment to the whiteboard and what Willard had written there. Words he'd memorized long ago, but it wasn't until now that they'd hit home with an impact that almost took his breath away. Words that offered life and promise. And one other thing.

Consequences.

Fredrik smiled. Ah, but wasn't that always the way of Scripture?

As though confirming the thought, the words from the whiteboard drifted through his mind: *"If you need wisdom…ask God, and he will gladly tell you. But be sure you expect an answer, for a doubtful mind is as unsettled as an ocean wave driven and tossed by the wind. Doubters waver back and forth in everything they do. Such people should not expect anything from the Lord."*

Fredrik walked from the building out into the sunshine. *If you need wisdom…ask.*

This he could do. This he would do.

And God, as sure as the sun would rise on the morrow, would answer.

THIRTEEN

"When evil men plot, good men must plan. When evil men burn and bomb, good men must build and bind. When evil men shout ugly words of hatred, good men must commit themselves to the glories of love."
MARTIN LUTHER KING JR.

"Its walls are patrolled day and night against invaders, but the real danger is wickedness within the city."
PSALM 55:10

These old fools were going to answer for their stubborn stupidity.

King K leaned against the side of the building, thumb flicking across the point of his butterfly knife, pondering what he'd just overheard. Good thing they were too stupid to close the windows during their meeting. Made it easier to listen in, find out what was happening.

He'd expected them to bail. Walk away. They had to know the fire was set. Had to know it was a warning. Get out before things got worse. Leave now. No harm, no foul.

But no. These stupid white fogies were going to pray. Think about it and pray.

King snapped his wrist, flipping the knife until it folded up, and slid it into the side pocket of his pants. So. They were going to pray. Maybe stick it out.

Fine. Just meant he had some planning to do.

He turned, then froze. A form slipped out of the shadows. His hand slid toward the knife he'd just pocketed.

"It was you, wasn't it?"

Fingers tensed, then relaxed as he recognized the voice. "What are you doing here?"

"Watching out."

King's lip curled. "For what?"

"For you."

The boldness of the words, the pointed intensity, drew his fingers into a fist.

"You did it, didn't you? You set the fire."

King didn't dignify the question with a response. Just stood, arms crossed, features bored.

"You proud of yourself? Settin' fire to a *church*?"

That was enough. More than enough. "What you doin' here, L'il Man?"

"More to the point, what are *you* doing here?"

Anyone else dared to question him, King K would put the fool down. Instead, he spread his hands out, palms up. "Just walkin' my turf. Makin' sure everything's cool."

Tarik's lips thinned, but King didn't take the bait. Let the boy get upset. He wasn't backing down. He let his posture say as much—for all the good it would do. This boy didn't scare.

He would have made a great 22.

King K shook the thought from his head. No. Not this one. The life wasn't for him. Sure, he'd been mad when L'il Man walked out on them. Or so he'd made it appear. Couldn't let his crew know how relieved he was Tarik was gettin' out.

Tarik turned to look at the burned section of the church. King studied the younger boy's profile. Kid got more handsome with each year. Stood taller too. He might be young, but it was clear to any who looked at him that Tarik was a man.

"You've gone too far, man."

King narrowed his eyes. "No such thing. I go as far as I like in my own crib."

Tarik spun to face him. "This isn't your crib! It's God's. Don't you see that? You're not going against me or these people. You're going against God. And that's a stupid play, even for you."

Nobody called him stupid. Nobody. King K took a step forward. Let his words hiss though clenched teeth. "You're as much a fool as those old men, *Tarik*." He spat the name.

The boy didn't flinch. Just squared off. "I can only pray I'm one-tenth as good as those men in there. Those men you tried to kill."

King K let his mouth curve at the accusation. "I don't *try* to kill nobody." Anger flowed, turning to venom that dripped from his words. "I *kill*. Period. I want someone dusted, they gone. You got that?"

Silence. No sign of fear. Not even a flicker in those dark eyes. Had to admire the kid's guts. King's sneer almost slipped. Almost.

"I got it."

Tarik's voice, low and firm, sounded so old. And cold. King K could remember a better time…that voice young, laughing…

He turned and walked away. No point thinking about the past. Old business. Over and done with. All that mattered was here and now. And taking care of today's business.

No matter how hard—or messy—it got.

FOURTEEN

"Evil is easy, and has infinite forms."
BLAISE PASCAL

"What does this bunch of poor,
feeble Jews think they are doing?"
NEHEMIAH 4:2

I can't believe the mess you've made of this. You're telling me those old men haven't given up?"

"Maybe if your boy had done his job—"

"Think carefully before you finish that sentence."

The man on the other end of the phone call fell silent. Good thing. One more word and he'd have had to find another lackey.

Because that one would have been dead.

"Now, let's do this again. I ask the questions, you answer them. Short, concise answers. Have they given up?"

"No, Mr. Ballat."

Good. Tone and words both restored to the proper level of respect. "Do they have the resources to continue?"

"It's tight, but…for now, yes."

His lips pressed together so hard it made his jaws ache. *Relax, Samuel. You'll win. You know you will. Just consider it a challenge that it's taking longer than you thought.* "What do you mean, 'for now'?"

"They almost gave in. Their funds really are close to gone. But Fredrik Tischler…he drew them back."

"And how"—he didn't try to keep the ice from his tone—"did you let him do that?"

"It wasn't something I could stop!"

So. His weapon wasn't as effective as promised. "Then what am I paying you for?"

"Look, I'm doing all I can. But you can only get so far in the face of Bible verses and prayer. Not when people really believe in them. These men, they're dinosaurs! They don't even know how extinct they are."

Sam's lip twisted. "You listen to me, my friend, and listen close. I expect this job done on time. Failure on your part to do what you've promised will cause…dire consequences." He let that sink in, then softened his tone a fraction. "Success, though, will make me very happy. And if I'm happy, you will be as well."

The answering silence didn't bother him. He'd learned the value of silence, of letting people chew on the meaning—evident and hidden—of what he said to them.

"Don't worry. I'll get it done."

See there? Given a moment to ponder, the dolt on the other end of the phone line finally understood. It wasn't Sam Ballat's neck on the line. It was his.

Sam let the phone drop into the cradle, glad to be rid of any contact with the worm who'd come to him, hat in hand, promising all and, so far, delivering naught.

Maybe…

He fingered the phone receiver. Maybe he should make another call to an associate he *knew* he could trust. Send that person after the worm, reminding him that prayer didn't matter when you had no soul. Which the worm didn't. Because he'd sold it.

To Sam.

He let his hand fall away. *No, give him time. See what he does in the next day or so. You can always call later.*

Ah, the voice of reason. How he treasured it. What a pity those old fools at the church didn't do the same.

Prayer.

How fascinating that people still believed in such an archaic concept. Prayer to some supposed almighty being who watched over them, shifting lives like pawns on some celestial chessboard, all according to His children's whims.

Ridiculous.

He wove his fingers together, lips drawing to a smile as he remembered his grandmother teaching him an old poem.

"Here's the church…" Her soft voice warm in his ear, the hint of peppermint on her breath as she demonstrated hands, palm to palm, linked by interwoven fingers.

"Here's the steeple…" His child self had been captivated as she pressed her wrinkled forefingers tip to tip, thumbs side to side.

"Open the doors"—Paper-thin hands parted at the heel, rotating so soft fingers come into view—*"and see all the…"*

Fools.

He closed his eyes, brushing aside the tender voice of love. The voice that promised so much and delivered nothing.

His hands dropped to his sides as his smile slid from his face. Not, of course, the way his dear grandmother taught it. But far more accurate.

For who but simpletons and fools would believe some all-powerful being actually cared one iota about their pleas and requests. Still, there was a kind of poetic justice in it all, seeing as it was belief in prayer that had kept his enemies from taking any real action.

He splayed his hand out against the cool glass of the window. *Enemies* might be a bit harsh. *Opponents.* Yes, that was better. Though they could hardly be considered serious opposition. What he wanted, he got. It was just that simple.

He stood, walking around the massive teak desk, hand caressing the imported wood, and went to survey the world out his expansive window. Portland held such promise. So many opportunities for growth. For profit. Opportunities that were his, and his alone. Yes, because they brought him money. But not because of the money itself.

No, money was just a tool—admittedly, a very effective tool—for bringing his plan to fruition. And no one was going to stop his plans.

Not small-minded legislators—or their lackey inspectors—all of whom tried to impose ridiculous rules and regulations.

Not his competitors, who lacked the conviction to make hard decisions, no matter the cost.

And certainly not a bunch of silver-haired, wizened old men devoted to a so-called God that couldn't protect them. For a moment one hand clenched at his side, then he eased it open, flexing the fingers. His gaze drifted to the phone.

Perhaps it was time to flex something else.

Two strides carried him to his chair, and he reached for the intercom. His secretary's response was immediate.

"Yes sir?"

Satisfaction drew his lips into a smile. Let others set so-called reasonable hours. His employees stayed as long as he needed them. No questions asked.

Or they didn't remain his employees.

"Susan, get Mr. Wright on the line for me."

"Right away, sir."

Leaning back in his chair, he let his fingers tap out his impatience on the desk. Susan probably knew the number by heart. He used Mr. "Wright" more than any other associate. The play on words made him laugh. Or as close to laughing as he ever got.

Susan's voice came over the intercom. "Mr. Wright holding for you, sir."

Of course he was.

He hit the speaker button. "Wright?"

"What can I do for you?"

"Plenty." He explained the situation, and as he'd expected, Wright knew exactly what to do.

Which, he thought as he disconnected the call, was why he'd given the man that name.

His associate was, ever and always, the right man for whatever job came up. Few others were so dependable. So capable.

So willing to do whatever it took to get the job done.

Were he a man given to humor, he'd be laughing. Instead, he let one finger stroke the smooth wood of his desk.

The old fools could kneel until doomsday, whispering prayers until their voices gave out. Nothing they did would matter.

That property was his.

FIFTEEN

"A friend can tell you things you
don't want to tell yourself."
FRANCES WARD WELLER

"The heartfelt counsel of a friend
is as sweet as perfume and incense."
PROVERBS 27:9

A storm was brewing.

Rafe didn't need The Weather Channel to know it. All he had to do was look at the set of Tarik's shoulders. The grim glint in his eyes. The creases in his brow.

Oh yeah. The kid was bugged. Big time.

Rafe had been waiting all night for Tarik to start talking, but this had to be something big, because the boy didn't say a thing. Just sat there, school books open on the table in front of him, tapping his pencil against the page. The same page.

For an hour.

Finally Rafe went to take the pencil from the boy's fingers and set it on the table, then he shut the book.

Tarik sat back in his chair with a thud. "What? You got a problem?"

Rafe sat in the chair across the table and met the boy's burning gaze. "No. But I think you do. So spill. *¿Que pasa?*"

For a moment Rafe thought the kid would digress, jump up from the table like he used to in the face of any conflict or perceived slight. Maybe even send the table flying. He'd done that once or twice too.

Thankfully, the months of working through issues had had an impact. Tarik just leaned his elbows on the table, gripping his hands together. "The fire. At the church."

Rafe waited.

"It was the 22s."

So. That explained it. The heaviness in Tarik's tone, the furrows on his brow. "How do you know?"

Tarik's gaze shifted, fixed on the wall as though it held some answer to the questions churning inside him. "King K. I talked to him. Asked him right out."

"He admitted it?"

"Didn't have to. I saw it on his face." He lowered his head, rubbed his temples with fingers that trembled. Rafe laid a hand on the boy's sagging shoulder.

"You're not part of them anymore, Tarik. You got out. You did it on your own. And you're making your way. Doing all the things your mother wanted you to do. Finishing school. Getting the grades to go to college." He squeezed Tarik's shoulder. "You've done what's right. That's all you can do. King... He's the only one who can control his actions. Whatever he does, it's not on you."

Tarik swallowed and finally gave a slow nod.

Rafe pushed his chair back and stood. "Come on."

Tarik looked up. "Where?"

"I hear a Big Mac callin' your name."

The kid loved Big Macs. His lips lifted a fraction. "And fries?"

Rafe angled his head. "And...do I hear what I think I hear? Yes, I do! A milk shake. Chocolate, no less." He nudged the boy. "C'mon, kid. I'm buyin'."

Tarik stood and reached for his jacket hanging on the back of his chair. "You better be, man. I'm broke."

He fell into step beside Rafe, but when they reached the front door he hesitated.

Rafe glanced at him.

The boy stood tall, gaze unwavering. "Thanks. For listening, I mean. It helps to talk about things."

Rafe pulled the door open. Yes, indeed. The kid had come a long way.

~~

How was this possible?

Rafe glared at the TV screen, punching the channel button over and over.

More than a hundred stations on this crazy thing, and there was nothing worth watching.

Nothing!

Venting his frustration on a growl, he hit the power off button, pushed out of his recliner, and tossed the offending remote back on the seat.

This was ridiculous.

He couldn't sleep. Couldn't find anything to watch. Didn't feel like watching videos or DVDs. He'd seen them all over and over.

It was too late to start a book or phone a buddy. And food held no interest.

"Arrggh!" He slammed his cane against the seat of his recliner, which let him vent without running the risk of waking Tarik.

He turned and headed into his bedroom. He poked the power button on his computer monitor, waiting as the screen hazed to life. Yes, he'd just checked e-mail about ten minutes ago, but maybe something had come in since then.

A spark of relief burst to life when he saw one message waiting. From AngelEyes. He'd e-mailed her earlier about Kyla's visit to Cuppa Joe's.

> Hey, Asadi. So, YKW finally showed up again, did she? See? I told you you were getting all worried for nothing. You should have known she couldn't stay away from your coffee—or you—for much longer.

His snort was only slightly amused. Couldn't stay away from him, huh? She'd practically bolted from the shop to escape him today.

> Sorry to hear you've had nightmares again. I've been praying God would set you free from those.

Yeah, so had he.

> Had an interesting thought today, though. I kept wondering all day long who you have to talk with. About the dreams. About YKW.

About…everything. Do you talk with your sister about these things?

Not lately. He'd started to a couple of times, but other than letting her know he was worried when Kyla didn't come around for so long, he'd kept his struggles to himself. Which was odd, now that he considered it. He used to talk with Liv about everything.

I suppose talking with a woman might not be what you want to do right now. So how about a guy friend? Any of your Force Recon pals you can talk with? Or anyone from your church?
Don't know why this has been nagging at me so much today, but since it has, I figured I'd ask. I mean, I know it helps me to talk things through with someone. So hey, give it some thought, okay? Maybe the nightmares will ease if you can just put them into words with someone willing to listen.
Either way, know I'm praying for you.
A

Rafe leaned back in his chair, Tarik's words from earlier drifting through his mind: *"It helps to talk about things."*

He could call any of the guys from the Pride, but he hated to do that. They had their own stuff to deal with. Besides, it was too late to call any of them tonight. Lights out came early for Marines.

Which left one person. One whose ear he bent on a far-too-frequent basis. Still, the old man never complained. And if there was one thing Fredrik did well, it was complain when he didn't like something.

Which must mean he not only didn't mind listening to Rafe, he actually liked it.

Grabbing his cane, Rafe went to get his car keys and headed out into the night.

SIXTEEN

*"The most beautiful thing we can experience
is the mysterious. It is the source of all true art
and all science. He to whom this emotion is a
stranger, who can no longer pause to wonder and
stand rapt in awe, is as good as dead: his eyes are closed."*

ALBERT EINSTEIN

*"O LORD, God of heaven...the people you rescued by your
great power and strong hand are your servants. O Lord,
please hear my prayer! Listen to the prayers of those of us who
delight in honoring you. Please grant me success today."*

NEHEMIAH 1:5, 10–11

The night was creeping to a close. Dawn was only hours away.

Fredrik sat in the comforting cloak of nighttime, hands folded on his knees, eyes closed, mind and spirit focused on the only One who could help him now.

Father God, Adonai, help us. God of Abraham, Isaac, and Jacob, have mercy on us. Lead Your servants as we seek to obey You. We need Your intervention, Lord. We need Your angels to go before us. Better yet, to be with us, at our sides, watching over us.

His hand gripped the arm of the soft, worn chair as he prayed on, begging God for guidance. As the weight of reality settled upon him, his head bowed lower.

They had so few resources of their own. So little money, so few workers.

Those they had were willing, of course. But what could old men do? How could they shoulder all the work and accomplish the task in such limited time?

Father, send us aid. Please, send us the right person. An angel to fight for us and accomplish Your will—

A loud knock sounded on the door, and Fredrik jumped, almost slipping from his chair. *Who could be visiting him this time of…?*

He cast a glance to the heavens. *So why am I surprised? Someday, Lord, help me remember You don't fool around.* He pushed his old, aching bones out of the chair and made his shuffling way to the door.

At the sound of his slippered feet on the floor, he grimaced. When did it happen? When did he get caught in a body this old and unsteady? Time was, he stood tall and strong, could run and dance and walk with the best of 'em. Now…

Buck up, old man. Stop feeling sorry for yourself.

He slipped the security chain free, opened the deadbolt, started to pull open the door—then almost jumped out of his skin when a firm voice sounded from the other side of the door.

"Don't you dare open that door without looking through the peephole, Fredrik."

He stared at the door, then pulled a face. Of course. It was Rafe. The boy might be a good forty years his junior, but that didn't keep him from talking to Fredrik in that pseudofatherly, are-you-*out*-of-your-ever-lovin'-mind? tone. Fredrik shook his head. *You can take the boy out of the Marines…*

He did as he was told, squinting so he could focus through the tiny peephole. The fisheye effect on Rafe was slightly startling. The young man was imposing enough in and of himself. Add the slightly warped magnification of the peephole, and if Fredrik didn't know better, he'd think there was a thug on his doorstep.

Yes, indeed. Rafe Murphy was the model Marine. *But I don't see any wings, Lord. And I know for a fact this boy doesn't wear a halo. Maybe I'm wrong and he isn't the angel You sent me?* Well, only one way to find out.

Let the man in.

"Oh, look"—Fredrik spoke up against the door, keeping his eye to the peephole—"it's Rafe, come to visit an old man. So may I open the door now, Staff Sergeant, sir? Pretty please?"

Rafe's eye roll would have done any teenager proud. Fredrik opened the door and stepped aside so Rafe could enter. The young man came in, and Fredrik could tell from the storm in his eyes and his stooped shoulders he was troubled.

"*Sholem aleykham,* Rafe."

"*Aleyken sholem,* Fredrik."

Fredrik smiled. Yiddish always sounded good on a young man's tongue. And it touched him that Rafe remembered the phrases Fredrik had taught him. "So, tell an old man. What's on your mind?"

Rafe didn't answer. Instead, he made his way to Fredrik's kitchen, going to the ever-ready coffeepot, pulling a mug from the cupboard, and pouring himself a full cup of the thick black brew.

"I would think you'd get enough of that stuff at your place."

Rafe took a deep, long sip before he answered. "I suppose so. But nothing tastes quite like the coffee you make."

Fredrik came to refresh his own mug. "I notice you didn't say tastes as *good* as the coffee I make."

"You always have been an observant sort."

Fredrik eyed Rafe over the lip of his coffee cup. "I'm Jewish, my boy. We're like God; we notice everything." Good. The boy could still smile. So he wasn't too upset. "So, what brings you to an old man's apartment this late on a Friday night? I'd think you'd be out with some lovely lady, painting the town red—or whatever the appropriate color is these days."

A cloud settled on Rafe's brow. So, it had something to do with a woman. Of course. Wasn't it always a woman when a man was this restless and uncertain? "Don't tell me you're still mooning over that lady customer of yours?"

This time it was Rafe who eyed Fredrik over his coffee cup. "I. Don't. Moon."

Fredrik stirred his coffee with slow, measured care. "Of course you don't. I should have known big, tough Marines don't moon. My mistake that what you've been doing all these weeks, coming over here, talking about this woman until you're ready to cry in your coffee was mooning." He carried his coffee cup over to the couch and settled on the deep cushions. "So tell me, what *do* Marines do?"

A half smile lifted Rafe's lips. "Reconnoiter." Rafe walked over to the window and stared out.

"You'll forgive me for saying so, Rafe, but what kind of *mishegas* is that? Yes, fine, reconnoiter for a few days. But you've been doing it for weeks. Months, even. When is it time to stop thinking, stop evaluating, and actually *do* something?"

"I wish I knew." Rafe cupped his hands around the mug. "You remember I told you it'd been a little over two weeks since she came into the shop?"

"I remember you were about to call out the Marines." He realized what he'd said and grinned. "You should excuse the expression."

"I'd almost decided she wasn't coming back. And I'd almost decided how I felt about that."

"Which was?"

"Not good." He looked down into the coffee mug, as though the answer were somehow there floating on top of the dark liquid. "And then this morning, there she was. I could tell the minute she walked in she was unhappy." He ran a hand through his dark hair. "Kind of...unsettled."

As interesting as this was, Fredrik had to fight the urge to tell Rafe he didn't have time to listen to more rambling about this nameless woman. *Why* she'd remained nameless all these weeks was beyond him, but Rafe was adamant. The military seemed to have rendered the man incapable of sharing information unless he absolutely had to, so he hardly shared any details about her. Aside, of course, from the fact that she was driving him crazy.

Or, to be more accurate, that he was driving himself crazy over her.

At any rate, Fredrik had bigger worries now than Rafe's mystery woman. He opened his mouth to tell him so, but the words froze when a voice whispered through him.

Wait.

He crossed his arms. *For what should I wait? I've got no time for all this.*

Wait.

Fredrik clamped his mouth shut. God said wait. So wait he would.

Rafe tossed back the rest of his coffee, then set the mug on the kitchen counter. "The odd thing is, she should be happy. You know that new mall, the Mountain's Edge mall?"

Fredrik shook his head. *What do I care about a mall, Lord? What does this have to do with—?*

"Well, her construction company built it. And with all the accolades that mall and her company have been getting, shouldn't she be happy?"

Fredrik leaned forward. All those months of listening to Rafe talk about this woman, about his concerns for her. About the impact she had on him. On his heart. His spirit. And about her eyes. Those deep green eyes…

"Righteousness and justice are the foundation of your throne… Righteousness and justice…justice…"

Justice.

Understanding clicked. Pieces shifted and fell into place.

Lord, could it be? Was the answer there all along and I just forgot?

Heart rate accelerating, Fredrik turned to Rafe. "Are you saying this woman owns a construction company?"

As though realizing he'd given away something he shouldn't have, Rafe's protective walls slid back into place. Fredrik knew that look. All too well. That was his "name, rank, serial number" look.

Lord, we don't have time for this. He took hold of Rafe's arm, not even pausing when the muscles beneath his hand hardened to steel. "Listen to me, boy. God brought you here tonight for a reason. I was just praying, and here you are. With the answer I need. So tell me"—he gave that iron arm a shake—"and tell me true, is this woman Kyla Justice?"

Fredrik almost danced a jig at the astonishment on Rafe's usually controlled features. The boy's mouth opened, then clamped shut again. But it was enough.

"It is!" He clapped his hands, so overcome was he with delight at the wonders of God's ways. Why had he ever doubted God's timing? "So God shows Himself faithful again."

Rafe's confusion only increased Fredrik's delight. "Don't you see? God sees the whole of our lives. Beginning to end. Not because He's looking at the picture, but because He *painted* it. Every stroke. Every color. Every nuance of beauty. *He* put it there. As He put you in this woman's life. And in mine."

"Fredrik, *what* are you talking about?"

"Kyla Justice! You must not despair. Remember, 'The plans of the LORD stand firm forever, the purposes of his heart through all generations.'" *Abba, thank You for Your perfect plans and purpose!* Fredrik made a beeline for the phone book.

"What are you doing, old man?"

Not even the growl in that hard question could stop Fredrik now. *Righteousness and Justice. Kyla Justice. Yahweh, You had this in hand all along.* He gave Rafe a glowing grin as he lifted the phone from the receiver. "I'm calling Kyla Justice."

Rafe's eyes widened a fraction, but nothing compared to what they did when Fredrik went on.

"To set up a meeting for tomorrow. And you are going with me."

"You'll do no such—"

"*Sha shtil!* This isn't about you, Rafe. It's about God and His purposes."

Rafe watched as Fredrik pulled out the phone book and flipped through the pages to the *J*s. Fredrik found the number, jotted it down, then smiled at Rafe. "God has plans. And unless I've heard Him wrong"—which he'd bet the last hair on his head he hadn't—"those plans include the wonderful Miss Justice." He grinned. *Oy,* such a sense of humor God had! "And you. So go now. Go home. Get some rest. I'll call you in a little bit to tell you what time we're meeting."

"You're so sure she'll say yes."

"I'm so sure like I've never been sure before."

Rafe made his way to the door. "Yeah? Well, I can't say I share your conviction. And I'm not so sure I want to be a part of whatever plan that beady little brain of yours has hatched. What do you think about that, old man?"

"I think *gey gezunterheyt.*"

Rafe fixed him with a hard stare. "Sarcasm? You're giving me sarcasm?"

Fredrik shrugged, fighting a grin. "What sarcasm? Go in health, I tell you. This is sarcasm?"

Rafe jerked open the door. "You know as well as I do that's *not* what you said." An upheld hand stilled Fredrik's protest. "Okay, fine. Those are the words you spoke, but the true meaning of those words? Sarcasm."

The grin finally escaped. He'd taught the boy too well. Fredrik shuffled toward the man hovering in his doorway, then patted one strong arm. "You're a good boy, Rafael. God will speak to you, and you will obey. This I know."

Rafe threw a glance to the heavens. "You're crazy, my friend. Just do me a favor. Don't let this mishegas get you killed."

Fredrik just laughed. "What's foolishness to you is obedience to me. Now go home. Get some rest. Tomorrow, we have things to do."

He closed the door on Rafe's protest. From the sounds on the other side of the door, Rafe was telling Fredrik what he thought of him, which only made him laugh more. Chuckling, he made his way back to his phone, lifted the receiver, and punched in the number. As the phone rang, gratitude filled the prayers flowing through his mind and heart.

God was good.

And He was about to make things *truly* interesting.

SEVENTEEN

*"Even if you're on the right track,
you'll get run over if you just sit there."*
WILL ROGERS

*"Everything has already been decided. It was known
long ago what each person would be. So there's
no use arguing with God about your destiny."*
ECCLESIASTES 6:10

The jangle of the phone jerked Kyla from the warm folds of sleep. She groaned at the interruption. She'd been with him. Sitting. Talking. Letting herself get lost in the rich, sweet coffee he'd made, lost in those warm, welcoming eyes.

But the phone gave no quarter, and she finally pulled clear of the hypnotic dream.

Blinking to sluggish awareness in the dark room, she flung out a hand, seeking the offending sound. Her fingers curled around the receiver and she punched the Talk button and pressed it to her ear, even as her free hand stroked the kitten that was now wide awake and demanding her attention.

Her first attempt at *hello* came out as a groggy croak, so she cleared her throat and tried again. "H'lo?"

"Miss Justice?"

Even as her brain registered that the voice was masculine, her eyes fought to focus on the time projected on the ceiling of her room. 3:15. In the a.m.! Normally she'd just hang up on a male caller this time of night...morning…whatever. But something stopped her. This didn't sound like a masher or bored teenager.

"Yes?" Good, her voice was gaining strength.

"I don't know if you remember me—"

Kyla pushed to a sitting position, and Serendipity immediately hopped into her lap, turning circles before curling into a tight ball.

Fingers stroking the soft fur, Kyla frowned. At first she'd thought her caller was her age, but now she detected a slight tremor in the deep, calm tones. And an accent. One that stirred her memory…

"—but this is Fredrik Tischler. I knew your father. And you."

"Fredrik." Her brain clicked into search mode, pushing the last fog of sleep away and drawing out memories long forgotten: a smiling man who always brought her licorice when he came to see her father. A man whose eyes were as gentle as they were piercing. Who saw her heart from their first meeting. Who delighted in teaching her bits and pieces of Yiddish.

A man who accepted her for who she was.

Recognition shifted, then fell into place, eliciting a broad smile. "Uncle Ki!"

The chuckle was as deep and jovial as she remembered. "So you do remember me?"

Kyla opened her palm against the kitten's rumbling side—she loved it when Serendipity's purr got going like that—and cradled the receiver against her shoulder. "I remember asking Daddy once if God was as tall as you were."

"And I remember your awe when he told you God was even taller."

The giggle surprised her, but it felt good. How long had it been since she'd laughed this way, in sheer delight?

Too long.

"It's wonderful to hear from you, Uncle Ki."

"I'm sorry I'm calling so late—"

She shook her head. "No, it's fine." And, surprisingly enough, it was.

"But, my dear, I have a rather large favor to ask of you."

The suddenly serious tenor of his words gave her pause, but only for a moment. This was Uncle Ki. "Name it."

He started to explain, and Kyla did her best to just listen, not react. But she must have given her uncertainty away somehow, because in the middle of a sentence Fredrik stopped.

"Uncle Ki?"

A weighted sigh drifted across the lines. "You don't think it can be done, do you?"

She leaned back against the headboard. How to let him down easy? "That's hard to say without seeing the building—"

"Then let me show you."

Kyla bit her lip. "I don't know…"

"Please. I realize this is an imposition, but won't you meet me? Tomorrow—no, I guess it would be today."

Chagrin infused his realization, but Kyla just smiled. The least she could do was let him show her his dream. Dad would want her to do that much for such a dear friend of his. "Where and when?"

"Blessed Hope Fellowship Church, the corner of northeast 92nd and northeast Alberta. Say nine o'clock?"

Nine a.m. Well, she'd get six hours of sleep, anyway. "I'll see you then."

"Thank you. And *bubele?*"

"Yes?"

"Be ready. God is doing something wonderful."

EIGHTEEN

"Call on God, but row away from the rocks."
HUNTER S. THOMPSON

"Have mercy on me, O God, have mercy!
I look to you for protection.
I will hide beneath the shadow of
your wings until the danger passes by."
PSALM 57:1

Fredrik *had* to be kidding.

God was going to do something wonderful? Here?

Only if He were totally, completely lost.

She'd lain in bed, thinking over Fredrik's phone call, unable to sleep. A too-frequent occurrence anymore. Finally, when she'd stared at the ceiling for an hour, she got up, threw on some clothes, and grabbed her purse.

It couldn't hurt to check the place out before her meeting with Fredrik in a few hours.

When Fredrik recited the address over the phone, she'd had a vague idea that the area wasn't exactly the best in the city.

What she saw before her gave *understatement* a whole new meaning.

Block after block of run-down homes sporting boarded-up windows and an assortment of graffiti had escorted her to Fredrik's building. Now, sitting in her car beneath a pale, flickering streetlight, she checked the door locks once more as she peered out the window.

Cars that looked either abandoned or like they were on their last spark plug spotted the street on either side. Several had windows broken out, one had the bumper wired in place. And though she couldn't see anyone around her, she could swear she was being watched. Like a hapless rabbit that took a woefully wrong turn and hopped into a pack of hungry coyotes.

The idea sent prickles creeping up the back of her neck.

She pushed against the car seat, scrunching down a fraction. Times like this she envied her sister's height. True, Annot's five foot five wasn't technically petite, but it only missed the official designation by an inch. Either way, it was far easier to disappear when you were five foot five than when you topped five-eight.

And if there was one thing Kyla wanted to do right now, it was disappear.

So go. No one's holding you here.

Her fingers played with the car remote, dangled the ignition key. Temptation twitched her fingers, coaxing them to slip the key into the ignition, give it a quick turn, and drive away.

Just a minute more.

Are you looking to get mugged?

Kyla shook the silly thought away. She was locked inside her car. Besides, there wasn't anyone around but her.

Not that she could see, anyway...

Shivers skittered across her skin again as she peered, from her hunkered-down position, over the lower edge of the driver's side window. Someone was out there. She could *feel* it.

Oh, stop it. You're getting as fanciful as your sister.

Kyla pursed her lips. Maybe so. Still, scanning the area, one word kept creeping into her mind, over and over.

Dark.

Not just the-sun-has-set-and-it's-nighttime dark. But heavy, oppressive dark. Bad-things-lurking-in-the-shadows dark. Don't-go-there-alone dar—

Blaat! Blaat! Blaat!

Kyla jumped so fast and hard she slammed her elbow into the car door. Holding back the irritation perched on her lips, she grabbed at the remote and punched the panic button off. The piercing car alarm gave way to blessed silence.

She stared down at the offending remote, lip curling. Stupid contraption. As if she weren't doing a good enough job of freaking herself out. One bit of pressure in the wrong spot and wham! You deafened not only yourself, but anyone within a five-mile radius.

She slipped the remote and key back into her purse, where her nervous fingers couldn't get to it, then glanced at her watch. She really should go home. Try to sleep. And she would. Any minute now…

Her gaze drifted to the darkened street.

She'd go home. Right after she saw exactly what she was up against.

NINETEEN

> *"We must learn to live together as*
> *brothers or perish together as fools."*
> MARTIN LUTHER KING JR.

> *"It is safer to meet a bear robbed of her cubs*
> *than to confront a fool caught in foolishness."*
> PROVERBS 17:12

King K leaned against a concrete wall, where the shadows cloaked him, watching. And wondering.

The woman had been sitting there for fifteen minutes. Maybe more. She kept swiveling her head to look around the street, like she was scared out of her mind.

And so she should be.

She was on 22 turf. In the middle of the night. This was one gutsy woman. Either that or stupid. Really stupid. Whatever her story, she'd better stay in that nice car of hers. He'd hate to hurt her, but he'd do it. Couldn't let her just get by with comin' out here like she owned the place. Couldn't take the chance. Never knew who was watchin'.

He let out a silent laugh. That'd be a good tip for this woman: "Watch your step 'cuz you never know who's watchin'." Yeah, she should keep that in mind.

If she was lucky, he wouldn't be the one to tell her so.

With a flick of the wrist Kyla unlocked and opened the car door, stepping out into the street. *Okay. Just wait a minute. Listen before you leap.*

She did so, ears honing in…

The blackness around her held only silence.

Kyla reached beneath her driver's seat, pulling her flashlight free—the same solid black contraption her sister, Annot, had in her car. Their sheriff's deputy brother, Avidan, bought one for each of them. "Lights the area up like it's daylight, and the casing is steel. Good for both illumination and protection." The mix of delight and reverence in Avidan's tone as he told Kyla this still stymied her. It was, after all, just a flashlight.

Turning it on, she swept the beam around the area, eyes widening at how far the light traveled. Big brother was right. This thing was great.

King K flattened against the wood siding of the church, barely avoiding the bright beam of light the woman sent his way.

It was only there a second, and then it was gone—traveling along the side of the building. Good thing she didn't see him. He wanted to show himself in his way. His time.

Crouching low, he moved on feet trained in stealth, following the woman's rambling study of the building. What he saw was enough to convince him.

So, the man who called him earlier was right. Someone new was joining the battle. Trying to help the old men move in on the Brotherhood's turf.

King shifted to get a better view of the tall, slim woman walking along the building, her flashlight beam going here and there like a firefly on crack. She was new. He'd figured the old men would try again, even bring in some kind of help, but they had to be crazy if they thought this woman could change anything.

They were finished. Plain and simple.

The fire didn't stop them.

He pursed his lips. No…but then, it didn't do its work, now did it? How the firemen got there so fast, he'd never know. It was like these people had some kind of guardian angels watching over them—

Oh. Yeah.

King K shook his head at himself. Angels, demons…they were all just talk. So this was a church. So what? His *madre* may have believed in God, in all the supernatural hocus-pocus, but he knew better. There were no angels. No demons. No heaven or hell.

No God.

There was just here and now. Just the Brotherhood. That's all he had. All any of them had. But it was enough. And nothing—not these old men, not their make-believe God—was going to take one inch of their turf away from them.

They say the center will help the neighborhood. They say. Well, King knew how much he could trust what they said. What anyone outside the Blood Brotherhood said. And he knew what their precious teen center would do. It would pull new members away from the Brotherhood. Convince them there was something else.

Something better.

Let enough listen and believe that, and their crew would pay the price. You had to keep new blood coming in to replace those who fell. And you had to keep those who were in the Brotherhood from being drawn away.

Life in the 22s wasn't easy. Or safe. King K knew that better than anyone. But it was what kept them alive. Take away their turf, their members, and the Brotherhood would die.

And that was going to happen one way and one way only.

Over his dead body.

The thought made King K smile. Plenty of people had tried to take him out. But he was still here. As for his enemies, well…no one would find them anytime soon. So him being dead? Not likely. Others?

His gaze drifted back to the woman. Others wouldn't be so lucky.

Kyla swept the impressive beam of her flashlight along the building once more. Hmm…now this was different. It was all one building, but it looked to be three different structures in one. The burned-out three-story section making up—what? A home? The parsonage, maybe?—gave way to a long, single-story section. From the stained-glass windows, Kyla figured that had to be the sanctuary—

She froze. What was that? A scuffling sound behind her.

She spun, shining the light to the right. She'd heard something. She was sure of it. Furtive footsteps. Was someone following her?

But the flashlight revealed nothing.

Kyla hesitated, then drew the light back to the sanctuary. Her fears faded as she studied the structure.

How odd. The sanctuary gave way to what looked to be a two-story tower of sorts. Interest piqued, Kyla walked along the outside of the building, letting the light play along the walls, top to bottom, a list forming in her mind as she spotted problem after problem. Foundation, windows, glass, wood, roof, stairs...*everything* needed work.

No. Strike that. It needed to be replaced.

As the list grew, two things became abundantly clear. First, the job would be as huge as the structure itself. And second, this could *not* be a task God was calling her to. Oh, sure, she had most of what it would take to do what Fredrik had asked: finances, access to materials, workmen who were the absolute best, and the know-how. And if she had enough time, she could certainly pull it off. But the sense she had from Fredrik's call was that their time line was short at best, minuscule at worst. And if that was the case, then getting it done would take something Kyla couldn't provide.

It would take a miracle.

It was a miracle she hadn't spotted him that time.

How he'd missed the dip in the ground was beyond him. He knew better than to step out without checking the area in front of him first. But his foot hit the hole, and he'd stumbled. Good thing she'd swung the light at head level. He'd managed to crouch just in time.

She'd stopped walking, so he stayed that way as he watched her. One hand rested on the side of the building; the other eased behind him until he felt cold metal.

Fingers closing on the switchblade tucked in the back of his pants, he smiled.

Kyla had seen enough.

Regret dogged her steps as she headed for her car. She'd come in the morning, as she'd promised, and meet with Fredrik. But as much as she didn't want to disappoint him, she'd have to be honest. She'd have to tell him the job wasn't possible.

Is anything too hard for me?

Kyla's hand hovered midreach, just above the door handle. Shivers skittered across her skin. Where had *that* verse come from? She wasn't even sure if it was a Scripture verse. It sounded like one, but she couldn't place it.

She shook her head. She must be more tired than she realized. Time to go home and get some sleep. Her fingers closed on the door handle.

I am the LORD, the God of all the peoples of the world. Is anything too hard for me?

The words rang within her, as though someone had struck a large gong right next to her, sending reverberations coursing through her whole body. She grabbed the door handle, pulled the door open, and dropped onto the seat.

Leaning her head back against the headrest, she stared through the dark night at the building across the street. Another frown pinched her brow.

It would take so much work. Extra men, working nearly around the clock. Just getting the permits could take up all the time they had—

Is anything too hard?

Kyla gritted her teeth. No. Of course not. Nothing was too hard for God. If He wanted the youth center built, then it would happen. No matter what.

She released a sigh into the darkness, then leaned forward to slide the key into the ignition and put the car in gear.

Yes, God would accomplish His purposes for this church of Fredrik's. But what she still didn't know, she thought as she reached for the headlights—was if she was supposed to get involved—

"Oh!" Shock ripped at her nerves as she slammed on the brakes. Heart pounding, she sat there, staring out the windshield.

A dark form stood in the beam of her headlights. Right in front of her car.

"What on earth?"

Shrouded as much in the night's dark as in oversized clothes and a hooded sweatshirt, the form just stood there. Kyla's fingers tensed on the steering wheel. Should she honk? Open the window and ask if he…she…

She studied the stance, the build. Definitely a *he*.

So should she open her window and ask if he was okay? Maybe he needed help—That thought died as quickly as it formed, for the figure raised his head. Just enough for Kyla's headlights to illumine a pair of dark eyes.

Dark…cold…

Menacing.

Kyla's throat went dry, and her hand reached almost without thought to ensure the doors were locked. But somehow she had the sense that locks wouldn't stop this person. Not by a long shot.

A sense that doubled when her headlights glinted on something the form held up.

A knife.

Kyla's hand dove into her purse, seeking her cell phone, but she'd no sooner pulled it free than the form was gone. Melted into the night like a crocodile sinking into the murky depths, leaving not even a ripple on the water's surface to prove it had ever been there.

Fear spurring her on, Kyla hit the gas, sending her car shooting forward. She didn't slow until she was back in a well-lit, familiar area. The comforting glow of streetlights eased her grip on the steering wheel, though she couldn't help glancing in her rearview mirror to ensure she wasn't being followed.

Who was that back there? What did he want with her?

Kyla had no answers. She could only be grateful that she'd been able to get out of there before anything happened.

That and hope, with all her heart, that she never encountered that man again.

TWENTY

Morning dawned far too early.

Kyla woke before the alarm, thanks to a playful and hungry Serendipity. She opened her eyes with a groan and reached out to capture the pouncing kitten, holding her, closing her eyes, trying to recapture the dream she'd just lost.

Vague images flitted through her mind. It had started out more like a nightmare. She'd drifted off to sleep scant hours ago, falling into dark and ominous dreams peopled with hazy forms flashing knives in the moonlight. But just as the forms reached her, as she cried out her terror, he was there.

A new form. Tall, broad-shouldered. And protective.

Kyla smiled at the memory. Willed the images back into her mind. Saw again as he circled her with arms of steel, standing between her and her attackers. Though repeated blows fell on him, he didn't flinch. He kept his arms about her, and his rich voice told her over and over again that she was safe.

Funny thing was, she believed him. Though she knew it was one protector against many attackers, she knew he was right. She was safe with him. He'd never let anyone hurt her. And as soon as she realized it, the dark, menacing forms dissipated like fog pierced by the sun's warm—

A fierce yowl brought Kyla's eyes wide open. Serendipity squirmed, making her displeasure at being constrained known.

"Come on, kitty. Give me a break, will you?" She stroked the cat's ears, whispering soothing words. As Serendipity stilled, Kyla closed her eyes again.

The images were faint, but still there. She could see herself looking up at her rescuer. "Jesus...?"

A slow, sonorous chuckle wrapped around her, as warm and welcome as hot chocolate on a snowy night. She couldn't see his features, not clearly. But she sensed his pleasure.

"No. Just one of His warriors."

She wanted to see his face, to know who he was. Her hands reached, fingertips brushing his cheeks, his nose, his mouth. Feeling the warmth of his smile.

Her hands stilled. "I...I know you."

She tried, both her dream self and her real self, to see his features. Identify him. But just as it was about to come clear, Serendipity dug in. Kyla sat bolt upright with a yelp. Serendipity tumbled backward on the bed, righting herself with a hiss, pouncing on Kyla's pillow.

She grabbed the pillow and flipped off the cat. "One more minute. Just one more and I would have known who he was!"

Serendipity's only response was to swat a paw at her. Kyla glanced at the clock. Almost time to meet Fredrik.

So she'd needed to be up anyway.

Pushing aside her blankets—and her disappointment—she slipped from bed and padded to the bathroom.

Delighted that her mistress was up and about, Serendipity danced and tumbled, batting a stuffed mouse here, a furry rabbit's foot there. Kyla's irritation faded and she laughed at the cat's antics.

With each passing day the kitten grew stronger and more at home. Their first night together Kyla had fixed a nice, neat bed comprised of an extra pillow and some towels. She'd lifted the kitten into the makeshift nest, scratching her behind the bedraggled ears.

"Okay, little one. This is your bed. You be a good girl and go to sleep."

She smiled as the kitten snuggled into the pillow. Who said owning pets was hard? She crawled into her own bed, shut off the light, then, with a deep sigh, beckoned a night of deep, restful sleep.

The noise started within seconds.

Tiny mewling wails. Quiet at first, then growing in volume and discontent.

Kyla tried ignoring the little puffball.

Right. It was like ignoring fingernails screeching down a blackboard.

Plan B: Coo soft reassurances.

No go.

Plan C: A pillow over her head.

Plan D: Fingers in the ears.

Nothing held off the cries.

Finally, Kyla did the only thing her sleep deprived brain could conjure. She yelled. *"Go to slee—!"*

Something hit the edge of her comforter, tugging on it. Kyla scrambled to a sitting position, knees against her chest, and hit the base of the touch-lamp beside her bed.

There, scrambling up the comforter like a miniature Marine on maneuvers was the kitten. Kyla watched as she progressed, little legs trembling with the effort, but refused to let herself be impressed. She pointed toward the pillow. *"That* is your bed."

Not even a pause. Slow but sure, the kitten made her unsteady way to Kyla, mewling all the way.

"I will not have a cat sleeping in my bed."

Mew! It had reached her sheet-covered feet now.

"You are not going to get your way."

Mew! Mew! Mew!

The kitten's little claws gripped the sheet as it pulled itself up the mountain that was her legs, not stopping until it reached the tops of her knees. There, at last, the tiny animal halted.

They were almost nose to nose. Kyla narrowed her gaze. "Get down."

Mew!

"Look, I'm the human. You are the animal—"

Mew! Mew!

"—You have to do what…"

Mew!

"…what I…"

Oh, who was she fooling?

Kyla reached out and caught the little creature up, cupping it in her hands as she cuddled it close, stroking its trembling body. The kitten rubbed its head against her, eyes closed. Kyla surrendered on a long, deep sigh. "Okay, Serendipity. You win."

She held the kitten out so they were face to face. "But just until you're stronger, understand?"

Kyla turned off the light, then scooched down under the covers, keeping the kitten cuddled on her shoulder. She rested her cheek against the soft fur, whispering into the kitten's ear. "Trust me on this, kitty, this is *not* going to be your bed forever."

Serendipity didn't seem in the least concerned. She just curled against Kyla, a soft purr rumbling from that tiny chest.

Kyla smiled and closed her eyes.

Now, after just a few weeks of steady food, water, and shelter, of cuddles and nurture, scarcely a shadow remained of the bedraggled animal she'd first seen. In its place was a playful puffball that lived to entertain her.

And, of course, slept in her bed every night. But, as amazing as it was to Kyla, she didn't mind. Because she'd laughed more in the last week than she'd done in months.

Kyla looked down at her recalcitrant companion, who was, at the moment, sprawled on her back, paws up in the air. Kyla dangled her fingers, letting Serendipity bat at them. "You're good for me, you know that?"

The kitten arched, doing her best to capture Kyla's fingers. She patted the fuzzy head, then reached to pull back the sheets. Serendipity sprang up from the pillow, bounced stiff-legged across the bed, and made a dive at Kyla's hand. She pulled back, intent on avoiding more scratches—why hadn't anyone ever told her how sharp a kitten's claws were?—then burst into laughter when Serendipity's momentum sent her somersaulting off the bed.

The kitten landed on all fours, then shook herself, looking around as if to say, "I *meant* to do that."

Kyla pulled on her robe and headed for the kitchen, Serendipity right behind her. She pulled a can of cat food from the fridge—gourmet cat food, no less. Who knew such a thing existed?—and spooned some into Serendipity's dish.

She crouched, set the dish on the floor, and stroked the kitten's fur as it devoured the food. "How can Mason not like you?" How could anyone not love this little rascal?

She straightened, going to the cupboard to pull out some coffee. "I'm afraid neither one of us is winning brownie points with dear Mason lately, are we?" Kyla frowned. "But then again, he's not winning a lot of points with us either."

Oddly enough, she wasn't upset about it. She was just...nothing. She opened the bag of grounds. If she didn't know better, she'd think she didn't really care whether he wanted her to keep the cat or not.

Maybe that's because you don't.

Her hand halted, the coffee scoop suspended over the coffee maker. That was absurd. Of course she cared. She loved Mason, and what he felt, what he thought, mattered to her.

Not enough for you to give up the cat.

Yes, well, that was because he wasn't being reasonable. She scooped Serendipity up, putting them eye to eye. "I ask you, what kind of person detests cats? Even one as adorable as you?" Kyla set Serendipity down before the cat—or, more to the point, her mind—answered that.

Some things really were better left unsaid.

~⌒

"Hurry up, Fredrik."

The sun shone bright in the sky, and cars passed by Kyla's parked vehicle, but that didn't matter. She didn't want to be there.

Didn't want to risk running into her visitor from last night.

At the thought of him, Kyla glanced around her, as uneasy as a mouse in a room full of alley cats. "Come on, Fredrik. Please."

Daylight hadn't done much to improve the run-down buildings and graffiti she'd seen in the dark last night. In fact, it all looked worse, which didn't help calm her apprehension as she drove through the neighborhood.

Worst of all, since she'd parked in front of the church, she would swear she was being watched.

You're getting paranoid.

Yeah. Well. Just because you were paranoid didn't mean someone wasn't out to get you.

"Any time now, Fredrik."

As though he'd heard her whispered plea, an old Buick pulled up behind Kyla's car and the door opened. Despite the passing years, she would have known him anywhere.

She opened her own door and stepped out.

"Kyla, *mein kind.*"

My child. How long it had been since she'd heard that phrase, that voice... that warmth.

Kyla walked into the old man's embrace, and his solid arms around her took her back to the safety and joy of childhood. Fredrik had been so much a part of her youth. How could she have forgotten about him?

You've forgotten many things.

"Let me look at you." He held her at arm's length. "Such a beauty you've become. So tall. And skinny." He shook his head, which was crowned in thick white hair. "What? They don't feed you at home?" His impish grin peeked out from the neat white beard and mustache.

Kyla laughed. "There is no 'they,' old friend. It's just me."

His head tipped at that. "So? No Mr. Wonderful in the wings?"

Mason. Tell him about Mason.

She tucked her arm into his. "Just you, *Zeyde.*"

Before that inner voice could question her reluctance to talk about her beloved, Fredrik swatted at her hand where it rested on his forearm. "Grandfather, eh?" He nodded. "It's good. You remember your Yiddish."

It was coming back to her. Somehow just being with Fredrik drew it from the dusty corner of her memory.

"So." He turned to survey the building across from them. "What do you think?"

Oh dear. How to answer that? "It's large."

"Close to four thousand square feet all together." They started across the street. "Or it was, before the fire. This was our church home for over forty-five years. And now, dear child, we'd like to make it into a youth center."

Kyla tipped her head at that. A youth center… She studied the structure. Yes, she could see that. It looked large enough, anyway.

"Come. Let's go inside."

As she followed Fredrik up the steps, a movement to the side of the church caught Kyla's eyes. Five teens stood there, watching them, leaning against the concrete warehouse next to the church. They wore the usual low-slung, baggy pants and oversized football or basketball jerseys kids sported lately; all had cigarettes hanging either from their mouths or their fingers. A veritable cloud of smoke drifted up from their gathered circle, as though staking claim on even the sky.

Kyla made eye contact with one of the boys and felt herself go cold inside. She looked from one to the other and saw the same thing. Their expressions, like their stances, sent clear messages. Defiance. Challenge. Threat.

"Be ready. God is doing something wonderful."

Kyla barely restrained a shaky laugh at the echo of Fredrik's assertion. From what she'd seen last night and so far today, this was the last place God would work a miracle.

She watched the fixed stares follow her and Fredrik up the stairs. Were those kids angry? Curious? Stoned?

"The church building was donated years ago, before I came here, by a couple in the church. The Maisels. Lovely people. Salt of the earth. Hard workers who made their money with integrity. They loved God and devoted this property to His use and purposes."

Fredrik's words drew Kyla's attention away from the teens. "So that's why you want to make it into a youth center, now that it's no longer going to be a church?"

"Yes."

If those sullen kids were representative of the teens in the neighborhood, a youth center was not just a good idea, it was a necessity. They reached the sanctuary doors, and Kyla hesitated. "So when does the renovation need to be done?"

Fredrik pulled open the double doors and held them for her to pass through. "Well, we've been working on this for almost a year."

She did her best to hide her surprise at that, but his wry smile told her she'd failed.

"I know, I know. You can't tell from looking, eh? Well, it's not from lack of trying, *kinder*. I'm afraid we've had a bit of…resistance."

His words reached her but didn't really connect because her attention was captured by what she saw before her. She'd guessed the building was fairly old as she inspected it last night, but she'd had no idea the beauty contained within the structure. The sanctuary boasted lovely, rich wood paneling—not veneer, but real wood. Knotty pine, from what Kyla could see. The stained-glass windows were tall and stunning, and the pews, done in the same knotty pine, were worn but inviting. She walked along, trailing a hand across the back of one of the pews, loving the feel of the old wood.

Her attention drifted from one unique quality to the next, and Kyla caught her breath at the quickening in her spirit. Her mouth fell open as understanding struck home.

This was it. This was the job she'd been waiting for.

Excitement building, her imagination slammed into overdrive as she considered the possibilities, what they could do with this room…

"It's beautiful, yes?"

Kyla's smile was immediate. "Yes."

"I knew you'd see the beauty, the potential here. Now we just have to figure out how to get everything done in the time we have left."

Kyla turned to face her old friend. "About that. Exactly how much time are we talking about?"

Fredrik lowered himself onto one of the pews. "First, let me give you some background. The Maisels donated the building and land on the condition that both would always be used for God's work. But there was a provision."

Uh-oh. Provisions were seldom good news.

"If the building ever stood idle, or if it was used for something other than God's work, after one year, the title would revert back to the Maisels. Of course, they're gone now, so that means ownership reverts back to their grandson, Sam Ballat."

Fredrik watched her expression as he spoke the name. Kyla guessed he wondered if she recognized it.

She did.

Sam Ballat was one of the most successful businessmen in the Northwest. His holdings were almost as well known as his cutthroat business practices. The man was a mogul, one who did not tolerate fools or resistance.

"So Ballat would own the property. Which means…"

Fredrik stood and led Kyla to the back of the sanctuary and up a stairway leading to three rooms that had served as Sunday school classrooms. "You know property in this area has appreciated."

Now *that* was an understatement. Though this wasn't the most desirable neighborhood for homes, it was a mecca for industry. From what Kyla had seen as she drove here this morning, there were as many concrete warehouses in the area as there were run-down houses. Maybe more.

Ah. Of course. "Ballat wants to sell."

"Raze the church and build another warehouse or two." His tone turned mordant. *"Genug shoyn* with the warehouses. Like a hole in the head this neighborhood needs another warehouse."

She followed Fredrik back down the stairs. "Ballat's a businessman. He'd make a pretty penny if he sold."

"That he would." Fredrik fell silent, his gaze sweeping the sanctuary. "But that's not why he wants to sell."

Kyla crossed her arms. "Then why do it?"

Fredrik indicated the pew next to them, and Kyla sat. She had the sense he wasn't quite certain how much he should share. "As much as Harriet and Caleb Maisel loved God, that's how much their grandson hates Him."

"Hates Him?"

"Passionately. With a devotion I've rarely seen, not even in God's faithful. For him, this isn't a place of worship and beauty, but a chamber of lies and deceit."

"But…" Kyla looked around the sanctuary, trying to imagine how one couldn't see the beauty here. "Why?"

"His parents, Martin and Rose Ballat, God rest their souls, gave everything to God. Including their lives. Missionaries, they were, in the sixties. In the Congo." Sorrow weighted his words, and as though it did the same to his head, he lowered it. "Such an endeavor back then, it wasn't safe. One night rebels attacked their home. Took them prisoner. For days we heard nothing. For weeks no word of hope. No word even of death. Then…"

The pain in the old man's voice was so deep, so profound. She placed her hand over his, where it rested on the back of a pew.

As though plucking the powerful emotions from his heart and setting them on a shelf, just for a moment, Fredrik gathered himself, lifted his head, and continued. "The pictures came."

Dread gnawed on Kyla's nerves. "Pictures."

"Martin and Rose. Dead. Tortured. Mutilated. Though their faces were untouched, it was clear they were dead."

"Oh, Fredrik."

This time it was his hand that patted hers. "We don't know who took the pictures. Some thought it was a mercy for the family to know what happened to them."

Kyla gripped his hand. "And you?"

"Such things, no one should ever see." He shook his head, as though to send away the images lurking within. "With the pictures was a letter. The English was far from perfect, but the message was clear. Martin and Rose—their bodies were thrown into a river. With the crocodiles. There…was nothing left to bury."

God…God… Kyla had rarely felt such sorrow. And yet she knew what washed over her was a fraction of what this mother and father must have experienced. *How did the Maisels endure it? How do Your people survive, hold to their faith, in the face of such brutality?*

"So, Ballat. He blamed God?"

"With every ounce of his being. And though he was only ten when his parents were murdered, he nurtured his anger, his pain, like a man grown old on rage. Nothing his grandparents or I did could get through to him. He didn't even come to his grandparents' funerals. The only time he's contacted us in the last twenty years was when he had his corporation send us a letter a month ago."

Kyla didn't have to ask. She knew what that letter must have said. "He's claiming ownership."

"Two months. That's all we have left. If we haven't finished the renovation by then, all our history, all his grandparents dreamed and intended for this place…all the years of God's work here will be lost."

Kyla wanted to say something. But two words stuck in her throat, blocking her voice.

Two months.

Two months?

Kyla gripped the back of the pew with both hands. Had the room suddenly gotten smaller? "Excuse me?"

Fredrik's steady gaze didn't falter. "You heard me right. Two months."

She looked around them again, this time in a new light. The light of impending doom. "Why did you wait so long to bring in a contractor?"

"We didn't. You're the fourth contractor to try and make this place over as we'd like."

That didn't surprise her. It startled her. "The fourth?"

"We hired the first more than a year ago, before the church actually closed. He didn't last long once the threats started."

She tried not to let him see her alarm. "Threats?"

Fredrik lifted his shoulders. "I couldn't blame him for leaving."

Neither could she.

"The second contractor kept saying there were delays. Unavoidable delays with materials. Workers. Permits." His white head shook back and forth. "Such a list he came up with. And nothing we said or did made a difference. He took his time and our money, but as you can see, neither was used well."

Obviously not.

Kyla could see spots where work had been started, but nothing was really finished. And now, with the fire…

She couldn't help but wonder if the best thing to do wasn't to just bulldoze the place.

"Finally we fired that contractor. But we'd lost so much money. So much time."

Two things you couldn't afford to lose with construction.

"The third contractor seemed more promising. But once they started on the work…" He shrugged again.

His sigh seemed to bear the weight of the world in it. Discouragement warred with frustration in the old man's wrinkled features. He lifted his shoulders, the shrug eloquent. "Things happened."

That didn't sound good. "'Things'? What kinds of things?"

Fredrik was about to answer when an odd sound caught her ear. A kind of step-tap, step-tap. She turned, senses going on alert when she saw a man walking toward them. The sunlight flowing through the stained-glass windows—Annot would love those windows—illuminated him from behind, making it impossible to see his features.

"Ah, Rafe, my boy. It's about time."

Kyla glanced at Fredrik. The old man's face was wreathed in a smile, and there was a definite twinkle in those clear eyes. Like he'd just told the best joke ever.

"Kyla, meet a friend of mine. Rafael Murphy."

Kyla froze. She could see his face clearly now, but she blinked all the same. It couldn't be. But it was. Kyla blurted out the first thing that came to her astonished mind. "It was you. You were the one in my dream."

TWENTY-ONE

Rafe and danger were old friends.

Bombings, strafing, sniper fire, ambushes. He'd faced them all and come out alive. A little worse for the wear, maybe, but alive. The sound of rapid gunfire didn't even make him flinch anymore.

But those seven words— *"You were the one in my dream"*—from that particular woman?

Almost sent him scrambling for cover.

Which, the strategist within him pointed out, was absurd. Talk about a perfect opening. One witty response and he'd set them down the road that led beyond being mere acquaintances. Just give her a glimpse into his feelings, a hint of what she meant to him…

But even as he acknowledged all that, his features fell into a polite smile. One that greeted even as it kept distance.

"Miss Justice."

And then he put his hand out. Yup. A handshake, grip firm, but not lingering. Quick, professional, disconnect.

And above all, unemotional.

What was it Olivia said about him? He was too tough to express his emotions? Oh, how he hated to prove his sister right.

When Kyla turned away from him, her cheeks tinged with red, he pretended not to notice. Better to focus on the matter at hand.

Safer.

"Rafe owns a coffee shop downtown," Fredrik was saying. "Cuppa Joe's, I believe."

Kyla nodded, though her focus seemed fixed on the wall. "Um, yes. I've been there."

"Oh? So you two are friends?" Fredrik took their hands and tugged them together, joining them. "That's good. Two such attractive single people should be friends. Maybe more. Only God can say."

Rafe wanted to pop the old guy on his white head. Kyla's fingers in his were rigid, and her cheeks flamed. What was Fredrik trying to do? Give the poor woman a heart attack?

As though they'd choreographed it, they pulled their hands apart and launched into clarification.

"Well, not *friends*, exactly—"

"Kyla comes in to buy coffee—"

"I mean, I *have* a man friend—"

"She's a customer—"

"Well, not a friend, really. A boyfriend, I guess. Yes, I suppose that's right."

"We just know each othe—" Rafe's words caught in his throat as her last comment registered. He turned to Kyla. "You do?"

Kyla blinked, as though Rafe's abrupt question caught her as off guard as Fredrik's earlier comment. "I do what?"

"You know. What you just said. You have a—"

"Did you know Rafael works with the gangs in the area?"

Both Kyla and Rafe stared at the man standing between them.

"It's true." Fredrik bobbed his head, as if that would make his off-the-cuff comment make sense. "He volunteers his time to help kids caught up in gangs. Don't you, Rafe?"

Where on earth was *this* leading? Rafe narrowed his gaze. "You know I do, old man."

"You've gained the trust of those in leadership, yes? Acted as a mediator when needed. Established yourself in the minds of the police and those who live in the neighborhood as a force for good. And then there's your background in the Marines, hmm?"

This was starting to sound like some kind of bad political ad. *I'm Rafael Murphy and I approved this ad.* "Fredrik, what on earth—?"

"What do you think, Kyla? Quite the man, isn't our Rafe?"

Poor woman looked as confused as Rafe felt. She managed a nod, but her cheeks were approaching meltdown red.

"Fredrik, *what* are you talking about?"

The old man waved a veined hand in the air, brushing off Rafe's question as though it were a pesky gnat. "I'm just explaining to our new contractor here why I've invited you to come here for this meeting, that's all. So she can know she's safe with you here. A woman should know that, yes? That she's safe."

Rafe looked from Kyla—whose expression resembled someone who'd just swallowed the pesky gnat—to the old man who surely had gone completely around the bend. "Of course she should."

"Good. Then it's settled."

"I…what?" If Rafe didn't love the old coot so much, he'd throttle him. *"What's* settled?"

"As long as you're here, Kyla can know she's safe."

Thus assaulted by Fredrik's so-called logic, Rafe responded in the only way he could. He fell into military posture—back straight, arms crossed over the chest, feet planted a foot or so apart. He directed his best staff sergeant glare at the old man—a look that had stopped many a Marine in his tracks.

A look that had no impact whatsoever on Fredrik.

"So, as I've been saying, Kyla, the ministry here isn't done. We've made some ground on the renovations. Or we had, until the fire."

Kyla's features as she studied the sanctuary reflected her sadness over what was lost. "And how did the fire happen?"

"An accident?" Fredrik's doubt suffused both his tone and features.

A fact not lost on Kyla. "You don't believe it?"

Rafe couldn't take it any longer. *"No*body believes it."

Those beautiful eyes swiveled to his face, but Rafe didn't let them stop him. This was not the time to mince words. "That fire was set. I hate to tell you this, Kyla, but our friend here is wrong. You're not safe. No one is. Because as determined as Fredrik and his friends are to make this youth center happen, there are others equally determined to stop it." He held her increasingly troubled gaze. "And they won't stop at anything."

Her eyes widened a fraction. Well, good. At least he was getting through to her.

"Anything?" Her brow puckered. "Are you saying…?"

Best to hit her with the truth now, before she got sucked in on a project doomed to failure. Really, he was only doing this for her good. "I'm saying they'll do what it takes. Theft. Arson—"

"But these people—" The pucker deepened. Apparently she was having a hard time getting her mind around what he was saying. "How serious a threat are they really?"

He hardened his tone to honed steel. "Serious. As we said, we're sure they were behind the accidents, so we know they don't mind hurting people. And if you take this project on, you can be sure of one thing."

Her chin tipped a fraction at his tone, and she squared off with him. "And what, *Mr.* Murphy, might that be?"

Each word clipped, like jagged shards of ice. Hmm. The lady was getting irked. Fine. Match ice for ice. "That you, Miss Justice, will become their prime target."

Kyla stared at Rafael. She couldn't tell if he was being hard for her good or just condescending. Either way, his tone sent irritation snaking through her. If he thought she would be scared off by his dire pronouncements, well…

"Just one more thing, Kyla."

"Yes?" She matched him, crossed arms for crossed arms. Men didn't have a corner on the tough exterior market.

"Go home."

"I—excuse me?" Kyla stared at the man in front of her, the man she'd spent months thinking about, who'd been kind and encouraging, who'd so disturbed her dreams last night that she'd been unable to shake the effect all day.

The man whose nose she'd love to smack right now.

A soft *tsk* drew her attention from Rafael's scowl. Fredrik stepped between them, patting the muscled arms crossed over Rafe's chest.

"Now, Rafael, please. You paint too dark a picture, I think."

The younger man didn't give an inch. "And you paint it too bright."

Kyla couldn't deny the relief when Rafael's gaze shifted from her to Fredrik. Or the touch of umbrage when Rafael's hard features softened. Why glare at *her* and not Fredrik?

Rafael's arms fell to his sides, the barrier broken. When he spoke again, his tone was gentle, but firm. "You have to tell her the truth, old friend."

At the misery on Fredrik's face, Kyla stepped forward and linked her elbow with his. "He's told me all I need to know."

"I'm only trying to ensure you know all the facts."

Kyla heard the concern in Rafael's voice, but it made no sense. "What are you afraid of, Rafael? If I didn't know better, I'd almost think you were trying to undermine this project."

That ruffled his feathers. His brow darkened. "Don't be absurd."

She stepped away from Fredrik—and closer to Rafael. "One thing I have never been, sir, is absurd. I'm only telling how it seems to me. Clearly, this is God's call to Fredrik and the church people. And yet when you arrive, rather than offering constructive suggestions, you spout dire warnings—"

"Kinder, please."

"—and act as though you're the only one with a rational thought in his head. Even you—"

The frown between those dark brows deepened. "Even I?"

"—must see how odd that is. Which leads me to wonder at your motivation."

"Really, both of you—"

Rafael's sharp words sliced through Fredrik's objection. "What are you trying to say?"

"Only that Fredrik trusts you implicitly, and I hope he's right to do so. Because all I've heard today seems to imply that, for whatever reason, you're part of the opposition." She made her own gaze as pointed as she could.

"And all I've heard proves you haven't a clue what's going on here. Which makes you more dangerous than the gangs."

"Please, don't you two see how wrong it is?"

Kyla shushed Fredrik with one hand, even as she demanded Rafael's attention by laying the other on his arm. "And what is that supposed to…to…"

She swallowed whatever she'd been about to say. The moment her hand touched Rafael's arm he'd flinched, then gave her what she wanted.

He looked at her.

Right into her eyes.

And suddenly all words were gone. Melted away in a gaze so intense it made Kyla pull back as though she'd touched fire.

Which, from the heat in Rafael's eyes, she might have done.

The only question now was if that heat was intimate…or incendiary.

TWENTY-TWO

"He is a fool who thinks by force or skill
To turn the current of a woman's will."
SAMUEL TUKE

"I have seen that fools may be successful for
the moment, but then comes sudden disaster."
JOB 5:3

What was *wrong* with him?

Here he'd spent all these weeks thinking and praying about Kyla, and now that he was face to face with her, all he could do was antagonize her.

He might as well be twelve years old again.

Still, as much as he wanted to stop what was happening, her defiant accusation stuck deep in his gut. The idea. That he'd undermine God's work.

If she'd been a man, she'd be on the ground. Nursing a broken jaw.

"Rafael!"

He started at Fredrik's harsh tone, but before he could ask what the old man wanted, his arm was gripped by aged fingers and he was led to the side, away from Kyla.

Probably a good thing right now.

"You must listen to me, Rafe. *Listen and hear.* You are not at war here. And this woman? She's not some target to be taken off—"

"Out."

"I…what?"

Rafe's lips twitched. "Taken out. You take targets out, not off."

Fredrik's head wagged back and forth. "Out, off…oy! Such a *schmendrik,* when you want to be. But this stops now. No more, my boy. All you've been doing is hearing words. But you must listen to a woman's heart to hear what she means."

"Fredrik…"

"No. On this I insist. Go now, back to mein kind, but this time not so much of *this*"—his finger poked at Rafe's mouth—"and substantially more of this"—a finger jabbed at Rafe's ear. "Because then, dear boy"—Fredrik laid his hand over Rafe's heart—"this will know what to do."

Ancient eyes rested on his face. Eyes holding such wisdom. Rafe pursed his lips, then gave one slow nod. He turned and walked back to Kyla.

She stiffened at his approach, and he forced a calm he did not feel into his voice. "I'm not against the youth center, Kyla. I'm only concerned."

Her posture relaxed a fraction. "About what?"

"Did Fredrik tell you that there's one very determined, and even more dangerous, man out there who will do everything he can to keep this center from being built?"

She nodded. "He did."

That wasn't the answer he'd expected. "He did?"

"Sam Ballat. Yes, Fredrik told me."

Rafe couldn't remember the last time he'd felt this way. Sheepish. Foolish.

Or could he? Actually, if he were honest with himself, he'd have to admit something he'd been trying to ignore. He'd been feeling foolish for months. Ever since the day Kyla Justice walked back into his life. Fascinating how a man's fury could go from zero to sixty and back in a matter of seconds.

"I'm sorry, Fredrik." There was no doubting the sincerity in Rafael's voice. "I misjudged you."

Kyla almost snorted, ready to point out Fredrik wasn't the only misjudged soul here today. But before she got a chance, the old man rested a hand on Rafael's shoulder.

"No need for apologies, Rafe. I know what all this means to you. God made you a passionate man—"

Passionate? Was that what you called it?

"—and I wouldn't change that about you. Besides, you were right." At this, Fredrik came toward Kyla, holding his hands out. She placed her hands in his, noting the strength in his grip. "I wasn't completely forthcoming, my dear. I didn't want to frighten you away before you caught the vision for what God has called us to here."

She tugged at Fredrik's rough hands. Hands that had helped so many. "So tell me now."

He did so, explaining the obstacles they'd faced since beginning the project—which, Kyla had to admit, were many. Minimal funding, suppliers who seemed hesitant to deal with them because they didn't want to cross Sam Ballat, dissension within the elders, who were overseeing the project...

Kyla patted Fredrik's hands. "You're right, it's a lot. But it's nothing we haven't dealt with before on other projects." She offered him as encouraging a smile as she could. "That's all just a part of construction, Fredrik. Nothing that you've told me sounds all that terrible."

"He's not finished."

She looked from Rafael to Fredrik. "You're not?"

Clearly, the older man didn't want to go on. But Rafael placed his hand on Fredrik's shoulder. "You have to tell her all of it."

Fredrik nodded. "We have a certain group here in the neighborhood..."

"A group?"

Rafael's patience was wearing. Kyla could tell from the increased tension in his voice. "A gang."

Kyla's eyes widened at that. "A gang."

Misery rested on Fredrik's features. "A gang, yes. But not one involved in truly serious crimes. At least, not murder." He pointed at Rafael. "You told me that yourself, Rafe. They aren't like those violent prison gangs or the violent gangs immersed in the drug trade."

Thank goodness for that.

"No, they're just a violent gang bent on defending their territory."

Kyla turned to face both men. "Their territory being?"

Rafael didn't flinch. "This neighborhood."

So. If she took this job she'd be facing tight deadlines, high expectations from the church leadership, and resistance from a bunch of hoodlums. She should just turn and walk away. Kyla opened her mouth to say she was going to do just that, but what came out instead was, "Tell me about this gang."

Fredrik took her arm, tugging her toward a pew. "Come, sit. I will tell you all I know."

She followed him, lowering herself onto the cushion. *Lord, a gang? This is the project You're calling me to? One where I have to deal with a gang?*

"They call themselves the Blood Brotherhood."

She focused on Fredrik's somber words.

"They started a number of years ago and have been growing a bit as each year passed. We've lost a number of the youth from our church families to this gang."

Kyla folded her hands in her lap. "What do they want?"

Rafael spoke up. "They consider this neighborhood their territory. Their turf, they call it. And they want to keep it. Every inch of it. Having a youth center here, it might pull some of the kids away from them. So, as you can imagine, they're less than enthusiastic about the proposition."

"I thought you were working with them. Had gained their trust. Can't you talk with them? Explain that a center might actually help them?"

Rafael's gaze narrowed, and she had the sense he was trying to determine if she was criticizing him. But when he spoke, his voice was calm. Assured. "I've done exactly that, and while some may want to buy into it, unless the leadership does so, it's a no-go."

"The leadership?"

Fredrik leaned toward her. "One young man." His gaze traveled to Rafael, who nodded.

"Tell her."

Oh dear. This didn't sound good. "Tell me what?"

"The leader, his name is King K."

"Fredrik."

The old man bent his head at Rafael's scold, then heaved a deep sigh. "Which stands for King Killa."

"King Killa." Kyla had the sense that should mean something to her. She looked from Fredrik to Rafael.

The latter shook his head at her apparent thickness. "Killa is gangspeak. For killer."

She stiffened. "You mean…has he really killed?"

Rafael's shrug was as eloquent as it was dismissive. "No one can prove it, but he claims six kills." He angled a look at her. "That's how he made his bones."

"Made his…?"

"Got into the gang. You know, 'Blood in, blood out.'"

Her confusion must have been plastered on her features, because he went on.

"Only way in is to kill. Only way out, be killed."

"I thought that was just the Mexican mafia."

Mafia? Kyla stared at Fredrik. There was a mafia involved?

Rafael shook his head. "Other gangs have taken it up. With King Killa in charge, you know the Brotherhood won't let anyone out without spilling blood."

All they were saying was utterly terrifying. If she had a brain in her head, she'd turn and walk away. And yet as she listened, she felt a quickening deep within. Against all common sense, a certainty grew.

This was the kind of project she'd been asking God to bring her. And though her mind told her to run and not look back, her heart had other ideas. "Let me pray about it."

Another snort from the peanut gallery. Kyla pinned Rafael with a glare. "You have a problem with prayer?"

"Me? No. But then, I'm not looking for it to justify a bad decision."

Oooh! That man was impossible! She turned her back on him and focused on Fredrik. "I'll get back to you in a week."

"If you're smart, you'll say no."

She turned back to Rafael Murphy. How had she ever thought this man appealing? "Perhaps so. But I'm far more concerned, Mr. Murphy, with being obedient." She just barely withheld the "So there!" perched on her tongue.

"Come, kinder. It's time we should leave, while everyone is still alive."

Fredrik's tone almost made her laugh out loud. It reminded her of her mother's voice when she moderated childhood battles between Kyla and her siblings.

From Rafael's expression, he recognized the tone as well. A wry smile teased his lips, and he put a hand on the older man's shoulder. "I'm sorry, Fredrik. We…*I* got a little"—his gaze slid to Kyla, apology clear in his eyes—"out of control."

She inclined her head and linked her arm in Fredrik's. "*We* got out of control. It won't happen again, I promise."

"*Got zol ophiten.*"

God forbid? Kyla stared at her friend.

"Such *aftselakhis* I haven't seen since I was a boy in the old country."

Now that one Kyla didn't recognize. She looked to Rafael, but he just shrugged. Apparently he didn't recognize it either. Fredrik didn't notice their confusion—either that, or he didn't care to enlighten them. He just went on.

"It did this old *kvetcher*'s heart good. Not happen again? *Feh!* It will happen again." Chuckling, he patted her cheek, then turned and headed for the door. "But such entertainment you couldn't find on television."

Kyla stood there, mouth hanging open. Rafael appeared as nonplussed as she felt. They exchanged a look.

"What was that all about?"

Rafael shook his head. "I have no idea. But I'll tell you one thing"—he fell into step beside her as she followed Fredrik out of the sanctuary—"I'm gonna look up *aftsela…*"

"Aftselakhis."

"Right." He stared after Fredrik. "That word. I'm gonna find out what it means."

"Just be sure you tell me too."

"Oh, you can count on it."

As they walked the rest of the way in silence, Kyla wished that was all she could count on. But she couldn't help feeling something else awaited her.

Trouble.

In abundance.

TWENTY-THREE

*"Latent in every man is a venom of amazing bitterness,
a black resentment; something that curses and loathes life,
a feeling of being trapped, of having trusted and been
fooled, of being the helpless prey of impotent rage,
blind surrender, the victim of a savage, ruthless power that
gives and takes away, enlists a man, and crowning injury
inflicts upon him the humiliation of feeling sorry for himself."*

PAUL VALERY

*"Look after each other so that none of you fails to
receive the grace of God. Watch out that no poisonous root
of bitterness grows up to trouble you, corrupting many."*

HEBREWS 12:15

See? I told you there was trouble."

He watched King K step forward, studying the three people exiting the church. Three people seemingly determined to make his life difficult. They'd have to pay for that.

All of them.

"So this lady"—King nodded toward Kyla Justice with his chin—"she's someone who can help them?"

Such menace in the question. In the gaze King kept trained on the good Ms. Justice. Ah, manipulation. It was a thing of beauty. "She's eminently qualified—" He bowed his head. "I'm sorry. *Very* qualified."

The second King K turned to him he knew he'd made a tactical error.

"I know what *eminently* means." Those dark eyes narrowed. King's menace was now aimed squarely at him. "What? You see the way I live, you just assume I'm stupid?"

He kept his gaze down. "No, of course not. I know you're intelligent. A stupid man could never lead people the way you do. I simply didn't want to seem pompous in my word choices."

"Yeah, well, too late for that."

He forced a smile to his face. "Indeed. But as I was saying, Ms. Justice is a contractor, one of the best. If anyone can pull this job off for the church, she can."

King K's gaze swung back to Kyla Justice, who was getting into her car. "Well, we can't have that now, can we?"

He let himself smile, create a sense of camaraderie. "Indeed, not."

"It's done."

The finality of that surprised him. "How can you be sure?"

"Hey. I *said* it's done."

He considered pushing but decided it wouldn't serve his purposes to aggravate his volatile associate further. That, and the awareness that somewhere on his person King K harbored a knife. Inclining his head, he turned to go back to his own car. "I'll be in touch."

"You do that."

The young man's glib tone set his teeth grinding. How he longed for the day when he wouldn't have to put up with this street scum any longer. As soon as he had his way, he'd be on the phone to the police. He'd turned a blind eye to the thefts from his warehouses, but only for so long as he needed the gang.

His lips twisted in a smile. King K and his like were finished.

They just didn't know it yet.

King K watched the rich fool drive away. Man was gettin' on his nerves. Yeah, he was good for business. But once this was over, once he and his crew had their payoff, King and the rich man were gonna dance.

"I'm sorry. Very qualified."

Like King had never heard *eminently* before. Yeah, well, no one treated him like an idiot and walked away from it.

No one.

He turned back toward the church and the more immediate concerns. No one was moving in on them either. He'd tried to make that clear. Tried to show the old folks they needed to stop. Ballat's man did his part, messin' up the orders and stuff. King and the 22s, they took care of makin' sure that old saying "Accidents happen" came true. A lot. And then, finally, they set the fire.

King shook his head. These old guys were like that stupid rabbit with the battery in his back that never quits.

Well, time was up. Them thinkin' they could just keep pushin', just keep bringin' people in to help, that had to end.

Now.

He turned and sauntered down the alley.

Yeah. It was time to show the church folks that he and his crew, they'd do whatever it took to protect their turf.

TWENTY-FOUR

*"Only two things are certain: the universe and human
stupidity—and I'm not certain about the universe."*
ALBERT EINSTEIN

"Give me an understanding heart."
1 KINGS 3:9

Rafe poured himself another cup of coffee. "It was like I was a crazy man."

"Rafa, tell me something, okay?"

He stirred thick rich cream into his coffee. "What?"

";Por que un hombre no puede ser guapo e inteligente a la vez?"

His spoon stopped midstir. What did *that* have to do with anything? He looked at his sister. "What are you talking about?"

"Just answer the question, porfa."

Rafe took a sip of his coffee and leaned back in the chair. "I don't know, Livita. Why can't a man be both good-looking and intelligent?"

"Porque entonces sería mujer."

Because then he'd be a woman.

The thought of tossing his coffee on her drifted through his mind, but he dismissed it. He'd just have to clean up the mess himself. And though they had a break in customers right now, they likely didn't have long until things got busy again.

"Very funny, Livita. But not much help."

"Actually, it is. You're all upset because you acted *a lo loco* with this woman. But Rafa, men, they have trouble thinking straight when things aren't right with a woman. You come to a meeting with Fredrik, and there she stands. In a place you know she isn't safe. So what do you do?" She waved one hand in the air. "You get angry. Say things a *cretino* wouldn't say. And so? She's angry too. *Todos* are angry, and nobody's talking."

He was all set to argue, but the words died on his lips. She was right. The second he saw Kyla standing there, he'd lost it. Rafe took a long drink of coffee.

"Am I right?"

He hated admitting it, but… "You're right." He shot her a glare. "*¿Aqui entre nos, entiendes?*"

She laughed. "You think I want to tell anyone my big, brave Marine brother is afraid of a woman?"

"I'm not afraid of her."

Liv bobbed her head, her long black hair bouncing. "Okay, then, you're afraid of telling a woman the truth. That you love her with all your soul, *verdad?*"

He considered arguing the point but didn't have the heart. "Verdad."

Liv patted his shoulder. "Don't fear, brother. Love isn't fatal." With that, she went back to the counter, leaving him to sit with his thoughts.

Not fatal, eh? You couldn't tell it by him. Right now it felt like it was cutting him to pieces. Kyla Justice had been part of his life for as long as he could remember. First as a baby-sitter, who cuddled him and read him stories as he drifted off to sleep. His smile broadened. Ah, the blissful heaven of childhood.

Then, when Rafe and Annie struck up a friendship, Kyla was his buddy's older sister. The five-year age difference between him and Annie never seemed to matter much to the two of them. They just liked hanging out together. As for Kyla, he knew she was there, on the fringes of his world, but he never really thought about her that much.

Then came that fateful day when he saw Kyla—really saw her—for the first time. When he realized she wasn't just a neighbor, but something beautiful and fine. He'd been outside, playing croquet with Annie. The sun was just beginning to set, and Annie had just beaten him for what was probably the tenth game.

"You lose, Rafa. I'll take ice water this time."

He tossed her a mock grimace, but he didn't really mind. It was the rule: losers fetch drinks, and he'd definitely been the loser that day. So he trotted to the house, pulled the sliding-glass door open, went into the kitchen—and the sight that met his eyes stopped him in his tracks.

Kyla was there, standing by the sink, looking out the window. The colors of the sunset streamed in through the glass, touching the highlights in her auburn hair with fire, caressing her face with light. It was though she was bathed in gold.

Eyes closed, soaking in the warmth, she looked so serene, so incredibly beautiful, that it took his adolescent breath away.

Even now, all these years later, the memory of her that day moved him.

That was when everything changed. When he could no longer look her in the face, for fear she would recognize his feelings. When he ached to see her, even as he dreaded it. And since Rafe's family lived a few houses down from the Justice family and Rafe and Annie were pals, he got to see her often. A fact that both delighted and tortured him.

He had one ally in his struggle: Annie. One look at him as he stared at Kyla, and she knew the lay of the land. Imp that she was, Annie did everything she could to throw Rafe in Kyla's path. More than once he threatened to pound her, but she'd just grin at him.

Of course, Kyla was oblivious. At twenty, she was making her mark in college. To Rafe's deep relief, she decided to commute rather than live in the dorms. But then disaster struck.

Kyla started dating Rafe's jerk older brother, Berto.

He couldn't believe his eyes the first time he saw them together. Sure, Berto was handsome and the girls flocked to him. But Kyla? She was smarter than that!

And yet, there was Kyla, tall and confident beside Berto. Rafe's one consolation was that she didn't hang on his handsome brother's arm like most of his simpering girlfriends. That and the fact that he knew, deep inside, it wouldn't last.

Because Kyla was special. And Berto didn't treat her the way he should.

Unfortunately, Rafe was as outspoken at twelve as he was now, as determined to speak truth without the garnish. So whenever Kyla came to their house, Rafe let it be known he didn't think she should date Berto. Which had the effect of convincing Kyla that Rafe didn't like her.

Which was as far from the truth as it got.

Rafe shook the memories away. No point going over it again. He'd accepted long ago that Kyla Justice was as out of his life as she was out of his reach. That didn't keep him from staying in touch with Annie. They'd been e-mailing each other since he left home. She even stayed in touch while he was overseas, which mattered more than she knew.

But for all of his friendship with Annie, Rafe knew he had to accept the facts: Kyla was out of his life.

Which was why he'd been so stunned when she walked into Cuppa Joe's a few months ago. He'd recognized her the moment she came in. Age, hairstyle, clothes…they were all different. But it was Kyla. She still had that look about her, the look that told him she was something special. And the sight of her gave him that same jolt.

And then some.

He'd stood there, waiting for her to look at him, to remember—but she never did. At first he was disappointed, and then two noteworthy points set in.

She didn't recognize him.

He was no longer a kid.

Suddenly opportunities seemed endless, so he gave her a warm smile and fixed her the best mocha he'd ever made. She'd been coming back almost every day since. He hoped it was as much for the smile as the mocha.

"Rafa, if you're done daydreaming, you have customers waiting."

He looked up. Sure enough, three people were standing there. He hadn't even heard them come in the door. Gripping his coffee like it was the elixir of life, he stood and headed to the counter, painfully aware he didn't have any answers where Kyla Justice was concerned. But he'd better find them. Soon.

Before his feelings drove him straight over the edge.

TWENTY-FIVE

*"Those that set in motion the forces of evil
cannot always control them afterwards."*
CHARLES W. CHESNUTT

*"What sorrow awaits you who lie awake at night, thinking
up evil plans. You rise at dawn and hurry to carry them out,
simply because you have the power to do so. When you want
a piece of land, you find a way to seize it. When you want
someone's house, you take it by fraud and violence. You cheat
a man of his property, stealing his family's inheritance."*
MICAH 2:1–2

Sam Ballat walked into his office, headed straight to the bar, and poured himself a brandy. It was good to be back on his own turf, to steal a colloquialism from the King K.

He settled into the leather executive chair behind his desk, letting his fingers tap out his thoughts on the side of the tumbler. King K had been quite definite. Still, the thug and his gang had let him down a number of times already. As much as he'd like to believe this new wrinkle was taken care of, he didn't dare.

He hit the intercom. "Susan, I need Mr. Wright on the line. Now."

"Yes sir, right away."

He leaned back in his chair and waited.

Mason Rawlins knew he'd had a worse day, but he couldn't remember when. First there were problems at every site he visited. Problems and frustrated clients. And while he prided himself on his ability to work through issues with people, by the time he returned to his office, he felt utterly chewed up.

And then there was Kyla.

They were supposed to go out for dinner tonight, and he'd been trying to call her all morning. He'd left several messages, but she hadn't called him back.

He was just reaching for the phone to try her again when it rang. This had to be Kyla.

Mason lifted the receiver, her name on his lips, but a glance at the caller ID stopped him. Sam Ballat.

Shifting gears so fast he stripped them, he fell into professional mode. "Mr. Ballat. Good to hear from you again."

"Mr. Wright. I'm calling about that project I mentioned to you the other night."

"Yes?"

"I know I said I wanted you to oversee the whole thing, but there's a small problem."

Mason picked up a pen, drawing lines on the pad of paper in front of him. "Oh?"

"Yes, you see, the people who still own the building won't accept they've run out of time. And now I understand they're bringing Justice Construction in on the project."

Mason's pen froze. "Excuse me?"

"Really, Mr. Wright, I'd think you'd be worried about someone so important to you being in that neighborhood. Did you know there's a gang down there determined to keep the youth center out? Taking that project on certainly doesn't sound like a wise move to me."

Mason pressed his lips together. "Or to me." *What* was Kyla thinking?

"Exactly. Which is why I thought I should let you know. That property should just be razed. And when it is, you and I will have some serious business to discuss."

"We will?"

"The owners have already agreed to sell me that property."

"But I thought you said the owners had contacted Justice Construction."

A pause. Mason frowned. Sam Ballat was seldom at a loss for words.

"The current owners, yes. But that will change soon. It's a bit…complicated. At any rate, you can trust me on this, Wright. This isn't a safe project for your Miss Justice. You'd do her—and yourself—a true service to use whatever influence you have to sway her away from the job. That is, assuming you do have influence?"

Mason bristled. "One usually does with his fiancée."

"Fine." He could hear the smug smile in Ballat's tone. "Well then, I'll leave this with you. I know you'll do what's right."

Mason hung up the phone. So Ballat knew he'd do what was right. If only he were as certain what, exactly, that was.

TWENTY-SIX

*"Snarling at other folks is not the best way of showing
the superior quality of your own character."*
CHARLES HADDON SPURGEON

*"Have I now become your enemy
because I am telling you the truth?"*
GALATIANS 4:16

Kyla couldn't wait to see Mason.

She'd called him that afternoon to make sure they were still on for dinner.

"Kyla! Thank heaven."

She frowned at the relief in his voice. "Mason, is everything okay?"

"Yes, of course. I'm just…I'm happy to hear from you!"

Such an effusive reaction to her call just wasn't Mason. "If you're sure?"

"Absolutely."

They finalized their plans for dinner, but before they hung up, she told Mason she had something exciting to tell him.

"I'll look forward to hearing it."

The words were right, but the tone was suddenly dry. Almost sarcastic. She let it go, though she couldn't help a tinge of frustration. Were all men confusing and frustrating?

By the time her doorbell rang that evening, she'd all but forgotten her question. She opened the door and ushered Mason inside.

He pointed to his watch. "Our reservations are in a half hour."

"I know." She tugged him toward the couch. "This won't take long. I just want to tell you what God's done."

His brows lifted as he sat on the couch. "God has done something?"

"Oh yes!" She perched on the chair next to the sofa, letting her excitement spill over as she filled him in on the project Fredrik had brought to her. She'd expected him to share in her enthusiasm, to be happy for her, but the more she talked, the more agitated he seemed. When she asked him what he thought, his brow was positively thunderous.

"Isn't that an area where gangs are active?"

"Well, yes, but—"

"Kyla, why would you put yourself—and our future together—at risk like this?"

"It's not a question of my putting anything at risk. It's a question of obedience."

"So what you're saying is, you'd rather take on this lost cause than marry me?"

Kyla stared at him. Was the man totally nuts? "No, that's not it at all."

He stood and paced the room, jittery energy barely contained. "Then what is it? Please, help me understand why you insist on staying involved in this business. Especially for a project that's doomed from the beginning."

She rose and went to take his hands in hers. "Mason, don't you see? This is what's been missing in my life. A project that *means* something." She released his hands, and this time it was she who paced. "I'm so tired of building things that look great, make lots of money, but don't help anyone. With this project, people will benefit. *Children* will benefit." She stilled and faced him. "How can I walk away from that? From the certainty inside that Fredrik isn't asking me to do this." She held his gaze. "God is."

They stood in silence for a moment, and she watched for emotions on his features. But his expression was neutral. Almost…concealed.

The troubling thought dissipated when he came toward her. Putting his hands on her arms, he drew her close. "I'm sorry. I shouldn't have reacted the way I did. Of course you should do this if you feel God calling you to it. But Kyla, I'd like you to consider something."

She leaned back, looking up into his face. If only she could read what he was feeling. "What?"

"Go ahead and take on the project. But if you can't get it done in the allotted time, no matter what the reason, will you at least consider selling your construction business and marrying me?"

Apprehension tripped across her nerves. "Mason, you know how much can go wrong—"

"Are you saying you don't think you can do it? Meet the deadline?"

Was that what she was saying?

"Kyla, if you don't think you can do what Fredrik and the church need you to do—"

"No. That's not it." She stepped away from him. She needed to think. Was he right? Was it time to consider a change? Was this a way to determine whether or not she should walk away from JuCo?

Was she ready to risk everything for this project?

Risk it? What kind of way is that to talk about marriage?

Kyla closed her eyes. She was so tired of doubting herself, her motivations, her feelings.

"Kyl—"

"Yes." She opened her eyes and found Mason staring down at her, serious eyes wide. She nodded. "Yes, Mason. Yes. If I can't get this job done on time, I'll know it's time. Time to think seriously about selling you JuCo. Time to marry and focus on being a wife."

"If you can't do it, no matter the cause?"

The words were as unsettling now as when he'd first said them, but Kyla pushed her feelings aside. She shouldn't be worried about this at all. If, indeed, God wanted her to take this job—to stay in the business and to focus on projects more like this one—then He would make sure they succeeded. He would see to it that the youth center was completed. On time.

And if she truly believed He was calling her to this, then fear had no place in her heart—or decisions.

Kyla lifted her chin. "No matter what."

He nodded, sealing the deal. "Well, then, what say we go to dinner?"

She nodded, letting him take her arm and lead her to the door. Wondering, as she did so, if she was following him as well to a future she wasn't entirely certain she wanted.

TWENTY-SEVEN

*"Dare I? Of course I don't. But I'm going
to anyhow because I have no choice."*
MADELEINE L'ENGLE

*"The God of heaven will help us succeed.
We, his servants, will start rebuilding."*
NEHEMIAH 2:20

The phone rang at 8 a.m. on the dot. Fredrik didn't mind. He'd been up for hours, seeking God's guidance. When he heard Kyla's voice on the other end of the line, he knew he'd received it.

She got right to the point. "I'll take the job."

He wanted to accept her right away. But he had to make sure she understood. "You realize the deadline is less than two months away now."

"Yes."

"And that we're desperately short on funds."

"Not a problem."

"And that you may well have to deal with the Blood Brotherhood?"

Her answer came out sure and strong. "I understand."

"And Rafe. On an almost daily basis."

Wry laughter tinged her voice. "I already told you I'm going to be good, Fredrik. I even promised, remember?"

More foolish than that, a promise didn't get. But he didn't tell her so.

"You've been up-front with me, Fredrik. I know what I'm getting myself and JuCo into. And so does God."

It's beautiful, Father. To see a true calling. "Wonderful. I'll set up a meeting with the elders at once."

"I'll look forward to it."

Fredrik set the phone in its cradle and lowered himself to his knees. "Thank You, Father. Now be with us…as we go into battle."

~~~

Kyla wasn't sure what she'd expected when she met the elders. But it certainly wasn't this group of sweet-faced, grandfatherly gentlemen sitting around a table, staring at her.

Fredrik introduced each of them, and Kyla noted the mixture of hope and doubt in their eyes. She couldn't help wondering if that was because of all the opposition they'd experienced—or because their new contractor was a woman.

"Of course"—Fredrik offered her a bright smile; at least he was happy to have her here—"we don't expect you to remember all the names right off."

"Just the important ones."

She smiled at the man teasing her. Don, if she remembered correctly. His brother, who sat next to him, nudged him in the arm. "So you don't want her to remember your name?"

Kyla's tension began to ease. She was going to like these men.

"And, of course, our dear Hilda D'Angelo. She's been the organist and pianist and head deaconess—"

One of the elders—Steve? Was that his name?—gave a good-natured snort. *"Only* deaconess, you mean."

"—for years. And that large ball of fluff in her lap is Doggy Dog."

At its name, the dog lifted its head, laying a long, sleek snout on the table and peering at Fredrik. He came to lay a large hand on the dog's head, scritching its ears. "Doggy has been coming to our church for what?" He looked down at Hilda. "Ten years?"

The woman's smile was as sweet as her features. A halo of white hair framed her slightly lined face. "About that."

Fredrik walked back to where Kyla stood. "Hilda's really the one who watches over all us old men, making sure we don't get in deeper than we can get out of."

"I'm afraid I didn't do a very good job of that this time." Hilda's soft voice held an underlying strength.

"You did as well as you could, considering this stubborn bunch."

Kyla's gaze drifted to the back of the room. Her first reaction at seeing Rafael standing there when she came in was pure pleasure. Then she remembered their conflicts—and her devotion to Mason—and grabbed the reins of those runaway emotions, giving them a mighty jerk. She was going to see Rafael on a regular basis. She'd have to keep her traitorous emotions in severe check if she wanted to get through it unscathed.

She turned her attention back to the elders, noting again the lack of enthusiasm in their gazes, the tension in the way they sat there, looking from her to Fredrik. Before she could ask about it, one of the elders spoke up.

"I want to apologize, Miss Justice. I'm sure you can tell we're somewhat reserved."

"I had noticed…Steve? Is that right?"

The man's angular face lit up. "Your memory is exemplary. And it's not that we're not glad you're here, but we haven't much money left in our building fund. We spent most of our resources on the last contractor—"

"At least Lawton was better than the nimrod before him. Took our money and gave nothing in return." This muttered comment from Wayne, his grizzled features stormy. "Rotten crook. He should rot in sheol."

Steve hardly broke stride. "As will we all."

"Oh, don't start that again!"

Kyla lifted her brows at Fredrik, who leaned toward her and explained. "Wayne says *sheol* is hell, the place where the evil are punished for eternity. Steve says it's the grave, plain and simple." He shrugged. "But don't let the outburst worry you. They've been fighting over this for more than forty years."

Steve went on. "So I'm afraid we really can't pay you."

"Or your crew," Sheamus piped up.

"Or buy supplies," Von added.

Kyla almost burst out laughing. It was like working with the seven dwarfs!

"I don't even know why we're doing this again." Wayne crossed his arms and pushed back in his metal folding chair, lifting the front legs off the ground. Kyla was sure he'd tip over backward, but apparently the old gent had better balance than she'd estimated. "Didn't we lose enough last time 'round? And we haven't got it to lose this time. I don't know about you all"—he nodded his head at those gathered—"but I don't much care to donate my social security to this project. Man's gotta eat."

"And remember that the community won't be much help this time."

Oh joy. Another bit of encouragement from Little Mary Sunshine. "Why is that, Rafael?"

"Those who came forward to help the last three times paid a high price."

Sheamus let out a heavy breath. "Their homes were vandalized. Graffiti drawn inside and out."

"And they received phone calls, threatening them if they didn't back off." Fredrik's tone showed just the faintest hint of anger.

Well. At least she could put one concern to rest. "You don't have to worry about the cost."

"Easy for you to say."

Kyla studied Wayne, careful to keep her expression calm. She'd run into more than her share of naysayers on other projects, so this was nothing new. "You know, my father started Justice Construction. He's the one who brought me into the business, who taught me how to run it. How to lead well." She straightened, infusing her words with as much confidence as she could. "And something that he taught me early on was to set aside a certain percentage of company profits for the important jobs—the jobs God wanted done but circumstances or finances said it couldn't happen."

She nodded. "Jobs like this one. So when I say you don't have to worry about the cost, I mean it. JuCo will provide the crew and supplies."

Astonishment traveled the faces watching her. And hope.

They all started speaking at once.

"That's too generous!"

"God will bless you, young lady."

"That's far more than we ever could have hoped."

"Maybe this will work after all."

Everyone was talking, except Hilda. She just sat there, tears coursing down her sweet face.

Finally, Fredrik got them settled down. "So, it looks as though we're back in business. Kyla, when can you have everything ready to go?"

Normally she'd need ample time to get a crew together, but time was short. Ridiculously so. It'd be a stretch, but... "Give me two days."

"Fine. Two days it is. We'll all gather here, all of us and you and your crew, for the blessing ceremony."

"Blessing ceremony?"

Hilda patted Doggy Dog. "To dedicate the project—"

"And its completion, no matter how unlikely."

She ignored Sheamus's sour comment. "—to God and His protection. We'll pray, you'll dig a shovelful of dirt for a memory book photo, and then you can start."

"Sure, okay." Kyla tipped her head. "But you know, it's not really a ground-breaking. We're not going to put up a new building."

Hilda nodded. "I know. But we've taken the same picture the other three times, so why break with tradition now?"

Because tradition has been that the project fails?

Kyla didn't say it out loud. She nodded and said that would be fine. Sometimes it just wasn't helpful to point out the obvious.

TWENTY-EIGHT

"When you invite trouble, it's usually quick to accept."
QUOTED IN *P.S., I LOVE YOU*

*"When arguing with fools, don't answer their foolish
arguments, or you will become as foolish as they are."*
PROVERBS 26:4

M ost holy God, we beseech Thee, walk among us today in power and
protection…"

Warriors.

That's what Kyla was listening to, as sure as if they'd come decked out in
shields and swords. But these people didn't fight with weapons of steel and
wood. They used words. Powerful, heartfelt words.

"…that all may know this, Thy house, stands by Thy almighty will."

Prayers to a God far more powerful to them than the obstacles standing
in their way. Prayers for His presence. His overshadowing.

His blessing.

"Work within us, gracious Father, that we might serve Thee with our tal-
ents and skills."

The task was as large as ever. Kyla still didn't know how they were going
to rebuild the burned-out church into a youth center in a matter of weeks.
Contrary to Hilda's assertion, they weren't the *Extreme Makeover Home Edition* crew. Nor did they have the show's budget.

Which made it all the more odd that Kyla wasn't worried. Because the
prayers—and the pray-ers—had made her realize this wasn't her task.

It was God's.

"Lead us in going beyond our own strength so that we might rely on Thee."

Good thing too. Because it was certain they wouldn't get much help from the neighbors. The church folks were all here, of course, and her crew, hard hats in hand, ready to get started at the "Amen." But despite church members putting up fliers about the dedication, even going to visit the homes of those they knew, only a handful from the neighborhood showed up. It would seem Rafael was right.

The Blood Brotherhood had everyone scared.

An elbow nudged her side, and Kyla turned to the man standing beside her, Grant Wilson, her first-line supervisor. "We've got an audience."

"Let us see not only this task, but all involved with Thy eyes of love and compassion."

She followed his gaze to a young black man standing on the fringes, watching, listening. She took in his attire—and ground her teeth.

Fine.

The Blood Brotherhood…22s…whatever they called themselves, didn't want the neighbors around, and yet they had the gall to be here? If she wasn't afraid it would disrupt the ceremony, she'd march over there and tell that thug exactly what she thought of him. Since she couldn't do that without drawing attention from the prayers, she'd have to settle for making her feelings clear in her gaze.

"And should any of us walk in ways contrary to Thy will, pull us back, holy God, but do so with love and compassion…"

While she wouldn't want that old adage "if looks could kill" to come true, she wouldn't mind if they managed to wound this hood and his buddies a bit.

"…for we are all Thy children, dearly loved by Thee and called to Thy service. All this we ask in Thy Son's most precious name…"

The target of her attention looked up. His eyes collided with hers, and even from this distance she could see him start. Good! She narrowed her glare. Take tha— "*Oomph!*"

She glowered at Grant, who'd just jabbed her a good one in the side. "What?"

He jerked a nod toward the elders and hissed at her. "A-men."

"Amen?"

"They said it twice now, boss. They're waiting for you to take the shovel."

Sure enough, Fredrik and the elders were standing there, watching her.

"Oh! I'm sorry. I…" She clamped her mouth shut. No way she was going to admit she wasn't listening. Cheeks on fire, she hurried to take the shovel from Willard and dig it into the ground. But as she lifted the pile of dirt, she didn't look at Hilda, who was taking pictures of the event. Instead, she glanced past the little woman to the cause of her humiliation.

And almost dropped the dirt.

"Smile, Miss Justice."

Even as the camera snicked, she knew what crossed her face was more grimace than grin. But that was the best she could do.

Because the gang member was no longer alone. There, right in front of God and everyone, stood Rafael Murphy. Next to the enemy. And from the looks of the two of them, the conversation wasn't only civil.

It was downright friendly.

~~~

"So, you gonna stick around all day?" Rafe kept his stance relaxed as he glanced at the tall young man beside him.

"Don't know. Just figured I'd watch until I got bored."

That wasn't likely to happen anytime soon. Even Rafe was all but mesmerized as he watched Kyla and her crew go to work. He'd never seen such precision and energy before—at least, not outside of the military. "They're pretty impressive."

"They?" Tarik slanted him a bland look. "Or her?"

Sometimes that kid saw entirely too much. "I was surprised to see you at the dedication ceremony."

Tarik shrugged. "I wasn't really at it."

"Okay…I was surprised to see you around it."

Another shrug. "I decided I should. Just in case."

Made sense. If the Brotherhood showed up, Rafe and the others would need Tarik. Big time. Which, unless Rafe missed his guess—which didn't happen often—was why Tarik was still here.

Just because the Brotherhood didn't show up at the ceremony didn't mean they weren't coming.

"You know this is trouble."

Rafe didn't deny the boy's quiet words. "Has it started yet?"

Tarik slid his hands into his pockets. "There's a lot of trash talk going on, but nothing definite. Not yet."

"Any chance of heading it off?"

"Your Marine buddies going to show up?"

Rafe's lips twitched at the irony in the boy's words. "No."

"Then no. The Brotherhood can't let this one go. If they do, it's like saying they're down with it. And that would mean there's an option."

"To joining the gang."

Tarik's nod was barely perceptible.

"So you're the exception to the rule."

The boy's mouth compressed. "So far."

Rafe wanted to throw an arm around Tarik's shoulders, to tell him how proud of him he was, but pride wouldn't allow such a gesture. Besides, it could very well bring Tarik even more attention from the Brotherhood.

Rafe glanced at the buildings around them. The gang members might not be visible, but he had no doubt they were around. Somewhere. Watching. And they wouldn't take kindly to an outsider buddying up to one of their own. Doing so meant trouble.

For everyone.

~~~

He'd been doing it all day.

Every time Kyla glanced up from her work or from a discussion with her crew, she saw Rafael. And every time, regardless of his location or involvement, he'd been doing the same thing.

Watching her.

After a day of being scrutinized by those dark eyes, she was about to jump out of her skin! Finally, a few hours ago, a voice called to Rafael from across the street. A young man, probably no more than nineteen, waved him over.

She watched as Rafael laid down the tools he'd been using, then headed across the street, his movements graceful despite his cane and limp. And there he'd stayed, talking with the boy.

And watching her.

By the time the men finished up for the day she was so antsy she could happily spit nails.

"So you want me to pick 'em up tonight?"

She spun. "What?"

Grant eyed her. "The nails. The 316s. I told you we were gonna run short if we didn't pick some up."

"Oh. Right." She swallowed back her embarrassment. Why did she let Rafael get to her this way? Grant must think she'd gone totally nuts. "I thought you left already."

The frown deepened. "Told you I was gonna check in before I left."

Okay. Nuts and stupid.

He held up a hand, forestalling any explanation. "You and those old folks best be gettin' outta here."

Kyla glanced back at the church elders. Steve and Von had left, but Willard, Wayne, and Sheamus awaited her. Along with, of course, the ever-present Hilda. "We're just going to do a quick walk-through of the site, see what we got done today. Then we'll leave."

Grant's features creased as he studied the skyline. "Yeah, well, you don't wanna be out here after dark." He hesitated. "Want me to wait?"

She waved him off. "No. Go home. We'll be back at it early tomorrow morning, and you need your rest."

He nodded. "Whatever you say." He started to turn, but she couldn't let him go. Not yet.

"Grant. I'm sorry I was so…distracted earlier."

He pulled a piece of gum out of his pocket, unwrapping it and sticking it in his grinning mouth. "Yeah"—he looked across the street to where Rafael stood—"I noticed. And you're not the only one." He turned back to her. "Been noticing you both. All day."

"I—" Well, really. What could she say? The man was spot-on.

"Boss, no worries. We been together too long for me to think anything but the best of you." He unhooked his tool belt and draped it over one shoulder. "Besides, I figure it's about time. None o' my business, but to my way of thinkin', you been alone too long." His firm gaze stopped the protest perched on her tongue. "You know it as well as I do. Your dad would'nta wanted you to be alone."

With that, he made his way to his car, leaving Kyla to do the only thing she could think of in the face of such a comment.

Glare at Rafael Murphy.

"She's watching you."

Tarik's words jerked Rafe's attention toward the church. He was right. Kyla was watching him. For a moment pleasure flooded him, only to slam into a dam of reality when he saw the storm creasing her features.

She might be looking at him, but she wasn't happy.

Not by a long shot.

"Guess you'd better go see what's up with your lady."

Rafe allowed himself a small smile. His lady. Would that it were true. "Guess I'd bett—" His words stilled when Tarik grabbed his arm. Rafe looked at his friend and found the tension in the boy's fingers mirrored in the dark eyes beneath the ball cap.

Only one thing could get Tarik that upset that fast.

He spun, his gaze racing back to Kyla, his worst fears confirmed by Tarik's dark tone.

"They're here."

TWENTY-NINE

"If the enemy leaves a door open, you must rush in."
SUN TZU

*"Don't be afraid of the enemy!
Remember the Lord, who is great and
glorious, and fight for your friends,
your families, and your homes!"*
NEHEMIAH 4:14

They were surrounded.

Ten…no, twelve Blood Brotherhoods circled Kyla and the elders. She hadn't even seen them move in. They just appeared, a terrifying barrier cutting Kyla and the elders off from the shelter of the church.

She scanned the faces staring at her—the wall of red and black clothing, bandannas, tattoos. Her heart pounded in her chest.

What are you afraid of? These are kids. No more than early twenties, Rafael said.

Maybe so, but there was nothing youthful about them.

Chests out, chins up, arms crossed. All of them, from what she could see of their eyes in the growing dusk, ice-cold.

For a heartbeat, no one spoke. Kyla's hand inched toward her pocket, to her cell phone, but firm fingers closed over her arm.

Willard.

He gave one shake of his head and met her gaze with his own. *Wait.* The warning was as clear as if he'd spoken. *Just…wait.*

"Why you dissin' King K like this?"

Kyla didn't have time to figure out who spoke. Words spat from every direction.

"He said no center, foo."

"Dat means no center."

"You dumm too? 'Cause you know you deaf."

"What this crew think they doin'? Think they can do this in a week if they pray?"

"Don't matter. They usin' wack goods. Stuff other people used and pitched."

"Building'd fall down if a pigeon pooped on it."

"Nah. That's what's holdin' it together."

The mockery crescendoed; the comments grew more violent. Vitiating. Behind her, Hilda gasped. Kyla turned and saw Sheamus's and Wayne's white faces. The anger burning in their aged eyes. Anger and something more…

Despair.

The ugliness rose on a swell of dark anger, washing over Kyla until she could bear it no more. She had to do something.

Be still.

It whispered through her—low, calm, but a command all the same.

Listen to them, Lord! They are mocking us. Mocking You!

Be still…

She wanted to scream. To hit something. Didn't God understand? People like this, they didn't care. Didn't respect you unless you made them.

Be—

No! Fury set her feet in motion. Willard grabbed her arm again, but she pulled away from him. "Those punks aren't in control here."

Willard's eyes pierced her. "Neither are you."

"No"—the words seeped through gritted teeth—"but I work for the One who is." She held his gaze, and his hand fell away.

"If He's calling you to this, then I won't stand in your way."

If He's calling me…

Kyla jutted her chin and stepped forward, sensing more than seeing the elders fall in behind her. A line of warriors. "Be not afraid." That's what God said, right? Fine.

She'd show these thugs she wasn't afraid.

⁓⁓〜

"Where you two tinkleberries think you goin'?"

Rafe wasn't surprised when three 22s blocked their way. He'd expected it sooner. King K always had lookouts. Big ones.

These three were no exception.

He stopped in front of the guy who'd challenged them. The kid's stance—chin up, eyes at half-mast, arms crossed over his chest—that and the fact that he was the largest of the three marked him as the leader of this little outing.

Good. Saved Rafe time. He didn't have to guess who to take out first.

He fell into his ready stance. Loose. Hands clasped together in front of him, atop his cane, like he was having a nice little talk with his grandmother. Deceptively relaxed. "Tinker Bells."

The kid looked at him like he was nuts. "What?"

"Tinker Bells, genius, not tinkleberries. Tinker Bell was a fairy, which I assume is what you want to call us. Tinkleberries don't exist. Get your insults straight."

His adversary's lips parted to show one gold tooth. "You talk tuff for a gimp." His gaze dropped to Rafe's cane.

"I have one good one." He tapped his strong leg. "That's all I need for someone like you."

The smile turned decidedly nasty. "Oh, you a smart boy. I bust grapes on smart boys."

"Well"—Rafe shrugged—"you can try." He tensed, watched the kid's eyes, waited…

There.

A flicker in the kid's eyes just before he moved. Rafe deflected the fist aimed at his face, then used the momentum to flip the crud off his feet, onto his back. One strike with the cane to the back of the kid's head as he fell.

He was out before he landed, hard, on the concrete.

Rafe looked down at the still form. It was over. Ten, fifteen seconds tops.

He was slowing down.

He turned to the others standing there, eyes wide. But they weren't looking at Rafe. They were staring at the boy beside him.

"Tarik."

The taller of the two remaining gang members put his arm in front of his buddy, and the two of them stepped aside.

Rafe and Tarik ran. But even as they did so, Rafe heard a sound that turned his blood cold.

Kyla's voice. Yelling for King K.

God, why did You let me fall for a crazy woman?

"King K!" Trepidation tripped along Kyla's nerves as she called out the gang leader. Whispers of alarm shot through her.

Not smart, Kyla. Not smart at all.

Yeah well, so what? She wasn't putting up with this foolishness a moment longer.

"King K! If you have something to say to us, step up. Say it." She let a sneer twist her mouth. "Or are you just going to let your lackeys speak for you like some kind of coward?"

She didn't see who hit her.

The blow drove her to her hands and knees, and for a moment she thought for sure she was going out. But the stars that had burst to life in her head circled, then faded. She caught the sound of someone yelling. A voice she recognized—

Wayne hit the ground beside her, blood streaming from his nose.

God, no…don't let them be hurt because of me! Dimly she realized someone's hands were on her shoulders, her head. Stroking her back.

"Willard, no more." Hilda's voice. Choked with tears.

"Tell them it's over." Kyla started at the voice right next to her ear. Sheamus. Kneeling beside her. "Tell them they've won."

Though her jaw felt as though it were going to fall off her face, Kyla clenched it. "No!"

The hands gripped her.

"Miss Justice—"

"No!"

She pushed their hands away. "Take care of Wayne." She waited as they helped him to his feet, then drew a breath.

Stood.

Prayed no one could see how she trembled.

Another kid, hands fisted at his sides, started toward her, but before he came two steps, he yelped and flew backward. The thug beside him followed suit. Before Kyla could figure out what was happening, two forms strode through the line. Kyla knew one of them right away.

"Rafe!"

Rafe.

Not Rafael. But Rafe. And the way she said it sent his pulse into overdrive. It took all his self-control not to gather her in his arms, to cradle her against him. But now wasn't the time.

Not if they wanted to get out of this in one piece.

He took up a stance on Kyla's right. Tarik moved to her left. The message was clear: You want her, you go through us.

"Sorry I didn't get here sooner," he ground out of a suddenly dry throat. "We met with a little resistance."

Her wondering gaze swept from Rafe to Tarik. "I thought…"

Tarik didn't look at her, but then, he didn't need to. What she'd thought had been clear in the glares she'd directed at the two of them all day. To the kid's credit, there was no resentment in his voice when he spoke.

"I'm not in the Brotherhood."

Kyla wavered and alarm stung Rafe. *Keep her on her feet, Lord. Don't let her fall. If she goes down, they'll move in.*

His leg was already aching, just from the little dance he'd done a few minutes ago. He'd be able to take out one or two, maybe three. But ultimately…

Forget it. Don't think about ultimately.

Just think about survival.

Kyla fought the wave of dizziness. She was not going to fall. She needn't have worried. The boy to her left shifted closer, just enough to support her with the side of his crossed arm.

He and Rafael stood there, arms crossed, feet planted. Two men of muscle and sinew. Strength personified.

An angry rumble sounded from the line circling them, and Kyla tensed. Waiting. *Here they come. God, help.*

"Step off."

The low words worked a miracle. Within seconds the aggressors vanished into the night.

Kyla blinked. "What…?" She turned to Rafael. "What happened?"

"King K."

This from the boy to her left. She shifted to get a better look at him. "How can you tell?"

Something crossed his features. Anger? Pain? Maybe both. "I know his voice." He nodded to the nonexistent line. "And so do they."

An arm came around Kyla's waist. Rafael. She should protest but was shaking too hard to speak. In fact, she was shaking too hard to stand.

Rafael caught her as she fell, sweeping her into his arms as though she were a feather. He nestled her against his chest, his arms a protective barrier around her.

"One of those animals hit her!"

Her eyes had drifted shut, but she felt him nod to Hilda.

"I know. I saw."

The raw rage saturating his hoarse reply sent shivers across her nerves. His arms tightened around her, their strength and warmth seeping into her cold body.

"Let's get you inside."

Tenderness. Protectiveness. Concern. It all resided in those few words, and as he carried her up the stairs and into the church, Kyla had to fight the powerful urge to press her face to his shoulder…

And weep.

THIRTY

> *"The greatest glory in living lies not in never falling, but in rising every time we fall."*
> NELSON MANDELA

> *"So be strong and courageous! Do not be afraid and do not panic before them. For the LORD your God will personally go ahead of you. He will neither fail you nor abandon you."*
> DEUTERONOMY 31:6

Rafe cradled Kyla close, his arms locked around her. He'd have to put her down in a minute, but until then…

He wasn't letting her go.

"Lay her here."

He walked to the pew Hilda indicated, then hesitated for a moment. He wanted to keep her right where she was. Where he could keep her safe.

In spite of herself.

Hilda touched his arm. "She'll be fine, Rafe. Just lay her down so we can see to her injury."

He set Kyla on the cushioned pew and started to straighten, but her fingers gripped the front of his shirt. He met her gaze.

"Stay."

She didn't have to ask him twice. He eased onto the pew beside her, careful not to crowd her too much. Hilda hustled about, dispatching the others for water, ice, a washcloth, and other things. Rafe sat beside her, then glanced back. Kyla turned and saw the boy standing there, shifting from one foot to the other.

Rafe inclined his head to the boy. "Wait for me outside, Tarik."

The boy turned and started to walk away.

"Wait!"

He turned back, brows arching when Kyla extended a hand to him. He came back to her and let her take his hand.

"Thank you." She brought her other hand to grip his as well. "Thank you so much. And…I'm sorry. For what I thought."

His dark eyes rested on her face as though he sought something. Then he spoke, his words firm but without anger. "You saw what you expected. 'Cuz you looked with your eyes. If you're gonna make it here, you better start looking with His." He gave one brief nod toward the cross at the front of the sanctuary, then pulled his hand free and walked back outside.

Willard handed him a basin of water and a washcloth. Sheamus appeared behind him, holding out what looked to be a small bag of crushed ice.

Rafe took the items. "Did you call the police again?"

"Ag'n?" Suddenly Kyla's mouth wasn't working right; she felt like she was talking around a mouthful of rocks. But Rafe seemed to understand her.

"I called them when Tarik and I saw the Brotherhood move on you and the others." He dipped the washcloth into the water, then wrung it out.

"It all hap'n so fas'—" She gasped when he pressed the washcloth to her face.

"I know. It usually does." He pulled the washcloth from her cheek and dipped it back in the basin of water. She was shocked to see the water turn red.

Rafe lifted the washcloth to her face, and she winced. He reached out his free hand to brush her hair back with gentle fingers. "I'm sorry. I know it hurts. But that bas—" he drew in control on a deep breath—"jerk who hit you must have been wearing a ring, because he cut your cheek. We need to get it cleaned out."

Tears slid down her cheeks as she managed a nod. Moments later, he lifted the ice pack and pressed it to her jaw. "Hold this here."

Kyla squared off with Rafe. "You th'nk I c'n't han'le a buncha hoods on my own?"

Heat flickered in his features, and then his pointed gaze rested on the ice pack. "I know you can't."

How could mere words hurt so much? More than she'd ever thought possible. "Thanks for the vote of confid'nce."

A nerve jumped in his jaw. "Look, these aren't some TV sitcom thugs. These guys mean business. And their business is hurting people who get in their family's way."

"Their family?"

"See? That's why you don't belong here. You don't even understand the basics!"

She struggled to sit up. "Th'n explain it to me." She laid her hand on his arm. "Tell me."

He seemed to struggle within himself for a moment, then gave in. "The gangs are like a family. Once you're in, you belong for good. The OGs—"

She held up a hand. "OGs?"

"Old gangsters." He grunted. "Of course, most of them are all of midtwenties, but life expectancy for kids in a gang isn't high. Gangs like the 22s, they're all about turf. About keeping it, protecting it from anyone who might invade. Might take it away from them. They've fought off other gangs, and they sure have no qualms about taking you out if they need to."

What kind of craziness had she gotten herself into? "Don't they know they'll get caught?" Oh, thank heaven. Her mouth seemed to be back in gear.

"They know. They don't care. Not unless it's a three-strike situation."

Kyla hated to show she didn't understand yet another term, but it was the only way she'd learn. "Three-strike?"

"We don't have it here in Oregon, but in a number of other states, including California, if you're convicted of a serious criminal offense on three or more separate occasions, you're done. The courts are required to lock you up for a long time. But the gangs get around it. If they've got a two-striker about to go down, one of the young members will cop to the crime."

Kyla couldn't believe what she was hearing. "Are you saying someone would go to prison for a crime he didn't commit?"

"Without hesitation." He ran his hand through his hair. "That's what I'm trying to get you to see, Kyla. This isn't about a group of kids being troublemakers. These gangs, they're solid. They're organized. They have their own list of commandments."

"Their what?"

He held up a hand, counting off on his fingers as he spoke.

"Thou shalt not snitch.

"Thou shalt get thy respect.

"Thou shalt be down for thy homie, right or wrong.

"Thou shalt be down for thy set, thy hood, thy crew.

"Thou shalt handle thy business.

"Thou shalt have money."

Kyla's head felt like it was spinning. It was too much. Too much to comprehend. To absorb and sort through. These people were crazy. Dangerously so.

"Are you okay?"

His concern was both touching and irritating. She held up her hand, warding off any more questions. "I just…I need to think a minute."

She swung her legs off the edge of the pew and sat there, head in hands, willing the chaos to still. But it all swirled around her, amping up her tension.

Maybe Rafael was right. Maybe she should leave. Get herself and her people out of here before something terrible happened.

So it's time, then. To make a change. To sell JuCo to Mason?

Just…shut up.

Time to get married. Settle down to being a wife. A mother of his chil—

"Stop!" Rafe started as she came off the pew. "Just stop." She turned to face him. "I know, okay? I know I'm in over my head. I know this crazy bunch of people is out to get me for helping the church, but it doesn't matter."

"Kyla—"

"No!" She imposed an iron control on her raging emotions. She wanted to run. More than anything she'd ever wanted in her life. But there was no way those thugs were chasing her off. "I'm not leaving. God called me to this; He'll protect me."

"He expects you to arm yourself. To gain the knowledge you need. To enlist the help of others you can trust."

Emotion swept over her at his words. She wanted to fall into his arms, let him protect and shelter her. Instead, she stiffened. "I appreciate your concern. But I can deal with it."

Bold words from a heart that was quaking in its shoes. But she couldn't let him see that.

"Not by yourself, you can't."

Yes, by herself. Always by herself. Because that was the only person she knew for certain she could trust. "I'm not afraid. Not of the Blood Brotherhood. Not of King K." She shifted, trying to find a stance that didn't hurt. "Not even of your dire warnings. None of it worries me."

The last remnants of warmth dissipated from his eyes. "Then you are an utter fool."

With those chilled words hanging in the air, Rafe turned and walked away.

THIRTY-ONE

"I will love the light for it shows me the way,
yet I will endure the darkness because it shows me the stars."
OG MANDINO

"What sorrow for those who say that
evil is good and good is evil."
ISAIAH 5:20

Tarik listened as the angry voices faded, replaced by rapid-fire, retreating footsteps.

Wow.

So that's what being in love did to you, huh? He'd seen Rafe angry before, but he'd never heard him like this. He was going to have to ask Rafe—

"Why you got to be here, L'il Man?"

Tarik didn't even turn. "I wondered when you'd come back."

"How many times I gotta tell you, stay away from these dead men."

"I can't do that, Jamal. You know it; I know it."

A powerful hand grabbed his arm and spun him to face the man standing at his side. "I don't know it. No reason you can't jus' walk away."

Tarik didn't flinch. "Yes, there is. These people are my family."

"I'm you're family, little brother. And stop callin' me Jamal. My name is King Killa."

"That's your street name. I prefer the name Mama gave you."

Jamal's face twisted. "Yeah, well, Mama ain't here now, is she?"

His brother's cold tone would have hurt if Tarik hadn't known the pain that fueled it. "No, Jamal. She isn't. These streets killed her. Like they're going to kill you one day."

His brother didn't argue. He knew as well as Tarik that it was true.

Tarik turned back to look at the church. "Can't you let this one go? These people are good, Jamal. They just want to help."

No answer, but then Tarik hadn't really expected one. He knew the fine line his brother walked. Knew it angered some of the Brotherhood that Tarik wasn't a member. Made no sense to them that the leader's little brother wasn't connected. Only the OGs understood.

They didn't want their kid brothers or sisters involved in gangs either.

Fortunately, those who might grumble knew better than to question King about Tarik. You challenged King K and you got a full dose of wrath. No one was willing to risk that. So they let it go. For now. But one mistake on King's part, one sign of weakness...

"This will happen."

Tarik looked up at the night sky. What was it like to live someplace where you could see the stars? Where the streetlights didn't obliterate them? "I know, brother."

"You stand on the wrong side when the judgment comes, you go down with them." Jamal lifted his chin. "Won't be nothin' I can do."

Spoken so matter-of-fact. But Tarik knew what those words cost his brother. "I know."

Jamal nodded, then turned and walked away. But his voice drifted back through the night. "I love you, L'il Man."

Tarik closed his eyes. "I know, brother. I love you too." When his whispered response was met with silence, Tarik opened his eyes, ignoring the tears that slipped free and ran down his face. He gazed back up at the sky.

Someday, he'd really like to see the stars.

THIRTY-TWO

*"[God] will not necessarily protect us—not from
anything it takes to make us like His Son.
A lot of hammering and chiseling and purifying
by fire will have to go into the process."*

ELISABETH ELLIOT

*"When [our enemies] heard that the work was going
ahead and that the gaps in the wall of Jerusalem
were being repaired, they were furious. They all made
plans to come and fight against Jerusalem and throw
us into confusion. But we prayed to our God and
guarded the city day and night to protect ourselves."*

NEHEMIAH 4:7–9

S top the work."

Kyla blinked in the darkness of her bedroom, struggling to comprehend
the words coming across the phone line. The jangling phone had jerked her
from sleep, and she grabbed at the receiver, fearing, as anyone does at a call
in the middle of the night, bad news from her family.

Instead, a low, threatening voice filled her ears. "Stop the work. Or we'll
have to stop you. Permanent."

"I…what?" Kyla pushed to a sitting position. "Who is this?"

Obscenities flew then, and Kyla jerked the receiver from her ear and
slammed it down in the cradle. She pushed back against her pillows, trembling, not just because of the foul words thrown at her, but also at the violence behind them.

She should have known this was coming. They were making real progress on the church, so it only made sense their opponents would resort to such tactics. But that didn't make it any easier to endure.

A soft mew drew her attention, and she scooped Serendipity up, holding her close, letting the cat's rumbling purr—and her own fervid prayers—replace fear with calm.

～∾

Progress. It was a beautiful thing.

Kyla studied the papers in front of her. Invoices, schedules that had been worked and reworked and…

Okay, so there had been a few delays.

More than a few.

Their two largest shipments of materials were delayed, though the companies couldn't explain why. One shipment just disappeared. "Lost," Kyla was told when she called for the umpteenth time to check on it.

"Lost?"

"Yup."

Apparently the company she'd called didn't hire folks for their scintillating conversational skills. "So…will a replacement shipment be sent?"

"S'pose so."

Drawing a deep breath, Kyla counted to two hundred. "I paid for expedited shipping on that order. I assume the company will absorb those costs and get this replacement to me ASAP?"

"Well, don't know if we can do that without knowing whose fault it is."

"Whose fault? Sir, it has to be on your end."

"How do we know that? How do we know it isn't there already?"

"If it were here, I wouldn't be calling you!" She sucked in some measure of calm.

"You never know, miss. Could be someone signed for it and just set it aside."

"Set it aside."

"Yup."

"An entire shipment of windows." Kyla wanted to pound her head on the desk.

The conversation went downhill from there. It took Kyla another fifteen minutes to get a supervisor on the line. And another half hour for him to figure out the issue and assure her the replacement shipment would go out that same day. ASAP.

At their expense.

What drove Kyla nuts, though, wasn't just that the shipments were messed up. It was that no one could offer any explanations. Just apologies.

Lots of apologies.

The first few had some calming effect. After hours upon hours with her ear glued to the phone—maybe Annie was right; maybe it was time to go Bluetooth—Kyla was certain if she heard one more "I'm awful sorry" or "I don't know how that could have happened," she was going to erupt.

She'd almost done so when one customer service rep, whose company did manage to deliver on time, but whose entire shipment of plumbing fittings was the wrong size. Another lengthy phone call revealed what they'd received was one letter off the unit number they'd ordered. When the rep finally figured it out, he spoke the words that almost pushed Kyla over the edge:

"You must have ordered the wrong thing."

Kyla squelched that almost the second the words came through the phone line.

Her people were the best. They checked and double-checked before orders went out. Especially on this job. Because they knew time was at a premium.

But now things were starting to click. They'd finally received almost everything they needed and the project was well underway. The floors, walls, and old ceiling were stripped from the sanctuary-cum-gymnasium. The walls between the upstairs classrooms were history, as was the old wiring. New insulation was in place, and they were all set to start putting in the new double-paned windows today.

And they were only a week behind schedule.

Normally a week's delay was no big deal. With this project it could have been disastrous. Had her crew been any less skilled, they'd never have made up that time. But her guys were amazing. They'd worked almost around the clock getting the building gutted, and now they were back on schedule. Almost.

At this point, "almost" was great. For the first time in days, Kyla felt as though she could breathe.

"The windows arrived."

Kyla looked up from her desk. If the dark cloud on her foreman's face meant anything, her relief was about to die a grisly death. "Dare I ask?"

Grant snorted. "They're all the wrong size."

She stared at him. She couldn't have heard right. "All of them?"

"Off by a quarter inch. Every last one of the da—" He caught the warning of her arched brow and clenched his teeth. "Dratted things."

Grant was a tough old bird. He'd been with the company since she was a teen. Knew all the workers by name, and despite his gruff exterior, treated people like gold. Kyla considered him one of JuCo's greatest assets. Sure, his language got a bit salty now and then. But he'd worked hard to restrain himself, knowing how much she—and her father before her—didn't care for vulgarities.

However, she had to admit she understood his desire to use stronger language right now. Too well. Kyla wasn't inclined toward obscenities, but more than once lately she'd wanted to scream. Really, really loud.

Instead, she held her hand out for the invoice.

"You gonna call 'em?"

She gave his bland question a nod. "I'm gonna call 'em."

"Sure you don't want me to do it?"

That brought her gaze to his. The man hated the phone as much as she detested technology.

"Company's based in Shy Town, right?" His face was a study in innocence. "I can be real persuasive."

Kyla's frustration gave way to laughter. "Let me guess. You're from Chicago. You know people."

"Uncle's a Gambini."

"Uncle who? Guido?"

He didn't even crack a smile, though she knew it had to take some serious effort to prevent it. "Close. Giovanni. He's a very tactful fellow."

"Only breaks bones that heal quickly, huh?"

"Miss Justice, you disappoint me. Such flagrant stereotypes don't become you." The pure delight in Grant's broadening smile belied his chastisement.

"Tell you what"—she lifted the phone receiver—"let me give it a shot. If they don't make this right, we'll call in the…cavalry."

He bowed his head, ever the gentleman. "I live to serve."

Question was, would those he dealt with while serving survive? Kyla didn't care to test the theory. Well. Not yet, anyway. But the next company that messed up an order or hit a snag in delivering on time?

She just might give good ol' Giovanni a call.

～

Mason got the call just before the end of the workday.

"You haven't stopped Kyla Justice."

Controlled fury singed Mason's ear. "Mr. Ballat, I never said I'd stop Kyla. I said I'd check into the situation."

"Perhaps"—the snide edge to the words set Mason's teeth grinding—"you've lost your edge with the good Ms. Justice—"

"Look. My relationship with Kyla is none of your—"

Ballat didn't even pause. "—considering the fact…" Now he hesitated, as though making sure he had Mason's full attention.

Which he did. Because Ballat sounded even more supercilious than usual. And that was not a good sign. "Yes?"

"Oh, nothing really. Just that there's another man beside her all day." The suggestion was as ugly as the smile he could hear in Ballat's slimy tone. "Close beside her. And Mason?"

"Yes?"

"She seems to like it that way."

THIRTY-THREE

"Better an honest enemy than a false friend."
GERMAN PROVERB

"Let him not deceive himself by trusting what is worthless, for he will get nothing in return."
JOB 15:31 (NIV)

Mason was well aware Sam Ballat was not averse to fabrication when it served his purposes. But to try and manipulate him with such a bald-faced lie? "Please. I've seen you use your inflammatory tactics too often to be influenced by them."

"Are you implying that I'm fabricating lies to get my way?"

"I know you are. There is no other man in Kyla's life."

"I see. Then you've been down to the construction site?"

Mason spread his fingers on his desk, letting the cool of the wood transfer itself to his temper. "Of course not. I'd never intrude on one of Kyla's projects. Not without an invitation."

"Ah. Which means you haven't received one? Don't you find that... intriguing?"

Mason's irritation perched on his lips—and halted. Kyla always told him he was welcome to come to her sites. He'd been so busy lately that he hadn't realized it was different this time.

Which, much as he hated to admit it, begged the question: Why? What made this job different from any of the others?

What...or who?

"You might want to check out your facts, Wright." Smug triumph oozed through the words. Then Ballat's tone hardened. "But you definitely want to do what you guaranteed. You said you'd take care of this situation. I depend on you to do what I need. If you can't take care of this woman, I'll find someone who can."

Ballat was a valuable client. One who brought him more work than any other.

But enough was enough.

"What you need is for this project to fail, correct?"

"Isn't that what I've been saying?"

Mason met belligerence with pointed logic. "Then that, Mr. Ballat, has been taken care of. Your focus, sir, is on that fact. Not"—warning seeped into his next words—"on Kyla Justice."

Silence met his assertion. Mason waited. Ballat was free and easy with threats. Well, this time he was the one who needed to understand. Nobody was going to "take care" of Kyla. Nobody but him.

"I see."

"I hope you do, sir. Because if anything happens to Kyla Justice, I will hold you accountable."

"Are you threatening me, Mr. Wright?"

Warning was evident in that low question, but Mason didn't flinch. "I am, indeed, sir. You and I both know how close we've come to the line of what's legal and what isn't. I haven't crossed that line." Mason let his implied message—You have—sink in. "As a professional, I've kept thorough documentation on all of our business ventures."

"All?"

Mason smiled. "All."

"I see."

Mason was sure he did. He'd have to be an idiot not to, and Sam Ballat was no fool.

"Well, Mr. Wright, I hear your message loud and clear."

"As long as that message is simply that you don't need to worry about this project, that's fine. You and I have been working together a long time, Mr. Ballat, you know you can count on me."

"I always have. I'll talk to you later."

Mason hung up, keeping his hand on the receiver, tapping one finger on the smooth black plastic. He'd just taken a risk that could either pay off—or ruin him. But that didn't concern him. Not nearly as much as Ballat's snide words about another man…

He stood, grabbing his suit coat off the coat tree on the way out his office door.

Time to see exactly what was going on with Kyla Justice.

THIRTY-FOUR

*"There are always uncertainties ahead, but there is
always one certainty—God's will is good."*
VERNON PATERSON

*"Though I am surrounded by troubles, you will protect me
from the anger of my enemies. You reach out your hand, and
the power of your right hand saves me. The LORD will work
out his plans for my life—for your faithful love, O LORD,
endures forever. Don't abandon me, for you made me."*
PSALM 138:7–8

Kyla Justice was amazing.

Rafe had known that for years, but this? He never would have believed it if he hadn't seen it with his own eyes.

He stood inside what used to be the church sanctuary, surveying the progress Kyla and her workers had made. The burnt-out parsonage was gone, replaced by the framing for a two-story office building connected to the old sanctuary. The sanctuary was getting ever closer to completion as well.

Justice Construction had accomplished more in just under one month than all the other contractors together had done in nearly seven.

"So, what do you think?"

Odd how the sound of her voice seldom surprised him. Then again, it wasn't odd at all. It made a world of sense. He heard it so often, anointing him in his dreams, resonating in his heart, it had become a part of him. He turned, taking in the welcome warmth of Kyla's smile. They hadn't spoken much the last few weeks. After that last blowup, they seemed to have reached a tacit agreement to avoid one another.

He was glad she'd decided it was time for that agreement to end.

Kyla came to stand beside him, looking up at the new twenty-foot ceiling now sporting shiny new vapor lights. The old flooring and walls had been removed. And today the beautiful stained-glass windows, which were slated to go in the office building, had followed suit. It was an amazing thing, the way the workmen removed the windows. Not one was damaged. They'd been wrapped, crated, and set at the back of the sanctuary, ready to be picked up tomorrow and taken to a secure storage.

Good thing. Those windows were over a hundred years old. They'd cost a fortune to replace.

"So?"

Rafe let his gaze drift from the room to Kyla. "You and your crew have done a great job."

Pleasure flooded her features. "Thanks." She surveyed the room in front of them. "They've really worked hard. You know something?"

"What's that?"

Her smile was one part relief, one part triumph. "I think we're going to make the deadline." She let out a long sigh. "Good thing too. I really wasn't ready for what I'd have to decide if we failed."

Rafe frowned at the low words, spoken almost as though to herself. "What you'd have to decide?"

"Oh." She turned to him, eyes wide, the proverbial child caught with a hand in the cookie jar. "Never mind."

The sudden red glowing in her cheeks stirred his curiosity even more. "But you said—"

"Did you hear that?" She stared over his shoulder.

He turned, studying the empty room. "Hear what? I don't hear anything."

"I don't know. I thought I heard someone call me."

Her pleased tone and easy shrug as she turned and started walking toward the exit were a dead give-away. Rafe shook his head. Of course. Distraction. He should have recognized it the minute she cut his question off.

In two long strides he was walking beside her. "So, you were saying?"

"Hmm. No one's come to pick up the windows yet? I'll have to give them a call."

Oh, no you don't. I'm not giving up. "About what was riding on getting done on time?"

"Hmm? What?" The wide eyes she aimed at him were the picture of confused innocence. Her hand was on the doorknob, pulling it open. "I'm sorry. Did you say something?"

His mouth opened on a pointed retort when the phone jangled. She grinned and hurried to pick it up.

Rafe leaned against the doorframe. "You could let the machine get it, you know."

The phone at her ear, she wrinkled her nose at him. "Kyla Justice."

With a muffled chuckle, Rafe waited for her to finish the call. She walked to the office window, looking outside as she talked. When she ended the call and set the phone in the base, he readied a new rally, but she held it off by speaking first.

"They're out there again."

He moved to stand beside her, following her now unsettled gaze. His own mouth tensed when he spotted the young men congregating across the street.

The Blood Brotherhood. Five or six of them. They weren't making any effort to hide the fact that they were watching the church.

Apparently Rafe wasn't the only one to notice the progress Kyla and her men were making.

Without thinking, he put a hand on her shoulder. "Don't worry, Kyla."

She turned to him, so close he could breathe in the fragrance of her hair. Those beautiful eyes looked up at him; worry weighted the edges of her brow. "How can I not? You know what they're capable of. If it's not sabotage, it's vandalism. Or threatening phone calls in the middle of the night."

"What?"

"They've been calling me. Almost every night now."

Every night? And he was just hearing about it now? "Why didn't you say something?"

"What could you have done, Rafael? Stay at my house every night?

Hover over the phone until they called? And then what? There's no way to prove who is making those calls. I finally just turned off the ringer."

Anger burned deep in his gut. "You shouldn't have to deal with something like that."

"I'm not nearly as worried about me as my men. I don't know if they can take another catastroph—"

His fingers against her lips stopped the rush of words. Whatever assurances he'd been about to give her fled his suddenly sluggish brain. The feel of her lips against his skin sent heat raging through him. He looked deep into those wide eyes of hers and saw the same blaze burning there.

His free hand moved up her arm, fingers trailing along the line of her neck, burying themselves in her silken hair. A multitude of rapid-fire sensations assaulted him—the feel of her, the sweet fragrance of her, the fact that she wasn't moving away—and all thought, all reason dissipated like a hapless fog in the Iraqi sun.

Her lips parted, and, eyes locked on hers, he lowered his head.

With a gasp, Kyla brought her hands to his chest, pushing away. "No!"

The word was ragged, a bare whisper, but it was enough. Because it contained something that held him fast.

Fear.

He had the strong sense, though, that the fear wasn't of him, but of herself. Regardless of the cause, he stepped back, hands falling to his sides.

"I'm sorry."

"No." She lay a trembling hand on his arm. "I'm sorry. I never should have…I mean, it was wrong of me…"

His hand settled over hers. "It's okay." He patted the back of her hand, making the action as patronly as he could. "We're both tired, we just got a little carried away, that's all."

He'd hoped his semiglib tone would put her at ease, but couldn't tell if it was successful. Probably better to leave and give her some time to work through whatever was troubling her.

He only hoped the whatever wasn't him.

"I'd better be going."

She swallowed. "I'll see you tomorrow?"

Was that hope hiding in those words? "Bright and early."

He waved good-bye, then turned and made his way back into the sanctuary. His footsteps echoed in the large room, the sound haunting. Lonely. He stepped up his pace. But no matter how fast he walked, he couldn't escape the realization gnawing at him.

Kyla Justice was drawn to him.

And that fact terrified her.

How did she let that happen?

Kyla leaned against the desk, watching Rafael's retreating back. She should have stayed the course. Continued forcing herself to head the other direction whenever she saw him. But she hadn't realized how much she missed being with Rafael, just talking. The fighting, now that she could do without. Still, when she checked to make certain she'd locked the door into the sanctuary today and saw him standing there, that thoughtful look on his face...

She just couldn't resist. She'd wanted to be with him. Talk with him. See his smile, the light in his eyes when he looked at her.

Wanted it more than she'd wanted anything in a very long time.

So, taking a risk that they could be in the same room together without irritating one another, she pulled the door open and went to stand beside him.

Well, the risk paid off. At least where irritating one another was concerned. But it had opened a whole new Pandora's box.

She picked up a pencil, drawing circles on a piece of paper as she recalled their lighthearted banter. She hadn't realized she'd spoken aloud when saying how relieved she was about meeting the deadline. Then, when Rafael asked her about it, well—mortified didn't begin to cover it. The last thing she wanted to do was tell him what she'd agreed to.

Because the more she thought about it, the more she realized how foolhardy she'd been to make such an agreement. If she married Mason—

If? Not *when?*

She clenched her teeth against the dratted questioning. If she married him, and if she quit JuCo, she'd do so for the right reasons. Because she loved Mason and wanted to concentrate on being a wife and mother. Not because she'd failed.

What about what happened in here tonight—?

Kyla pushed away from the desk. Nothing. Nothing happened.

Okay, then. What almost happened. And what about how relieved you are that you'll meet the deadline? Doesn't that tell you anything?

Of course it told her something. That she was a professional who wanted to do what the client needed.

Uh-huh.

She grabbed the paper she'd been doodling on and thunked it into the in-basket. This was silly. Her negative feelings about missing the deadline didn't have anything to do with marrying Mason. Of course not.

Yeah. Right.

"I love Mason."

Which is why you can't wait to get married, right? Why you were going to let another man kiss you?

Kyla clenched her teeth. Enough was enough. "I love Mason and I'm going to marry him!"

"Well, I'm happy to hear it."

She spun with a gasp. "Mason!" Her gaze flew past him, to the sanctuary. Relief filled her when she saw it was empty.

Mason's furrowed brow told her the reception she'd just given him was far from pleasing. She forced enthusiasm to her words. "I'm so happy to see you."

One neat brow lifted. "Indeed?" His eyes searched the office. "Who were you talking to?"

"Hmm?" She followed his gaze. "Talking to?"

"Just now, when you announced your undying love for me."

Ah. Yes. "No one." Okay, from the way his eyes were narrowing, that wasn't enough. "I just"—she looked around the room…no help there—"I just like saying it." Yes. Good. She'd go with that. She met his gaze and put on her most brilliant smile. "Out loud. I love you, I love you, I love you." She took his hand, hanging limp at his side. "See? Sounds wonderful, doesn't it?"

He stared down at her, and she felt shame heating her cheeks. One lean finger traced the line of her jaw, and then he gathered her to him, arms folding about her and holding her close. "I love you too."

Kyla closed her eyes against the sudden sorrow that assaulted her. Because she could tell from his voice that Mason meant it. Meant every word.

She pushed back from him, looking up into those blue eyes. "I don't deserve you."

An indulgent smile lifted his lips. "Perhaps not, but you've got me."

Tell him. Tell him you're not sure. Tell him you're confused. Tell him that he's not the man who occupies your thoughts, your heart—

"No!"

Mason started, then his arms fell away. He stepped back, studying her. "No?"

"I…" She rubbed her suddenly burning eyes. "I don't know." Could she feel any more miserable? "Mason, I—"

Gentle hands took hold of her fingers, pulling them away from her eyes. "Dear, you're exhausted. You've been working too hard. Why haven't you enlisted more people from the church to help you?" He studied her face, an odd light in his eyes. "Surely there are some men with the church who aren't octogenarians?"

The truth perched there, right on the edge of her lips, ready to set them both free. "I…no."

"No?"

Kyla, tell him.

"No." She lifted her head. "They're not all in their eighties."

He stiffened. "They're not?"

"No. Some of them…" *Just say it!* "…some of them are in their seventies." Defeat shuddered through her. She couldn't do it. Just couldn't bring herself to let go of what they had.

And what is that? Safety? Complacency? A so-called love that will never hurt you because you aren't passionate about it?

Passion. She'd had her fill of passion! What had it ever brought her but pain and the gut-wrenching knowledge that she was a fool? Passion. She wanted to spit the word out. Instead, she reached for her purse.

"How would you like to buy an exhausted woman dinner?"

Mason's gaze rested on her face for a few moments longer, then he bowed. "Of course, darling. It would be my pleasure."

Let others live and die for passion. Kyla didn't need it, nor did she want it. What she wanted was peace. Security. Stability. And a man who would give her all of that.

Which clearly was not Rafael Murphy.

THIRTY-FIVE

> *"God and devil are fighting,*
> *and the battlefield is the heart of man."*
> FEDOR DOSTOEVSKI

> *"In your strength I can crush an army;*
> *with my God I can scale any wall."*
> PSALM 18:29

"Serendipity, I swear, it's a good thing you're so cute."

Kyla glared at her cat from where she knelt on the carpet, cleaning up yet another mess the little scamp had made. The calico mewed, circling Kyla, alternately butting its head against her and rubbing its side along her.

"Shoo." Kyla waved a hand at the cat. "You're in my way."

With a final head butt, the young cat jumped up on the couch, grace personified, then folded herself into a sphinx position to watch her mistress, amber eyes blinking.

Kyla shook her head, and dipped the cloth into water, then dabbed at the carpet again, grateful there were cleaning products that worked as well as they did. Who knew cats made such disgusting messes?

Funny thing was, Kyla didn't really mind. Well, not now. She'd minded a great deal the first few times this happened, especially when she discovered one of these little treasures with her bare foot in the middle of the night. But as the weeks went on, she found herself less and less upset.

Amazing what love could do to one.

She pushed to her feet, gathered up the cleaning products and went to put them away in the cupboard below the sink. Serendipity bounced off the couch, dancing around Kyla's feet as she walked.

Kyla laughed, and leaned down to scoop her multicolored rascal up into her arms. This action was rewarded by a mighty purr—and another gentle head butt to her chin.

"You're crazy, you know that?"

Serendipity didn't argue.

Kyla grabbed her now-cool coffee from the counter, where she'd set it when she discovered the cat's little gift, and padded back to the couch. She settled on the cushions, legs curled beneath her, cat cuddled in her lap. Lifting the remote in her free hand—the other was occupied with scratching those velvety ears—she aimed it at the CD player and hit the power button.

Rachmaninoff filled the room with power and passion. Kyla closed her eyes and leaned her head back against the cushions.

At last. After all these months. The work was nearing completion. Her worries were no more.

She could finally relax.

~~

"Relax, Sarge. You need us there, we'll be there."

The confidence in Thales's voice tugged Rafe's lips into a smile. "How many of the guys are stateside?"

"Well, lessee. Last I heard, not too long ago, ol' Monroe and Jesse was trainin' at ARS in Coronado."

Amphibious Reconnaissance School. Rafe remembered it well. Of course, before a Marine reached ARS, he had to qualify. First there was the standard PFT. If the series of a three-mile run, sit-ups, and pull-ups didn't do him in, the Marine moved on to the pool. Decked in cammies and boots, the candidates went into the water for aerobics and underwater push-ups.

Then came the brick.

Rafe remembered how weary he was by that time. But weary didn't matter when you knew you were meant for Force Recon. So he led the others in diving after a ten-pound brick. He had his up and to the far end of the pool first. Oo-rah!

"Sabada's still running that martial arts school of his."

Rafe nodded. Sabada had left the service at the end of his last tour, six months after Rafe's injuries. That had surprised Rafe since Sabada had been in the Corps longer than anyone else in the unit.

"You sure you want to do this?" he'd asked his friend when he called Rafe to tell him what he planned.

"I'm sure. Time to focus on life, Asadi. Not death."

Rafe knew Thales was a Marine through and through. But he understood. Rafe had seen too much. Things he'd never forget, no matter how much he wanted to. Sabada? Rafe couldn't even imagine all he'd seen. And done. "What about Rashidi?"

"I'm not exactly sure, sir. I'm thinkin' he's still in-country."

"Thales, you outrank me now. What's with the sir?"

"Shoot, Asadi, you'll always be sir to me. And the other guys too."

Rafe knew his friend was right. Though most of the others from their unit had passed him up in rank these last few years, they still saw him as their unit leader. Always would. Just as he still saw them as the best of the best.

Always would.

"You want us out there now, Sarge?"

Did he? Rafe shook his head. "No, not yet. I just need you to be ready if I call."

"You got it. I'll call the team. Those who can will be ready."

"Thanks, Thales."

"Naw, Sarge, thank you." Rafe could hear the grin in the big guy's words. "Sounds to me like these yahoos deserve some serious pain, and I ain't put a good whompin' on anyone in too long. Comes right down to it, you doin' me a favor."

Rafe rang off, Thales's deep chuckle echoing in his mind. A good man. All good men. As solid and tough as it got. And when they got to town, one thing was certain.

The 22s would be very, very sorry they'd messed with Kyla Justice.

THIRTY-SIX

*"Those who will play with cats
must expect to be scratched."*
CERVANTES

*"Our enemies were saying,
'Before they know what's happening,
we will swoop down on them
and kill them and end their work.'"*
NEHEMIAH 4:11

Is someone messing around in the church?"

Fredrik paused, hand on the handle of his car door. He met Don's gaze in the darkened interior of his car. "Messing around? Why?"

Don's gaze was fixed past Fredrik, out the car window. "Maybe Miss Justice is still there, then?"

Fredrik turned, peering through the night at the church building. "She should be inside this late? I don't think so." He and Don had just arrived for their late-night walk around the church. They'd hoped that coming down every night would let any unsavory sorts know there was no opportunity for…for…

He frowned.

The church windows were dark, as they should be this time of night. Except for what appeared to be streams of light dancing around in the sanctuary.

"Flashlights."

Apprehension seized Fredrik's heart. Of course. It had to be. He reached into his coat pocket and pulled out his cell phone.

"You calling the police?"

"I'm calling the police."

Don nodded. "Good." His gaze traveled back toward the church. "Tell them to hurry."

~~⌒

He was always at church after dark.

But then, darkness was home as far as King K was concerned. It covered and sheltered. Even kept him alive a couple of times when rival gangs came after him.

He was too good in the dark for anyone.

So was his crew. The walls, covered with graffiti, proved that. So did the crates, riddled now with bullets and bits of pillow stuffing. King smiled. Pillows weren't great silencers, but they were good enough for this.

"He's gone be happy, like fo sho." The OG next to him grinned, one gold tooth shining in the darkness.

"Who you talkin' 'bout, Dancer?"

"Ballat. He said the work had to stop." Dancer's hand swept the room. "Well, it stopped cold now."

Killer's nod was slow. "True dat."

"We done good, word?"

"Word."

A high-pitched wail drifted on the night breeze, and King K lifted his head. Listened. Turned to Dancer. "Time to jet. Someone dropped a dime."

Dancer nodded. "Yo! Dip!"

Empty spray paint cans clattered to the ground and slammed against the walls as the 22s threw them, their hoots of laughter echoing in the room as they ran for the back door.

King hesitated. He wasn't ready to dip. Not yet. He waited, smiling when he heard the first of the cop cars scream to a halt outside the church. His fingers tightened on the piece stuffed in the back of his pants.

"C'mon, King! Popo gonna see you!"

The cops see him? Not in a million years.

The sound of heavy footsteps drew nearer.

"King!"

He spun, glaring at Chato. "Get out."

"But—"

King pulled his piece, aimed it right at Chato's stupid head. "You lookin' to die, Chato?"

He heard the boy swallow, watched him step back with slow, careful steps. "Jus' don' want you caught, man."

King's reply hissed through clenched teeth. "Ain't nobody catching me. Now get out or go down!"

Chato ran.

King turned back, listening. Voices sounded on the other side of the room. They were inside. He tipped his head back, closed his eyes, and waited. Listening. Footsteps sounded closer…closer. Then halted.

King smiled, opened his eyes. A cop stood not twenty feet away, the beam of his flashlight coming straight at King. With one silent motion, King slipped out the door, pressed his back to the wall, and stood to the side, out of sight.

"Hey! Was that somebody standing there?"

"Where?"

Lights shone through the doorway, dancing in the darkness, searching— but not finding. King wanted to laugh. Instead, he slid his piece into his pocket and slipped away, returning to the welcoming arms of the night.

THIRTY-SEVEN

*"We can't complain and whine about
where we're at. We've got to go forward."*
JOE RANDA

"Then the people of [God] began to complain..."
NEHEMIAH 4:10

Kyla hugged her arms around herself.

She couldn't breathe. Couldn't think. All she could do was stand there,
surveying the damage. The walls, the floor, the lights...all ruined. And the
windows. Those beautiful windows they'd been so careful to remove and
store.

Angry tears trickled down her cheeks, but she didn't wipe them away. She
let them flow, hoping—no, praying—they would wash the rage from her
heart.

Jesus, how could You let this happen? Where were You!

"Sholem aleykham, Kyla."

Peace be with you. How could Fredrik still say such a thing? Though the
words stuck in her throat, Kyla managed to force out the response: "Aleyken
sholem."

"Such a mess they made, heh?"

The only response she could muster was a nod.

His arm came around her shoulders, and she leaned into his strength. A
strength born of faith and endurance. Age couldn't take away from a strength
like that.

"I guess you need to call a meeting of the elders."

"I already have."

She wasn't surprised. Unfortunately, he was about to be. She turned to face him. "Fredrik, I can't replace what's been ruined here. I have enough to finish the work, but to redo it? To replace the fixtures and walls?" She shook her head. "I can't do it."

She waited for Fredrik's reaction, his disappointment. But he just stood there.

Smiling.

"Fredrik, are you listening to me? Did you hear what I just said?"

"Your father, he was a special man."

She blinked. "Yes, he was."

His aged eyes came to rest on her. "And he raised a special daughter. One with a heart of love."

Apprehension skittered though her. He wasn't making sense. Had this latest attack sent her beloved friend over the edge?

"But you know what I like best about you?"

She laid a hand on his arm. "Fredrik, come sit down. Maybe a nice drink of wat—"

"You're just as *eingeshparht* as your father was."

Eingeshparht? She knew she'd heard the word before, but couldn't recall what it meant. "Fredrik…"

He held up a hand. "No, don't deny it. You know it's true. Getting your father to do anything he didn't want to was like trying to get a donkey up a ladder."

Ah. Eingeshparht. "Yes, you're right. Daddy was stubborn. As stubborn as it gets sometimes."

"And you." His eyes were twinkling. "You share that side of him. And making you stop when you're determined?" He shook his head. "I should sooner get water from a stone. But it's good, this trait."

Now she was almost smiling. "It is, huh?"

"Because I'll tell you a secret. Me? I'm just as eingeshparht as your father. And as you." He looped his arm in hers. "These *schmegeges*? They think they can stop God's work?" He squeezed her arm. "They don't know us. And they don't know God."

The sound of approaching footsteps drew Kyla's attention. The elders walked toward them, necks craning as they looked first this way, then that, surveying the Blood Brotherhood's handiwork. Fredrik opened his arms. "Welcome, my friends. Come, let us talk together."

Without another word, Kyla fell into step with the elders as they all followed Fredrik into a room off the church office.

"I told you this was foolishness."

Such anger. Kyla hadn't expected that from these men. Anger and hopelessness.

Wayne slammed his fist on the table. "We should just give up and get it over with."

"Maybe Wayne is right." Steve leaned over his folded hands where they rested in front of him. "Miss Justice's resources have been strained, her workers are weary. I don't see how we can overcome this setback."

The furrows in Don's forehead deepened as he listened. "But does any of this mean God has released us from His call?"

His brother looked down at the pencil he'd been rolling between his fingers. An action Kyla recognized all too well as an attempt to release tension. "I don't think it does."

Kyla waited for Fredrik to jump in, but he just stood at the back of the room, expression serene. How could he stay so calm in the face of all this struggle? And how were these good men going to make the decision it seemed they had to make?

How could men like this abandon God's call?

How can you? Do low funds and short deadlines change the fact that God called you to this?

The thought stiffened her spine. But how could she continue? Was she supposed to go in hock to make this work?

Has the call changed?

Frustration surged through her. Of course it hadn't. But she couldn't do this! Her men couldn't do it. It was impossible. Fiscal suicide. Utterly cr—

"Crazy. That's what this is. Crazy."

Kyla started, and turned to Wayne, who seemed to be reading her troubled mind.

Wayne surveyed the men around the table. "Can any one of you give us a good reason for staying the course?"

Before anyone could respond, Willard laid his large hands on the table in front of him and pushed himself out of his chair. He stood there. Just…stood there.

One by one, the others fell silent. The stillness was jarring, and Willard let it continue for a good three or four minutes before he finally spoke. "I will praise the LORD at all times. I will constantly speak his praises. I will boast only in the LORD; let all who are helpless take heart."

The words struck Kyla's heart, colliding with her frustration. *Lord, I know all this. But come on—*

"Come, let us tell of the LORD's greatness; let us exalt his name together." Willard's gaze swept those gathered in the room. When his eyes came to rest on Kyla, her chest tightened, the ache so deep she wanted to cry out.

When the old man turned his gentle gaze from her, she almost wept her relief.

"I prayed to the LORD, and he answered me. He freed me from all my fears. Those who look to him for help will be radiant with joy; no shadow of shame will darken their faces."

No shadow of shame. Kyla closed her eyes. She couldn't remember the last time she'd been free of that shadow.

"Look, Willard, it's all fine and good to quote Scripture"—Sheamus's tone was as tight as Kyla's chest—"but we've got a serious problem here. What are we going to do?"

Willard considered the man, then went on. "In my desperation I prayed, and the LORD listened; he saved me from all my troubles. For the angel of the LORD is a guard; he surrounds"—he paused, letting his gaze touch each person—"and defends all who fear him."

Willard laid his hand on Sheamus's shoulder. "Taste and see that the LORD is good." He moved until he was behind his two sons, then laid his hands on their heads. "Oh, the joys of those who take refuge in him! Fear the LORD, you his godly people, for those who fear him will have all they need."

"What we need is money." Wayne's words were a plea. "And a good deal of it. Where are we going to get that?"

Willard's slow gait carried him to Wayne's side, and he looked down at the man he must have known for longer than Kyla had been alive. "Even strong young lions sometimes go hungry, but those who trust. In. The. LORD"—each word infused with strength, with a power that stemmed from the man's utter belief in them—"will lack no good thing."

"What you're saying has nothing to do with any of this."

Now Fredrik stepped forward, that same calm smile on his features. "Come, my children, and listen to me, and I will teach you to fear the LORD."

Willard took up the call. "Does anyone want to live a life that is long and prosperous? Then keep your tongue from speaking evil and your lips from telling lies! Turn away from evil and do good."

Fredrik's eyes rested on Sheamus. "Search for peace, and work to maintain it. The eyes of the LORD watch over those who do right; his ears are open to their cries for help."

This time it was Don who joined in. All hesitation, all doubt had fled. His voice was sure and strong. "The LORD hears his people when they call to him for help. He rescues them from all their troubles."

"The LORD is close to the brokenhearted"—Steve's mouth lifted in a rueful smile as he took up the chorus—"He rescues those whose spirits are crushed."

Von stood and went to his father's side. "The righteous person faces many troubles, but the LORD comes to the rescue each time"—they finished together, their combined voices ringing with such certainty that chills danced through Kyla—"For the LORD protects the bones of the righteous; not one of them is broken!"

"Please, brothers, listen to reason."

Kyla studied Wayne. He sounded almost desperate as he went on.

"Those thugs out there, they don't care about what Scripture says. All they know is what they want, and that's for us to fail. And you know as well as I that they'll do whatever they think they must to make that happen."

Willard walked to the window and looked across the street to where the gang members had been gathering to watch each day's work. "Calamity will surely overtake the wicked, and those who hate the righteous will be punished." He turned back to face his friends, and his voice rang out in the room. "But the LORD will redeem those who serve him. No one who takes refuge in him will be condemned."

The promise resonated deep within Kyla, leaving her both shaken and heartened. Whatever these men decided, she knew what she had to do. Willard moved back to his chair. He lowered himself, age evident in the movements, and yet as Kyla watched him she didn't see an old man. Rather, she saw a warrior. One who stood tall in the most fierce battle of all.

The battle to hold fast to faith.

Once again, silence reigned. But this time it wasn't because the elders were frustrated. Kyla could see on their features that they were pondering the words they'd just heard—words from the heart and soul of one who'd struggled as they had, to trust, to hold to God's call.

David was clearly a hero of the faith, and yet he'd fallen, time and again, to despair and fear. Oddly enough, Kyla found that comforting. But this man, this weak king chosen by God to placate a stubborn people, was considered God's friend.

Which meant there was hope for her.

But Lord, how am I going to do this? If I had months, I could do it. But all we have left is weeks! How can I do all that needs to be done in that amount of time?

She waited, hoping for an answer. None was forthcoming.

What did stir, though, was a soul-deep certainty. One that, in the face of reality, made no sense. But Kyla knew it was right.

Knew it was God.

Drawing in a deep breath, she let that knowing fill her with purpose. *Okay, Lord. I have no idea how I'm going to pull this off. But here goes.* "Gentlemen, I believe my path is clear."

Wayne looked up from his study of the tabletop. "What are you saying, Miss Justice?"

She stepped forward. "That God set me on this path, and until He—not the Blood Brotherhood, but God—directs me otherwise, I will continue."

"How?"

She met Sheamus's incredulous question with a shrug. "I have no idea. But you can count on this much. I'll do everything I can to make it work."

"What about the money?"

She turned to Wayne. "I'll take care of it."

"And the workers? You'll need more than you have now to make up time."

Sheamus was right, of course. She'd realized that. She just wasn't sure how she was going to deal with it. Still, she forced a confidence she was far from feeling into her assurance. "I'll take care of that, too."

"No."

Kyla's head came up and she fixed Fredrik with a hard stare. "What?"

He inclined his head, eyes kind but firm. "No, bubele. You won't take care of it. This is too much for you." She started to protest, but his next words stopped her. "But for God?" He waved a hand. "*Psheh!* All of this? It's nothing for God." His gaze held hers. "So we seek Him together, yes?"

Kyla looked around the room, then gave a slow nod. "Yes."

"*Gut!* Sit. We'll take this to Him together and seek His guidance. His provision."

Kyla did as her old friend asked, but even as she bowed her head, she knew. Prayer was fine, but it was going to take more than that to get this job done on time. It was going to take long hours of hard work. And while God would bless and guide them, He wasn't going to step down from heaven to oversee what had to be done.

No, that little task rested squarely in one person's lap.

Hers.

THIRTY-EIGHT

*"We are sisters. We will always be sisters.
Our differences may never go away,
but neither, for me, will our song."*
ELIZABETH FISHEL

*"We have sworn loyalty to each other in the
LORD's name. The LORD is the witness of
a bond between us and our children forever."*
1 SAMUEL 20:42

Her eyes had to be deceiving her.

Annie Justice stared at her computer screen, reading the e-mail again. True, she'd read it at least four times now, but it still didn't make sense.

An e-mail from Kyla that was not only long and detailed, but actually emotional? Annie glanced out her window, cocking her head to listen. It had to be coming. The trumpet sound heralding the end of the world. That was the only explanation. Kylie didn't emote in person, let alone in e-mail!

What was going on with her sister?

A long snout pushed at her hands where they rested on the keyboard. "Kodi, knock it off. I'm busy."

The snout landed in her lap this time.

"Kodi, come on."

The black shepherd pulled back and circled next to Annie's chair, wagging her head back and forth to show her displeasure. "Arrowww-row!"

Annie gave up. She hit the power button on the monitor and stood, grabbing Kodi's Frisbee as she walked out of her studio. Kodi danced along beside her, all delight now that she'd gotten her way.

Sending the Frisbee flying, Annie kept walking as Kodi raced after the disk.

"Hey, hon!" Jed waved at her from the doorway of her house. "Are you okay?"

Annie smiled. Amazing. He could read her so easily. "Not really, but how did you know?"

"Simple." He nodded toward the yard. "Kodi just made a great catch and you didn't even notice."

She came to stand beside him, leaning against him. "I got an e-mail that bothered me, that's all."

"About your sister."

"From her, actually."

His brows arched. "She wrote you a real e-mail. Not just one or two words added to a forward?"

"Right again."

"Look, why don't you give her a call? You've been wanting to for days now. It's time to just do it, even if she gets on your case for being worried about her again."

He was right. She wouldn't be happy until she talked with Kyla herself. She went up on tiptoe to plant a kiss on his cheek. "Thanks."

Jed tugged at a short strand of hair. "Any time."

It only took her a few seconds to dig her phone out and punch the speed dial. It barely rang twice before Kyla picked up.

"Annot, if you're calling to ask if I'm all right, just do us both a favor and don't."

Well. There was a happy greeting. "Hello to you too." Annie walked back outside, watching Jed, who'd taken over throwing the Frisbee for the inexhaustible Kodi.

The moment's silence told Annie she'd made her point. As did Kyla's apologetic tone. "You're right, and I'm a grouch."

Annie chuckled. "Agreed on both counts. Now tell me, what's happening with you?"

"Well, at least you didn't ask if I'm doing okay."

"Hey, I can learn."

"Hmm. As for what's happening here…"

Annie straightened. Her sister really didn't sound right. "Kylie?"

A heavy sigh drifted through the phone. "I don't know. Things have just gotten so…complicated."

Annie waited, and was glad she did. Because it was as if her normally reticent big sister had an emotional dam break. "We were making such great progress, you know? I told you about that last week?"

"Right—"

"And than wham! It's like God is delighting in putting obstacles in my path. And now, even with this disaster, we're supposed to move forward. I'm supposed to just keep on going, pushing myself and my workers to meet an absolutely impossible deadline—"

"Kylie."

"—with not enough men or supplies—"

"Kyla, hang on—"

"—or funds. It's insane!"

"Kyla!"

"What!"

Annie let out a breath she hadn't even realized she was holding. "You've lost me, Kylie. What obstacles? And what happened to your funds? I thought you had plenty for the job."

"We had visitors last night."

Annie didn't like the sound of that. Any more than she liked what Kyla went on to tell her. But it was what Kyla didn't say as much as what she did say that put Annie on alert.

Clearly, something was going on. Something beyond what Kyla was telling her.

"Anyway, I have an impossible amount of stuff to do in an impossibly short amount of time."

Annie knew better than to question, but she couldn't help herself. "You have to do it all?"

"No one else here can do it."

"But isn't there someone who can help—"

"Annot, please. I don't have the energy to argue with you. Just trust me on this. Now, I've got to go. I have I don't know how many more phone calls to make before I go for the day. I'll talk to you later."

Annie's good-bye was still perched on her tongue when the dial tone sounded in her ear. She stared at the receiver for a moment, then hit the Off button to disconnect the call.

"Problems with Kyla?"

Annie let her fingers trail along the receiver as she turned to face Jed. This call to her sister ended as almost all of them had over the last few weeks. With Kyla just a tad too vague, and Annie a tad too unsettled. "No…maybe." She tried to shrug her anxiety off. "I don't know."

"And that's bothering you."

She plopped down on the couch next to Jed. "Yes." No point in denying it. He could read her emotions better than anyone. "You know, Rafe and I have been friends for a long time." She managed a smile. "Kyla even said it was too bad he wasn't a couple of years older."

"Why?"

"So he could be my boyfriend. I informed her it would take more than a couple of years. When you're seventeen, five years is forever. You know what Kyla said to me?"

He slid his arm behind her, letting his fingers massage the back of her neck. "Something terribly logical, I'm sure."

Annie turned on her seat, facing him. "No, that's just it. She said, 'Love doesn't see age. It sees the heart.'"

Jed's mouth dropped.

Annie laughed. "I know, I know. Not the kind of thing you'd ever expect to hear from Sister-Mommy. But she was different back then. Softer. And then…"

Jed took her hand and gave it a gentle tug. "Then?"

Heart heavy, she settled back against the couch cushion. "That's just it, I don't know. Something happened. Something bad. But I haven't a clue what. All I know is Kyla was Kyla one day, and then she wasn't. She was harder. More controlled."

"Sister-Mommy."

Annie nodded. "Exactly. But lately, I've been getting glimpses of Kyla from back then. The softer Kyla. What's more, I think she's been getting those same glimpses"—she met Jed's tender gaze—"and it's scaring her silly."

Without a word, Jed rose and went to pluck the receiver from its cradle. He came back and held it out to Annie.

She looked from it to him. "What? I can't call Kylie back—"

"Not Kyla. Call your brother."

"My...?" Annie's head tilted. "Why?"

Jed sat on the couch beside her. "Look, you've been anxious for weeks now. And you've shared those concerns with Dan, right?"

"Right."

"You need to see your sister, hon, and I can't get away right now. But I'm willing to bet your brother is as ready for a drive north as you are." He held out her hand and dropped the phone receiver into her palm. "Call him."

Her fingers curled around the phone even as the truth in Jed's words curled around her heart. She hugged the phone to her chest.

"You call, I'll go get us some coffee."

Jed rose and headed for the kitchen as Annie settled into the corner of the couch. She dialed her brother's number, then dropped a hand to Kodi's broad head, her fingers scritching just behind the dog's ears, as she waited for Dan to answer. "You ready for a visit to Auntie Kylie, Kode?"

The dog's thumping tail was all the confirmation Annie needed.

Twenty minutes later, it was all arranged. Dan would pick her and Kodi up first thing tomorrow morning. Annie's heart was lighter than it had been in weeks. Maybe even months.

"All set?"

Annie set the phone aside and accepted the hot mug of coffee Jed held out to her. She waited until he was situated beside her, then leaned into the curve of his arm, resting her head against his solid shoulder. "I'm so lucky I have you."

His lips caressed the side of her face. "And don't you forget it."

As if she ever could.

THIRTY-NINE

*"Your willingness to wrestle with your
demons will cause your angels to sing."*
AUGUST WILSON

*"Suppose you make a foolish vow of any kind,
whether its purpose is for good or for bad. When you
realize its foolishness, you must admit your guilt."*
LEVITICUS 5:4

Rafe hadn't heard a sound like this in a long time.

Not since the last time Olivia was furious with him.

But frequency didn't matter. Once you'd heard that sound, you never forgot it. The clear, unmistakable tones of a woman in total meltdown.

"I don't *care* if it's impossible."

The furious words scorched the air as he walked across the floor of the new gymnasium.

"I'm the customer; you are the supplier. If you want to continue doing business with Justice Construction, you will give me what I need when I need it!"

At the sound of a receiver being slammed back in the cradle, he stepped into the office. Kyla sat at the desk, head in her hands.

It took all his will to not cross the room and pull her into his arms.

"Bad day?"

She lowered her hands with a start, eyes wide. "Oh! Rafael. I didn't hear you come in."

His gaze rested on the phone. "You were occupied."

Pink bloomed on her smooth cheeks and she leaned back in her chair. "I was pretty awful to them. They didn't even deserve it. I just..." She rubbed at the back of her neck with one hand. "Yes. It's been a bad day."

"Seems you've had quite a few of those this week."

Something in her features seemed to harden. "There's just a lot to do. And I'm doing the best I can to take care of it all."

"You. By yourself."

This time there was no mistaking the anger in those beautiful eyes. "Now, don't you start."

Before he could ask what she meant, Kyla stood and brushed past him, shoving the office door open and going into the old sanctuary. Rafe caught the door with his cane, pushed it open, and followed her.

"Look at this place! It's still a mess, and I've got just over two weeks to get everything done."

"You do."

She spun to face him. "Yes! I do. God called me to this. I have to see it through. Even though it's going to cost me everything."

"You really think God wants that? For you to lose all you've worked so hard to build?"

Something flickered in the depths of her eyes—something more akin to fear than anger—and then it was gone. "I have no idea what God wants!" She waved her hands. "All I know is I'm supposed to do this job."

"Are you sure that's what God called you to? Finishing a job? What if it's more than that?"

Her gaze narrowed. "What do you mean?"

He lifted his cane, sweeping it in an arc, indicating the room around them. "What if God's call has nothing to do with this project? What if it's more about you. Your heart. Your ability"—he pinned her with a hard look—"or lack thereof, to trust."

"Trust? How can you say I don't trust?"

"Do you think it's trusting to try and do everything yourself?"

Kyla squared her shoulders. The woman was ready for a fight. "I think God has other things occupying his attention. Sure, building a youth center, especially in a neighborhood like this, is important. But what is that compared to children starving? To people dying from AIDS?"

"God cares, Kyla. Big problems or small ones, He cares."

"Well then, where is He?" The fact that she'd raised her voice didn't bother him half as much as the desperation he heard in her tone. "I don't see Him stepping in to stop the 22s."

"I wouldn't be so sure about that."

"Don't you *get* it, Rafael? This has to be done! And I'm the one who has to do it."

"Why?"

She froze, mouth hanging open. *"Why?"*

"You heard me." He wasn't backing down. "Why?"

"Can *you* do this job?"

He ignored the sarcasm in her tone, making his reply calm and level. "No."

"Can any of the elders? Fredrik? Willard?"

"No."

She crossed her arms over her chest, chin lifting. "Then please, tell me, who will do it if I don't?"

He took in her posture, the emotions on her expressive features that betrayed her, though he was sure she didn't realize it. She probably thought she was as controlled as always. "Must be tough."

Kyla tensed. "What?"

Rafe gentled his tone, but didn't hold back the bald truth. "Thinking you have to take everyone's problems on your shoulders and handle them. Alone."

She gave an angry huff, lowering her arms. "Yes, well, that's how it is. How it's always been."

"Not always."

Kyla hesitated, her eyes searching his face. A slight pucker tugged at her brows, and for a heady moment he thought she knew. Thought she remembered. Realized who he was.

But then she turned away. "Always."

So much contained in that one word. Hopelessness. Despair. The echo of a little girl lost in the dark. He longed to go to her, to comfort her. But he couldn't. For her sake as well as his own. "Kyla, do you really think God has called you to bring this about yourself? What about all the others? The neighbors? Businessmen in the town? How do you know He hasn't called any of them to be involved?"

She kept walking back toward the office, tossing her sarcasm over her shoulder. "Of course! Why didn't I think of that. Oh—because they're nowhere to be found!"

He followed her back into the office. "Have you called any of them?"

She sat down and grabbed the phone. "I really don't have time to deal with this, Rafael."

He laid his hand over hers, where it clutched the receiver like a lifeline in a storm-tossed ocean. "No. What you don't have is the time to *not* deal with it." Before she could let fly with the anger he knew was building, he went on. "Think about it, Kyla. You know the construction community. Are there any other construction companies in town that might possibly be willing to help?"

She stared at their hands for a moment, then finally looked up at him. "Maybe."

The hint of concession, grudging though it may be, energized him. "Then call them." He stopped her refusal with a raised hand. "Just one call. To someone you really think might help. Lay it all out—everything that's at stake—and see what happens." He pulled his hand away from hers. "Make that call, Kyla, and if they refuse, I'll back off."

Interest sparked at that. "You'll back off?"

"All the way."

She lifted the receiver. "You're on."

Rafe stepped back. Curiosity nudged at him when she hit a speed-dial button. She had a competitor on speed-dial?

"Mason, hi. It's Kyla"—her gaze drifted to Rafe—"Kyla Justice, of Justice Construction? Right, I'm fine. Thanks for asking. Listen, I have a question for you."

Rafe left the office, then pulled up one of the old metal folding chairs and sat down, massaging his leg. Better to give her some privacy than hover like some kind of vulture.

At the sound, a few minutes later, of the door opening behind him, he turned. The frown on her face wasn't encouraging, but he asked anyway. "So?"

She didn't answer. Just stood there, seemingly lost in thought.

"Kyla."

Still no response.

He pushed out of the chair and started for the office.

"Where are you going?"

"To hit redial on the phone and ask the guy myself what he said."

"Okay, okay."

Rafe turned to face her, and he could tell she had no desire to say whatever it was she had to say. "You were right."

He tried to restrain the grin. Really he did.

"He agreed to help. Said it was an important cause, and he'd be happy to contribute materials and workmen. Even funds, if we needed." She swatted his arm. "Stop looking so smug!"

Rafe held up his hand. "Sorry. I was trying not to gloat."

"Yes, well, you were doing a lousy job. Besides, Mason is my…a friend of mine. So of course he'll help. But even with what he'll bring to the project, it's not going to be enough."

"Miss Justice."

Kyla and Rafe both turned. It was the church elders. Walking toward them with what seemed to be very definite purpose. Kyla went to meet them.

"Hello, Don. Von. Gentlemen. What can I do for you?"

"The question is"—Steve slid his hands into his pockets—"what can we do for you?"

Rafe cocked his head. This should be interesting.

"Do for me?" Kyla looked from one man to the other. "I'm not sure I understand."

"Well, ma'am," Von's easy drawl held a hint of humor, "it's like this. We've been talking, and we've all agreed. You won't have to deal with any more problems"—he looked at the walls, which still bore signs of the graffiti—"like this."

"I won't?"

Don joined the conversation. "No, Miss Justice. You won't. Because we're going to stand watch. 24/7. We're going to patrol the area and, if need be, protect it." He nodded toward her. "And you."

Kyla stared at the man as though he'd suddenly turned green and sprouted an eye in the middle of his forehead. "Protect me."

"That's right." This from Wayne. "You may not know it, Miss Justice, but we were all in the service at one time or another. Proud to do so, you know. To stand for this country and freedom."

Rafe's grin grew. He liked these men more and more every day.

"So we're going to put our training to use."

Rafe looked beyond the elders and saw Sheamus just coming to join them.

Von nodded at his friend, then leaned toward Kyla. "Just call us the Silver Squad."

Kyla tossed a plea over her shoulder, but Rafe just smiled. She might not think these men could handle the kind of trouble that most likely was headed their way, but he knew otherwise. Age might slow the reflexes, but it brought something to the table that was far more important.

Experience. And an understanding of human nature.

Besides, he'd felt the grips these men still had whenever they shook his hand. These guys might be a bit beyond their prime, but Rafe would hate to go head to head with them. In a fair fight, they'd be odds-on to come out on top.

Of course, the Blood Brotherhood wasn't exactly well known for fighting fair.

Rafe moved to stand beside Kyla. "Well, gents, sounds pretty good. But I think there's actually something else you can do that might be of even more help than patrolling."

The elders gathered around Rafe and Kyla, and Don nodded. "You just tell us what you need."

Rafe looked from them to Kyla, who struggled between relief and confusion. He smiled. She wasn't going to like this, but...

"Miss Justice was just getting ready to put together a list of folks to call, to ask if they can help us out."

"Folks?"

"That's right, Wayne. Professionals she knows in the construction field."

"Now that's a good idea."

The others echoed Von's approval.

"So, when Kyla gets that list put together, which she'll do right away"— he tossed her a "won't you?" look, and she had the grace to nod—"if you gents will take to the phones, that will be a great help."

"We can do that." The wheels in Steve's mind were turning already. "You've all got your cell phones, right?"

Wayne huffed. "You *said* to bring them so we could call 911 if we needed to."

"Okay, then, let's go get the meeting room set up as a call center."

The men moved away, their excitement palpable in their animated discussions and straight backs. When they were out of earshot, Rafe leaned his head toward Kyla.

"*This* is what you can do that no one else can."

"What?" She didn't look at him, and Rafe had the sense that was because she was struggling with her emotions.

"You know the right people to call. You know what's needed and who can supply it. And"—he took hold of her shoulders, turning her to face him—"you can let a group of men who have spent their lives serving God know that you need them. Because you do. Get your list together, Kyla"—he smiled—"and let the Silver Squad have at it."

She held his gaze, but only for a moment. Then she looked down. "You really think this will work?"

"I really do."

With a slow nod, she stepped back from him and headed back toward the office. "I'll have the list in a half hour at the most."

She wasn't happy letting go of this. Shoot, this woman wasn't happy letting go of any little bit of control in her work. But that was okay. Because Rafe was as certain as he'd ever been that she was doing the right thing. No matter how much she didn't want to.

FORTY

He didn't want to think about what he'd just done.

Mason's fingers tapped an uneasy cadence on his desk. He'd been confused at first, what with the way Kyla identified herself. Like a stranger. But he'd heard the plea in her tone, and that held off the questions he wanted to ask.

Then she told him why she called.

Excuses raced through his mind. Everything inside urged him to say he couldn't do anything. That he didn't have men available. That there was no money for such things. That—and this was the one that finally did him in—it wasn't ethical to get involved in her project.

Ethical.

The word stuck in his throat.

It wasn't until he spoke that he realized he was going to help her. But the minute he said he would, he knew he meant it. Not because it was Kyla.

But because it was the right thing to do.

It was about time he reminded himself what that was like. Doing the right thing.

He looked at the phone for a moment, thinking. But there was no denying what he had to do next.

Lifting the receiver, he punched in the number. The answer was swift.

"Ballat here."

"Mr. Ballat."

"Ah, Mr. Wright. I hope you're calling me to confirm all is as I requested."

It's not too late. You can still back out. Call Kyla back and say you were mistaken. Don't burn this bridge!

Mason flicked a torn piece of paper from his desk. "No, sir. I'm afraid not." His voice grew stronger, more certain as he went on. "I don't think there's any way to stop Kyla Justice."

"Is that right?"

Normally the threat in those quiet words would have given him pause. But now? It just made him smile. "No sir. You see, she's enlisted help."

"Help?"

He was flat-out grinning now. "Yes sir. From me."

"Help?"

"Yes. From me. And Rawlins Building."

"I see. So. Fiancée trumps long-standing customer, eh?"

"I'm afraid so."

"Well, I won't say I'm pleased. But I do understand. I've been in love a time or two myself."

Mason didn't comment. He just bid Ballat good-bye—aware he was doing so to the business the man had brought his way all these years.

Oh well. It was time for a change.

Although…that call was a good deal easier than he'd expected. In fact, it was too easy.

Could it be…?

No. Mason shook his concerns from his mind. Ballat might bend the rules. He might even break them once in a while. But hurt Kyla to keep the job from completion?

Ballat would never go that far.

Not if he knew what was good for him.

~~~

Well. Mr. Wright had become Mr. Wrong. All because Mason Rawlins had his limits. Who knew?

He'd just have to contact someone who didn't share Rawlins's compunctions. He flipped through his Rolodex, then dialed the number.

"Hello?"

"It's time."

A rustle of sounds came over the phone, and it was a few seconds before the man spoke again. "I *told* you not to call me on my cell!"

"Yes, well. You shouldn't have given me the number, then. I take it you can't talk freely."

"Of course not." The voice dropped to a hiss. "I'm at the church!"

"Then I won't keep you. But know this, my friend. You came to me. I've given you guarantees of very healthy returns provided you deliver on the promises you made."

"I know that. Listen, I have to go. They're looking at me—"

"You have to go after Kyla Justice."

The lack of response told Ballat this might take some convincing. He picked up a pencil, rolling it between his fingers, waiting. Let the weasel get his thoughts together.

"Are you sure that's necessary?"

Ballat snapped the pencil in two. "Positive."

"How far do you want me to go?"

Hmm. Intriguing question. "What do you mean?"

"Do you want her just frightened? Or out of the scene entirely?"

"I want her stopped."

"So you're authorizing violence?"

The man was a fool. Ballat made a mental note to dispose of him once this ugly affair was over. "I don't want details, you idiot. I just want her *stopped.* Do we understand one another?"

"Perfectly."

"I hope so. Or your fifteen minutes of fame will be for some very unpleasant reasons." Ballat ended the call, grabbed up the pieces of the pencil, and threw them into the trash.

One way or another, this was over. Kyla Justice. Those old fools at the church. The man with the cane. Even Mason Rawlins. He'd take them all out if he had to.

Whatever it took to make it clear.

This stubborn, stupid church was done.

FORTY-ONE

"When we are afraid we ought not to occupy ourselves with endeavoring to prove that there is no danger, but in strengthening ourselves to go on in spite of the danger."
MARK RUTHERFORD

"They will come from all directions and attack us!"
NEHEMIAH 4:12

It was done. Fifteen minutes, and he was inside Kyla Justice's home. Shouldn't have taken more than five, but some old coot was outside, walking a white puffball of a dog. At least, he figured it was a dog. Looked more like some kind of mutant hamster. Either way, the old fool took his time, letting the little rat sniff every bush along the walkway. Watching the slow progress, he'd almost lost patience, but calmed himself by lifting the gun and fixing his sight on the rooting runt.

By the time man and puffball finally passed by, he'd nailed the midget a dozen times. In his mind, of course, but that was sufficient.

Once the coast was clear, he made his way to the fence bordering the town house's backyard. Scaling it was a cinch, and within moments he was at the back door. He'd already checked to see if the Justice woman had any kind of electronic security. She didn't, which had pleased him enormously. He loved it when his marks made his job easy.

Getting inside held no challenge. He just slipped the torque tool into the deadbolt, inserted the pick, and within seconds had the pins set. The lock slid open, as obliging as a sycophant at the feet of a rock star.

He eased the door open, then slipped inside.

All was calm. Silent.

Perfect.

Thanks to waiting for the old guy and his so-called dog to pass by, his eyes were accustomed to the dark. He took his time walking through the silent rooms, picking up a knickknack here, moving a photo there. Nothing too obvious.

Just enough to let her know he'd been there.

He loved this part of the job. Planting fear was such a personal thing. Had to be tailored to each mark. What made one person edgy might not even faze another. So he always made sure to study his prey, to know them inside and out.

Kyla Justice, for example, was a neat freak. A place for everything, and everything in its place, as his mother used to say. The thought of his mother brought a smile. He'd practiced his skills on her long before he even knew what he was doing. All those little pranks, moving things from where they "belonged," pushing pictures just a fraction crooked on the wall, spilling just enough granules of salt on the table to irritate the subconscious…

His smile widened. He could still see his mother's features, the furrowed brow, the clenched jaw, the glaring eyes. She never did figure out it was him doing it. She just thought she was losing it.

Kind of amazing when you thought about it. His talent far excelled anything others claimed. Born to be wild? Child's play. Born killer? Too messy. Let others embrace those clichés. No, he thought as he lifted a photo from the top of the TV—the shot was of Kyla Justice, a younger woman, and a large black dog. His was a talent of distinction.

Born to torment.

He smiled, setting the photo down on the bookcase next to the television.

Silent as the shadows, he traveled from room to room, making his tiny adjustments, saving the best for last. Finally, it was time for his favorite.

The bedroom. Where she, even as he walked toward the door, slept.

Turning the doorknob always made his heart accelerate. Every knob was different. You could never tell for sure what was too fast or too slow, what would send a loud click echoing into the silence, spoiling the game.

Easy…easy…

Relief flowed as the door slid open without a sound. He stood for a moment, listening. Kyla Justice's breathing was low and even. The sleep of innocence. He almost hated to disturb…

Almost.

Stepping into the room, he moved on feet well trained in stealth, heading for the bathroom. Opening that door was even more nerve-racking—and even more satisfying when he did so successfully. He took his time here, smelling her shampoo and then her perfume as he traded their locations. He resisted the urge to open the medicine cabinet. Too much risk there. Even someone as organized as Kyla Justice could have a messy medicine cabinet. Opening that could bring any number of things tumbling down. No, as much as he'd like to get inside it, he'd best leave it be. He didn't want to risk alerting her too soon.

Because that, he thought as his gaze traveled to the door, would spoil all his fun.

Back in the bedroom, he paused, savoring the moment. Then, with slow and careful steps, he made his way to the side of her bed. He stood there, looking down. His gaze followed the line of her face in the darkness, then traveled lower. The sheets moved up and down with each easy breath.

Oh, the beauty of the human form in repose. So relaxed, so at peace.

So in his control.

He lifted a hand, let it flow, an inch or so above her, along the shape of her body beneath the covers. He didn't touch. Never touched. That was uninspired. Loutish. No, it was far more exciting to stir the subconscious. To get just close enough to spawn a subtle awareness, a vague unease.

He crouched, bringing his face within inches of hers. Watched, heart leaping, as his breath caressed her hair. Moved a strand just a fraction. He closed his eyes, let himself luxuriate for just a moment in the act of creation.

In these moments, he was god. Master. Creator. Almighty. All-powerful. He breathed, and fear lived.

But he gave himself only a moment to savor. Any longer and he'd miss it. Miss seeing his creation come to life. So his eyes opened, and he watched. Breathed a second time on her smooth face. Watched, seeking…

There! Subtle, but real all the same. Kyla Justice's breath caught. Her eye movement shifted. And then he saw it. The very moment awareness tugged at her, even through the folds of sleep…

Saw it…and smiled.

Kyla's eyes flew open.

She flailed in the sheets, pushing herself to a sitting position. Back against the headboard. Fingers digging in the blanket.

What…?

She blinked, trying to see in the darkness of the room. Her hand finally released the blanket and reached for the light. Tapped the metal, and drew a grateful breath as light sprang to life.

Nothing. There was nothing there. She frowned. She'd had such a strong sense…as though someone was there, standing over her. She pulled her knees to her chest, listening.

No sound reached her.

A sigh escaped her, relief tinged with frustration, and she let herself relax and slide back under the covers. She'd leave the light on, just for a bit.

Just enough to dispel whatever had invaded her dreams.

He amazed even himself.

His timing was impeccable. He'd stepped back, easing out of the room just as she stirred. Heard her panic as she fought the sheets. Reveled in the sound.

He was a conductor, guiding her in a symphony of fear. And she was playing the piece to perfection. Now, though, was the tricky part. While she was awake. Aware. Listening even when she wasn't conscious of doing so.

Now was the time to bring her panic to a crescendo. To let her know he was there. That she was not alone. Was not safe.

Now was the time he relished most.

It had taken awhile, but her breathing was finally slowing down. Silly how worked up one got because of a dream. But it had seemed so real…

I swear, I'm getting as fanciful as Annot.

Shaking her head at herself, Kyla turned onto her side and curled around her pillow, her eyes drifting shut as she burrowed deeper under the covers. If there was one thing she hated, it was waking up when she didn't need t—

Her eyes flew open. What was *that?* A soft sound. Muffled.

Was that a *footstep?*

Heart pounding, Kyla threw back the covers and perched on the edge of the bed, hugging herself, arms a barrier between her and whatever she'd heard. Whatever—or *who*ever—was out there.

A quick glance around the room confirmed she was alone. And that didn't seem right. But why—

Oh.

Of course.

A shivery laugh washed over her. The cat. The cat wasn't in her spot, on the pillow next to her. She looked to the bathroom door, and frowned again. She was sure she'd closed it.

Right. And the cat opened it? Come on. She's not that clever.

Letting go another sigh, she slid from the bed. Best to corral the critter and get her back into the bed. No telling how much trouble the silly thing could cause roaming free.

She took hold of the bedroom doorknob, then froze. That door, too, was open. She *knew* she'd closed it. Remembered doing so.

Kyla tried to swallow, but her mouth was suddenly as dry as sawdust. Her voice lodged, trapped by the fear that had suddenly dug its claws into her chest. Breathing erratic, she pushed the door open and stepped out into the next room.

"Hello?"

The word sounded like a mix between a croak and a cough. Kyla cleared her throat and tried again. "Is…is somebody there?"

Idiot! What will you do if someone says yes? Go back in the bedroom and call the police!

A reasonable suggestion, but Kyla couldn't get her feet to obey. Because as she peered into the dark room, she realized someone was there. A form, silhouetted against the drapes over the french doors that led to the backyard.

A man.

Kyla felt a scream crawling past her fear, scrambling toward freedom. But before it could escape, two things happened at once. The form took a step toward her—and something from behind the form flew screaming out of the darkness.

She just caught a glimpse of white, black, and tan leaping from the top of the draperies, and then, with a screech so unearthly it chilled her to the bone, the dervish was on the man's head.

The man bellowed rage and pain, slamming back into the french doors. The draperies went flying, and another screech tore through the room. The bedeviled man grabbed at his attacker even as he fumbled with the french doors. Kicked at the bar holding them fast.

Then, suddenly, the doors were open—and the man was gone.

Gasping, still barely believing what had just happened, Kyla slapped at the wall switch behind her. Light flooded the room and her eyes widened as she realized what had attacked her invader.

There, on the floor, still spitting fury, legs stiff, hair puffed out like a demented porcupine, was Serendipity. Kyla ran to the cat, scooped her up, and pressed her to her chest. She half expected her to sink angry claws into her, but instead she just leaned against her, that deep purr rumbling in her chest, and bumped her head along her jaw.

Kyla could swear she was asking if she was okay.

Shaking so hard she almost couldn't stand, she shoved the french doors closed and slid the lock into place. Then she forced her trembling legs to carry her through the house, double-checking each door. She sank onto the couch and buried her face in soft fur. Several gasping breaths later, reason returned. Cradling Serendipity in one hand, Kyla grabbed up the cordless phone from the coffee table and punched in 911.

"Nine-one-one, what's your emerg—?"

"There was a man in my home!"

"Was? Is he still there?"

"No." Suddenly she was crying. Great heaving sobs. "No, my cat attacked him. She scared him off. I mean, I know it sounds crazy, but…" She wiped at her streaming eyes. "Please, please just send someone."

The woman's assurances that a squad car was already on its way were confirmed by the distant wail of a siren. The woman stayed on the line until a heavy pounding sounded on Kyla's front door.

"Ma'am, the officers are there now. Go let them in, and then I'll hang up."

Kyla stood, not entirely certain her legs would support her. But they did, and she made her way to the front door. She pulled it open, and the two officers standing on her stoop were as welcome a sight as she'd ever seen. Thanking the woman dispatcher, she hung up—and promptly burst into tears.

An hour and a half later, Kyla was once again alone in her apartment.

Well, not entirely so. Her protector was there, too, weaving in and out between Kyla's feet, purring up a storm.

Looking down at the now-content kitty, Kyla would never have imagined it could turn into a whirling dervish of claws and yowls. The memory of the police officers' faces when Kyla explained what Serendipity had done still made Kyla smile. But traces of blood on Serendipity's paw and on the curtains bore mute testimony to the cat's prowess as a protector.

Kyla lifted the cat to her lap, giving those soft ears a gentle scratch. "Looks like God brought you to me for a reason, huh?" Serendipity leaned into her fingers, purr going double time. "Well, I think you deserve a treat."

Scooping the cat into her arms. Kyla went to pull the container of cream out of the fridge. She filled a bowl, then set it and Serendipity on the floor. The cat didn't hesitate. She started lapping up the cream with gusto.

Kyla leaned her elbows on the kitchen counter, watching Serendipity, pondering the night's events. If only she could have seen who her intruder was, but she never got a clear look at his face. Of course, the fact that police found graffiti sprayed on the outside walls of her home was a pretty telling clue.

Kyla had gone outside with them to see the images. The number 22 was everywhere, along with other numbers she didn't understand.

"Looks like gang tagging to me. Some kind of warning." He nodded toward the spray-painted image in front of them. "The *22* refers to the gang itself, the—"

"The Blood Brotherhood," Kyla supplied.

The officer glanced at her, interest in his blue eyes. "You know them?"

Kyla looked down. As much as she wanted the police to help, she didn't want them linking her with the gang. Last thing she needed was a leak to the media about all of this. Neither she nor JuCo needed that kind of sensationalistic press.

When she met the officer's eyes, she schooled her features into the epitome of innocence. "I believe they're a gang on the northwest side of town. A friend of mine attends a church in that area, and he's mentioned them to me."

"Hmm." The officer looked less than convinced, but apparently decided not to push. Good thing. After all, *she* was the victim here! "Those other numbers? They're from the Oregon penal code."

Kyla frowned. "The penal code."

"Yup. The codes for breaking and entering, and murde—"

"Jensen."

They both turned at the warning tone. The other officer, clearly the elder of the team, was frowning at his younger partner. "Let's not trouble Ms. Justice with unnecessary details tonight."

Red tinged the man's cheeks when he turned back to Kyla. "Oh. Right. Sorry, ma'am. I didn't mean to frighten you."

Kyla waved her hand. "I'd say the intruder did that far more than anything you could say, officer."

Pushing away from the counter, Kyla went to pull coffee from the cupboard. No way she was going to get any more sleep tonight. As she readied the coffee maker, she thought about the graffiti.

So, the 22s had left her a warning. The more she thought about that, the angrier she got.

Who did these people think they were? First the phone calls, and now breaking into her home, terrorizing her. She slammed a coffee cup down on the counter.

"Enough is enough!"

Spinning on her heel, Kyla marched to the phone, picked it up, and jabbed in a number. It was picked up on the second ring.

"Hello?"

She'd expected a sleepy voice. But Rafael didn't sound as though he'd been any more asleep than she was. "I have something to tell you."

There was a pause. "Kyla?"

"Yes, it's Kyla." Her heart pounded out a furious beat. "I want you to go tell your pals that it's not going to work."

"My pals? What pals? What are you—"

"Your gang buddies. The Blood Brotherhood. The 22s. The Dippity-Dos, for all I care. You tell them I'm not backing down."

"The 22s are not my pals."

"Look, I don't need to hear your denials. You just let them know I don't scare off. I've taken this job and I'm going to complete it. On time!"

"Kyla, what on earth—"

She slammed the phone back in its cradle.

When it rang a few seconds later, she turned her back on it and strode back to bed.

FORTY-TWO

"The truth is sometimes the funniest joke in the world."
GEORGE BERNARD SHAW

"Then everyone who has eyes will be able to see the truth,
and everyone who has ears will be able to hear it.
Even the hotheads will be full of sense and understanding."
ISAIAH 32:3–4

Rafe's back was up.

He knew it, just as he knew he shouldn't go to the construction site until he cooled off.

Tarik looked up from his bowl of cereal when Rafe walked into the kitchen, and his eyes widened a fraction. "I do somethin' wrong?"

Rafe barely kept the irritation from his tone. "What? No, why?"

"'Cuz you look like you're about to take my head off." He dug a dripping spoonful from the bowl and chomped it down. "Jus' wanted to know why before I died."

Rafe grabbed the mug of coffee he'd just brewed and tossed back a swallow. First his tongue, and then his throat, wailed when the scalding-hot liquid hit.

"Prob'ly shoulda let that cool some, huh?"

He started to bark a response, then stopped. There were others far more deserving of his foul mood than Tarik.

The teen carried his now empty bowl to the sink. "Whatever she did that got you so salty, man, you best chill before you talk to her."

Good counsel. Which he completely ignored.

By the time he drove to the church, he was ready to chew nails. And spit them out as tacks.

He found Kyla, deep in conversation with her foreman. He waited, aware she didn't even realize he was there, just barely resisting the temptation to tap his cane on the new wooden floor of the sanctuary-turned-gymnasium. She finished the discussion and looked up. Their gazes collided—and her eyes went wide.

"Rafae—"

"We need to talk."

"I know. I'm sorr—"

"Now."

She fell into step beside him, not questioning when he directed them outside and across the street. Away from anyone who might overhear them. Not until they were far enough away to ensure privacy did he face her. "*What* was last night about?"

"I've been *trying* to explain."

"Well, try harder."

A deep red seeped into her cheeks, and he waited. Expecting an explosion. Instead, she looked away and sucked in a breath.

One beat. Two. Then she let the breath out and turned back to face him. "I'm sorry. I don't blame you for being angry. I would be too if someone treated me the way I treated you last night."

There were tears in her eyes! Rafe's well-stoked anger fizzled, even as his concern came alive. "Kyla, please. What's going on?"

"Someone broke into my home last night."

The words, spoken in a hushed horror, rocked him. He listened as she went through it all, from waking up to the intruder to staying up all night after the police left. All of which explained not only the crazy call last night, but the exhaustion in the sag of her shoulders, the droop of her head. As he stood there, listening, watching her, one glaring truth speared him.

He was an idiot.

How could he not have realized something was seriously wrong? That Kyla wouldn't make a call like she had last night without reason. Speaking of which...

"When you called last night, you said something about my pals."

She passed a hand over eyes so weary it broke his heart. "The Blood Brotherhood. I know they're not your pals, I was just—"

"Angry."

"Frightened." She looked away, fighting whatever emotions still assaulted her. "I was terrified."

Rage surged through him again, but not for her. This time it was wholly aimed at whoever put that look of fear on this woman's face. That man, whoever he was, would be sorry.

"Kyla, do you mind if I go by your place? Take a look around?"

She swallowed and shrugged. "Sure, go ahead. But why?"

He wanted to see for himself if the graffiti was signature 22. It seemed too convenient. Why, if the gang was involved, would they leave such a blatant calling card? But he didn't want to tell Kyla that. Didn't want to risk her thinking he didn't believe her.

"I'd like to double-check a few things."

"Like what?"

He considered a white lie. Saying he wanted to check her security. But only for a moment. "To see the graffiti for myself."

Her brows drew together. "Because...?"

Rafe shifted. Well, no avoiding it now. "Because it doesn't make sense. That the 22s would go that far off their turf. Not even to terrorize you."

The storm he'd feared settled in those beautiful eyes, but only for a moment. Almost immediately something in her features shifted. "So you don't think it was the gang?"

"I don't know. That's why I'd like to check it out. I mean, think about it. The 22s are all about their territory. They don't let others on it, and they don't drift far from it."

Doubt painted lines across her brow, and Rafe frowned. "What?"

"I...I don't know. I just...the officer seemed so sure. Doesn't it make more sense to trust a seasoned police officer? You are kind of..."

"Kind of?"

The words rushed out. "Young. Okay, there. I've said it. It's simply common sense to trust an officer who's been on the job awhile rather than a coffee barista barely out of his twenties."

Barely out of his twenties? She was playing the *age* card? After all they'd gone through?

"I'll have you know I haven't seen my twenties for years—"

"Years." She rolled her eyes, and he was sorely tempted to tell her *she* was the one acting like a child. "So you left the twenties behind what? Two years ago? Three? *Much* more mature. Face it, Rafael, you're scarcely more than a kid."

"Better than being forty and acting like you're ready for the nursing home."

That stopped her. Cold. A tiny voice told him it was enough. More than enough. Downright mean, in fact. But he was on a roll.

"And I may be younger than you, but at least I haven't let my heart dry up into some hard, bitter stone. You're so tied up with fear and regrets you can't even trust yourself, let alone anyone else. As for God? I don't see you leaning on Him either."

"My faith is none of your business!"

Her choked words drew a harsh laugh from him. "Your faith? *What* faith? The only God I see you relying on is the one you see in the mirror every morning. Look, I know you've taken some hard hits—"

"You know *nothing* about my life!"

He ignored her, in part because he still had things to say. Mostly because she was wrong.

About a lot of things.

"But who hasn't?" He lifted his cane. *"Mira,* you think I *like* having to use this thing? That this is what I wanted for my life? You think I couldn't be bitter? Then think again, mija."

She hugged her arms around herself, and he realized she was trembling. Words caught in his throat, and he looked away. What was he *doing?*

And how many more times was he going to ask himself that?

Here she was, frightened, terrorized, and all he could do was spit judgment at her. "Kyla." He reached for her, but she jerked away as though his touch stung even more than his words.

"No!" She took two steps away from him, holding her hands out as a barrier. "Please…just…no. I can't…"

The rasping words tore at him. He started toward her—when a loud, deep bark sounded, followed by a cheerful voice ringing out.

"Kylie! *Rafa!*"

They both turned, and Rafe stared, not believing his eyes.

"Annie!"

"Annot!"

He and Kyla spoke together, and Rafe realized too late he'd given himself away. He caught just a glimpse of Kyla turning confused eyes his way—before a petite bundle of energy launched herself into his arms and hugged the stuffing out of him.

Annot. Hugging Rafael.

This made no sense at all.

Admittedly, Annot was as friendly as the summer day was long, but still. To hug a total stranger with such abandon? That went beyond the pale, even for her sister.

"Hey, sis."

Kyla pulled her gaze from the curiosity in front of her and felt a smile lift her face—and her heart. The first smile she'd really felt in the last few days.

"Avidan!"

Her brother's arms closed about her, and she leaned into him, grateful for his strength surrounding her. She hugged him. Tight.

"Hey, easy! I need those ribs."

Kyla stepped back on a shaky breath. "I'm sorry. I'm just so… It's great to see you." She turned to Annot, who had slipped up beside her. "Both of you."

Annot embraced Kyla, then stepped back to control an excited Kodi. When Annot looked at her again, her smile was pure sunshine. "Why didn't you tell me Rafa was here? I wouldn't have been near as worried if I'd known you had a Marine watching over you while you were at the site."

Kyla blinked. Rafa? Annie knew Rafe?

Dan came up, tight-lipped. "Murphy." He nodded to Rafael. "Been a long time."

A long…? Kyla stared at her siblings. Had they completely lost their minds?

"Kyla—"

Whatever Rafael had intended to say was lost in the music of Annot's laughter. "Kylie, it's Rafe. Rafe *Murphy*. You remember the Murphys. They lived down the street from us."

You remember the Murphys…

Kyla felt her face drain of color. Her head spun as though she'd taken a ride on a turbocharged merry-go-round. Her gaze went to Rafael. It couldn't be…

Annot's eyes widened at Kyla's clear confusion, then she looked back to Rafe, who Kyla suddenly realized was quite red-faced. "You…" She turned back to Kyla. "You don't know who he is. And you"—she turned an intrigued gaze to Rafael—"didn't tell her. Oh, Rafa." Annot shook her head. "What were you thinking?"

By now Kyla was downright miffed. "Of *course* I know who he is. He's Rafael Murphy, he owns Cuppa Joe's coffeehouse." Her words seemed as out of control as her emotions. "He makes marvelous coffee and he loves to say terrible things to me and drive me absolutely insane."

Annie took Kyla's arm, but Rafe forestalled whatever explanation she was about to offer.

"No, I should tell her."

Kyla did something she hadn't done since childhood. She stamped her foot. "Tell her *what?* And stop talking about me like I'm not here!"

Rafael straightened. "Like Annie said, my family used to live down the street from you."

But only one family lived down the street. A family she'd sworn to forget. A family she'd thought she would join. Prayed to join.

A family that destroyed her life.

Suddenly the pieces fell into place.

Of course. "Rafa."

Rafael inclined his head. "That's what Annie"— those dark eyes—eyes that had blazed with anger, eyes that burned with other emotions she hadn't dared define—"and you used to call me. I'm Berto's brother."

Berto.

No. Oh, no. It couldn't be. It just couldn't.

But it was.

The name she'd banned from her mind hit Kyla with the force of a jack-hammer. "You…" Long-buried memories surged to the surface, struggling to break free. Kyla did the only thing she could.

Shove them away using the one emotion more powerful than her pain. Anger.

FORTY-THREE

> *"Passion, it lies in all of us, sleeping…waiting…*
> *and though unwanted…unbidden…*
> *it will stir…open its jaws and howl."*
> JOSS WHEDON

> *"The discerning heart seeks knowledge."*
> PROVERBS 15:14 (TNIV)

Anger. Betrayal. Sorrow.

Annie watched, amazed, as these emotions touched her sister's features, colored her voice. Listened as she lit into Rafe, accusing him of everything from lying to causing global warming.

Okay, that last one was an exaggeration. But not by much. To say her older sister had lost it would be an understatement. And that told Annie more than anything else could have.

Dan moved as if to intervene in the heated exchange between their sister and Rafe, but Annie stopped him with a hand on the arm. "I think they need to work this through."

He glanced from them to Annie. "If they don't kill each other first."

She smothered a smile—no way she wanted Kylie to think she was enjoying all this. She leaned into her brother and pursed her lips. "So this is what it's like."

Dan cocked his head. "What's that?"

"Watching two people in love doing everything they can to not admit that's where they are."

Dan's eyes widened a fraction and he turned back to their sister. "In love? With Rafael Murphy?"

Annie heard the hesitation in his tone. "Dan, Rafe isn't Berto. He's a good man." She angled a look up at him. "A really good man."

He didn't say anything for a moment, just watched the two in front of them. "I thought you said Kyla was practically engaged to this Mason guy."

True enough. But come to think of it, Kyla hadn't said anything about Mason the last few times they'd talked. Of course, she hadn't said Mason was out of the picture either.

"Well, I'll tell you one thing."

Annie inclined her head. "What's that?"

"Your buddy Rafe had better be a *strong* man." He shook his head. "Or dear Sister-Mommy is going to eat him alive."

"Annot!"

Annie jumped, and found Kyla glaring at her.

"Are you two ready to go?"

"We're not finished here."

Kyla turned to Rafe. "Oh, yes we are." She aimed a hard stare at her siblings, Sister-Mommy in full view. "You two, meet me at my place."

Not waiting for a response to her overly harsh command, she walked away. Annie looked from her to Rafe...and grinned.

She'd known something was going on with her sister. But she would never, in her wildest imagination, have guessed it was *this* interesting!

FORTY-FOUR

"The final mystery is oneself."
OSCAR WILDE

*"Then will the eyes of the blind be
opened and the ears of the deaf unstopped."*
ISAIAH 35:5 (NIV)

Look, if she doesn't want to talk with him, I don't think she should."
Annie shifted in the car seat to face her brother as he drove. Why was he
so angry? "Of *course* she needs to talk with Rafe—"

"Why? It's not like Kyla has any reason to trust *any*one in that family."

Ah. So that was it. "Dan, Berto is the one who hurt Kyla, not Rafe.
Rafa...he'd never do anything to hurt her." She laid a hand on her brother's
tense arm. "He loves her. Has since we were kids."

The look Dan gave her would have given a bonfire frostbite.

Annie settled back in the seat, a sudden thought niggling at her. "Is there
more to this whole Berto thing than I know?"

A veil dropped over Dan's features. "What do you know?"

"That's not an answer."

"Neither is that."

Annie pulled her feet up to rest them on the dash, only to have her
brother swat at her ankles.

"Do you mind? I'd rather not have your footprints on my glove box."

She wrinkled her nose at him. "Whatever you say, *Brother-Daddy.*"

"Ha-ha."

"Okay, fine. What do I know about Berto Murphy and Kylie? They dated. She loved him. He dumped her and broke her heart." She arched her brows. "Anything I forgot?"

For a moment she didn't think Dan was going to answer. "No. That pretty well sums it up."

Her brother wouldn't lie to her. And yet…she had the distinct sense he wasn't telling her everything. She settled back into her seat. Dan could be a regular Fort Knox when it came to keeping people's secrets. That had worked in Annie's favor in the past, but now? Well, Kyla was her sister, for Pete's sake!

"Come on, Dan. What gives?"

He kept his eyes on the road, ever the diligent sheriff's deputy. The man never ate or drank while driving, and cell phones? Not on your life. He said they were the worst thing to happen to driving. If he'd said it once, he'd said it a gazillion times: *More accidents happen every year from people talking on their cell phones while driving than happen as a result of driving drunk.*"

"You're not going to tell me, are you?"

He hesitated. Then lifted his shoulders in a slight shrug. "It's not my story to tell."

Ah ha. So there was more to it than she knew. Fine. Then she'd just go to the source. "Do me a favor, okay?"

"What's that?"

"Give Rafe a chance."

This time Dan did look at her. Just for a moment. "You're sure he loves her."

Oh yeah. "Definitely."

"And she loves him?"

Annie slapped her hand to her forehead. "Duh! Did you *see* them out there? When was the last time you saw Kylie lose it like that?"

"Never."

"Exactly my point."

Dan's confusion creased his forehead. "So if a woman screams at you, she's in love?"

"No. But if Miss Iron Control screams at you?" Annie looped her arms around her legs. "Time to order china patterns."

Dan shook his head. "I'll never understand women."

"Of course not." Annie gave his arm a comforting pat. "You're a man."

He turned a corner, and Annie saw they were almost to Kyla's house. "So you'll leave things with Rafe alone? Let them work it out?"

Dan pulled his vehicle into the driveway of Kyla's town home, put the gear into park, and turned off the ignition. He leaned against the door, studying Annie. Then he gave a slow nod. "But if Rafe Murphy hurts her like his brother did—"

"It won't happen." Annie didn't back down from her brother's hard glare. "Dan, you have to trust me on this. I know Rafe, and he's nothing like his brother. He'd cut off his own arm before he'd hurt Kyla."

They both jumped when they heard a car screech into the driveway. Kyla's driver's door flew open, she shoved out, then slammed the door and made her way to the town home. Dan arched a brow and his doubting gaze swung back to Annie. "Maybe you'd better tell *her* that."

Annie grabbed the door handle. "I plan to tell her exactly that."

And a good deal more.

~~

Dan was so smart.

He'd dropped Annie off, saying he would just leave the women to talk. "Better not to have a guy underfoot while you two figure things out." His brows waggled at her. "Besides, I spotted a new military surplus store on the drive here."

"Oh goody!" Annie clapped her hands together, not even trying to hide her mockery. "New stuff to shoot with."

"Brat." Dan gunned the engine, then leaned out the window. "Go tend to your sister."

Annie tried. Several times. But Kyla was having none of it. She just kept pulling food from the fridge to fix dinner, saying over and over that she was fine.

"I'm fine. Everything's fine. Really. Absolutely fine."

Annie might have believed it if not for the fact that Kyla was moving like the Energizer Bunny on speed. If this woman wasn't running, Annie's name wasn't... Well. Annie.

"You know, I'm glad you're here."

Annie perched on the stool, doing her best to stay out of her sister's frenetic way. "Oh? Why's that?"

"Mason and I are doing so well together, I think it's time we set a date." She gave Annie a rapid look, then turned back to the eggs she was whisking. "Next month would work." *Whisk, whisk, whisk.* "No, better yet, maybe next week." *Whiskwhiskwhiskwhiskwhisk!* "I'm pretty sure Mason is free—"

"Kyla Marie Justice! Shut *up!*"

Her sister turned, mouth hanging open. That sight alone was worth listening to her sister's craziness.

"I beg your pardon?"

"You heard me." Annie hopped off the stool and went to pluck the whisk and bowl of abused eggs from her sister's hands. "I want to know—and you're going to tell me, right now"—Annie cornered her sister with a look that let her know she was serious as an accountant on Tax Day—"*what* in heaven's name is going on?"

Kyla stiffened, then sagged back against the kitchen counter. Her hands came up to cover her face. Annie set the bowl on the counter, then took her sister's hand and led her to the living room couch. She settled the two of them on the cushions, side by side, holding Kyla's hand in hers.

It took a few moments for Kyla to get herself under control—another first for Annie…usually she was the one crying all over the place.

She liked it better when that was the case.

Watching Kyla struggle was hard. She wanted to hug her, to tell her it would all be okay. But something told her that wouldn't help. That what was needed here was some gut-honest talk. So Annie waited.

"I don't know what's wrong with me."

Okay. That was a start.

"I've been so restless lately. Feeling like nothing is right." Kyla's hazel eyes were troubled. Annie let her encouragement show with a gentle squeeze of her hand.

"Work hasn't felt right. It's been so empty. And Mason." Kyla wiped a tear from her cheek. "He's a good man, Annot. And he seems to love me."

"Seems to?"

Kyla fell silent and looked down at their joined hands. Annie wanted to jump in, to prod. But something restrained her.

No…make that Some*one*.

"You're so lucky." Kyla lifted damp eyes to Annie's. "You and Jed, you fit together so well. You complement each other, and you have so much fun together. I watch you two and"—her face crinkled up with such sadness that Annie could hardly stand it—"I want that, Annot. I want it so much!"

Tears threatened, but Annie held them at bay. "There's no reason you can't have it, Kylie."

"You don't understand." She pulled her hands away, hugging herself as she had when talking with Jed. Annie reached out and pulled her sister's arm away from her. "Don't."

Kyla tilted her head.

"Don't put a barrier between us."

Emotions flooded her sister's features again, and Annie thought she would dissolve into weeping. But she drew a shaky breath and went on. "You deserve the happiness you have with Jed, Annot."

"You deserve that kind of happiness too."

Kyla shook her head. "No." She met Annie's gaze, and the hopelessness in her sister's eyes left Annie stymied. "I don't."

"But why?"

"Because." Kyla closed her eyes, and Annie had the most powerful sense that her sister was actually afraid. *Lord, please. What could be so terrible that she's afraid to tell me?*

"You'll hate me."

Oh, this was too much. "Nothing could make me hate you. Kylie, you're my sister. I love you."

"How can you *not* hate me, Annot? When I hate myself so much?"

"Kylie, please, what are you talking about?"

Tears slipping down her pale cheeks, Kyla folded her hands together in her lap, staring down at them. "I did something. Something I never should have done. Annot, I—"

The doorbell rang, the sound so unexpected that they both almost leapt off the couch. Their nervous laughter brought them a modicum of relief from the intensity of the moment, and Annie patted her sister's arm. "I'll see who it is and send them away."

Kyla nodded.

Annie jumped up, trotted to the front door, and peered out the peephole. Then stepped back, looking at her sister.

Kyla frowned. "Who is it?"

"Rafael."

Kyla was off the couch like she'd sat on a bee. "No!"

Certainty filled Annie. A certainty so strong she knew it wasn't from her. "Kyla, you need to talk to him."

Her sister came to stand beside her. She looked through the peephole, then leaned her forehead against the door. "I don't want to."

Annie laid a gentle hand on her sister's shoulder. Let the touch communicate her love and support. "Kyla."

Her sister lifted one hand to rub the remnants of tears from her pale cheek, then put her hand over Annie's. Her nod was barely perceptible, but it was there. Annie turned and walked toward the doors to the backyard. "I'll be out here if you need me."

As she stepped outside Kyla's soft whisper followed her: "Oh...help."

Annie sent up a prayer echoing the request, knowing the only One who could do so was not only listening, but already on the job.

FORTY-FIVE

*"We have two ears and one mouth so that
we can listen twice as much as we speak."*
EPICETETUS

*"Let the wise listen and add to their learning,
and let the discerning get guidance."*
PROVERBS 1:5 (NIV)

It took more courage than she'd ever shown in her life for Kyla to open that door.

Rafael stood there, regret bright in his eyes. "Kyla, please. We need to talk."

She drew a deep breath, then turned to call her sister. Annot was back inside in an instant.

"Everything okay?"

Kyla angled a look at her. "What could have happened in the two minutes you've been outside, Annot?"

Her sister's shrug spoke volumes. "You can never tell."

"Rafael and I are going to the church." Had the situation not been so tense, the mischievous spark in her sister's eyes would have been comical. Kyla let censure fill her gaze. "To talk. That's all."

"Take your time."

Shaking her head, Kyla stepped through the door. She and Rafe walked in silence to the street. He held the passenger's door of his car for her, and she slid inside. Oddly enough, the drive back to the church was almost peaceful.

Amazing. Even now, in the midst of such emotional turmoil, how this man affected her. Like peace flowed from within him to lift and calm her.

Yeah, you were calm when you were screaming at him.

She lowered her head. No, she hadn't been calm then. But she was starting to suspect something. Something that troubled her deeply.

That anger, that heated emotion that surged through her so often when she was with this man...

It was camouflage. A powerful way to hide things she didn't want to admit. No, more than that. Things she didn't want to feel.

Because if she did that, let herself feel, she'd be vulnerable.

And that was utterly terrifying.

~~~

Okay, they were here. In the church. Together.

Rafe drew in a shaky breath. *Now what, Lord?*

"I remember you."

Kyla's admission caught him off guard. "You do?"

"Berto's little brother. Annot's shadow." Her eyes softened. "You two were like peas in a pod. I even thought you might..."

"End up together?"

She nodded.

"No. We're just friends."

"I remember something else too."

Rafe could tell from the tone of her voice this wasn't something pleasant.

"You didn't like me."

"No."

She took it wrong. He could see it on her face—the hurt that cut across her features. "Fine. Like I said."

The ache underlying her defiance cut deep. He ground his teeth. "No, *you* don't understand."

"Look, it's fine. You have a right to your—"

"Stop it."

"What? All I'm saying is—"

He'd had enough. Enough meaningless words—words that said nothing and yet everything as they struggled to conceal her pain. So he did the only thing he could think of.

He grabbed her.

Circled her upper arms with his fingers, intending to give her one quick shake. Nothing hard. Just enough to stop the maddening flow of nonsense. But she fell silent, her mouth forming a mute *O* the moment he touched her. Which was understandable—especially if the contact gave her the same electrical jolt that nailed him.

Her wide and startled eyes locked with his. Rafe felt his grip ease, soften. His hands seemed to develop a mind of their own as they slid from her arms to her back. He didn't take his eyes from hers as he drew her closer.

He wanted to kiss her. Wanted it so much that he ached. Wanted it more than he'd wanted anything in a very long time. And she would have let him. He was sure of it. And yet...

No.

That same still voice within him was firm.

Not like this. Not in anger.

As much as he wanted to argue, he knew it was right. And so, even as everything within him screamed for him to taste that taunting mouth, to show her just how wrong she was about his feelings for her, he drew her close, nestling her against his chest, resting his chin on the soft hair crowning her head. For a moment she stiffened, and then, like the winter welcoming spring, she melted against him. He closed his eyes, pressed his cheek to her hair, let himself breathe in the heady fragrance.

And held her. Just...held her.

Time lost all meaning. They could have stood there minutes or hours, he didn't know. All he knew was that this was right. This was what she needed.

Almost as much as he.

Tell her.

He didn't argue this time. He simply started talking.

"I always liked you, Kyla. Too much. From the first time I saw you, all I could think of was you. You filled my heart and mind, fired my imagination. I was just a kid to you, but in my heart, I knew we belonged together."

"But"—her words slipped out, muffled against his chest—"you were so…"

"Mean?"

She nodded against him, and he smiled. "I didn't mean to be. I was so confused. All I wanted to do was make you see that Berto was wrong for you."

Her head lowered, as though a weight pressed down on her. "Because I wasn't good enough for—"

This time he did shake her. *"No!"* He gripped her arms, holding her away from him, just enough to look deep into those eyes. Eyes that had haunted his dreams for so many years. Eyes that had reminded him, when he felt lost and alone in the Iraqi desert, that it was all for a reason.

To protect her. To protect all women like her.

He gentled his tone. "No, Kyla. Not because you weren't good enough for Berto. But because *he* wasn't good enough for *you.*" His jaw tensed. "Because I knew he'd hurt you. And I couldn't let him do that. Not without trying to stop him."

Tears glistened, and she blinked them back. "I thought…I thought you just wanted to get rid of me."

How could such a smart woman be so dense? "Yeah, well. You were wrong."

Something flickered in the depths of her gaze. Something troubled. She looked down. Picked at a button on his shirt.

"Kyla." He covered her hand with his own, pressing her palm to his chest—and immediately regretted the action. The warmth of her hand over his heart was enough to make his knees weak. *Buck up, soldier!* He pulled in a deep breath, steadied his pulse rate. *Focus on what she needs, not on your stupid feelings.* "Kyla, what's wrong?"

She pulled away from him, shaking her head. He didn't move. Didn't want to crowd her. "Tell me."

At his low command, she spun back to him, fire returning to her eyes. "I'm not one of your soldiers."

That all-too-obvious truth almost tugged a laugh out of him. She *definitely* wasn't one of his soldiers. Good thing, too, considering the way one look or word from her could get to him. He'd never have been able to function. He inclined his head, conceding the point. "I'm sorry." He held her gaze. "Kyla, you know you can trust me."

The barest nod answered him.

"Then please, tell me."

She struggled for another heartbeat, her arms coming up to hug herself. Rafe understood what she was doing, probably better than she. He took two steps forward and placed his hands on her arms. With gentle force, he removed the barrier she'd created. Keeping one of her trembling hands nestled in his, he led her to a chair. They sat, side by side, and the words came out in a tumble.

"I did something. Something I'm so ashamed of."

Misery punctuated the words, but he didn't try to soothe her. She needed to get this out. No more delays.

"When Berto and I were dating, I"—she closed her eyes and exhaled, then finished on a whisper—"I got pregnant."

Her eyes came to his face then, seeking, probably for any sign of shock or condemnation. But she'd find none.

Because Rafe already knew.

FORTY-SIX

> *"You might have loved me if you had known me. If you had only known my mind. If you had walked through my dreams and memories, who knows what treasures you might have found. Yes, you might have loved me if you had known me. If you had only taken the time, you might have loved me."*
>
> GENEN GAINES

> *"No eye has seen, no ear has heard, and no mind has imagined what God has prepared for those who love him."*
>
> 1 CORINTHIANS 2:9

She'd come.

Rafe knew fifteen was too young, in some people's minds to have the feelings he did for Kyla Justice. But they were there. Had been since he was twelve. Little wonder, then, that he knew the moment Kyla walked into their house for his fifteenth birthday party.

And that something was wrong.

He read it in her every movement, heard it in her voice. Berto, of course, was clueless. All through his party, Rafe watched Kyla, anxiety growing ever stronger. What could make her look so miserable?

So frightened.

His hands fisted at his sides. Had Berto done something to hurt her? His fingers clenched so tight they ached. If so, he'd have Rafe to answer to.

Rafe had never understood what Kyla saw in his older brother. That they'd been together for a little over three years utterly stymied him. But it also worked in his favor at times, like tonight. With the connection through Kyla and Berto, both of their families had gathered at Rafe's home to celebrate his fifteen birthday. And that meant he got the best present of all.

The chance to see Kyla.

At one point, Rafe spotted her sitting by herself. Screwing up his courage, he grabbed a cup, filled it with punch, and carried it to her. She started when he thrust it toward her, then offered him a wan smile and took the cup in both hands.

"Thank you."

Her words were as troubled as her expression. Rafe wanted to soothe her, to take away whatever troubled her. But his tongue wouldn't work, and so he ended up just standing there.

"Hey, little brother"—Berto's too-loud voice grated on Rafe's nerves— "just 'cause it's your birthday, don't think you can get away with mooning over my girl."

Is that what she thought he was doing? Humiliation washed over him and Rafe turned and walked away, his brother's raucous laugh echoing in his burning ears. But he couldn't shut out her voice...

"Berto, that's mean. He wasn't mooning—"

"Forget him. You should be focusing on me, Kylita."

Why did she let him talk to her that way? Didn't she know she deserved better?

The party was winding down when Rafe realized Kyla and Berto were missing. Normally, he would have just marked it up to Berto wanting time with his girl. He didn't like sharing Kyla with anyone, not even their families. But the look in her eyes when she arrived wouldn't let him go. And so Rafe went searching.

It wasn't hard to find them. All he had to do was follow their raised voices. He stood just outside the doorway of his father's library, listening. Not to eavesdrop, but to be ready. Just in case. Berto's temper, as unpredictable as it was fierce, decided to make an appearance.

"What do you *want* from me?"

Kyla's response was equal parts anger and agony. "How can you ask that? This didn't just happen to me, Berto! It happened to us!"

"You want me to be sorry? Well, I'm not! I'm glad. You were stupid to let it happen in the first place."

Rafe planted his hands on either side of the door. It took all his control not to burst into the room and shove his brother's scornful words down his throat. But Berto wasn't finished.

"It's good that thing is gone."

"*Thing?*"

The ragged pain in Kyla's wail pierced Rafe's gut. *What* was going on? When she finally spoke again, her words were soft, broken.

Like grief come to life.

"That *thing* was your baby, Berto. And now it's dead. Our baby is dead."

Her sorrow became his own, loosing tears to course down Rafe's face. He put his hand on the doorknob…everything within him needed to go to her. To comfort her. To ease her pain. But he was halted by his brother's hissing response.

"Did I *ask* for a baby? No! I told you to be careful. But you let this happen, so it's on your head. I *told* you, chica, I wasn't going to let you or some screaming brat ruin my life. I've got a future, and your baby was not a part of it."

"My…*my* baby?"

Rafe's throat was so tight he could scarcely breathe. *Listen to her, Berto! Don't you hear the pain? Pain* you *are causing…*

"I'm just glad that thing is out of my life. You should be glad too."

The silence that followed Berto's words was heavy. When Kyla spoke, Rafe barely recognized her voice. The words came out flat, emotionless.

Dead.

"And will you be glad when I'm out of your life as well?"

Rafe could just see his brother's reaction. The curled lip; the derision. No woman had ever left him. No matter what he'd done or said.

Sure enough, Berto's tone shifted, turned low and husky—the voice he used to sway women. "Don't be silly, *cara.* Te amo. You know I love you."

Rafe closed his eyes. It wouldn't work. Not this time. No amount of charm could erase what Berto had said. Not from the way Kyla's voice had sounded—

"Good-bye, Berto."

Rafe barely had time to step back before Kyla burst through the door. She jerked to a halt when she saw him there. Those deep green eyes, drenched in tears, stared at him. The seemingly limitless sorrow he saw in those depths pierced his heart. For a moment the pain was so intense he thought he might be having a heart attack. But no pain could keep him from wanting to reach out, to comfort her. Words balanced on the precipice of his tongue, waiting to take flight. Assurances that she was better off without his jerk of a brother. That any man would be blessed to have her love.

But before he could coax them forth, she folded her arms around herself and dropped her gaze to the floor.

"I guess you're glad to see me go."

No! He wanted to scream it out. To tell her how he felt. That she owned him. Owned his heart. But the words wouldn't come. They just tangled up inside him. Left him standing mute while she bit her lips, fighting against the pain, then gave one final nod.

"Good-bye, Rafa."

And with that she was gone.

The moment the door closed behind her, Rafe came back to life. "No!" He started after her, but someone grabbed him from behind, jerking him off his feet.

"What do you think you're doing?"

Berto.

Rafe spun, striking his brother's arm, knocking him away.

"¿Por qué andas tan brava? What's wrong with you?"

Rafe met anger with anger. "Why am I angry? What's wrong with *me*? How could you *do* that? How could you treat her that way?"

Berto's eyes—eyes women swooned over—narrowed. "Were you listening, *tarado?*"

His brother was bigger and stronger than he. Rafe knew he'd lose in a fight. But he didn't care. That his brother had done this to such a woman.

He couldn't bear it.

"Women think you're so wonderful, but you're *nada!*"

"Be careful, little brother."

"Or what?" Rafe pulled himself to his full height. "I'm no woman you can knock around."

Berto smirked. "Or knock up."

Rafe didn't know he was going to hit his brother until it happened. But hit him he did, with the full fury of his outrage and sorrow. All the shame, the anger, congealed within him, drawing his hand into a fist that flew through the air with such force he heard his brother's jaw break when it connected.

Standing there, staring down at his brother where he lay sprawled on the floor, Rafe knew his life was over. Not because of what he'd done here. Berto deserved it. All that and more.

No, what cut to the quick, what stole the future he'd dreamed of since he was twelve, was the shame of what Berto did to Kyla Justice.

And the sure knowledge she could never, ever want to see any of them again.

FORTY-SEVEN

"Life is all about timing…the unreachable
becomes reachable, the unavailable become
available, the unattainable…attainable.
Have the patience, wait it out.
It's all about timing."
STACEY CHARTER

"God has made everything beautiful for its own time.
He has planted eternity in the human heart."
ECCLESIASTES 3:11

I never expected to see you again."

Kyla couldn't speak. Could barely think. Rafael knew her deepest shame. The secret that had taunted her for all these years with her own imperfections. Her stupidity. "You…you knew?"

"I was worried about you. I could tell you were upset that day when you got to our house."

The irony was almost too much. "You could tell I was upset. And Berto didn't even notice."

"Berto was too focused on himself to notice anyone else." He caught himself. "I'm sorry. I shouldn't talk about him that way. I know you loved him back then."

"I thought I did."

"So you can imagine my astonishment when you walked into Cuppa Joe's. Just walked in one day."

He knew what she'd done. How foolish, how out of control she'd been. "The moment I saw you, I knew. It was another chance."

Lord, I can't bear it.

And yet, as she sat there, Rafael's tender voice washing over her, the memories she'd avoided for so long—feared for so long—didn't seem as devastating as she'd thought they would. In fact, with Rafael's dark eyes on her, so full of compassion and care, she realized she was wrong.

She could bear it. At least for now.

Why? Because you think you can trust him? Why? Don't you realize he's known all this time and didn't say anything? Didn't tell you who he was. How can you trust someone who keeps secrets like that?

The dark thoughts pulled at her. "Why didn't you tell me?"

He didn't need to ask what she meant. "I wanted to get to know you again. To let you get to know me. As adults. Not as a kid and his brother's girl. But as friends."

Friends.

As she thought about it she realized it was true. Rafael was a friend.

"I was afraid if I told you who I was, all you'd see was Berto. That you'd never see me."

What a loss that would have been. The thought, as unexpected as it was true, startled her.

Rafael leaned forward, massaging his knee. "Annie stayed in touch with me all these years. She e-mailed me while I was overseas."

Kyla looked up at that. "The Marines."

He nodded. "I joined right out of high school. You were gone by then."

She curled her legs beneath her on the chair. "I left just a few months after…" Kyla plucked at the pillow next to her. "After I lost the baby."

She'd said it. Actually spoke the words aloud. She waited for the relief, the sense of freedom.

There was none.

Only a deep, aching sorrow.

"I'm so sorry."

She met Rafael's eyes, and saw it was so. "My parents were gone when it happened. And Annot was off doing"—she surprised herself by smiling—

"whatever it was Annot did back then. I was so wrapped up in my own world, my own tragedy, I don't think I even saw her."

"You didn't see a lot of things."

She didn't disagree. "The pain started late in the morning. By the afternoon, I knew what was happening. Thankfully, my brother was there with me. He stayed with me, took care of me…" She was not going to cry again. Unfortunately, the tears streaming down her face didn't seem to know that. "Held me and prayed with me when I told him what had happened. I begged him not to tell our parents. Or Annot. I couldn't bear it."

"Did you ever tell them?"

Kyla shook her head. "I went away to college, and soon it was as though it never happened. As though it happened to someone else. Which, in a way, it did." Misery sidled through her. "Because that girl, the one who loved your brother with such abandon? The one with such a tender, giving heart? She died, right along with her baby."

"Kyla—"

"It's true, and you know it. I'm changed." A harsh laugh forced its way free. "And not for the better."

"I know different."

Poor, poor Rafael. Sitting there, watching her with the eyes of his youth. But she had to tell him. Had to let him know the worst.

The very worst.

"I'm not. I wish I were, Rafael, for you as much as for me." He started to speak, but she stopped him. "Do you know how I know I've changed? Why I'm so certain?" The terrible truth tightened her chest. She pulled her hand free from his and gripped the back of the chair in front of her so hard that her fingers ached. "You tell me, Rafael. What kind of woman am I?" She squeezed her eyes shut, wishing she were somewhere else. Some*one* else. Longing for an excuse, any reason to stop the words she was about to say. To put off the confession she knew she had to make.

But there were no excuses. No more delays. No more denying. It was time to let him see who she really was.

"Because when I realized I'd lost my baby, I was glad!" Her agony rang out in the empty church, sailing to the rafters and beyond. Pounding at the gates of heaven.

"What kind of woman is glad that her own baby is dead?"

Such pain.

Rafael had seen young men die. Heard them cry out to God for mercy as the breath left their bodies. He'd helped bind wounds, forced to ignore the screams as they dragged an injured Marine to safety as shots peppered the ground. But he'd never heard such depth of pain as he heard now.

He longed to speak peace to her. To ease the grief and shame tearing at her. But for all that he'd give his very life to set her free, Rafe knew it would never be enough. He couldn't heal Kyla Justice.

Only God could do that.

Father, help her.

It wasn't eloquent, as prayers went. But it was as sincere a prayer as he'd ever sent heavenward.

He took her hand, easing the clenched fingers open, pressing his palm to hers. "What kind of woman? Shall I tell you the kind of woman I see in you, Kyla Justice?"

She made a wounded sound and turned her head away, but he didn't let that stop him. He had to say this. Needed her to hear him. "Because I see you, Kyla. I always have. I see your heart and your kindness; I see the glow of love inside you. Yes, it's been hidden beneath layers of self-protection. But it's there."

She let out her scorn, and he tugged her hand gently. "I saw it the day you brought that bedraggled kitten into the coffee shop. It shone on your face. Sparkled in your eyes." He looked at the room around them. "I saw compassion and determination every day you came here. With every obstacle you faced, every danger, you could have turned and walked away. No one would have blamed you. But instead you showed strength and courage."

He reached to touch her face, turning it so their eyes met. "Say what you want, Kyla, but I know the truth. You're still the amazing woman I fell in love with when I was twelve."

She didn't speak, but she leaned forward, letting him close her in the circle of his arms. She nestled against him, and silence settled over them.

She'd listened. Whether she really heard or not was in God's hands. But she'd let him say what was on his heart. And she hadn't walked away.

For the moment, that was enough.

FORTY-EIGHT

*"When one door closes, another opens; but we often
look so long and so regretfully upon the closed door
that we do not see the one which has opened for us."*
ALEXANDER GRAHAM BELL

*"I am feeble and utterly crushed; I groan in anguish of heart.
All my longings lie open before you, O Lord; my sighing is not
hidden from you.… I am like a deaf man, who cannot hear,
like a mute, who cannot open his mouth; I have become like
a man who does not hear, whose mouth can offer no reply.
I wait for you, O LORD; you will answer, O Lord my God."*
PSALM 38:8–9, 13–15 (NIV)

She couldn't get enough of the silence.

Kyla walked through the silent building, oddly at peace. She'd asked Rafael to leave, to give her some time alone to think, to pray. He'd refused until she agreed to let him sit outside until Annot came to pick her up. It was like having her very own walking, talking guardian angel. And she had to admit, she liked it.

Maybe too much.

She watched him leave, torn by the desire to call him back. To ask him to say all those things to her again. Until she heard them. Really heard them. But she knew his saying them a thousand times wouldn't make a difference.

Not until she changed inside.

How do I do that, God? I've held on so tight for so long. How can You expect me to just let go?

If she'd expected some heavenly response, she wasn't going to get it. What she did get was silence.

She made her way up the new stairs, leading to the offices on the second floor of what used to be the old parsonage. Walked along the new floors, ready at last for the carpeting that was to be laid in the morning. Went into the main office and turned on the lights. Then, steps slow and thoughtful, went to stand before the beautiful stained-glass windows.

Kyla laid her hand on the cool, colored glass. She'd been so sure they were all destroyed. And then, several days later, Fredrik came to her, eyes shining. He led her to a back room where he pointed at two large crates leaning against the wall.

Heart leaping, Kyla found a crowbar and pried the first crate open. The window inside was a heart-wrenching depiction of the crucifixion. Though delighted to find a window undamaged, Kyla couldn't deny a tinge of disappointment. She'd hoped for something more…encouraging.

Upon opening the second crate, all her hopes were realized.

There, carefully wrapped and stored, was a window bearing a glorious depiction of the resurrection. Easter lilies danced along the border, outlining the empty tomb in one panel, and Jesus ascending to heaven in another.

She'd wanted encouragement. What she got was that and more. A gentle but undeniable reminder that God was God.

Her fingers traced the shape of a lily. *I know that, Father. I believe it. But I can't help wondering…what are You doing? What were You thinking, bringing Rafe into my life this way? How could You let me feel the way I do about him?*

Her hand stilled. How did she feel?

Nothing. Rafe is a friend, nothing more.

Rafe. Not Rafael?

My heart is devoted to Mason. Period.

Liar.

End of discussion.

Coward.

"Leave me alone!"

"Okay, okay. You don't have to yell."

Kyla jumped back, then blew out her relief when she saw her sister in the doorway of the room, Kodi at her side. "I was worried about you. I saw the lights come on and figured you were in here."

"How long have you been here?"

"Oh, maybe ten minutes." One side of her mouth lifted. "I relieved Rafe."

Kyla didn't deign to respond to so obvious an attempt at gathering information. "I see you brought your furry shadow."

"You think I'd come here after dark without her? Hardly."

Pounding footsteps coming up the stairs startled them both. Kodi lowered her head and uttered a low warning growl.

"Hey! Call off the beast!"

Tarik! What on earth was he doing here? Kyla went to meet him at the top of the stairs. "Is Rafael still here?"

"Nope. I saw him pull away just as I was comin' 'round the corner."

Kyla flipped off the light in the office, then followed Annot and her dog to the stairs. "Coming around the… Did you ride your bike all the way here? This late at night?"

Humor tugged at the boy's lips. "Wow, you weren't kidding, were you, Miss Annie?"

"Nope. I told you she was a Sister-Mommy."

Fine. Now people outside the family would call her that awful nickname. "Did you come to find Rafael?"

Tarik started back down the stairs, Kyla and Annot right behind. "Yeah, but then I saw the lights come on and got a little worried."

"Seems to be an abundance of that going around."

A growl sounded, low and menacing, sending chills across Kyla's shoulders. "Annot, please. Control that dog."

Usually her sister did as she was bid. But this time, Annot hesitated. "Kyla, I think she hears something." Annot's gaze traveled past them, toward the front door. "Outside."

Kyla looked down at the dog, and stilled. Kodi's head was low, the black hair at the back of her neck standing up like a furry cowl. The chills skittered across her nerves again, then went into double time when they heard a sound outside.

Glass breaking.

"Oh, no! Not again!" Kyla's emotions surged into righteous anger, and she headed for the front door at a dead run. "Annot, call the police!"

"Kylie! Where are you going?"

"To stop them! They're not going to destroy our work again!"

Her sister cried for her to stop, but Kyla didn't break stride. As she hit the front door, bursting into the night, one thought pulsed through her mind.

I wish Rafael were still here!

FORTY-NINE

"We are not born again into soft and protected nurseries, but in the open country, where we suck strength from the very terror of the tempest."
DR. JOHN HENRY JOWETT

"By faith these people...shut the mouths of lions, quenched the flames of fire, and escaped death by the edge of the sword. Their weakness was turned to strength. They became strong in battle and put whole armies to flight."
HEBREWS 11:33–34

Kyla's car was still there.

When Rafe got home and found the note from Tarik, he turned right around and headed back to the church. Crazy kid. He was not riding his bike all the way home this late at night.

Rafe stepped out of his vehicle and frowned. Why was it so dark? Before he had a chance to figure that out, he heard a door open and saw Kyla step out of the church.

He started toward her, then halted when his feet crunched over something in the street. He stopped, looking around—and then up. The streetlights. They'd been shot out.

Dread weighing on him like a snagged anchor, Rafe spun back toward Kyla. She was crouching in the street below another light, fingers to the ground. Her name had just formed on his lips when she stood and started to run back to the church.

"Annot, get back inside!"

Her alarmed voice slammed Rafe's pulse into overdrive, and he ran toward the church—just as a shot rang out.

No!

His frantic gaze sought Kyla, and relief swept him when he saw her standing—then fled when he realized she and Tarik had Annie in their arms. They dragged her back inside the church as Kodi's howl sounded.

"I'm sorry." Kyla's voice, grief-stricken, drifted through the night. "Oh, Annot, I'm so sorry."

"Not…your fault."

Rafe almost faltered at the sound of Annie's voice. He'd heard voices like that before. From mortally wounded Marines.

He took the steps two at a time and halted at the sight that met him in the vestibule.

Annie, lying on the floor, covered in blood. Kyla, hands pressed to her sister's injury. Kodi leaning into Kyla watching her mistress. Kyla looked up when he came in. The fear in her eyes melted to relief. And something more.

He didn't have time to absorb that now, so tucked the awareness away until he could ponder it.

Kneeling beside Annie, he took hold of Kyla's wrists. "Let me see."

"No! I have to keep the pressure on."

"Kyla." He bent to draw her focus, captured her gaze. "Let me see."

Biting her lip, Kyla nodded and moved back, arms circling Kodi, hugging the dog close. Rafe's dread eased. The bullet had gone completely through. No telling, though, if any organs were hit.

"Am I gonna make it?"

"Hey." Rafe smiled at Annie. It was so like her, to attempt humor at a time like this. "You think somethin' as minor as getting shot can stop the likes of you?"

"Nah." The word wisped out on a shivery sigh.

The sound of a siren split the air, and Rafe took Kyla's hands and put them back in place.

"Will she be okay?"

He wanted to reassure her. Oh, how he wanted to. But he'd learned long ago not to promise what only God could deliver. "Just keep the pressure on. I'll be right back."

Rafe was out the door and down the steps, waving down the ambulance. Praying every step of the way for God's mercy.

And a miracle.

FIFTY

"I believe that unarmed truth and unconditional love will have the final word in reality. This is why right, temporarily defeated, is stronger than evil triumphant."
MARTIN LUTHER KING JR.

"'Wherever you hear the sound of the trumpet, join us there. Our God will fight for us!' So we continued the work with half the men holding spears, from the first light of dawn till the stars came out. At that time I also said to the people, "Have every man and his helper stay inside Jerusalem at night, so they can serve us as guards by night and workmen by day." Neither I nor my brothers nor my men nor the guards with me took off our clothes; each had his weapon, even when he went for water."
NEHEMIAH 4:20–23 (NIV)

It was a miracle she could hold the phone, let alone dial it. Kyla listened as her phone rang. Answer. Please, answer—

"Hello?"

She cupped the receiver, knees almost giving way at the relief of hearing his voice. "Avidan."

"Kyla? What's wrong?"

Little wonder he asked. Fear choked her voice. "It's Annot. She's been hurt."

"Hurt?"

"Shot. S-she's been...shot." Spoken aloud that way, the words still didn't make sense. Kyla gave Avidan directions to the hospital. "I don't know how bad it is. You need to come." She gripped the receiver. "Right away."

"I'm on my way."

Kyla leaned her head against the wall next to the pay phone. She needed to hang up the phone, but couldn't seem to lift her hands to do so. Gentle hands moved over hers, taking the phone from her, hanging it up.

She knew who it was without looking, and turned to bury her face in his solid chest. "Rafe…"

He led her to nearby chairs, and they sat together. Rafe's arm about her, his whispered encouragement, fed her starving spirit. But only for a moment. Soon she could stand it no longer and stood, pacing.

"It's my fault! I never should have been down there that time of night. After all that's happened—"

"There was no way you could know."

She shook her head. "I should have sent Annot home the moment she arrived. I was just so glad to have her here…" Would she never be able to escape the consequences of her foolish decisions? Would she always be haunted by what she'd done to herself? And now to others?

God! Kyla put her hands over her face. *God, it should have been me. Please, please, take me. Just let my sister live!*

He couldn't take it. Couldn't take her tearing herself up like this.

Rafe had been giving her space. Letting her walk off the fear, the nervous energy, but now he pushed out of his chair. In two strides he was at her side, his hands pulling hers from her face. "Stop it!"

She tried to break free, but he gripped her arms. "Your sister never would have left, and you know that. Don't you know how much Annie loves you? How much I—"

"Kyla?"

Rafe frowned at the man approaching them. Why did he sound so…*proprietary* when he said Kyla's name? Rafe glanced at Kyla, and what he saw on her features made no sense.

Guilt.

~~~

Kyla wanted to find a hole someplace and crawl in. But since no bottomless holes seemed available at the moment, she freed herself from Rafe's steadying hands and turned to face Mason.

"Kyla, the police called me..." He stiffened when Rafe came to stand beside her. "Who is this man?"

She was backed into a corner. The words slipped out before she could stop them. "No one. Just...a friend. Of Annot's."

This time it was Rafe who stiffened. Kyla spun to face him, to take the words back, but he was already walking away.

Pain seared through her, and she was certain her heart was tearing in two. She turned to Mason, offered a quick, "I'll be right back," and ran.

He was rounding the corner when she caught up to him. "Rafe!"

He stopped, but didn't turn.

What could she say? She longed to excuse her careless words, but knew there was no defense. She'd taken the coward's way out.

Something Rafael would never do.

"Rafe...where are you going?"

He came about, eyes studying her. She tried to read the emotions there, but couldn't. He'd put up a wall, and she couldn't get through. "To find out what happened out there."

He turned and walked away, leaving her to puzzle over what that meant. Find out what happ—

No!

Cold iced her spine. There was only one way Rafe could do that. He was going to talk to King K. Panic ripped through her and Kyla ran after him. She pushed through the outside doors—just in time to see his taillights heading down the street.

With a cry, she sank to her knees.

"Kyla!"

She didn't look up, not even when Mason took hold of her arms and pulled her to her feet, and then into his arms. All she could do was press her face against him.

"Who was that?"

She pulled back, meeting Mason's eyes. "Rafael Murphy."

Mason's mouth thinned. "A friend of yours."

Tell him. You owe him the truth.

Yes, she did. But not yet. Not now. She just shook her head and walked back toward the waiting room.

"Kyla?"

She waved Mason's question away. She couldn't deal with it. With him. With them.

All she could do right now…was pray.

~~~

Rafe had only come to the BB's crib twice before, and both times by invitation.

As he approached the building, a tall form stepped out of the shadows.

Tarik.

"I knew you'd come here."

Rafe squared off with the boy. He was in no mood for reason. "Don't try to stop me."

Tarik fell into step beside him. "Stop you? Man, I'm here to join you."

Together they walked to the entrance into the 22's main crib. Two hulking gang members stood on either side of the door, arms crossed. Rafe recognized them from the night the gang went after Kyla, outside the church.

They were the two he'd stomped.

Apparently they recognized him as well, because they both dropped into a defensive posture.

Nimrod #1 popped off first. "What you want here, tinklebe—" He swallowed what he'd been about to say, pressing his lips together. "What you want?"

Rafe leaned on his cane, gauging the best assault, should it come to that. "I need to talk with King K."

"You got an appointment?"

This from Nimrod #2. Rafe was about to respond when Tarik stepped forward. "You tell him L'il Man wants to see him."

Both of the gangstas hesitated, then peered at Tarik. Rafe could understand their confusion. Six months of exercise, sleep, and good food had stood Tarik in good stead. He'd bulked up considerably in the muscle department.

Nimrod #1 finally gave an abrupt nod. "Been awhile, L'il Man."

"Not long enough. We in or not?"

The two stepped aside. "You in."

As Rafe and Tarik walked through the door, Nimrod #2 piped up. "You in, a'ight, but question is, you comin' out?"

Good question.

Especially considering the number of gang members milling around. Had to be a good two dozen around them as they walked through the warehouse-cum-crib. Rafe scoped out the different exit routes available, and his jaw tensed when he realized there weren't any.

A nudge from Tarik focused his attention to the right, to a leather couch. King K sat there, women on either side.

"Well, well, look who come to visit."

Rafe stopped in front of King, planting his feet. He rested his hands on his cane, which he kept between him and King. "I'm here about what happened at the church."

King's eyes narrowed. "And so?"

"Were the 22s involved?"

King stiffened at the threat in Rafe's tone. "If they were? You gon' do somethin' 'bout it?"

Solid tactic. Don't admit or deny. "I just want to know if you were involved."

King leaned forward. "Why?"

"Because he's been standing for you, that's why."

King's gaze shifted to his brother, and Rafe saw something that gave him the first hope he'd felt all day. A softening in King's eyes. "You lookin' good, L'il Man."

"Yeah?"

Rafe's hand shot out to grip Tarik's arm. The sarcasm in the kid's tone wasn't what they needed right now, and he communicated that with a hard squeeze.

Tarik fell silent. He was a smart kid.

King K relaxed back against the couch cushions, his arms draped over the women at his sides. "I'm not saying we did or didn't do nuthin', but I will say this. Those church people got what they deserve for moving in on our territory."

Rafe's anger had him stepping forward, but Tarik cut him off. He faced his brother. "Are you saying this was your doing?"

Rafe had never heard the boy's tone go so hard. Like honed steel. He'd better be careful, though. He might be King's brother, but the gang leader wouldn't let Tarik go too far over the line. In fact, from King K's angry eyes and tense mouth, Rafe was pretty sure Tarik had gotten as far as he was going to get.

"What if I am?"

Tarik's reply matched his brother's tone, ice for ice. "Then you tried to kill me."

King K's arms fell away from the women, and he stood, a frown crossing his features. "What you talkin'?"

"That shot, big brother." Tarik took another step forward, putting his face right in his brother's as his words hissed out. "The shot that took out Miss Justice's sister. It was meant for me."

Outrage. Vengeance. Betrayal.

All those and more flooded the gang leader's features. "I don't believe you."

"Your belief doesn't change the truth, *hermano*." The term dripped sarcasm. "Miss Justice's sister, she heard the first shot and jumped in front of me. If she hadn't taken the bullet, it would have hit me"—he pressed a clenched fist to his heart—"here." Raw emotion turned Tarik's voice hoarse. "Was it you? Did you try to kill me?"

For a moment, silence, thick and heavy, fell over the room. The 22s watched King K for any signal to take out the intruders. Rafe tensed. He wouldn't go down without taking a few of them with him.

But the signal never came. Instead, King K reached out to grab his younger brother's shoulder. "*Nunca*, hermano. I'd never hurt you." His fingers gripped Tarik's shirt. "On Mama's grave, *lo juro*. You hear me? I swear it. Whoever did that woman, it wasn't the Blood Brotherhood."

"Where were you last night?"

King K's gaze cut to Rafe, and his features hardened. "You callin' me a liar?"

Rafe didn't back down an inch. "Answer the question, King. Unless you've got something to hide."

King let go of Tarik's shirt and took a step back, his chin lifting a fraction as he studied Rafe down his nose. Rafe's muscles tensed. This was it, that crucial moment when things either eased up or got worse.

Much, much worse.

He knew it. King knew it. And from the way the 22s were watching their leader, they knew it. Rafe didn't let his gaze flicker. He would not be the one to give way. If he did that, he'd lose any chance of getting to the truth.

"We were here." King's soft words split the silence like an explosion. Rafe let himself relax. The slightest flicker in King's eyes said he'd seen Rafe's tension, and his relief. "You don't believe me"—his stare drilled into him—"you go ask the 5-0. They were here too."

Tarik frowned. "Why were the police here?"

A gang member behind them spoke up. "They always droppin' by when we just chillin'."

Hoots sounded from all around. "Yeah. 5-0 tryin' to bust up on us."

King K held up his hands, and the room fell silent. "Like I said, you got someone other than us to worry about."

Rafe believed him. "Thanks." He nodded to Tarik, and they started to turn. But King's voice stopped them.

"Mr. Marine."

Rafe turned, not sure what to expect. King's expression was hard. "You find out who did this, who tried to take my brother out, you let me know."

"I'll make sure the person responsible pays."

King didn't like his answer, but he didn't argue. "One more thing."

Rafe waited.

"You tell the builder lady we're done."

"Done?"

"We out of it. Her sister saved one of ours. We won't come against her and hers. Not no more."

There were those who might doubt a gang leader's word, but Rafe knew if King was saying it, he meant it. Because of Tarik.

"I'll tell her."

"You do that. And you tell her somethin' else."

"What's that?"

"Watch her back." King was dead serious. "'Cuz they be comin' for her. Soon."

~~⁓~~

Rafe and Tarik walked back to Rafe's car, but before they reached it Tarik stopped him with a hand on his arm. "What are you going to do?"

"What do you mean?"

The kid snorted. "Don't give me that. I know that look. You've decided something."

Yup. No doubt about it. Tarik was smart. And altogether too perceptive. "Yeah, I have." He started walking toward his car again.

"So?"

He didn't look at Tarik as he answered. "It's time."

"Time? For what?"

Rafe pulled his driver's door open. "To call in the Marines."

FIFTY-ONE

"We make war that we may live in peace."
ARISTOTLE

*"Sanballat and Geshem sent me this message:
'Come, let us meet together in one of the villages on
the plain of Ono.' But they were scheming to harm me."*
NEHEMIAH 6:2 (NIV)

Like any good Marine, Thales was ready for Rafe's call.

"I need you here. Now."

"Will four more Marines do the job, sir?"

"Five Marines against a whole gang?" Rafe smiled. "Well, I hate to over-power them, but that's just the way it goes, oo-rah?"

"Oo-rah, sir. It'll be Sabada, Monroe, Rashidi and me. Green's been deployed, so he can't make it. But the rest of us will be there soon as we can."

Rafe filled Thales in on where he'd meet them at the Portland airport, then hung up.

"You weren't kidding? You really called the Marines?"

Tarik stood behind him. Rafe leaned back. "You listened in?"

"Naw, but you gettin' all oo-rah means Marines."

Rafe let a slow grin travel his features. "Yeah, it does."

"The whole team—"

"Unit."

"—unit comin'?"

Rafe studied the boy. Was Tarik frightened King might show after all? If so, would Tarik warn his brother reinforcements were on the way?

"Don't sweat it."

Rafe tipped his head. "Don't sweat what?"

"I ain't—"

"I'm not."

A long-suffering sigh. "I'm not askin' so I can warn anyone. Jamal's my brother, but if he goes against his word, he's on his own. I just want to be sure you're, you know, covered. And to let you know I'm with you."

It took a moment before Rafe could respond. "Thanks. That means a lot."

"Yeah, well, you done"—he caught himself and grinned—"did a lot for me. So you and the Marines, you gonna be on the front lines, huh?"

Rafe digested that fact. Back on the front lines. He thought he was done with all that. "Looks like it."

"Then I'll stay in the background." The boy's eyes, so full of knowledge a boy that age shouldn't have, met Rafe's. "To watch your woman."

Rafe arched a brow at that. "My woman?"

The kid's grin was all boy now. "C'mon, man. Don't try to tell me she ain't…isn't your woman. You get all googly-eyed when you talk about her."

"Googly-eyed?"

"Yeah, like this." Tarik pulled a hilarious face, and Rafe cracked up.

"I have never looked like that in my life."

"Just every time you talk about Kyla Justice." Tarik stood. "But it's okay, man. I like it that you got a good woman to love." He punched Rafe's arm. "Just promise you'll name your first kid after me, a'ight?"

Rafe did his best not to let the boy see what that idea—having a family with Kyla—did to him. But from the laughter brimming in Tarik's eyes, he figured he blew it. "Uh-huh. Tarik Murphy. Just sings off the tongue."

"Tha's what I'm talkin' 'bout, Mr. Googly Eyes."

Rafe stood, and Tarik signaled his surrender. "Okay, okay, I'm going to my room. Do the homework. Don't get all up in yo' testy self."

The boy's laughter echoed down the hallway as he headed to his room, and Rafe welcomed the sound.

Almost as much as he welcomed the boy's idea.

He and Kyla getting married. Having a baby. Tarik Murphy…

More unlikely things have happened.

Not many. The image of the man at the hospital drifted into his mind. Kyla's voice taunted him: "Just a friend of Annot's." Yeah, unlikely. That was the word for it.

But it's not impossible.

Well, no. Of course not. Nothing was impossible with God. Rafe pondered that thought. Nothing was impossible.

This time the voice echoing in his head was Fredrik's: "The plans of the LORD stand firm forever, the purposes of his heart through all generations."

The plans of the Lord. The purposes of his heart.

And timing. God's perfect timing.

All that swirled around in Rafe's mind and heart. He stood, stretching, and headed down the hallway to his room. But right on his heels was a thought he knew he shouldn't entertain. But one that wouldn't go away.

Maybe…just maybe…this would turn out right after all.

FIFTY-TWO

> *"If only. Those must be the two saddest words in the world."*
> MERCEDES LACKEY

> *"I know that you can do anything, and no one can stop you.
> You ask, 'Who is this that questions my wisdom with such
> ignorance?' It is I. And I was talking about things I did not
> understand.... I had heard about you before, but now I
> have seen you with my own eyes. I take back everything
> I said, and I sit in dust and ashes to show my repentance."*
> JOB 42:2–3, 5–6

What have I done?

Kyla Justice leaned her head back against the wall, grateful for its support. Her fingers gripped the hard chair that held her, keeping her from collapsing into a heap on the floor.

She wanted to get up. To go look through the glass at the still form that lay there. But she couldn't. Couldn't stand to see the tubes. To hear the beeping monitors. All that terrifying equipment that said, as clear as day, "This is your fault."

God! The prayer catapulted her from her chair. *Help me!*

But He wouldn't. How could He, when she'd gone so wrong? She'd known what He wanted her to do. Known the right thing to say and do. But no. She had to do things her way. Always her way.

Kyla's feet halted their agitated pacing, and she sagged against the hard wall of the intensive care waiting room. Her mother used to tell her disobedience had a cost. Now...

There was no doubting it.

Her mom was right.

Weary to her soul, Kyla rested her burning cheek against the cool wall, then pushed away and let her slow, leaden feet carry her through the double doors, back into the ICU, past the nurses' station, and into the doorway…

Beep. Beep. Beep.

The steady sound should be reassuring. Instead, it grated on Kyla's raw nerves. Yes, the heartbeat was regular and strong. But what difference did that make if Annot wasn't awake?

Never woke up again.

Jesus, no…

The same plea she'd been making for days now. The same plea God seemed to be ignoring.

Scenes and sounds flooded her mind, a terrifying video projected on the black screen of her closed eyelids. The heavy darkness all around, and then the explosion of sound. The sight of her sister, slumped, eyes wide, hands pressed against the ribs. Trying, but not succeeding, to stop the red flow as it stained the white shirt, seeped through the pressing fingers…

The pain that pierced her then had nothing to do with guns or bullets. Everything to do with guilt.

Kyla forced her reluctant eyes open and moved to the spot that had been her whole world for the last three days.

Three days. Kyla frowned. Had it really been that long? Three days. A heartbeat in time.

An eternity.

She sank into the chair and reached for the still hand resting on the bed, cradling it, stroking the fingers that held such talent. That created such beauty from glass and metal.

Tears burned at the back of her eyes, and Kyla lifted the hand, pressing it against her cheek. "Please, open your eyes." She stared at the stubborn eyelids, willing them to open, willing the slack mouth to lift and smile. How Kyla loved that smile. The thought that she might never see it again dragged another hoarse whisper from her.

"Please, Annot…wake up." No response.

Kyla pressed her forehead to her sister's still fingers and let the ragged prayers flow.

～～

It was late—or was it early morning? She wasn't sure—when Kyla finally made her way home.

She'd just let poor Serendipity out of the bedroom when the phone jangled, assaulting her already frayed nerves. Apprehension soared when she realized it must be the hospital. She grabbed the phone up before the second ring died.

"Hello?"

"Kyla?"

She didn't recognize the voice. "Yes?"

"It's Sheamus. From the church?"

Of course. She brushed a hand across her weary eyes. "What can I do for you, sir?"

"I just wanted to let you know we received a tip tonight. That gang is sending someone after you. Tomorrow night. You'd better call in the police. Get them to go after these thugs where they live. That's the only way they're ever going to stop."

Kyla put a steadying hand on the wall. She couldn't deal with this tonight. She was too tired. Too empty. "Thanks for letting me know."

She didn't wait to hear his good-bye. Just hung up, and sank on the couch.

A moment later she lifted the receiver again, ready to dial Avidan. But he was at the hospital, and she didn't want to disturb him. Fine, she'd call Mason. Her finger hovering over Mason's speed dial, but before she realized what she was doing, she'd punched in Rafael's number instead.

The phone rang once when she remembered how late it was. Before she could hang up, she heard his voice. Warmth surged through her at the sound. In a few short sentences, she explained the call from Sheamus.

"I'm coming right over."

Kyla didn't argue.

~~~

Rafe sat on Kyla's couch, studying her home.

It suited her to a tee. Beautiful and elegant, and yet warm and welcoming at the same time. Her kitten—make that cat…amazing how much this animal had grown—perched on the arm of the couch, leaning against him, purring up a storm.

"Oh, tell that silly cat to get down if she's bothering you."

Kyla carried two mugs of cocoa in from the kitchen. Rafe reached over to scratch the purring feline's soft ears. "She's just fine. I like her being here."

Something flickered in Kyla's eyes at that, but she didn't say anything. Just handed him the mug and sat in the chair beside the couch. "So what do you think I should do?"

Rafe sipped the rich chocolate. "I don't think Sheamus's information is correct." He'd told Kyla about the visit he and Tarik paid to the gang. "King meant what he said. I don't think the 22s are the problem."

Kyla leaned back in her chair. She looked so weary, so worn. Annie was still in a coma, and that had to be driving her crazy.

"How can you be so sure?"

"They gave me their word."

Kyla's mouth dropped open. "And you *believe* them?"

Rafe watched her a moment. "You don't trust anyone, do you?"

"I don't trust thugs!"

"Amazing. You can look at the structure of a building and see all it can be when it's done, but when it comes to people, you focus on the surface." He stood. "You've got to decide, Kyla."

"Decide what?"

"Did God call you to this project or not?"

She looked away.

"If He did, seems to me you should be more at peace in His protection and presence."

She met his eyes. "My sister is in the hospital, in case you forgot!"

He gentled his tone. "I know that, Kyla. But that doesn't mean she isn't in God's hands."

"And if God didn't call me?"

Rafe considered that. "Then you'd better get out. Now."

He went to put the mug in the sink. When he came back, Kyla hadn't budged. It only took a quick glance to see why.

She was fast asleep.

He walked down the hallway until he found her bedroom, then went back to the living room. His movements slow and careful, he slid his arms beneath her and lifted her, cradling her against his chest. Serendipity danced around his feet as he carried Kyla down the hallway and into her bedroom. He laid her on the bed, then pulled the quilt up over her.

She moved, restless, and he laid his hand on her head, stroking her hair, whispering soothing words. With a small sigh, she relaxed. Standing there like that, his hand on her soft hair, Rafe closed his eyes, letting his heart pour out prayers for wisdom, safety, and peace.

When he opened his eyes, Serendipity had settled down on the pillow, next to Kyla's head. With a final scratch on the cat's ears, Rafe walked back through the town house and let himself out.

But all the way home, he kept up his prayers. Because if he'd learned anything over the years, he'd learned this: the minute you relax your guard, the enemy strikes.

And he didn't think Kyla could take another hit.

FIFTY-THREE

*"The forceps of our minds are clumsy things and crush
the truth a little in the course of taking hold of it."*
H. G. WELLS

*"You have heard the law that says, 'Love your neighbor'
and hate your enemy. But I say, love your enemies!
Pray for those who persecute you!"*
MATTHEW 5:43–44

I t hit her square between the eyes around noon the next day.
Shortly after Annot regained consciousness.

It happened the day Jed arrived from down south, which didn't surprise
Kyla one bit. Annot's eyes had been moving more, as though she were trying
to pull out of the deep sleep her assaulted body had put her in. But despite
coaxing from both Kyla and Avidan, Annot's eyes stayed closed.

Until Jed leaned close and whispered in her ear. At the sound of his voice,
Annot's eyes fluttered…and opened.

Those green eyes, almost as familiar to Kyla as her own, were a more welcome sight than anything she'd ever seen. Kyla wanted to run and dance and
sing.

She settled for hugging her brother and Jed so tight they couldn't breathe.

Now, two days later, as the three stood by Annot's bedside, Jed held her
hand, stroking his fingers along the back. Annot tired easily, so they told her
they would only stay a short while.

"But I'm so bored."

"I think the word you're looking for is tired."

Avidan added his agreement to Kyla's statement. "More like exhausted."

"Worn out," Jed supplied.

"Peaked—"

"All right, you guys. Enough, already." Annot pouted prettily, all for Jed's benefit, Kyla was sure. But she didn't mind. Her sister could pout all she wanted.

For a good two or three more days, anyway.

As Kyla and the men were leaving the room, she heard Annot call her name. She turned and went back to take her sister's outstretched hand.

"Kylie, something occurred to me."

"Hmm? Did you have a dream?"

Annot's eyes lowered as she fought the need for sleep. "I don't think so. I think it was more of an epiphany. But not for me." Her sleepy eyes settled on Kyla. "For you."

Kyla leaned close. "What is it?"

"You need to see the King. Talk to him."

The king? "You're not making sense."

The pout was back. And Jed not here to see it. What a pity. Kyla smiled and patted her sister's hand. "Get some rest."

"No. Not yet. Kylie"—a wide yawn struck her—"you need to do it. Go see King."

King.

King K.

Her sister was telling her to go see a gangster?

She started to say how absurd the idea was, but Annot was already asleep. Kyla left the room, deep in thought. And, as little sense as it made, the more she considered the idea, the more certain she was Annot was right.

It's too dangerous! There's no way you can be sure of your safety. You're not just walking into the lion's den, you're sticking your head in its mouth!

All true. Which sent her pulse pounding, and yet she couldn't deny what she knew.

It was time to see the King.

〜〜

"It's not happening."

Rafe took in Kyla's stubborn countenance. Looked for the disbelief he felt in Tarik's and Fredrik's faces. But it seemed he was alone in his stand. Well, so what? He could be stubborn too. First Kyla called and asked him to meet her here at the church, then she blindsided him with this crazy request. Take her to talk with King K?

She was out of her mind.

Besides, Thales and the others would be arriving later this afternoon. He didn't have time to take Kyla Justice on a fool's errand.

Especially one that could get her hurt. Or worse.

"Rafael, please. I can't explain it, but I know this is something I'm supposed to do."

"Do you know how dangerous this will be for you?"

Kyla's jaw set in the stubborn line he was coming to know so well. "I thought you said they weren't going to cause any more trouble?"

"Here!" Rafe indicated the building. "Where we're working. But this? You're invading their crib. Without an invitation."

"Like you did?"

Rafe didn't let Tarik derail him. He kept his eyes on Kyla. "That was different."

Tarik wasn't about to be ignored. He sauntered over to stand beside Kyla. "How? You think you some kind of Superman?"

"You're."

Rafe and Kyla said it together, and Tarik looked from one to the other, shaking his head. "We talkin' 'bout life and death here, and all you two can do is correct my grammar?" He waved them off. "You two deserve each other, you know that?"

Rafe drew Fredrik into the fray. "Will you talk some sense into her?"

"Rafe, this has the ring of truth, this thing she's asking."

Okay. No help whatsoever from that corner. "You...well, who asked you?"

Tarik's brows lifted. "You did."

"Look, all of you. It's not happening. Let it go." Ignoring their protests, he left the room, then the church, walking out into the morning chill. *Lord, give me strength!*

Words whispered through his mind. *Listen carefully to the voice of the* LORD *your God and do what is right in his sight.*

Rafe froze at the top of the stairs. Stairs he'd all but flown up a few nights ago. Stairs that led him to a bleeding Annie Justice. *You can't be serious.*

Not exactly a reverent response, but God had to admit it was an honest one.

If you are careful to obey me, following all my instructions, then I will be an enemy to your enemies, and I will oppose those who oppose you.

Rafe sat down on the top step. He was a Marine. In service or out, always a Marine. As such, he'd been asked to do a lot of things. Dangerous things. Seemingly crazy things.

And yet he followed commands. Because he knew what his eyes saw was just a piece of the puzzle. But those giving the orders…they saw the picture in its entirety.

Be strong and courageous, for you must bring my people into the land I swore to give them.

The words struck deep, resonating within him.

I will be with you.

So be it.

Rafe stood and walked back inside. Kyla, Tarik, and Fredrik were still sitting there, talking, but they stood when Rafe approached. He stood, silent, then inclined his head. "Tarik, set it up."

"Do you mean…?"

Such hope in her tone. "I'll take you to talk with King K." He folded his hands over the lion's head of his cane. "I just hope you're ready."

Tarik snorted. "You kiddin'? I hope King is ready." He sprawled in the chair as only a teenage boy could do, directing a wry grin at Kyla. "'Cuz, Miss Builder Lady, I don't think he's *ever* met anything like you."

~⁓~

I'm not ready for this.

The thought kept running through Kyla's mind as she walked between Rafael…

No. Kyla almost smiled to herself when the realization hit her. Not Rafael. Not any longer. He'd become Rafe, in her heart and in her mind.

She walked between Rafe and Tarik now, through a gauntlet of red and black.

The old Stealers Wheel song kept running through her mind, but with a new twist: *22s to the left of me, BBs to the right, here I am, stuck in the middle with You.*

Heart pounding, she kept putting one foot in front of the other, holding her chin high. Ignoring comments tossed her way. Tensed for the attack she was sure was coming.

Lord, why did You do this? Why send me here? What if they jump us? Rafe can't fight them all. And what about Tarik? He's just starting to understand life outside of this world. What if he gets hurt here, because of me?

Good thing these people couldn't see beyond her cloak of confidence, couldn't hear the anxious questions tumbling over each other in her mind.

Good thing they didn't know she was about a heartbeat away from turning and running as fast as her legs would take her. But that surety within didn't let her go.

Not by a long shot.

A touch on her arm startled her, and she looked up. Rafael tipped his head to the side. "King K."

She turned, and saw the gang leader sitting on a large leather couch, arms spread out along the back. A lounging sovereign, surveying intruders to his land.

Oh…help.

Tarik's elbow poked her. "Go on. He's waiting."

Sucking air through lungs that suddenly felt too tight, she did as she was bid. Walking forward until she stood in front of the man who'd been determined to destroy her work.

And her.

He leaned back, looking her over. "Your dime, lady. You wanted talk." His lip curled. "So talk."

Kyla indicated the couch. "May I?"

A glimmer sparked in his eyes, but she couldn't tell if it was respect or outrage. He pursed his lips, then slid over—but just enough for her to sit right next to him.

His slow smile almost did her flagging courage in, but she forced herself to sit. She pushed her back against the arm of the couch, then turned to face him. Far closer than she liked. But faced him, nonetheless.

Of course, she kept her gaze fixed somewhere in the vicinity of his chest. She had no desire to look a cold killer in the eyes. *Lord, what do I say?*

No reply but the ache in her heart.

Which was all the reply she needed. Setting her shoulders, she let the words pour out. "I know you're against what the church is trying to do, but I'm asking you, think about the kids. Your kids. Brothers and sisters. Children." She spread her hands. "You *know* you don't want this life for them."

King didn't reply. Just kept those cold, empty eyes fixed on her. Kyla tried again. "How many have you lost, King? How many children have died, shot down in the streets for no reason other than they live two blocks one direction or another? You know there's a better life for them out there." She met his gaze for a heartbeat, then looked away. Forced herself not to flinch at the violence burning in those dark depths. "That's why you let Tarik go. Why you let him live with Rafael."

King's chin lifted a fraction, but he held his silence.

Lord, help me. Give me the right words. "Don't you see? Fredrik and the others, they're not trying to take over your turf. All they want to do is save the children. To give them a place to go that's off the streets. To get them involved in things that will bring life, not death."

King K crossed his muscled arms over his chest. The power this man held was amazing. Physical power. Emotional power. Kyla knew he could break her in half without even trying. But she willed herself not to waver. Not to show fear.

She *had* to get through to him. Yes, he'd said they were done. That the gang wouldn't interfere in the building. But what about after that? What about when the center opened, and young people starting coming?

If he didn't stop the opposition now, all of it…if the 22s didn't back off, the church, the center, *they* were done. The youth center would fail. And all those children would be lost. As Kyla looked around the room, she saw faces far younger than she'd expected. Tarik had told her the OGs didn't want their younger siblings in the gangs, and yet here they were.

Why couldn't the 22s see that these precious little lives hung in the balance?

Suddenly Kyla realized she was crying. She wasn't making a sound, but tears had gathered in her eyes and spilled over onto her cheeks. She wiped the moisture, staring down at it with a frown.

"Why you cryin', woman?"

"I…" Kyla looked from her damp hand to meet King's sneer.

"If you think you gon' get your way by cryin', you wrong. I ain't some white boy gets all gushy inside when a woman cries."

Kyla straightened her shoulders. "I'm not crying for you. I'm crying"— she looked past him at two gang members who couldn't be any older than eleven or twelve—"for them."

King turned, following her gaze. When he faced her again, a frown creased his brow, and he fell silent for a moment. "Why you care what happens to the children here?" He jerked his chin toward the direction of the church. "That place ain't your crib. This ain't your turf. You a hired gun, is all."

"You're right."

His carefully schooled features lost their bored look at that, but just for a moment.

Kyla went on. "I *was* a hired gun when I first started this job. All I cared about was getting the project done on time. Proving I could do what the other contractors couldn't."

A sneer twisted across his mouth. "You gon' tell me all that changed now?"

"Yes." Even as she said the word, Kyla felt the confirmation inside. She was telling the truth. It had changed. *She* had changed. That's why she was crying. Not because she wasn't getting the project done, or because her reputation, business, and freedom were at risk. None of that mattered.

No, the only thing that mattered, she realized with stunning clarity, was the children.

Mouth open on a silent *O,* Kyla looked at the man sitting beside her. A man old before his time. Scarred, inside and out, from scrapping to gain every bit of respect. Every bit of turf.

Get it and hold it.

"You're right, too, when you say I don't know what it's like here. What your life is like. But I'm asking you to believe me on this. We, the church people and I, we're trying to help, not hurt you. Look at the children! Your sisters and brothers. Don't you see what a place like this could do for them?"

"What you afraid of?"

Kyla stopped. "What do you mean?"

"You sit here talking, lookin' all 'round the room. At everyone here. Everyone but me. Why you look away every time you start to look me in the eye?"

She should have known. Should have realized he wouldn't miss the slight. Fear whispered along her nerves, but she knew she could hide no longer.

Kyla looked up.

Their eyes met—and suddenly all of her fear melted away. Because there, sitting in front of her, was not the monster she'd created in her mind. But a young man. And when she looked into those dark, haunted eyes, it was as though God opened her heart and let her see.

Really see.

Brokenness. Hopelessness. Pride. Determination.

All the same things she saw in her own eyes when she faced herself in the mirror—

No!

Kyla pulled back. She was not like this man! She'd never tried to hurt anyone. Never killed. Never broke the law. How could anyone think she was like him?

She stood, hands clenched at her sides. *Was this why You brought me here? To tell me this? That I'm like...*

"Kyla?"

Rafe's voice jerked her focus back to the present, and she met King's eyes again. No. She was *not* like this man.

"You want me to look at you?"

King's features hardened at the derision in her tone. She felt a hand on her arm, but shook Rafe off without even looking his way.

"Fine! I'm looking. And you know what I see?"

King's lip curled. "Do tell."

"A man who cares for no one but himself. Who uses his followers to his own ends, to commit crimes and cause others harm."

The storm brewing on King's face should have stopped her cold. Instead, it only fed her growing fury.

"You've done everything you can to destroy what good people are trying to do. And why? Because it's your turf?" Her laugh held no humor. "I don't buy it. You want to know why I think you've done all this? Why you've vandalized. Why you broke into my home. Why"—she was shaking now—"you almost killed my sister."

King was on his feet now. "Yeah. I want to know."

"Because you, King Killa, are a coward."

Someone grabbed her from behind, jerking her back. She spun, ready to fight, only to find Rafe glaring down at her. "What are you *doing?*" He hissed the words at her.

"Nah, man." King lifted his chin. "Let her go. We not done here."

Kyla pulled free, knowing as she did so that it was only because Rafe let her. She could tell, from the blaze in those eyes, that he was moments away from hauling her out of there.

And she couldn't blame him. Kyla held her hand up, then turned back to King. "I'm sorry."

He didn't react. *Oh God, what have I done? See what happens when I let my emotions go? I destroy what You're trying to accomplish.*

But even as the thought formed, she knew it was a lie. That it wasn't her *emotions* leading her astray. It was one emotion. The one that had plagued her since the day she realized she was pregnant with Berto's child.

Fear.

Whether it masqueraded as anger and rage, or ushered in its playmates depression and hopelessness, fear was always there. Taunting her. Pushing her to utter stupidity.

She faced King K square on. "I came here to talk, not accuse. I'm sorry. I…" The admission caught in her throat, but she lifted her chin and forced it out. "I was afraid. When I looked at you, I saw something I didn't expect. And…it frightened me."

Still no reaction from him. Just one question. "What'd you see?"

Are you asking this of me, God? Must I confess my failings in this place, to this man?

She knew the answer before she asked. Straightening her back, she met his eyes. "Myself. I saw myself."

That got a response, though Kyla wasn't sure if it was good or bad. King tipped his head, eyes narrowing. "You know what, Builder Lady?"

"What?"

"You whack."

"I'm...what?"

"You whack. You standin' here, thinkin' you know us. Know me. And you ain't got no clue. Not who we are or what we do. And I got a news flash for you. We didn't do it."

"Didn't do what?"

"Your sister, that is. We didn't shoot her."

Kyla folded her arms over her chest and jutted her chin out. How stupid did this thug think she was. "Oh, please."

King's eyes narrowed to slits. "You callin' me a liar?"

Her arms fell to her sides and she stepped toward him. "I'm calling you a ruthless thug who will do whatever it takes to get what you want. You didn't do it. How stupid do you think I am?"

Steel settled in those eyes. "Don't know." His gaze swept her. Insolent. Disdainful. "Depends on whether you take another step or not."

Rafael stepped in, one hand halting Kyla before she could follow her impulse to put her face right in King's. "No."

She glared at him, but he just gripped her arm tighter. "Like you said, you came here to talk. Now can you do that or not?"

Kyla put her hand over his. "I can do it." *God, help me do it. Stop the fear, Lord. Stop the anger. Give me Your words, because mine are just messing everything up.*

As she turned back to King, the truth of that hit her. Every time she opened her heart—and mouth—to fear, destruction followed.

King K sat back down, eyes wary. "You listen close, Builder Lady. The 22s don't play no games."

"I don't understand."

"Listen!" His finger jabbed at her, adding emphasis to the word. "If we came to your crib, you'd *know* it. Everyone would."

"You mean because of the graffiti."

He waved her words away. "Naw, man, you don' get it. I mean 'cuz you'd be done."

Horrific words, and not just because of the meaning. The relaxed, off-handed way he spoke them was far more terrifying. As though killing meant nothing.

"Are you trying to scare me?"

He jabbed his hands in front of him. "See? You ain't listenin'! *We. Don't. Play. Games.* If I wanted you scared, you'd be there. No need to ask. If we come to your door, we don't leave you standing. And we sure don't let no *kitty-cat* scare us off."

Wait a minute. How did they know about Serendipity if they weren't the ones who...

She looked over her shoulder at Tarik. He shrugged. "Hey, it was a great story. So I told a few folks."

Kyla sat back down on the couch, and this time when she turned to face King K, it wasn't so unnerving. "If it wasn't any of you, then who on earth was it?"

The gang leader pulled a toothpick from his pocket and stuck it in his mouth, chomping down on it. "Don't know. But we fo' shizzle gonna find out."

Now *she* narrowed her gaze. "Why? What do you care?"

"I don't. About you. But whoever tagged your crib, tried to make it look like it was us. I'm bettin' they the same ones shot at L'il Man." Death glinted in those hard eyes. "And they gonna pay."

Murmurs sounded all around them, and Kyla didn't doubt what he said was true.

"Your sister. She gonna make it?"

Emotion flooded Kyla's throat, closing it off for a moment. She forced ragged words free. "She'll be fine. Thank God."

"She saved L'il Man. Don't think I don't know it. That's why I tol' Rafe—and why I'm tellin' you now—what your sister did? For that, you and the 22s, we done."

Kyla folded her hands in her lap. Never would she have imagined sitting here, talking to this man, in this place. And not being terrified. "Done?"

Rafael stepped forward. "He's saying you can finish the job on the church and the Brotherhood won't cause any more trouble."

"Tha's what I said, man. We done. Out of it. Them that want to stop this thing with the church, they on their own. We don't stop them, we don't stop you."

Kyla risked looking at the gang members gathered around. Watching. Listening. "Are you saying the others in your gang will just stop? They'll leave us alone?"

He stiffened, his jaw going tight. "They do what I say."

"And if those others you mentioned, who want to 'stop this thing,' if they're the ones that shot at your brother?"

Kyla always thought of anger, hatred as heated emotions. White hot. But now, looking into those eyes, she knew different.

Rage was ice-cold.

"Then they die."

FIFTY-FOUR

> *"Am I not destroying my enemies
> when I make friends of them?"*
> ABRAHAM LINCOLN

> *"Go and celebrate with a feast of rich foods and sweet drinks,
> and share gifts of food with people who have nothing
> prepared. This is a sacred day before our Lord. Don't be
> dejected and sad, for the joy of the LORD is your strength!"*
> NEHEMIAH 8:10

Why didn't this neighborhood just accept the inevitable and die?
Ballat hated coming here. As soon as the church was his, he was selling it. Already had the buyers lined up. Soon, every last trace of the place would be gone.

Shoving the door of his Jaguar open, Ballat stepped outside. Two hulking brutes met him, eying the car.

"Watch it."

They didn't react to his command, but he didn't care. So long as they obeyed. And obey they would, because they knew King was Ballat's man.

At least until this ugly business was over. Then, the gang was gone. Ballat had that arranged too.

Smiling, he reached to push open the door, only to have it pulled from his hand. King K stood there, looking decidedly unfriendly.

"King." Ballat didn't let his surprise show. No point chumming the waters. These sharks were too ready to attack, even on a good day. "You called?" A fact that still stuck in his craw. That this uneducated lackey would call and demand *he* come down here.

"You gone far enough." King's words were curt. "Jus' wanted to tell you to your face. We not your boys no more."

"Not my…" What was he talking about?

"The church, man. We out of it."

Anger stirred, but Ballat kept it from his features. "Is that so?"

King leaned against the doorjamb. "Yeah. That's so. So you know now. Get offa our turf while you still can."

Ballat didn't understand what was behind this turnabout, but that didn't matter. The threat in the gang leader's tone was clear as day. Without another word, he turned and walked back to his car.

He drove away without looking back. This was unexpected, yes, but not insurmountable. In fact… Ballat reached under the passenger's seat and pulled out a city map. Yes, there it was. Three blocks over.

So the Blood Brotherhood were out of it, were they? Ballat fingered the map.

He was about to show that upstart King K just how wrong he was.

FIFTY-FIVE

"Why love if losing hurts so much?
We love to know that we are not alone."
C. S. LEWIS

"But the wisdom from above is first of all pure. It is also peace
loving, gentle at all times, and willing to yield to others.
It is full of mercy and good deeds. It shows no favoritism
and is always sincere. And those who are peacemakers will
plant seeds of peace and reap a harvest of righteousness."
JAMES 3:17–18

This was wrong.

Mason's arm around her shoulders as they looked over the schedules and details of the finishing work. His head close to hers as they discussed potential issues and progress. His proprietary air whenever someone came into the office where they stood together.

Nothing unusual. All things she'd allowed from Mason in the past six months. So why now did it all feel so…

Uncomfortable?

Kyla eased away from his arm, schooling her features to nonchalance as she pulled a folder from the filing cabinet. When she turned back, Mason's wry eyes were on her.

"It's finished, isn't it?"

She smiled. "Almost. I still can't believe it looks as though we'll make the deadline." She came back to the desk, opened the file, spread out the papers they needed to review, and bent over them. "I never could have done it without you."

"That's not what I meant."

Kyla straightened. Mason held his hand out to her, and after a brief hesitation, she placed her hand inside it. His fingers closed over hers.

"I mean us. We're finished." His eyes searched her face. "Aren't we."

No surprise in the words. No censure or anger. Just a simple statement of fact. Kyla looked down at their joined hands.

"Mason, I…" She felt a moment's squeezing hurt, regret for what could have been. She lifted her eyes to his. "Yes. I'm sorry, Mason, but yes."

He studied her a moment longer, then lifted her hand and pressed a soft kiss to the back of it. "I will always love you, Kyla. In my own way."

"How touching."

Kyla jerked her hand from Mason's and spun to face the doorway. Sam Ballat stood there, wry humor on those sardonic features. What was *he* doing here?

"I've just come to look over my property."

Surprise arched her brows, and her fingers itched to slap the smugness from his smile.

"I'm sorry I interrupted such a tender moment between you and your knight in shining armor."

Her cheeks burned at what this man had seen and heard.

"What do you want, Ballat?"

His features tightened as he turned his attention to Mason. "Why, Mr. Rawlins, how inhospitable of you."

He *tsked*, the sound utterly condescending. Why on earth was he here?

"You've never been so rude to me before, Rawlins. Not in all our years of working together."

Kyla snorted. "Mason, work with you?"

Ballat's tone turned unpleasant. "Oh, indeed, working with me. As recently as this last week." He cast a glance around the office, then out toward the new gym. "On this very project."

This was absurd! She turned to Mason, sure he was about to blast the man right out the door—and stilled. Mason was staring down at the desk, face crimson.

No. It couldn't be.

"But not to worry, Miss Justice." Ballat patted her arm, and she jerked back as if from a scorpion. "Your beau and I won't be working together any longer. You see, whatever I need, he delivered. But I'm afraid that didn't happen this time."

She wanted to scream at him to shut up. To get out and take his vile insinuations with him. But her voice was trapped in a too-tight chest.

"Ballat, you've said enough."

The man ignored Mason's hoarse assertion. He just stepped back. "No, indeed. He didn't deliver at all. And all I needed him to do—"

That cold gaze fixed itself to her, and despite her best efforts, Kyla shivered. It was like locking eyes with evil.

"—was stop you." He tipped his head, mock disappointment hissing out on a sigh. "You were too much for him."

He walked back toward the door. "I just wanted to drop in and offer my *sincerest* congratulations on completing the work. It's a lovely building." In the doorway, he hesitated, tossing one last baleful glance at them. "Oh, and be assured, I'm praying for you all."

"*Praying* for us?"

If the man's smile got any slimier, it would slip right off his face. "That nothing happens between today and tomorrow. That *is* your final deadline, is it not? Tomorrow, end of the day?"

"You know it is."

The smile faltered at her frosty tone, but only for a moment. "Indeed. I do."

Kyla stared after Ballat's retreating form. It was either that, or face the man she'd believed a friend.

And now knew to be a traitor.

Pieces suddenly fell into place. What had Fredrik said? It was as though those working against them knew what they were planning, even the minutest details of their schedules. As if they had access even to their orders, so they could transpose numbers.

Mason had all that and more. Because Kyla gave it to him.

Ice spread through her veins. It was her fault. All the delays. The church property almost being lost.

All her fault.

"Kyla—"

She turned, offering the same frosty tone she'd used with Ballat. "Am I correct that your crew is finished with their work?"

He stiffened. "All that's left is the final detailing."

"Which my guys can handle just fine."

Mason started to come toward her, but she stepped back. "Thank you for your help, Mason. I appreciate it more than I can say." She met his eyes, holding back nothing. Hurt. Shock. Betrayal. Loathing. "And now I'd appreciate it if you would leave."

"Kyla, please, it's not like Ballat made it sound."

Her jaw tensed. "Did you work with him?"

Desperation darkened his eyes. "Yes, but—"

"Did you agree to help him keep us from completing this job?"

He slammed a fist on the desk. "I've been here, helping! Remember? Working while you were at the hospital?"

She didn't give an inch. "Before that, Mason? What about before Annot was shot?"

His Adam's apple bobbed as he swallowed hard. "I...yes. I agreed to help him. But I couldn't go through with it."

"This time."

"What do you mean?"

"He said you'd always delivered before."

The words hung in the charged air. Kyla saw the truth on his pale face.

How had she been so *wrong?* So deceived? She thought Mason a man of character. Of integrity.

"So what you're telling me is you've been one of Ballat's hired thugs."

"I swear to you, I've never hurt anyone."

"Physically. But if you did to them what you attempted to do here, then Mason, you hurt people. Hurt them deeply."

His fist opened, and he placed his palm against the top of the desk, as though he needed support. "You're right."

The admission brought her no joy, no triumph. Only a heaviness that settled somewhere in the center of her chest.

He straightened. "I'm sorry, Kyla. For everything. But most of all, for hurting you."

She longed to forgive him. Maybe she would one day…but for now, all she could do was stand mute as he came toward her, pressed a gentle kiss to her cheek, and walked out of the office.

FIFTY-SIX

"Evil draws men together."
ARISTOTLE

*"O LORD, hear the cry of [your people],
and bring them together.... Give them strength to
defend their cause; help them against their enemies!"*
DEUTERONOMY 33:7

The Marines had landed.

Literally.

Kyla watched as Rafe's team came into the main terminal.

Even if he hadn't pointed them out, she'd have known it was them. Tall, straight, the unmistakable pride in those long strides.

These men were the real thing.

One of the men, a stocky blond who looked in need of a neck, was the first to spot Rafe. He grabbed the dark-haired man next to him and pointed. "Asadi!"

Kyla glanced at Rafe; he was grinning from ear to ear.

"Thales. Great to see you." Rafe held out his hand as the big blond came to meet him. Within seconds, a mass of tall, ramrod straight men surrounded Rafe, pounding his back, their laughter rich and deep.

"Hey, Sarge, you lookin' good."

"Course he is, *Mon*roe." The big blond punched the young man beside him in the arm. Kyla could scarcely believe the dark-haired man was a Marine. He looked so young! "You think the Sarge couldn't hack civilian life or somethin'?"

"No way, Thales. It's just good ol' no-necks like you who have trouble with that."

Thales turned back to Rafe. "Man, Asadi. Why'd you make me invite this farm boy? He don't do so well out in public, you know."

"Did just fine savin' your bacon a time or two, buddy."

A voice as smooth and soothing as honey rose over the horseplay. Kyla studied the darkly handsome Hispanic standing next to Rafe.

"Gentlemen, please. I doubt Asadi called us here to watch us fight among ourselves. In fact, I believe we have a whole new enemy to defeat."

"That we have, Sabada." He looked from one face to another, and Kyla couldn't miss the gratitude in his eyes. "Thanks for coming."

A lean black man, the last of the group to speak up, put a broad hand on Rafael's shoulder. "You needed us. We're here. It's that simple."

Such truth contained in those simple words.

"Rashidi, you always did have a way with words." Thales nudged the black man with an elbow, then angled a look at Kyla. "So, Asadi, who's the beauty?"

Kyla felt her face flame as all eyes—and a few cheeky grins—focused on her.

"Boys, meet Kyla Justice. Kyla, this motley crew"—pride and respect rang in his tone, belying the insult—"is the Pride. Tom Sabada, our point man and resident Taekwondo master; Rashidi Martin, my ATL—"

She frowned. "ATL."

"Assistant Team Leader, ma'am." Rashidi's voice was as warm as those brown eyes. "And honored to be so."

Rafe went on. "Kevin Monroe, a bit of a hothead, but the best navigator in the Corps. Oo-rah?"

"Oo-rah!"

Kyla jumped at the enthusiastic chorus. "And last but not least, our resident southerner, and communications expert, David Thales."

The big man's face split into a grin as he stepped forward to engulf her hand in his large paws. "Well, Sarge, I gotta say it, she's ever'thing you said she was. N' a whole lot more. Shoot, if *you* wasn't sweet on her, I'd have to step in."

There went the heat in her cheeks again.

"You?" Monroe hooted. "Like she'd look twice at you with Asadi around."

Thales elbowed his buddy. "Hey, some women prefer men like me, okay?"

"Like you? You mean like gorillas?"

Rafe's laughter, so full of delight, wrapped around Kyla. "Okay, gentlemen, that's enough of that."

"Hey, Sarge, what you think about Sabada's hair?"

Kyla followed Thales's nod, realizing Sabada was the only one among them who'd forgone the military buzz cut. His thick black hair fell to his shoulders.

Sabada shrugged. "I got tired of crew cuts."

Rafe's hair was short, but the other three Marines sported military cuts, hair shaved close to the scalp. It suited them. With their straight backs and square jaws, the air of power and confidence they exuded, Kyla had no trouble believing these men could overcome anything. Or anyone.

Rafe took Kyla's arm and turned her toward the exit. "Come on, boys. We're going to the church, where I'll fill you in on what's happening tonight."

"Tonight, huh?" Monroe whooped. "I was hoping we wouldn't have to wait long to rattle some cages."

"Not long at all, Monroe." He looked at the men flanking him. "It's time for the Pride to prowl."

～✺

"It's comin'."

Rafe almost jumped out of his skin. "Thales, you trying to give me a heart attack?"

The kid's teeth glowed white in the darkness. "Nah, Sarge. I'd just have to carry you to safety if I did that." He moved next to Rafe, shouldering his weapon. "Just come to let you know everyone's in position."

Rafe took in Thales's SitRep as he studied the sky. The sun was just dipping toward the horizon. Nothing would happen until full darkness provided their attackers cover. If only Rafe knew who was coming, and when.

He'd called the police, but without any real details, they couldn't promise much.

"You're saying someone may be comin' at some point tonight, but you don't know who or when?"

"That's right."

"Well, sir, I can't exactly send a squad out there for something you don't even know is going to happen."

The radio on Rafe's shoulder crackled to life. "Hey, Sarge."

Rafe keyed the mike. "Yeah, Monroe?"

"I'm hungry."

"You ate two steaks at dinner tonight!"

Sabada's voice joined in. "That was just the appetizer, sir."

"Keep eating like you do, Monroe," Rashidi added, "and you'll weigh four hundred pounds."

Thales grinned at Rafe and keyed his mike. "Now Rashidi, you know that boy is from Iowa. They got hollow legs there, as well as hollow hea—"

"Stuff it, Thales."

"Back atcha, *Mon*roe."

It was so familiar. The banter to ease tension. Standing shoulder to shoulder, studying the terrain as night began to fall. Like coming home. Rafe hadn't realized until this very moment how much he missed it.

No...missed *them*. The Pride. The Corps. The sense of belonging to something bigger, something that mattered in ways you couldn't by yourself.

All of it.

He lifted his gaze—and his sorrow—to the sky. *Where do I belong now? I want to belong.* No, more than that. *I need it.*

"Asadi?"

Rafe pulled his focus back where it belonged. "Right here, Thales."

The big man nodded, the matchstick between his teeth making a slow dip up and down as he chewed on it. "Sorry, sir. Just makin' sure." He didn't look at Rafe, but his concern came through loud and clear in his tone. "You seemed kinda gone for a minute there."

Rafe drew in the night air, letting it expand his lungs. A wry smile made its way across his mouth. "You saying I'm not as sharp as I used to be?"

This time Thales turned, his eyes wide as they met Rafe's gaze. "Nah, sir. I'd never—"

Rafe chuckled and waved the younger man's chagrin aside. "Never mind.

You were right. I was gone. But I'm focused now." He frowned, remembering. "Hey, you said something when you snuck up on me a minute ago."

"Didn't sneak, sir. You just wasn't payin' attention is all."

Rafe let that pass. Hard to debate the truth. "You said 'It's comin'.'"

Thales nodded. "Yes sir."

Rafe's frown deepened a fraction. "What is?"

Thales's gaze drifted past Rafe, to the street and beyond. He studied the night like a rabbit searched the skies when a hawk cried. "The storm. It's comin'." His gaze cut back to Rafe. "Soon."

Rafe wasn't afraid, but this wasn't Iraq, and it wasn't war. Not the official kind, anyway. Overseas, the enemy was clear; the objective honorable. He'd never doubted what they were doing, not for a second. In-country, it was kill or be killed. Right and wrong. Freedom.

Here…it was about real estate.

Money. Power. That young men were willing to kill, or be killed, for such things made no sense. Yes, Rafe had made every precaution to avoid having to take someone out. But if he'd learned anything in Iraq, it was that even seemingly perfect plans had a way of going wrong.

"Sure would feel better if our ammo was the real deal, sir."

Rafe agreed, but even blanks sound real enough when fired from an M16. And that's what they wanted: the convincing sound of automatic gunfire. Even the most battle-tested hesitated to move in on automatic weapons. That sound alone would give them time—maybe enough time for the police to deploy—before their attackers mustered the guts to come at them again.

Then the fight would be hand to hand.

At least they wouldn't be facing the 22s. King K was holding to his word—the Brotherhood was out of this fight. All Rafe knew was that another gang was coming.

Tonight.

Madness, Lord. This is madness. These young men we'll be fighting, they belong to You too. But they don't know it. Don't know You. Are we right to do this?

"I'm with you, Asadi."

This time Rafe looked at his friend, met the steady gaze. Eyes of iron, yet glowing with trust. Loyalty.

"They made this call, sir. Gave us no choice. You've done all you can to make sure no one gets hurt, but these men? They don't care. Life means nothing to them. They've proven that. So what you're doing here? It's the only thing a man could do."

"You're a good man, Thales. Thanks for being here."

Emotion flickered in those steady eyes. "Honored to stand at your side, sir."

"So are we."

For the second time that night, Rafe almost jumped out of his skin. He and Thales spun, weapons at the ready, then halted at the sight that met their eyes.

Fredrik and the elders stood there, feet planted, arms crossed, determination gleaming in their ancient eyes. Right beside them was Tarik, who Rafe had told, in no uncertain terms, to stay home. Apparently he'd neglected to tell Fredrik that. Just as Fredrik had ignored Rafe's request that the elders stay safe at home.

Why didn't anyone ever listen to him?

"What do you think you're doing?"

Rafe's outrage didn't faze them. They closed ranks, and Fredrik stood tall, white hair a gleaming halo in the darkening night. "We're here to stand with you."

Rafe pulled in calm. "Look, I don't have time to say this nice. You men are too old to fight these punks." He'd deal with Tarik in a minute. But he had to get Fredrik and the others out of harm's way. Now.

"Of course we are."

Rafe stared at Fredrik. "You are?"

"Old we may be, stupid we aren't. Fighting we shouldn't do. But prayer, my boy. That we can do. That we *will* do. We will uphold you and your warriors with prayer."

A cry split the air, stilling Rafe's response in his throat. Every nerve sharpened, and he and Thales moved as one, hunkering down, going back to back, weapons trained on the distance as they scanned the perimeter.

More yelling. Hoots and jeers assaulted the night. The sound of footsteps pulled Rafe's attention just behind the elders, and his blood ran cold when he saw Kyla step out into the night.

What *was* this? A *party?*

"Go back inside!" His order came out angry, which he didn't intend. For once Kyla didn't meet anger with anger.

Of course, she didn't obey him either.

"I'm not going anywhere."

"Child, listen to him—"

She halted Fredrik's wisdom with a hand in the air. "You and the elders go inside." She fixed a hard stare at Tarik. "And you go with them. The last thing we need is for you to get hurt."

Rafe arched a brow. Good. He didn't have to be the heavy for once.

Tarik's eyes narrowed. "I'm not afraid."

Kyla placed her palm over the boy's heart, and her voice, though still firm, softened. "I know that, Tarik. But we need you to stay safe. King K isn't working against us any more. That will change if you're hurt here."

Emotions played across the boy's features, then he looked down. "What about you?"

"I'm staying here."

Her words lit a fire in Rafe's chest. "You are *not!*"

"Rafe—"

He turned on her. "I can't focus when you're here, Kyla. Unless you want to get me or one of my men killed, get back inside."

Before she could launch the argument he knew was perched on her lips, another voice spoke up.

"Do what the man says, Builder Lady."

Rafe couldn't believe his ears—or his eyes. King K and his gang were suddenly just there. Like they'd slipped in on the darkness and materialized right in the midst of them. Rafe tensed, and King met his narrowed gaze without flinching. "We're not here for you." He jerked his head toward the darkness. "We're here for them. Nobody tries to take our turf."

Rafe took in King's stance, then relaxed. "Stand down, Thales."

Ever a Marine, Thales lowered his weapon.

"Who's coming?"

King came to stand beside Rafe. "The Nortes."

"The Nortes? Why?" The predominantly black gang usually stayed on their side of Alberta Street, too busy running a successful drug business to mess with a smaller gang like the 22s. As long as the Brotherhood stayed out of their business.

"Ballat. He got them all worked up about us moving in on their turf. Told 'em the youth center was really a front for the Man, so's cops could infiltrate the neighborhood."

"They bought all that?"

King shrugged. "Ballat knows how to make his case." He tossed a glance over his shoulder to Kyla. "This ain't no place for you, Builder Lady. You better get inside."

Kyla opened her mouth, most likely to argue, but King's hand flicked out a signal, and a hulking gang member came from behind to pluck her off her feet. Tossing her over his shoulder—obviously too stunned to express her outrage—the kid carried her back toward the church. "Perhaps we should go with them." Fredrik was trying to restrain a grin. "To calm troubled waters."

Wise, as always. Rafe squeezed his old friend's shoulder. "Thanks. I won't worry about her if you're in there."

When Fredrik and the elders were inside, Rafe turned back to King, who tensed the moment Rafe's eyes were on him. Rafe had the distinct impression the gang leader expected Rafe to come after him. Rafe just smiled.

"She's a fighter, your woman."

Truer words were never spoken. Rafe rested his hands on his weapon. "Yes, that she is."

"But she better off inside."

No arguing with the truth of King's assertion. "Yes, she is."

King looked over his shoulder, and his lips twitched. "Good thing Dancer come at her from behind. She saw him comin', I think she could take him."

Rafe's soft laughter echoed in the night.

~~~

Kyla roamed from one window to the next, peering out into the darkness, fuming. Her "jailer" stood guard, aided, apparently, by Fredrik and the elders.

A movement in the darkness caught her eye. Apprehension surged to life. "There's someone out there! I think they're coming."

Sheamus stepped back, away from the circle of elders. "We should call the police."

Fredrik waved his agreement. "Go, use the phone in the office, if they haven't cut the lines." Then he held his hand out to Kyla. "Come, bubele. The best thing we can do now is pray."

She tore herself from the window, taking his hand on one side, Don's on the other.

Shouts and loud, popping sounds drifted inside. Gunfire! Kyla started to pull away from Fredrik, but the old man's grip was solid.

"No, child."

"Please—"

He tugged on her hand, forcing her to look at him. "You must not. Rafe needs you in here, safe, to do what he must. Don't worry, child. God will protect."

Kyla grabbed onto that promise. As she held it fast in her terrified heart, Fredrik and the others bowed their heads—and lifted their voices in prayer.

~~~

The pride fired warning shots, sending the first wave of Nortes scurrying, just as Rafe had hoped. The gunfire sent them back once more before Rafe heard a Norte yell that it was blanks. No one was hurt. Rafe and Thales readied for combat as the next surge came. But just as Rafe focused on an advancing Norte—kid couldn't be more than seventeen—bodies raced past him. The 22s. They launched into the advancing line of Nortes.

Rafe slid his rifle to hang at his back, then nodded at Thales. "Ready?"

"Whenever you say, Asadi."

He keyed the mike. "Move in!" Adrenaline pumping, they moved into combat.

Cries of pain and rage echoed in the night air as bodies fell. Rafe fought with a twofold focus—to stay alive and kill only if it couldn't be avoided. He took one Norte down, then spun, only to find a gun pointed in his face.

The Norte's finger tightened on the trigger—just as he and the gun went flying. Rafe met Sabada's eyes over the subdued foe, and they shifted, back to back, not saying a word. Just standing ready.

A bellow from the left pulled his focus, and Rafe saw Thales go down under the force of four thugs who'd ganged up on him. He tensed, ready to go to Thales's aid, but before he could move, Monroe was there, kicking and punching, using the butt of his rifle to punishing advantage. Within minutes—maybe even seconds—all four of Thales's assailants lay motionless. Monroe reached down, took Thales's hand, and pulled the big guy to his feet.

"Asadi! On your six!"

Rafe spun, bringing his cane up, to block the knife slicing toward him. He parried the thrust, stepped back, then, when his attacker leaned in, dropped low and drove up with as much force as he could, punching the point of the cane dead-center into the gang member's chest. His attacker stopped, eyes wide, and then dropped to the ground like a discarded rag doll.

He started to turn back to Sabada, and just caught the glint of moonlight on a metal baseball bat. With a yell, he brought his arm up, but only managed to deflect the strike from hitting him square in the face. Instead, it connected at the side of his head.

Stars exploded in the night and sounds faded into silence as Rafe dropped to the cold, hard street.

"Rafe's down!"

Kyla's cry brought the others rushing to the window. She pointed to Rafe's inert form, finger trembling. *Jesus, please! What will I do if he's dead?*

Pounding footsteps brought her jerking around, and she saw Tarik racing for the doors out of the church. "Tarik!" She stepped forward. "No!"

But she was too late. He'd vanished into the night.

Kyla spun back toward the window, where Fredrik stood watching. His white face turned to her. "The boy…"

Kyla ran back to the window, peering out.

Fearing the worst.

～〜⌒

"Rafe! Wake up!"

The frantic command pulled him from the darkness, and Rafe rolled away from it, groaning.

Something grabbed at him, jerking him to a sitting position.

"Get up! Now!"

The scream made his pounding head feel like it was exploding. Anger flooded him, and with a roar he surged to his knees, eyes finally open, trying to focus on his tormentor.

Tarik.

The boy knelt beside him, a mixture of fear and relief on his features.

The sounds of battle reached Rafe then, and realization struck him low and hard. They were in the middle of the fight.

Training kicked in and Rafe flowed to a crouch, one hand grabbing his cane from where it lay on the ground beside him, the other arm moving to shelter Tarik. "I thought you were supposed to stay safe inside!"

"I thought *you* were supposed to stay alive!"

As though some evil force worked against both goals, two Nortes surged toward them, pipes raised. Rafe tensed for impact, but sudden gunshots barked out, and the two Nortes crumpled to the ground.

Behind them, handgun still pointing, was King K.

King jerked his chin toward the church. Tarik didn't argue. He stood and ran back toward safety. When he'd slipped through the doors of the building, King met Rafe's gaze. Then, with a slow grin, King turned and plunged back into the fray.

"Asadi, you okay?"

He took Sabada's proffered hand and stood. "I'm fine." He stared after King, heart aching. He hadn't wanted this. More bloodshed. More death.

"Asadi?"

Squaring his shoulders, he stared forward. Sabada fell into step beside him.

"Time to get back into it, sir?"

"No."

Sabada's surprise wasn't lost on Rafe. He met his friend's steady gaze. "It's time to end it."

～

Rafe didn't know how much longer they fought. Time slowed in life-and-death combat. Either that, or accelerated out of control. Nor could he have said how many Nortes he'd fought.

All he knew was the battle. The sounds and sensations, the pain when fists landed, the split-second reflexes that brought his cane up to keep iron bars and bats from ending him. That and the presence of his men.

Endless noise and fury swirled around him. And then, in one sudden moment that was shocking in its stillness, it was over.

Rafe and Sabada stood, still back to back, poised and ready for the next attack. It didn't come.

They scanned the darkness around them, watching, listening. And then Sabada's tension eased. "They're gone."

Bodies lay on the ground around them, some moaning, some ominously still. The only people standing were Rafe and the Pride, and King K and what was left of the 22s.

King K, his face already bruising, one eye closing, moved to stand over one of the moaning Nortes. He raised a hand, and Rafe realized he held a gun, now pointed at the Norte's head.

"No!"

King didn't look up. Just kept fierce eyes on his enemy. Rafe vaulted over the prone bodies in front of him, was at King's side in a heartbeat, then froze as the gun jerked up and trained on his chest.

FIFTY-SEVEN

"Having thus chosen our course, without guile and with pure purpose, let us renew our trust in God, and go forward without fear."
ABRAHAM LINCOLN

"But when I am afraid, I will put my trust in you."
PSALM 56:3

No!
This couldn't be happening!

Kyla gripped the edges of the window. At the sight of the gun trained on Rafe, her heart stopped, then slammed into overdrive. She spun, only to run into the hulking 22 who was her captor. She pushed back away from him. "I'm going outside!"

She was two steps from the door when he bellowed, "Stop!"

She froze, ready to fight if she had to, but he just walked past her and opened the door. "Mama always said to hold the door for a lady."

She brushed past him and hurried outside.

Rafe sensed more than saw his men start toward them, and gave the stop signal, all the while holding King's fierce gaze. "Lower your weapon, King."

"What? You think we on the same side now, soldier boy? That you can tell me what to do?"

"He isn't. But I am."

They both looked to the side. Tarik stood there, feet planted, arms crossed. "Drop it, Jamal. This man is not your enemy."

"No"—he jerked his chin toward the young man on the ground—"but he is. And he needs to die."

"No, he doesn't."

Rafe almost lost his composure at the sight of Kyla. What was she *doing* out here?

She stopped beside Tarik. "King, please. The police are coming. They'll take care of that man. And the others."

"We take care of our business our *own* selves."

Kyla started to speak, but Tarik stopped her by stepping forward. By doing what Rafe couldn't. Not without getting shot.

He walked to King and put his hand on the gun.

Kyla held her breath, heart pounding. *God, please! Don't let it end this way. Not before I have a chance to tell Rafe how I feel about him!*

"You don't want to do this, Jamal."

Tarik's low words held so much emotion, Kyla couldn't fathom his brother not being impacted. But King stood there, a statue in flesh and blood. For a moment the two brothers were locked in silent battle. Kyla risked a glance at Rafe, saw that his eyes were fixed on the gun.

And King's finger on the trigger.

"You wrong, L'il Man. I *do* want to do this."

Kyla almost cried out at King's hard words.

"But I won't." King lowered the gun.

Relief so intense it buckled her knees swept her, but she didn't go down. Rafe was there, arms around her, folding her close against that broad chest. "I *told* you to wait inside."

His breath warm on her face, Kyla felt her strength returning. She fixed King K with a glare. "Do you always manhandle women to get your way?"

"Only the stupid ones."

She tensed, but slight pressure in Rafael's hand stilled her. As irritated as she was with King, she wasn't ready to leave this man's arms.

Not even close.

~~~

He'd come so close. And now…

It was all ruined. All his work. All his careful planning.

Destroyed, right before his eyes.

He'd watched the Nortes fall back and run. Defeated. His last hope, defeated! Then new hope sprang to life when that useless piece of humanity, King Killa, aimed the gun at Rafe Murphy. *Shoot!* his mind screamed, willing the animal to listen. *Shoot him!*

But the gun lowered, and now they stood there, men who should be enemies, at peace. Peace! What *right* did they have to peace?

His gaze drifted past them, those disappointments. Those worms! And settled on one person. The person who caused it all, his loss and humiliation. His defeat. All because of one cursed woman too stupid to know she was defeated.

Kyla Justice.

How dare she?

How *dare* she!

Turn around. Walk away before they see you. Before they realize the part you played in all of this.

Impotent rage roiled through him, heating the blood flowing through his veins. Walk away? Slink into the darkness like some defeated cur? No.

Bile surged into his throat. *No!*

He'd almost won! She'd been afraid of him. He knew it that night in her apartment. He would have taken care of her then, if not for that blasted cat. A fine job he'd done hiding those scratches.

His feet moved as though of their own volition, carrying him closer to his tormentor. *His* tormentor. Raw laughter clawed at his throat.

I thought you *were the tormentor, they the ones who suffered. But here you stand, helpless. An old fool with nothing to show for his so-called genius.*

Words too foul to utter seeped through his heart and mind, poisoning whatever remnant of reason resided there. As it shriveled and died, vengeance rose with an unholy howl to take its place. It wound its way through him, energizing him, tightening his grip on the rifle in his hands.

The rifle…

They will kill you. That man of hers and his soldier friends. The minute you shoot, they'll retaliate. And they won't miss.

A gloating triumph bubbled up from within him as he lifted the rifle, fixed Kyla Justice in his sight. Death was a small price to pay for ending hers.

The cross hairs trembled, and he stilled, drawing in a steadying breath. There. A perfect sighting, right in the middle of her oh-so-smooth forehead.

His finger tightened, and he felt his tight mouth relax into a smile. "Good-bye, Miss Justice." He laughed, and it felt good. "I'll see you in hell."

~~

King K didn't know what made him turn.

A nudge, though he wasn't sure if it came from beside him or within. No matter. No time to think about it. There was only time to turn his head, but that was enough. Because there, just behind them, he saw what no one else did.

A rifle. Pointed directly at them. No, not at them…

King spun. No time for a warning. No time to do anything but throw himself at Kyla Justice. He heard her cry as he hit her. Almost smiled at the muffled outrage as he wrapped her in his arms, covering her with his body.

A heartbeat later he felt a sting at the back of his neck. Everything shifted. Slowed. He tried to move, to control his body, but it had stopped listening to him. Though he told his legs to move, they buckled, and he fell like a stone, taking Kyla Justice with him. Off in the distance chaos exploded. Angry voices. The *pop pop* of gunfire. A woman screaming. But it was all so tinny. So distant. And he was too tired to listen.

"Jamal."

This voice caught him. "Tarik…" He forced his eyes open, saw his brother kneeling beside him, tears streaking his face. "Don't cry, *hijo*. Don't cry."

Tarik's fingers dug into King's shirt. "Don't you leave me! You hear? Don't go!"

He wanted to do as his brother asked. No, demanded. But he was tired.

So tired. He focused his will on one hand, managed to lift it, lay it over his brother's. Their eyes locked. *"Te amo, hijo mio."*

His eyes drifted shut, and he sank into an engulfing void.

Kyla lay beneath King K's heavy form, too stunned to cry. His arms were locked about her, his body curled over her like a weighted, protective blanket. Eyes squeezed shut, she dug her fingers into the heavy leather of his jacket. Waited. Held her breath. Listened.

But she knew. There was nothing for her to hear. No breath. No heartbeat. No life.

King K was gone.

"Kyla!"

Rafael's voice came to her, frantic, pleading. But still she couldn't move. Couldn't make herself leave this one who had given all to save her. She'd only caught a momentary glimpse of the shooter before King hit her, but she'd seen all she needed to.

Sheamus.

The rifle in his hands trained on her. A bitter smile on his face.

"Kyla, please, mija! Talk to me! Are you all right?"

King K's body was tugged away from her. For a moment she resisted, held on to him, willing life back into his still form. *Live! Please, please, live!*

But other hands were stronger, and King was lifted away, leaving her exposed. She cried out, covering her face. Strong arms encircled her, cradled her close against a solid chest. Hands cupped her face.

"Kyla, look at me."

She looked into Rafael's eyes. Saw the fear, the worry, the burning anger. And, underlying it all, saw something that stole her breath.

Love. A deep, unwavering love that told her everything she could ever need to know.

She lifted a hand, pressed it to his face. "Rafe…"

"Are you all right?"

She swallowed at the raw, hoarse words. "I'm fine."

"You're not hurt?"

A shiver ripped through her, and she looked toward King K. Tarik was there, holding his brother's head in his lap, tears streaming down his face. Kyla groaned, and turned back to Rafe.

"He saved me."

FIFTY-EIGHT

*"For all sad words of tongue and pen,
the saddest are these, 'It might have been.'"*
JOHN GREENLEAF WHITTIER

*"Truthful words stand the test of time,
but lies are soon exposed."*
PROVERBS 12:19

Sheamus was dying. The thought filled Fredrik's mind as the scream of sirens sounded in the background, growing ever closer. The police. At last.

"Fredrik, I didn't have a choice."

He put a calming hand on Rafe's arm. "I know. You had to shoot. Now help me, please. I must talk to my friend."

Rafe helped Fredrik kneel beside Sheamus, the man's gasping breaths as heartrending as his betrayal. Haunting emotion burned in his eyes.

"What"—low and wheezing, the words carried as much emotional pain as physical—"do you want?"

Fredrik shook his head. "To understand why." He blinked back tears. "Why did you do this terrible thing?"

Sheamus squeezed his eyes shut and spat out an answer. "Two years! I spent two years preparing, working my way into your precious inner circle, gaining your trust…" A cough racked his body, but it was as though, once started, the tale demanded to be told. "I knew this day was coming, that we'd lose the church to Ballat. I'd been waiting years for it."

The anger was so deep. How could he not have known this was in Sheamus's heart? "But why?"

"All those years of paying tithes, of giving money to this place. I *deserved* something in return! And would have gotten it too. When we sold."

Fredrik shook his head. "No, dear friend. I told you, selling was not possible…"

"You made certain of that, didn't you? This stupid youth center of yours. You just had to see it built."

So many things made sense. All Sheamus did to discourage. How the saboteur seemed to know what they were doing and when.

"You left me no choice, Fredrik." The bitter accusation in Sheamus's voice struck Fredrik's heart. "I went to Ballat and offered my services. He understood what I was worth. Promised me a handsome sum, but only if he got the property."

"And you did your best to ensure that."

Hoarse laughter rasped free. "It wasn't hard. Making sure Ballat and that filthy gang knew what was happening and when. Transposing numbers on order forms. Sawing through the rungs on an old wooden ladder." His laugh deepened, brought on another coughing fit. "Arrange little accidents here and there. It was all so easy."

Yes, Fredrik knew he was right. Because they'd trusted him.

He jumped when Sheamus gripped his arm. "Don't you see? I would have had it all."

"Everything, old friend, but what matters most."

Sheamus opened his mouth, as though to refute Fredrik's words, but he didn't have the chance. With one final, gasping breath, his hand fell back to the ground…and he was gone.

Fredrik fought tears as he reached out to close unseeing eyes, took Sheamus's wrinkled hands, and laid them across the still chest.

Then, as the sirens crescendoed around them and red lights flashed through the darkness, Fredrik bowed his head and begged God for mercy on his friend's lost and tortured soul.

Kyla stood beside Rafe, waiting as Fredrik prayed.

The EMTs had done all they could to save Sheamus, but they were too late. The police had been there for what seemed like hours but couldn't have been more than twenty minutes, taking statements and photos. Then they told Rafe they were ready to "process" Sheamus's body and so she and Rafe walked over to tell Fredrik.

It was time to let Sheamus go.

The arm about Kyla was warm and strong, and she leaned close to this man she'd almost lost. This man she would never let go.

"Help me up, please."

Rafe gave her a squeeze, then moved to do as Fredrik asked. He kept his hand under the old man's arm as he led him to Kyla. She put her hands out and embraced Fredrik. "I'm so sorry."

His head nodded against hers. "Why such things happen, *nor Got vaist.* Only God knows." He patted her shoulder and she stepped back. "Come, kinder"—his voice was surprisingly strong—"let us leave the good police to do what they must."

The three walked toward the church, but as they reached the steps, Fredrik stopped and looked from Rafe to Kyla, a wonderful smile on his weathered features. "Oy, what a thought I just had!" He clapped his hands together, then reached out to them. Exchanging glances, they each took a hand.

"Mein kinder, what has happened has been so difficult. And losing Sheamus"—he faltered for a moment, then went on—"it's been a terrible trial. But God has breathed a thought into me. One that will bring joy to our hearts, and celebration to all who have worked so hard." He squeezed their hands. "But it rests with you to make this all so."

Kyla saw her confusion reflected in Rafe's dark eyes. "What do you want us to do?"

"You love each other, yes?"

Kyla couldn't help it, she giggled. Rafe's free arm slid around her, and those wonderful eyes, so full of love, looked down at her. His answer came sure and strong.

"Yes. Absolutely, yes."

"Then forgive an old man his foolishness, but let me marry you. Here." He pulled his hands free then spread them out, indicating the new building behind them. "In this place of new life and ministry."

Kyla looked at Rafe, taking in the slow smile that lifted his lips, the sparkle in his eyes. When one dark brow arched, she knew his answer. For once in her life, she didn't hesitate. Didn't think through all the pros and cons. She just stepped into those waiting arms and lifted her lips for his kiss.

"So? Is this a yes?"

Fredrik's tickled question almost set her giggling again, but she held it back, turning her head to deliver a stern glance. "No." Before Fredrik's face could fall any further, she clarified.

"This isn't a yes, it's a *you-bet-your life!*" She looked up at Rafe again. He hadn't missed a beat at her seeming refusal. But then, why should he? His smile said he knew her better than she knew herself. "I love you, Kyla. Now and always. Marry me."

She cupped his dear face. The face that had drawn her all those months ago. The face that had stayed with her all these years, even when she didn't know it.

The face of love.

"Just try and stop me."

His kiss made it clear he hadn't the slightest intention of doing so.

FIFTY-NINE

> *"If you were going to die soon and had only one*
> *phone call you could make, who would you call*
> *and what would you say? And why are you waiting?"*
>
> STEPHEN LEVINE

> *"And now, may it please you to bless me and*
> *my family so that our dynasty may continue forever*
> *before you. For when you grant a blessing to your*
> *servant, O Sovereign LORD, it is an eternal blessing!"*
>
> 2 SAMUEL 7:29

Wow.

Kyla blinked, trying absorb what she was seeing. But nothing had prepared her for this. She blinked again, but the vision before her remained.

She looked—

"Beautiful."

Kyla turned, her smile warm, but whatever she'd intended to say to her sister screeched to an astonished halt.

Double wow.

"Ohh...Annie, you look like a princess."

Annie came to slip an arm around Kyla's waist. "It still makes me grin to hear you call me *Annie.*"

Kyla tilted her head. "Who says God doesn't still work miracles?"

Annie chuckled, then turned them back toward the mirror. Joy inhabited her features. Kyla's smile widened at the equal measure of joy in her own.

And why not? She'd never been so happy.

Annie's arm hugged her. "I think we both look exactly as we should on such a wondrous day. Beautiful and utterly in love. So, are you ready?"

Kyla nodded. "More than I've ever been in my life."

"Rafe is a lucky man." Annie squeezed Kyla's hand, and a twinkle brightened her eyes. "And so are you. He's one handsome man."

Kyla didn't argue. How could she when she was flat-out grinning? "Yes, he is."

"Not"—Annie gathered the front of her dress and started for the door—"the *most* handsome man, mind you. *I'm* marrying him. But Rafe comes close."

"Close, schmose!" Kyla reached for the door and pulled it open. "Rafe is *the* handsomest man ever born."

"I couldn't agree more."

"Oh I don't know about that."

Kyla turned at the simultaneous comments, then swatted at Olivia and Shelby, who'd just come into the room. Olivia held the brides' bouquets; Shelby held a sparkling dog leash, which was attached to Kodi's flower-adorned collar.

Shelby glanced down at the German shepherd at her side. "You're sure she'll be okay?"

"Absolutely." Annie fluffed her dress out, then bent over to scratch her adoring dog behind the ears. "You're gonna be the prettiest flower doggie ever."

Kyla shook her head. "I still say Serendipity could have done the job."

Disbelief shone from her sister's eyes. "Hardly. Dogs can be trained. Cats?"

"Are cuter," Kyla finished.

Olivia held out the bouquets. "Mira, hermanas, you have other things to focus on now, si?"

"Yeah, you two," Shelby joined in, "no bridezillas allowed."

Kyla crossed her arms. "I can see you two are going to be a dangerous combination."

Olivia's shrug was eloquent. "I thought so, until she said my brother wasn't the handsomest man alive."

Kyla laughed. "That's just because she's partial to *my* brother."

"I'm warning you, Olivia"—Shelby actually managed to keep a straight face—"you have to stay on your toes with this crazy family."

"Well, with Kylie, maybe"— Annie smiled her thanks for the bouquet to Shelby. "But I'm so sweet you'll have *no* trouble from me." With that, she directed a stuck-out tongue at her sister.

"Now *that's* mature." Kyla bit her lip to keep from erupting into laughter. She tossed a sniff at Annie. "You're obviously ready to be an adult and get married."

"Oh, phooey on you."

"Yes, indeed. That's what I like to hear..."

At the deep voice behind Olivia, she turned. Dan stood there, tall and handsome in his tux, his gaze full of tender amusement. "The harmonious tones of my two sisters."

Moving as one, Annie and Kyla went to throw their arms around their brother in a tight hug.

Annie gave his arm a light punch. "Oh, you know we're just kidding."

He glanced past them to Olivia and his wife. "Prewedding jitters, I take it?"

"You know your sisters so well." Shelby stepped to the side as Kyla and Annie joined Dan in the hallway.

Dan held out his elbows to Annie and Kyla. When they each took an arm, he pressed their hands against his sides and planted a kiss first on Kyla's cheek, then on Annie's. "I love you both."

Kyla couldn't speak. How she wished their parents were still alive, able to join them in this celebration of what God had done. But since they weren't, she and Annie had agreed it was Dan who should walk the two of them down the aisle.

"Good thing you're marrying good, godly men." Dan's usually solid voice was just a bit gruff, as though he, too, was fighting his emotions. "Otherwise I'd have to haul you both out to my squad car and take you home."

Just then the wedding coordinator signaled to them from the sanctuary doorway. They watched Olivia, Shelby, and the bridesmaids line up.

"Oh! They look so pretty!"

"Soapity? For heaven's sake, Aggie, they're not even wet!"

"So *pretty! Pretty!* For the love of Puyallup, Doris, turn up your hearing aid!"

Kyla and her siblings turned to see two elderly women just entering the church. Kyla couldn't help a delighted cry. "Agatha! Doris! We're so glad you could make it."

Doris Kleffer turned to her best friend and constant companion, Agatha Hunter, with a huff. "I *told* you we'd be late. Why don't you ever listen to me?"

Aggie made a face. "Why couldn't I be the one with a hearing aid. Then I could turn you off entirely."

"Ladies."

They all turned at the low voice behind them. Jayce, Dan and Shelby's adopted son, stood there, taller than ever. Kyla wouldn't be surprised if he passed Dan's height in the next year or two. Jayce made his way to the two bickering women and held an elbow out to each. "May I escort you to your seats? We've saved two right up front."

Twittering their delight, Aggie and Doris did as Jayce bid, bowing their heads like royalty to the people in the pews as they made their way up the aisle.

Annie gave a soft laugh and leaned into Dan. "You've trained him well, Obi Wan Danobi."

The strains of music sounded, and Annie unclipped Kodi's leash, then directed her down the aisle. True to her training, the shepherd padded toward the doggie treat awaiting her at the front of the sanctuary.

As the bridesmaids started through the doorway into the sanctuary. Annie took a deep breath. "Show time."

Kyla noted the slight tremor in her sister's voice. "Nervous?"

She nodded. "Not about getting married. But walking in front of all those people…"

Kyla knew what she meant. She'd peeked into the sanctuary before she got dressed, and was astonished at how packed it was. "Forget the people," Kyla said, her smile both firm and tender. "Do what I plan to do. Focus on the wonderful man waiting at the end of the aisle. He's the only one who counts."

Annie couldn't restrain a grin, and Kyla knew exactly what was coming.

"Good ol' Kylie. Ever the Sister-Mommy." Annie touched Kyla's arm. "Especially when I need it. Thanks."

"Okay, you two." Dan looked from Kyla to Annie. "Here we go."

Kyla fell into step beside her brother, the regal tones of Wagner's wedding march ringing out around her as they started down the aisle. For a moment she caught her breath, aware of what seemed like a thousand eyes on her. Then she remembered her counsel to Annie, looked down the aisle, and felt her heart overflow.

Rafe stood there, Tarik at his side as his best man, so tall and strong. When Kyla's eyes met Rafe's, he smiled—and everything around them faded away. All her life she'd loved this man. Even before she knew he existed, she'd felt, deep within, the promise of him. Of the culmination of all God's promises and blessings. And now…

He was here.

And he was hers.

I am my beloved's and my beloved is mine.

The words had never rung so true.

Suddenly, Kyla realized they'd stopped walking. She found Rafe's gaze again, and the look in those dark depths made her heart pound.

Father, I don't deserve this man, but I'm so grateful You've brought him to me. Please…help me make him happy.

"Such beautiful women you two shmegeges don't deserve." A trill of laughter lifted in the audience as Fredrik, standing before them, a Bible in his hands, winked at Rafe and Jed. "But, since they seem determined to have you—?"

He arched his white brows at Kyla and Annie, and they responded together: "Absolutely!"

More laughter, and Fredrik lifted shoulders. "So, shows what an old man knows. You'll be good to them, yes?"

Now Rafe and Jed spoke together: "Absolutely."

"Oo-*rah!*"

This emphatic chorus of male voices almost brought the house down, and Kyla hugged Dan's arm at the sight of the men from the Pride, in full dress uniforms, standing beside her beloved.

"Who gives these women to be married to these men?"

Dan answered Fredrik's question, his voice strong and true. "On behalf of our mother and father and God Almighty, I do."

Kyla resisted the sudden tears stinging her eyes. She watched Rafe come down the steps, then held her breath as Dan turned to her. He lifted her veil and pressed a tender kiss to her cheek.

"God is with you, Kyla. Now and always."

She nodded, and he took her hand and led her a few steps forward. To Rafe. With tender reverence, Dan placed her hand in Rafe's, and then stepped back to Annie. As Rafe's strong fingers closed over Kyla's, liquid joy coursed down her cheeks. He reached up to capture the tears on a finger.

"Are you ready, mija?"

She tightened her grip on his hand. "Just try to get away."

His laughter enveloped her, wrapping her with warmth and joy and the sure knowledge that she was finally free.

From fear. From guilt. From the struggle against trusting herself and others. From the driving need for perfection.

In place of all that, God had given her the truest love she'd ever known. His—and Rafe's.

And that was the only perfection she'd ever need.

DISCUSSION QUESTIONS

1. Kyla, Annie (Annot), and Dan (Avidan) share a unique characteristic: Their parents named them intentionally with the prayer that God would show Himself true in their lives to the meaning of their names. *Avidan* means "God is just," so he dealt with issues of justice. *Annot* means "God is light," and she struggled with seeing herself through the light of God's grace.

   Kyla Marie Justice had a *lot* to live up to. *Kyla* means "victorious"; *Marie* means "the perfect one." And yet, in her own eyes, she was anything but victorious or perfect. What do the following Scriptures tell us about the source of our "perfection"?
   2 Samuel 22:32–34
   Psalm 18:29–31
   Matthew 19:20–21
   Romans 12:1–3

2. How important is the name we're given? Do you know the meaning of your name? What, if any, impact has the awareness of that meaning had on your life?

3. Kyla struggled with making a serious mistake when she was younger. In light of such Scripture as Psalm 24:3–6, how can those of us who haven't lived up to the requirements in this passage learn to forgive ourselves for wrong behaviors or decisions?

4. What Scriptures help you when you need to forgive yourself?

5. Rafael Murphy knew he was doing what was right in God's eyes through his service in the Marines. And yet he was injured and disabled, unable to continue to fulfill that role. What plans or

dreams have you had to let go of? What helped you do so and move forward into a different future than you'd envisioned?

6. What do the following Scriptures tell us about trusting God with our plans and dreams?
   Psalm 9:18
   Psalm 33:10–22
   Acts 2:25–26

7. Sam Ballat was consumed with bitterness because of his parents' seemingly meaningless death. How do we reconcile the truth that God calls people to the mission field—and that may well mean they pay for that call with their lives—with the reality of His love and provision?

8. Gangs are an ever-increasing problem in our cities today. Why do young people join gangs? What can we, as believers in Christ, do to help keep the young people in our lives from falling into this kind of violence and darkness?

9. King Killa told Kyla that once you're in a gang, you're in for good. Blood in, blood out. You kill to get in; you die to get out. What answer can we give to someone who feels he or she is trapped so completely?

10. Kyla had a difficult time trusting Rafael, or even herself, because of the way Berto hurt her and broke her trust. Has there been someone in your life who hurt you deeply? Broke your trust? What helped you open up to trust again?

11. Kyla judged Tarik (King Killa's younger brother) lacking simply because of his appearance. But Rafe saw something else in Tarik. He saw a young man willing to do what it would take to walk away from the life that trapped his older brother. Too often, we look at someone and assume, because of how he looks or where he

lives, that he's lost. What do the following verses say about how we should see and help others who may not look or live like we do?

Deuteronomy 10:17–19; 15:10

Psalm 82:3–4

James 1:27

James 2 (yes, the whole chapter ☺)

12. What can each of us do to help young people like Tarik? Have you ever considered getting involved in a ministry that deals with inner-city youth or even a prison ministry? If not, what holds you back?

13. The Justice clan was given a legacy of faith, not just in their names, but in the examples of their parents' lives. What can we do to leave a legacy of truth and faith for our children, or for the young people in our lives?

GLOSSARY

Yiddish Words/Terms

aleyken sholem—answer to sholem aleykham
baleydikung—insult, offense
bubele—darling, honey, sweetie (an endearment)
eingeshparht—stubborn
farshtaist?—understand?
gedaingst—remember
genug shoyn—enough already
gey gezunterheyt—go in good health
Got zol ophiten—God forbid
Loyzem gayne!—Let them go! Leave them alone! Let them be!
mein kind—my child
mishegas—foolishness
mitzvah—a good deed
schmegeges—goof, idiot
schmendrik—inept nincompoop
Sha shtil!—Be still!
Sholem aleykham—Hello, peace be with you
zeyde—grandfather
   (sources: www.bubbygram.com; www.askmoses.com; www.koshernosh
.com; www.yiddishdictionaryonline.com; www.linguanaut; *Yiddish Phrase-a-
Day 2007 Calendar*, Barnes & Noble: New York)

Spanish/Spanglish Words

abuela—grandmother
¿Aqui entre nos, entiendes?—This is just between us, understand?
hermana—sister
hermano—brother

jefe—chief

lo juro—I swear

'manita—an affectionate shortening of hermanita, which means little sister

mi amor—my love

mi corazon—my heart

mijo/mija—an informal term of endearment that can mean anything from my son/my daughter, to my friend, to my love.

mira—look; used as an exclamation or way to get someone's attention

nunca—never

porfa—"please," shortened version of *por favor* used in conversation with friends and family

¿Por qué andas tan brava?—What's wrong with you?

sabor a cielo—"taste of heaven"

Te amo, mi cielo—literal translation: I love you, my sky. *Mi cielo* is an endearment.

todos—all, everything

tu creo que—you think that…

una cretina, uno cretino—an idiot

vale—okay/sure

verdad—true

(sources: *Streetwise Spanish,* Mary McVey Gill and Brenda Wegmann, McGraw Hill, 2006; *Spanish Among Amigos Phrasebook,* Nuria Agulló, McGraw Hill, New York, 2006)

GANG TERMINOLOGY

beat down—a beating

cop to—admit to

crib—home

dance—fight

dime—a perfect 10; a good-looking person

dip—to run away fast

down with it—okay about something

drop a dime—snitch; call the police on someone

dumm—stupid

dusted—killed

fo sho/fo shizzle—for sure

front—to put on an act" ("Don't front with me!")

gangsta—gang member

homies—gang members/friends

jet—leave quickly

jumped in—accepted to membership in a gang through a beating

the man—person or people in authority

turf—gang territory

whack—crazy

word—term of agreement

popo—police

tat—tattoo

(sources: Urban Dictionary, Aaron Peckham, compiler; Andrews McMeel: Kansas City, 2005. www.urbandictionary.com; www.geocities.com/koogoomoofoo/hungcripad.html)

OWN THE PREVIOUS TWO

Dan is a small-town deputy wrought by tragic loss. Overtaken by bitterness, will he turn his lifelong devotion to justice into a quest for vengeance?

"*Shattered Justice* is for anyone who has ever known grief or asked God, 'Why me?'"

—TERRI BLACKSTOCK bestselling author of *River's Edge*

FAMILY HONOR SERIES BOOKS!

Annie Justice has always been different, thanks to a rare condition allowing her to see things others do not. Through a series of events, she is thrown together with Jed Curry, a producer of hit reality TV shows. Joined in a race against time and a cunning adversary, Annie and Jed struggle to work together because if they don't, it could cost them - everything.

"Karen Ball offers an intriguing story that kept me turning the pages and guessing the truth right up to the end."

—**TRACIE PETERSON**, bestselling author of *What She Left for Me*

OTHER TITLES

Anne's daughter Faith is the answer to her lifelong prayer to be a mother. But her dream is shattered when Faith rejects Anne's love and the love of God. After years pass, and God heals their relationship, Anne falls seriously ill. Faith watches her mother weaken, struggling with role reversals and leaning on God as never before. Through all the intricacies of their relationship, all the joys and trials, they learn that God is with them. He brings them peace in the darkness, joy in the midst of sorrow, and hope in the face of death.

FROM KAREN BALL

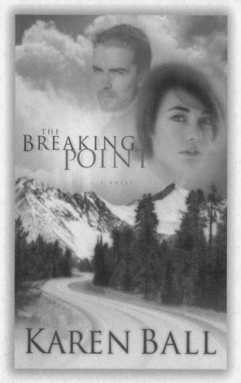

Gabe and Renee Roman are on the edge—relationally and spiritually. But after years of struggling in their marriage, their greatest test comes in the most unexpected of forms: a blizzard in the Oregon wilderness. Their truck hurtles down the side of a mountain, and suddenly they are forced to fight for survival by relying on each other. But both must surrender their last defenses if they are to come home at last—to God and to each other. Only then will they learn the most important truths of all: God is sufficient, and only through obedience to His call can we find true joy. Can the Romans overcome their greatest obstacle—themselves—in time?